DARK NORTH

Further Titles by Gillian Bradshaw from Severn House

THE ALCHEMY OF FIRE

DANGEROUS NOTES

THE WRONG REFLECTION

THE SOMERS TREATMENT

THE ELIXIR OF YOUTH

BLOODWOOD

DARK NORTH

Gillian Bradshaw

This first world edition published in Great Britain 2007 by
SEVERN HOUSE PUBLISHERS LTD of
9–15 High Street, Sutton, Surrey SM1 1DF.
This first world edition published in the USA 2007 by
SEVERN HOUSE PUBLISHERS INC of
595 Madison Avenue, New York, N.Y. 10022.

British Library Cataloguing in Publication Data

Bradshaw, Gillian, 1956-
  Dark north
  1. Romans - England - Fiction 2. Great Britain - History -
  Roman period, 55 B.C.-449 A.D. - Fiction 3. Historical
  fiction
  I. Title
  813.5'4[F]

ISBN-13: 978-0-7278-6524-3   (cased)

All Severn House titles are printed on acid-free paper.

Typeset by Palimpsest Book Production Ltd.,
Grangemouth, Stirlingshire, Scotland.
Printed and bound in Great Britain by
MPG Books Ltd., Bodmin, Cornwall.

One

The Alban Legion had posted sentries in front of its headquarters.

Memnon crouched in the shadow of one of the officer's tents along the Via Principalis and studied the pair of legionaries who stood guard. Their polished armour gleamed, their spears were perfect vertical lines, their bodies were relaxed in formal parade rest. The light from the torches burning to either side of them left their helmeted faces in shadow.

Personally, Memnon thought it very stupid to have torches burning when you were keeping a watch at night. The light destroyed your night vision and ensured that you could see nothing beyond it. He supposed, though, that having your face in shadow meant that you could drowse on your feet without anyone noticing. He grinned at the thought, then sobered quickly. Even if this pair was asleep, they would certainly wake up if they heard him, and he doubted very much that he could talk his way out of trouble at this time of night. They would be suspicious, and if they searched him and found what he was carrying, they'd be furious. He'd be arrested and flogged, and probably given a private beating as well. They might even kill him.

On the other hand, the night was overcast, moonless and dark, and none of the sentries on the perimeter of the camp had spotted him: this pair of ceremonial statues wouldn't, either. He turned his attention to the structure they were guarding.

It was a tent, of course. The Alban Legion – Second Parthica, to give it its proper name – had marched all the way from its base in the Alban Hills in the heart of Italy, sleeping in tents all the way. Now that it had arrived in Britain, those tents were showing signs of wear. The headquarters tent was big and grand, to be sure – oiled leather, painted red, with gold leaf around the entrance – but no tent that big and showy would take kindly to two months' worth of going up and down in all weathers. What was more, the legion had arrived at the camp only three days before. It had not had the opportunity to do much mending, and repairing a tent in which nobody actually slept had not been the top priority. Memnon's experienced eye noted two places where a splitting seam had been secured with an extra tent peg – and that was just on the tent's illuminated front.

He fell back behind the officer's tent, ghosted along behind it and its neighbour, then slunk forward again. The sentries stood stiffly in their places. Memnon knew exactly how much those fancy helmets blocked a man from seeing out of the corner of his eye even in broad daylight, and he grinned again as he walked easily across the muddy aisle that was the camp's Via Principalis. The sentries did not look round.

The layout of the legionary camp was familiar to anyone acquainted with the habits of the Roman army. The *principia*, the headquarters, stood in the middle, with the *praetorium*, the commanding officer's quarters, beside it. Memnon slipped through the staked-out workshops to the south of the *principia*. Everything was deserted at this time of night, but he was careful to move silently anyway, and to keep to the shadows: you never knew when you'd come across some trooper who'd got up to take a piss. He approached the headquarters tent again from its unguarded southern side and paused, straining his eyes to study the dark leather in the black night. There, against the blackness, a crack of gray. He crept forward and touched it and, sure enough, it was a hole large enough to allow a small man to slip through. He took the long bundle he carried and shoved it through the gap, then dropped to his knees and crawled after it.

The air in the big tent was close and still, and there was no sound beyond Memnon's own soft breath. Memnon picked up his bundle and crept silently forward, one hand extended, toes flexing in his boots as he felt for obstacles at each step. There were none. No sound came from the sentries only a few paces away on the other side of the leather walls: it was as though he had the camp to himself. After three steps his fingers brushed a canvas partition, and he felt his way along it. Where it ended, a light revealed itself as a single oil lamp, set on a stand. Facing it was a forest of gold. Memnon hurried forward, holding his breath.

The lamp burned alone before the legion's makeshift chapel of the standards. The proud banners reared up before it, a massed rank of gold and crimson. Second Parthica's eagle perched on the tallest post, a magnificent bird worked in pure gold, crowned with enameled laurel. Beside it stood the *signum* with the portraits of the Emperor and his family. A thicket of other standards crowded round the two, like children around the heads of a household, one for each cohort of the legion. And, there at the back, was what Memnon was looking for: Second Parthica's very own emblem, a centaur of gilded bronze, stepping proudly from the top of its tall post. A banner of crimson silk hung beneath it, painted with the same centaur rearing and the legion's name.

Memnon quickly crossed to the centaur standard. Holding his breath, he slid the heavy, awkward pole out from behind the others and lowered it carefully to the ground. The Emperor's portrait on the signum seemed to stare in disapproval, and he grinned and saluted it. He untied the standard's silk banner from the bronze cross-piece and rolled it up, then loosened the dark rag around the bundle he'd brought with him. Inside was another roll of crimson cloth – linen, unfortunately, since silk was expensive and hard to come by, but the colour was a reasonable match. He fastened the linen banner in the silk one's place and paused a moment to admire it.

The new banner also had a rearing centaur painted on it, but this one was holding a jug of wine and had a naked woman astride his back. It was, Memnon decided again, a much better painting than the original. He particularly liked the cheerful leer on the centaur's face, and the way the woman's head was flung back in a shriek of laughter. He glanced up at the signum again. The Emperor's profile frowned back, humourless dark eyes glowering above the curling black beard; his son, who as co-Emperor had a portrait just underneath, sneered in disgust. The Empress, on the other hand, seemed mildly amused: her large eyes smiled and her lips quirked up. He grinned and kissed his hand to her. Carefully, he tilted the bronze cross-pole, bunching up the cloth just a little – enough to obscure the design, but not so much that the standard-bearer would try to straighten it at once. With reasonable luck nobody would notice the change until they got the banner out into the open air; with real luck, anybody who noticed would be too surprised and puzzled to say anything until the legion paraded out of the camp for the next morning's troop inspection. Oh, please! he prayed silently, imagining the arrogant Alban Legion strutting proudly past all the assembled notables with that drunken centaur rollicking at its head.

It would still be a good joke, of course, even if the Albans spotted the switch right away. He imagined the uproar, the outraged officers, the stammering sentries, the frantic search for the original banner. They'd probably end up parading late and without their banner – and then everyone would want to know *why*. Yes! *That* would pay the legion back for its treatment of Memnon's own unit, those splendid auxiliaries, the Aurelian Moors!

He picked up the centaur standard and set it back in its place, then wrapped the legion's silk banner in the old dark rag and crept back out of the tent. He would stash it somewhere safe on his way out of the camp.

All the troops were to be inspected next morning, not just the legion. The Emperor had gathered a mighty army to subdue the troublesome barbarians in the north of Britain, and for the past month troops from all over the Empire had been arriving at the interim camp outside the provincial capital of Londinium. The Alban Legion had accompanied the Emperor himself, and had been the last to arrive. Now it was late in September, and everyone was here; now the Emperor would review the troops he had summoned from across the ocean. Second Parthica would parade first, of course: it was, as everyone knew, the Emperor's favourite. The detachments sent from other legions would follow it in order of seniority, and the auxiliary forces would follow them according to an arcane order of precedence.

The *numerus* of Aurelian Moors were irregular cavalry,

and thus would be near the end of the parade. Memnon saw
no reason to get up early: he doubted they'd make it on to
the parade ground until late in the afternoon. At first light,
however, Valerius Rogatus, the prefect, came striding through
the tents, slapping the entrance flaps with his riding rod.
'Up, children!' he shouted. 'Up, up, up! Atteeehn*tion!*'

The men groaned, but crept obediently out of their tents
into the cloudy light of the September dawn. They assembled sleepily, squadron by thirty-man squadron, dishevelled
and unwashed, pulling their boots on even as they took their
places. Memnon staggered to attention beside his tent-mates,
yawning and stiff.

Rogatus stopped in the middle of the camp and gazed about
himself with displeasure. He was a lean, white-haired man
of about sixty – city-bred, like most of the officers, with the
bronze skin of the Mauretanian coast rather than the darker
brown of more southerly parts. He'd served with the Aurelian
Moors since they were founded, though he'd only been
promoted to command them three years before. In more prestigious units such a promotion would have been unheard of:
prefects were generally appointed by the governor of the
province from the pool of ambitious men of rank who habit-
ually besieged him. Nobody had bothered to besiege him for
the post of prefect of the Aurelian Moors, however, so Rogatus
got the job. His men were, on the whole, very pleased. It was
true he was a strict, humourless old bastard, but he was sharp,
and there was no questioning his devotion to the *numerus*.

Flanking him were his officers, the unit's ten decurions,
most of them looking as sleepy as Memnon felt. Many weren't
even wearing the red sashes that denoted their rank. Saturninus,
however, the decurion of First Squadron, Memnon's own superior, was fully dressed and immaculate, like the prefect.
They'd probably hatched this wake-up call together. They were
thick as thieves, those two.

'Today,' yelled Rogatus, pitching his voice so everyone
could hear, 'we're seeing the Emperor *himself,* and you boys
need to look like soldiers!'

Memnon thought they already looked exactly like soldiers:
lean and tough and dirty. The Aurelian Moors had been assembled as a unit thirty-seven years before, cavalry scouts and

skirmishers specially picked for service on the Danube frontier. New recruits from Mauretania had joined them in a steady trickle, replacing men retired or killed, but the unit itself had remained constantly on the Empire's border. There might have been a couple of years when it saw no combat, but those had been the exception. They were a small unit – just over three hundred men, only three-fifths the strength of a regular cavalry wing – but they were, Memnon thought proudly, the best in the business.

Valerius Rogatus, however, did not look impressed with them. He gazed around at his command and rolled his eyes heavenward. 'Juno Caelestis!' he exclaimed. 'What just crawled out of a German brothel? No wonder the legion complained about "dirty Moors"!'

That created a silent stir of indignation. The Alban Legion had indeed complained about 'dirty Moors' – specifically, about the Aurelians having a campsite upstream from the one allocated to the Albans. 'Those dirty Moors and their ugly little horses will foul our brook!' the legion's camp prefect had been reported as saying. To pacify the legion, the Moors had been moved – to a site further from running water, more exposed, and generally less convenient. The Moors were furious about it. So what if they weren't all shiny-clean and fragrant like the fancy troops from the capital? They were soldiers of Rome; they'd fought to keep the border!

'You boys,' Rogatus continued, turning slowly on his heel to scan them all, 'make it look as though that bastard was *right*!'

There was another silent stir, this one puzzled. To be sure, the Aurelians were not normally much given to washing – but they'd been preparing for the troop inspection for days. This morning's grubbiness would quickly be wiped away, and all the parade gear was fresh and ready. Rogatus, Memnon decided with sudden sympathy, was just anxious. He'd resented the slur on his men, and he wanted to be sure that there was not one detail of their turn-out that would give any other unit an excuse to sneer at them.

The prefect paused in his survey, his gaze fixing on Memnon. 'You!' he barked.

Memnon straightened, bringing down his right heel with a thud on the muddy ground. 'Sir!'

'You're filthy, scout!' said Rogatus angrily. Memnon glanced down at himself, and saw that, yes, he had indeed collected some mud in getting in and out of the Alban camp. He hadn't bothered to wash when he got back; he had simply collapsed on to his bedroll, secure in the knowledge that his parade gear was clean.

Rogatus, though, realized that in his zeal he'd made a mistake. A man didn't get mud all over his front, knees and elbows by doing chores about the camp. 'Go clean up!' he ordered wisely deciding to say nothing more about the matter. 'And the rest of you clean up, too! We're going to show this army that the Aurelian Moors are a damned sight cleaner than those swaggering legionaries!'

The camp dissolved into a bustle of preparations. Saturninus, however, caught Memnon before he'd taken three steps. 'What've you been up to now?' he demanded.

Memnon gazed at him in wide-eyed innocence. 'Sir?'

Saturninus snorted. The drunkard banner had been prepared privately in Memnon's tent, but neither Memnon nor any of his tent-mates had felt competent to do the painting. They'd brought in Celer from Donatus's squad for that. Celer was a good painter, but he couldn't keep his mouth shut, and most of the *numerus* had traipsed in and out of the tent to admire his work. Saturninus would have had to be blind and stupid not to know that something was going on. He was neither: a thin, brown hawk of a man, with thirty years' experience in the habits of soldiers.

'The Alban Legion,' Saturninus said in a low voice, 'is the Emperor's own. Its commander is the Praetorian Prefect himself. If it's embarrassed it will want the man responsible flogged, and if it asked us to hand over a certain black-faced barbarian scout, we'd have no choice but to comply.'

Memnon maintained his black barbarian face in an expression of baffled attention. He'd left the silk banner stashed in a stack of firewood inside the Alban camp; the legion's officers would suspect the legionaries first.

Saturninus touched his arm. 'I would hate to see our best scout flogged.'

'So would I, sir,' said Memnon sincerely.

Saturninus's eyes searched his a moment. Then the decurion sighed. 'One day, Memnon, you'll get caught. Go on, then – clean up.'

The *numerus* spent the rest of the morning attempting to render themselves more shiny-clean than the men of a regular legion. It was, Memnon decided, an enterprise doomed from the start. The Moors simply didn't have the same amount of polishable equipment. A legionary had a cuirass of strip-armour, a helmet, shield, spear, javelin, sword and assorted belts. A Moorish cavalryman had two javelins and a knife: like all African light cavalry, the Aurelians wore no armour. Nor could they compensate for the lack of shiny plate by attention to their horses' harness. The small desert horses were ridden bareback without bridles, restrained by a rope about the neck and guided by the touch of a simple rod. There was a limit to how much even the most inventive trooper could titivate a riding rod.

Still, they tried. The unit's standard – a long white pennant topped by a golden star – had been washed the day before. The star – eight-pointed and set into a halo – was one of the symbols of the goddess Juno Caelestis, divine patroness of the province of Mauretania and claimed as protectress by the unit as a whole. Now the portrait of the emperor Marcus Aurelius, who had founded and named the Aurelian Moors, was annointed with oil and secured beneath the star. Duty to the standards completed, the men turned to their horses. The previous evening they had braided red and white cords into the animals' manes and tails; now they curried their surprised mounts until their coats gleamed, and painted their hooves with oil and lamp-black. Meanwhile water was heated in the big camp kettles, and after finishing with his mount, everyone washed and put on his parade tunic. There was some debate over whether to wear anything else: the garments – loose, knee-length shirts of fine bleached linen, with wide borders decorated in red – were designed for North Africa, not the British autumn, and the day was overcast and threatening rain. Living on the Danube had accustomed everyone to the use of breeches and cloaks. It was decided, however, that for the glory of the Aurelian Moors they could endure the cold.

They all had their ears pierced – a habit that was widespread among the men of the North African deserts – and each man made sure he had the gold star-shaped earring for the right ear that the *numerus* had long ago adopted as its unofficial badge. Most of the men were true Moors and Masaesylians, from the hills and plains of south-eastern Mauretania, and they beautified themselves in the traditional fashion of their tribes, braiding their long black hair in elaborate loops and adorning themselves with gold ornaments. Another third of the *numerus* were from tribes outside the southern boundary of the Roman province. They, too, prepared themselves as though they were going to a wedding, oiling their hair and pinning it and painting their eyelids blue. Creased leopard or lion skins were unpacked and draped over tunics, or fastened under quivers; ivory wrist-guards were secured with thongs of red leather.

Memnon came from still further south, one of a handful of Aurelian Moors from the tribes termed 'western Ethiopian' – people who were not merely dark, but black and woolly-haired. Watching his comrades prepare for the parade he felt suddenly left out. His own people, the Tebu, had been accustomed to paint themselves with ochre and chalk for special occasions, but he knew that would never pass here.

He had a sudden vivid memory of his father, face half red and half white, laughing as he danced at a festival, while the women sang and clapped their hands. Like all memories from his childhood, it brought a stab of pain. They were all dead, those people, their bones buried beneath the desert sands. He fingered his single earring, trying to push the memory away. He wasn't the boy he'd been – Wajjaj, son of Lianja, of the Tebu people. He was Memnon, scout for the first squadron of the Aurelian Moors.

Think about his joke, yes; think about the drunkard banner. Much better than remembering the past.

His tent-mate Victor, a Masaesylian, came over smiling. 'Here!' he said, thrusting a gold armlet into Memnon's hand. 'Borrow this.'

Memnon looked at the gold wire, then at his bare forearms. Ordinarily he tried to be as unobtrusive as possible, as befitted the unit's best scout. He dressed simply, wore his hair cut short, and avoided jewellery – it might catch in the undergrowth, or betray his presence to an enemy by reflecting light. When he was scouting he even removed his earring, and he had painted the blade of his knife black. On the other hand, he couldn't possibly let the *numerus* down by looking shabby on parade. 'Thanks,' he told Victor, and slipped the gold coil over his arm.

'I'll lend you one for the other arm,' said Himilis, another of his tent mates. He grinned. 'With a bit of work, you might look almost human.'

'Thanks,' said Memnon again, this time managing to produce a grin. 'Coming from you, Himilis, that's a real compliment. All the work you have to put into looking human makes you the expert.'

Victor laughed, and Himilis rolled his eyes.

Memnon retired to his tent that evening perfectly happy.

Not that the day itself had been perfect. About noon it had begun to rain, and by the time the Aurelian Moors at last had their turn on the parade ground, late in the afternoon, their finery was wet and bedraggled – best tunics, gold stars, braided hair, lion skins and all. When they returned shivering to their camp, there was nowhere to hang anything to dry. The damp parade gear had to be stowed under the roofs of the low tents, further decreasing the already cramped space and adding its own drips to the fug of moisture from the wet men crowded inside.

It didn't matter, though. The Alban Legion had marched all the way to the parade ground before spotting that their banner had been switched; worse, they had then dissolved in consternation and recriminations, delaying the whole parade and drawing the attention of everyone from the Emperor on down. Half the army was now greeting the men of the Alban Legion by miming a drink from a jug, and its officers were nearly apoplectic. The Aurelian Moors, delighted, had showered Memnon with wine and sweetmeats.

As darkness fell, he sat on his bedroll, head brushing the damp clothes above, and shared the gifts with his tent-mates – or four of them, anyway. The tents normally held six, but Castus, the last of their company, was on sentry duty. It was still raining, and the drizzle sounded softly against the leather roof. The concentrated body heat of the men inside held off the autumn chill, and the straw on the floor kept the bedding dry. The tent might be dark, and it might stink of wet leather, dirty straw, dirty woollens and muddy horsemen, but it was snug.

'I heard that the Empress laughed at it,' said Victor, taking a pull from the wine bottle. They were still discussing the banner, though it had been the main topic of conversation throughout the army all afternoon.

'One of her attendants was holding it,' said Honoratus, taking the wine from him.

They had all had a look at the imperial family as they paraded past – and a magnificent sight it had been. The troops had constructed a viewing stand: a four-square wooden platform, draped with purple and shadowed by a scarlet awning. The Praetorian Guard had stood in thick ranks around it, surrounding it with vivid crimson, gold and the sheen of armour. Raised above them like gods, seated on thrones of ivory and gold, had been the Emperors: Septimius Severus and his son Aurelius Antoninus. Their armour was gilded, glowing in the light, and their heavy cloaks were of rich sea purple. The Emperor's famous curling beard was white, not the jet black of his portrait on the signum, and the heavy-browed face familiar from a thousand coins and statues was puffy and lined – but it was recognizably the same man. Septimius Severus Augustus, conqueror of Parthia, Arabia, Adiabene; master of the world! Beside him was his son, young and vigorous, with curling black hair and a proud face: the promise of a secure future for the Empire.

The Empress Julia Domna had sat between and slightly behind her husband and her son, surrounded by a crowd of graceful ladies – one of whom had, indeed, been holding a roll of fabric dyed a familiar shade of crimson.

'She was holding something red, anyway,' agreed Himilis.

'It was the banner, for sure,' said Kahena. 'Rolled up.' He stretched a leg across the tent to nudge Memnon with a bare toe. 'Our banner's probably hanging in the Empress's bedroom right this minute!' he gloated.

Memnon smiled to himself in the darkness. He had a vivid

memory of the girl who held the banner – a tall, elegant dark-eyed creature in a long cloak of gray silk. He helped himself to a dried fig and said, 'Maybe that pretty lady wants to keep it herself.'

'She's a slave,' objected Honoratus. 'She wouldn't have taken it unless the Empress told her to.'

The others were all silent a moment, digesting this. Honoratus knew more about such matters than they did. He was a Roman citizen, and had grown up in Caesarea, the capital of Mauretania Caesariensis. There weren't many like him in the Aurelian Moors. Roman citizens who went into the army usually joined a legion, and even ordinary provincials preferred regular auxiliary forces to irregulars Honoratus, however, was a cavalryman born and bred: he had scorned the legions as mere infantry, and chosen the Moors because of their skill with horses. His choice had been honoured by immediate appointment as *optio*, or second-in-command of the squadron, though in the impecunious Moors this only meant he got pay-and-a-half and was obliged to share a tent like any other trooper. His tent-mates were respectful, though, and grateful for his superior knowledge.

'She was dressed like a rich lady,' objected Memnon at last.

'Slaves in the Household of Caesar *are* rich,' said Honoratus confidently. 'You remember Menophilus?'

There was a ripple of recognition around the tent. '*That* arse-licking bastard!' exclaimed Victor resentfully.

'*He* isn't a slave!' protested Kahena.

'He is,' replied Honoratus. 'Didn't you know that?'

'He *owns* slaves, lots of them!'

'Sure. He's Household of Caesar. They get paid, oh, twenty times what we do, even if they're not on the take.'

'*Paid*?' objected Kahena. 'Why would anyone *pay* a slave?'

'Because he's the *Emperor*'s slave,' said Honoratus. 'His master owns the Empire, and he's helping to look after his master's property. That's not like being somebody's goatherd, is it?'

'The Emperor's freedmen run everything,' commented Victor thoughtfully. 'Our Lord Severus keeps them on a short

chain, but they still control all the money. That's what they
say, anyway.'

'That's right,' agreed Honoratus. 'And the Emperor's
freedmen are nothing but his slaves who've been promoted.
That's how it works in the Household of Caesar: you're born
a slave, but you get rich and give orders to free men – and
then when you're thirty or forty you get freed and run the
Empire.'

'So the pretty girl with my banner was a slave?' asked
Memnon, getting back to a subject of more immediate
interest. 'A slave *and* a rich lady?'

'Certain to be,' said Honoratus.

'Was she pretty?' asked Victor. 'I didn't notice.'

'Pretty as a young palm tree,' Memnon informed him at
once. 'Weren't they a treat for the eyes, the Empress and her
ladies? – or slaves, if that's what they were.' He closed his
eyes and pictured the scene again: the Empress sitting on
her throne between the two Emperors, pearls dripping from
her ears and jewels glowing against her purple-draped breast;
the elegant silk-clad women standing behind her – with the
youngest, prettiest one holding his banner tucked under her
arm. He grinned to himself again. 'That was something!' he
said warmly. 'That was something, seeing the Empress of
the Romans, ah?'

There was a murmur of agreement round the tent. 'I don't
think even old Rogatus had seen an empress before!' said
Victor.

There was a stamp of feet outside the entrance to the tent.
'Castus?' called Himilis, expecting the returning sentry.

'No,' said a familiar voice, and the men all straightened
in alarm. The tent flap opened to reveal Rogatus the prefect,
holding a lantern. He scowled and gestured for them to let
him in, and the tent-mates all scooted hastily backwards.
Rogatus came crouching in and moved over to one side,
kicking some of the bedding up so that he wouldn't track
mud over it. Saturninus the decurion, who'd been holding
the tent flap for him, followed and settled down opposite his
superior. Rogatus set the lantern down in the middle of the
tent, carefully pulling the straw flooring away from it. The
prefect glanced over the tent's anxious inhabitants, then

allowed his stern gaze to settle on Memnon. 'Scout,' he said.

'Sir!' said Memnon, trying to come to attention while seated in a cramped tent with his head pushing into a pile of damp tunics.

'I am not going to ask any questions,' said Rogatus. The light from the lantern shone in his white hair; beneath that bright halo, his bronze face was expressionless and his eyes pitch-black. 'I will merely say that the Praetorian Prefect has been ordered by the Emperor himself to find out who tampered with Second Parthica's standard. The Prefect, in turn, has referred the matter to the Grain Commissary.'

There was a moment of shocked silence. The Grain Commissary might be an innocent-sounding title, but only a fraction of its work concerned grain: even barbarians from the fringe of the Empire knew that. Commissary agents were the Emperor's spies, responsible for detecting and suppressing treason.

Rogatus reached out with his riding rod and touched one of the unopened flasks of wine which sat in the middle of the tent. 'What's all this?' he asked. The rod moved on to tap the open jar of dried figs beside it. Kahena put the opened wine behind his back, and Rogatus shot him a look of disgust.

'It's a feast day for me, sir,' Memnon informed him earnestly. 'A Tebu harvest feast. Some of the others have given me presents to help me celebrate.'

'Oh, indeed!' said Rogatus. 'Well, I don't suppose there's anybody in the army who can contradict that: it may pass.' He paused, then continued, 'At the moment, the commissary suspect Second Parthica's own legionaries, not least because the sentries who patrol the perimeter of their camp swear that no one could have slipped past them.'

Memnon couldn't quite suppress a grin.

'Apparently their headquarters tent is also guarded,' Rogatus went on, 'so the theory is that the banner must have been changed by someone who had access to it. Since the standards had been sitting there since the legion arrived, however, and half the legion's been in and out of the tent for one reason or another, that doesn't help the investigation much. In fact, I don't think we'd have any trouble over this

– except that there's a *rumour* that it was one of *our* people who tampered with the legion's flag.' The prefect's dark look concentrated to a glare. 'One of those damned commissary agents has just been here, ordering me to make enquiries about it.'

There was a silence. Memnon had a sudden, dizzying fear that he would be hauled off immediately, questioned, and then thrown into a cell. He swallowed.

'I will, of course, report that I investigated the rumour,' Rogatus continued at last, 'and found that there was nothing in it. I will point out that all my men have been confined to our own camp at night, and that none of us has had any access to Second Parthica's camp even during the day. Obviously, no one in my unit had the opportunity to tamper with their standards.'

'Yes, sir,' said Memnon gratefully.

'I will not tell the agent,' Rogatus went on, glaring, 'that one of the men who couldn't possibly have touched that banner, once slipped through the entire Quadi army undetected.'

'No, sir,' said Memnon, and swallowed again.

'That was a damned foolish trick, scout,' Rogatus told him angrily. 'Standards are sacred things.'

'Yes, sir.'

'As for you, *optio*,' said Rogatus, turning the glare on Honoratus, 'you're supposed to keep an eye on troublemakers – not assist them!'

Honoratus opened his mouth, then shut it again. 'Yes, sir.'

'I'd set you both to digging latrines tonight, except that your decurion has other plans for the scout. Saturninus?'

'Sir!' replied Saturninus, smiling wickedly.

'Give him his orders.' Rogatus began to rise, caught his head on the wet clothes, grunted, ducked and shuffled backwards out of the tent, leaving the lantern.

Saturninus turned his evil smile on Memnon. 'We need to send a messenger to our winter quarters,' he announced. 'You're it.'

'Sir?'

'Now that the Emperor's reviewed us, we're moving north. We'll overwinter at a fort called Aballava. You're to go there, tell the residents that we're coming, have a look at the facilities, and report back to wherever we are by the time you're done.'

Memnon stared. Ordinarily this sort of errand would be given to a literate Roman like Honoratus. Messengers were normally given a written itinerary to follow on their journey, and Memnon couldn't read. He'd seen nothing of Britain but this muddy camp. He had no idea how he was supposed to find one particular fort in a huge unknown province full of them. He had no fear of getting *lost* – he was confident he could always retrace his steps – but finding a faraway destination was another matter.

He understood perfectly well that this errand was Rogatus's way of keeping him away from the commissary investigation, but there was a distinct possibility that it was also intended to punish him for his troublemaking. To wander the length and breadth of this wet muddy island as autumn closed in, asking everywhere for Aballava, sounded a pretty severe punishment.

'A number of other units are sending men of their own,' Saturninus conceded, after giving him time to get really worried. 'You'll ride with them most of the way. I'll give you your written orders in the morning.' He rose to a crouch, and smiled wickedly once more. 'I'd finish your harvest celebration now, if I were you. You'll need to be up early to get ready for the road.'

Two

Memnon said goodbye to his tent-mates at dawn the following morning and set out across the camp to report to the general staff for assignment to a travelling party. The rain had stopped during the night, and the first pink rays of sunlight showed that the clouds were starting to break up. Memnon's spirits rose. His horse, a small, sturdy gelding named Dozy, was well rested and eager to be on the move – and so was he. He had a supply of money in his purse, warm clothes on his back, and an unknown land to explore: what more could he want?

The Roman camp was vast. Riding across it, skirting the perimeter of one encampment after another, lifted his mood even further. The variety of men contained within the boundaries of the Empire had always been a source of delight to him, and here they all were gathered up together, one tribe jostling another: Africans and Italians; Syrians and Gauls; Arabs and Germans; Pannonians and Thracians and Iberians. Honoratus said that if you included the British legions there were a hundred thousand men committed to this campaign. A hundred thousand! That was such a big number, a man couldn't properly take it in – and yet all these men had their own encampments, their own supplies of food and tents and firewood. No one was hungry, nobody raided anybody else. What a wonderful thing the Empire was! What a marvellous thing was the Roman army, the most powerful force in the world – and he was a part of it! He almost felt sorry for those poor bastards in the north who'd provoked this.

Of course, it was one thing to admire the Roman army: it was another to expect it to run smoothly. Memnon was not at all surprised to find, when he presented his orders to the general staff in the Praetorian camp, that he was regarded as a nuisance. Nobody expected him so soon; nobody had arranged for him to travel with anyone. They were not happy to see him, either: black was an unlucky colour, and to meet a black man so early in the morning was a bad omen for the rest of the day. Come back this afternoon, he was told – or tomorrow afternoon; tomorrow would be better.

He knew how to deal with this, though: he identified which clerk could be plausibly held responsible for assigning him a group to travel with, threatened the man with Rogatus, then settled himself outside that tent to wait. He amused himself by gossiping with anyone going in to the tent and suggesting that the clerk might arrange journey-money or remounts as well as travel companions. After a couple of hours, the clerk came out, harrassed and short-tempered, and told him he could travel with Panthera's party, and here were his orders.

He was instructed to find Panthera's party outside the eastern limit of the camp by the bridge. This turned out to be the bridge that crossed the river Tamesis to the provincial capital of Londinium. Memnon looked across the river curiously; the assembled soldiery had been confined to the camp as too numerous and foreign for the city, and he'd had no chance to sample its delights. Nor would he have a chance now, he saw: a group which could only be his travelling companions had already assembled on his side of the bridge.

It was a motley and disunited group. There were eight men in the polished armour and blue tunics of legionary despatch riders, and one in the red cloak and purple-bordered tunic of a tribune, all on one side of the road; on the other side of the road were auxiliaries. There were two Germans on square, shaggy cobs, their fair hair tied back and their beards jutting; there was a Thracian in half-armour on a powerful black; a slim Syrian archer on an elegant Parthian mare, and a mustachioed Gaul on a restless bay stallion. A small wagon carried slaves and luggage that must belong to the tribune: legionary officers were aristocrats, and could not be expected to make do with what they could only fit in a pack.

Memnon trotted his horse up to the tribune and saluted. The tribune, a tall young man on a magnificent white charger, wore an elaborate breastplate rather than the usual strip armour – a breastplate which, Memnon noticed in dismay, had the centaur badge of Second Parthica prominent in its center.

The tribune looked down his nose at this small black man on a small brown horse. 'Yes?'

'Memnon, sir, First Squadron, *Numerus* of Aurelian Moors, sir! I'm to travel with your party, sir!' He held out the orders the clerk had provided.

'Oh, not *another* one!' groaned the tribune. He took the orders as though they were a dirty rag, glanced over them, grimaced, and handed them back. 'Very well, auxiliary. I am Flavius Panthera, a tribune of Second Parthica. You will obey my orders, or the orders of any of my men, or I will have you flogged. You can ride and mess with your fellow auxiliaries, and keep your unlucky face away from the rest of us. We have been assigned the task of escorting a palace messenger to the Emperor's new base in Eboracum: you are to stay out of his way, too, and behave with respect, if you know how. I hope your prefect gave you journey-money, because you're getting none from me!'

'Yes, sir! No, sir!' Memnon saluted again and trotted Dozy over to the auxiliaries.

The Germans, Thracian, Syrian and Gaul eyed him with wary curiosity. He grinned at them: he might as well try and make friends. The Gaul looked him up and down and commented disbelievingly, 'An Ethiopian?'

He grinned again. 'Been based on the Danube ten years now, most recently at Carnuntum. Memnon, a scout, *Numerus* of Aurelian Moors, bound to check out our winter quarters at a place called Aballava. You?'

The Gaul, slightly taken aback, considered a moment – then smiled back and held out his hand. 'Melisus, *optio*, First Gaulish Horse, out of Brigetio on the Danube, bound for somewhere called Uxelodunum.'

They shook hands all round, named themselves and their units. Memnon jerked his head in the direction of the tribune. 'He didn't seem pleased to see me.'

Melisus the Gaul scowled. 'He wasn't pleased to see *any* of us. Spoils his formation to have a disorderly rabble of auxiliaries trailing along behind it.'

'Ah. I thought maybe he was afraid we'd steal his jug.'

At this all the men laughed. They discussed the drunkard banner, then went on to comment on the parade and the British weather. They were just warming up when one of Panthera's legionaries came over and ordered them to fall into line and be quiet.

They obediently steered their mounts into some semblance of a line, and fell silent. Their horses shifted irritably under them and lipped the cropped grass of the roadside. From the fact that they were not setting off it was apparent that they were still waiting for somebody, presumably the palace messenger.

After a tedious hour or so, a very splendid enclosed carriage drawn by four fine mules rolled over the bridge and drew up opposite Panthera. A man leaned out the window. 'Greetings!' he called cheerfully. 'Are you our escort?'

The legionary tribune drove his charger over. 'You're the messenger from the sacred palace?' he asked. 'I'm Flavius Panthera, a tribune of Second Parthica. You're late.'

The messenger seemed a bit taken aback by this greeting, but replied mildly, 'I am pleased that you, at any rate, were on time. I am Septimius Castor, freedman of Augustus, *a memoria* and chamberlain to Our Lord Severus Augustus.'

It was the tribune's turn to be taken aback. An imperial chamberlain was a man of rank: freed slave or not, he was a member of the Emperor's personal staff. Memnon looked at the chamberlain with interest: he saw a stout fellow in his forties, with a round, snub-nosed, good-natured face and prominent front teeth, dressed well but soberly. He wondered what it meant to be '*a memoria*'. You reminded the Emperor of things, maybe?

'I hope we have a peaceful journey together,' the chamberlain was continuing. He glanced at the auxiliaries and added, 'You seem to have a very mixed assortment of men, tribune.'

Panthera snorted. 'I have a pack of stray curs! Apart from those, who are mine.' He indicated four of the despatch riders. 'The rest are messengers from their own units who were setting off this morning in the same direction as us. They've been foisted off on me because I'm the ranking officer.'

'I'm sure it's safer and more economical for soldiers to travel together where they can,' replied Castor pacifically. 'And we are all loyal to the Emperors, I hope.'

Panthera snorted again, then glanced into the carriage. He frowned. 'Here, what's that? You can't bring a girl along!'

A quiver of interest went through the watching soldiers. Castor frowned. 'This is a *secretary* of Our Lady the Empress Julia Domna,' he informed the tribune. 'She has been sent by her mistress on the same errand as myself.'

Memnon had had no idea that there were girl secretaries – though he supposed, now that he thought of it, that an empress ought to have them. He edged his mount forward a little to see if he could get a look at this exotic creature. There she was, sitting by the carriage window, her head turned toward Panthera, her straight back stiff with anger at being taken for a mere concubine. The rich brown hair and cloak of gray silk were familiar.

'You can't bring a *girl!*' repeated the tribune. 'It's bad for discipline. These mongrel auxiliaries will fight over her.'

'The *Empress* sent her, tribune,' replied the chamberlain, his voice cold now. 'Are you refusing to escort her? Do you wish to send to the palace and say so?'

The tribune surely knew that if he tried anything of the sort, it would be the end of his career. He glowered.

Memnon urged Dozy forward. The girl turned at the clatter of hooves, and he saw the dark eyes and pale oval face of the imperial attendant who'd held what might have been his banner. He grinned at her in delight. 'Sir!' he called across to the tribune, throwing in his best salute. 'None of us would insult this pretty lady by fighting over her like she was some barmaid. That would be an insult to the Empress, sir!'

The tribune glared at him, affronted. He looked as though he was about to say something about the Empress, but thought better of it. He scowled.

Memnon grinned again. The tribune wouldn't dare punish him for protesting loyalty to the Empress – not in front of the imperial lady's secretary, he wouldn't! 'I'll swear to it now, sir, if you like,' he offered happily. 'If I insult the lady secretary or her mistress the Augusta, the rest of the men can take me and put me head-down in the nearest latrine!'

He raised his right hand. 'I swear it by my ancestors!' He lowered his hand and added earnestly, 'But if there's no latrine nearby, there's no need to search for one. A dung heap would do instead.'

Grinning, the other auxiliaries echoed him, swearing by a variety of gods.

The tribune looked less than pleased, but he could not object. 'Very well!' he snapped. 'Let's get moving. We're late, and we need to reach Verulamium by evening.'

They rode out into a countryside of small hills, of fields dappled with patches of woodland, of fat cattle grazing in well-watered pastures. The clouds had given way to a warm September sun, and the land shone in the soft light, green grass gleaming with moisture, spiderwebs in the hedgerows glittering like so many jewelled necklaces. The air smelled fresh and damp. The harvest was in, the fields reduced to pale stubble, but in orchards along the road people were picking late apples. They watched the imperial party pass with the wariness farmers used toward soldiers all over the empire. Memnon waved to them.

Panthera's edict of silence was unenforceable on the road – and, in fact, from his position at the head of the party the tribune couldn't even hear the auxiliaries at its tail. By the end of the first hour, they were talking and laughing among themselves freely. They began by comparing itineraries for the journey. Most of them were bound for camps on the northern frontier of Britain, though the Thracian cavalryman, Sita, would be stopping at his own unit's base well to the south of it. Their route would take the rest of them to the northern army headquarters, a place called Eboracum, which was where the Albans and the imperial secretaries were bound: it would be the Emperor's base during the coming campaign, and the imperial staff members were undoubtedly going there to get things ready. It was about two hundred and seventy miles away, but they were expected to travel fast, and would cover the distance in seven or eight days. The imperial chamberlain had a licence to use the post, which granted him fresh mules for his carriage as well as accommodation at every posting inn along the way – and, as part of his escort, they would be staying at the posting

inns too. Memnon was much encouraged: all his travels hitherto had involved making camp at the day's end.

They began swapping stories of camps and officers – and
particularly about the pretensions of legionary officers, like
their temporary commander. Memnon informed his fellows that
the Empress shared their feelings – she must; she'd given that
very girl secretary the drunkard banner to look after; he'd seen
her holding it at the parade. The others were doubtful. At the
first halt – a posting inn twelve miles from Londinium, where
they paused to eat a light meal and to rest and water the horses
– they dared him to ask her about it.

He was always pleased to have an excuse to talk to a pretty
girl. He waited until the girl and the imperial chamberlain
were about to climb back into their carriage after the halt,
then marched up, taking along the Syrian and the Gaul as
witnesses.

The chamberlain noticed his approach first, and frowned.
Memnon met the man's eyes, saluted smartly, and was
rewarded with a perceptible relaxation.

'Excuse me troubling you, sir, lady,' he said, as polite and
amiable as he knew how to be, 'but we were wondering if
the lady secretary was the one we saw standing behind the
Augusta yesterday at the troop inspection.'

The young woman's face flushed slightly and she smiled
with pleasure. He guessed instantly that she was new to her
position, proud of it, and delighted that other people had
noticed she had it. Seen close up, she was even younger than
he'd thought; certainly no older than twenty. Clever girl, to
get a position with the Empress so young!

'Yes,' she agreed. 'I was there.' She had a clear, pleasant
voice, with an aristocratic Italian accent.

'We saw at the time that you were holding something red,
lady, and we wondered if – you know somebody changed
Second Parthica's banner? We wondered if that was what
you were holding.'

'Yes,' the girl said again, surprised. 'They brought the joke
banner over to show the Emperor, and my mistress the
Empress took charge of it. She thought it was funny.'

Memnon grinned triumphantly at his witnesses. Melisus
sighed. 'I never even saw it,' he said regretfully.

'I never saw it, either,' the imperial chamberlain said, unexpectedly.

'Oh, it was just a joke,' the girl said uncomfortably. 'It was like the real banner, except that the centaur was holding a jug, and he had a, um, nude woman on his back. Julia Augusta said it showed the legion's centaur "engaging in the legion's favourite activities".'

Castor gave a snort of amusement. 'I heard that Papinian suggested that it was a good omen, because it showed the centaur "enjoying a celebration of victory and peace". My patron the Augustus eventually decided to take it that way. They do know how to phrase things, these lawyers.'

Aemilius Papinian was one of the few imperial officials Memnon had heard of. As Praetorian Prefect, he was commander of both the Praetorian Guard and the Alban Legion. 'Papinian? The *prefect* said that, sir?' he asked, surprised. It was hard to reconcile the tolerant comment with the outrage of the Alban legionaries.

'Yes,' agreed Castor. He paused, looking at the auxiliaries with bright shrewd eyes, then continued in a low voice, 'You lads may be aware that before Papinian was appointed to the prefecture, the Albans were commanded by a man whose name and honours are now consigned to oblivion. That man passionately hated the Empress, and regularly abused her to his officers. I am not accusing any man currently in the legion of disloyalty, of course, I merely thought you should know that when you swore to punish anyone who insulted the Empress, you were touching on a sensitive subject. I don't want you to get into trouble with the tribune because of something you say out of ignorance.'

Memnon grinned. He'd been a bit dismayed about being under the orders of an arrogant Alban tribune – but he suspected now that he could have some fun. Expressions of admiration for the Empress were nothing Panthera dared quarrel with – but they would gall him mightily. Memnon felt himself becoming very loyal to the Empress. 'Thank you, sir, for warning us,' he told Castor sincerely, and grinned again.

Flavius Panthera stamped over to them at this point, scowling. 'Auxiliaries!' he snapped. 'What are you doing?'

Memnon stood to attention and saluted. 'Sir!' he said, beaming, 'please excuse us, sir. I'd thought I recognized the lady secretary from yesterday, when she was standing with the Empress, and we came to ask her if I was right. I was. We just wanted to be sure that we really do have the honour of guarding a woman who's close to Our Lady, the wise and beautiful Empress Julia Domna, Mother of the Camps. It will be something to boast about, sir, when we rejoin our units.'

Panthera's scowl deepened. 'Well, you're not to bother the slave girl, or the Emperor's freedman. That's an order. Go back to your places.'

Memnon saluted again. 'Yes, sir! Just let me say, sir, how glad I am to be serving in this escort, sir. The Empress's secretary and the Emperor's chamberlain, sir! You must be very proud.'

The tribune flushed angrily. 'Go!' he shouted.

'Yes, sir!'

Back at his horse, Memnon delightedly asked his companions, 'Did you see his face?'

Protus the Syrian shook his head indignantly. 'He is enemy of our Empress!'

'He doesn't like jumped-up slaves, either,' Memnon decided, 'but he doesn't dare say so, not in front of them. Ah, he's going to have a very miserable journey!'

The Gaul frowned at him. 'You mean to bait him?'

'Why not?'

'He could have you flogged!'

'For loyalty to the Empress? For praising the Emperor's staff? I don't think so!'

Melisus looked at him doubtfully. 'I hope you know when to stop.'

Memnon grinned again. 'Don't worry. I haven't been flogged yet.'

Londinium to Verulamium: twenty-two Roman miles. They did reach the city by evening, though it was dark when they arrived. Memnon had never stayed at a posting inn before, and enjoyed the experience. It was true that he and the other auxiliaries were required to bed down in the stables, but a clean, dry stable was a great improvement over a damp tent, and hot food fresh from the kitchen tasted better than rations cooked on a struggling fire.

Protus the Syrian objected to the stables, but that was more because the legionaries were allowed to stay in the inn than because he found the stables uncomfortable. Even he enjoyed the food. Each of the auxiliaries had been given journey-money by his own commander, and when they pooled their resources they found that they could eat well.

Memnon provided some entertainment to go with the meal: he told the innkeeper that Flavius Panthera would be pleased to be offered a jug of wine and a girl. In due course he was summoned to the inn's private dining room, where a red-faced tribune had been shouting at a pale and shaken innkeeper while the two imperial secretaries looked on with ill-concealed amusement. Memnon did his wide-eyed barbarian act: 'No, sir! Of course I wasn't trying to make fun of you, sir! Why, yes, sir, I had heard about the joke banner: that's what made me think you'd be pleased, sir. I thought it meant that Second Parthica knew how to have a good time. Don't you like girls, sir? Maybe the innkeeper knows of a boy who . . . no, sir! I'm very sorry, sir. It was never my intention to be offensive, sir. I was only trying to please, sir!'

It was a pleasure to use the wide-eyed barbarian act again: nobody who knew the Moors had fallen for it for years. It worked, too: the tribune dismissed him with nothing more than a snarled order to help the innkeeper with anything the innkeeper wanted done.

He apologized to the innkeeper – it was only fair – and pretended that he'd *thought* the tribune would be pleased. The innkeeper was sympathetic to a poor auxiliary who had to suffer such a humourless bear of a tribune, and did nothing worse than tell him to muck out the stables, which he and the lads had done anyway. Back in the stables, he recounted the scene in the dining room to his new friends, and they all laughed. He did not tell them his own part in the drunkard banner, of course – with near-strangers that would have been stupid. The others recounted similar pranks they'd played or heard about, and everyone went to sleep happy.

Verulamium to Magiovinium: twenty-five Roman miles. It rained again, and the tribune stopped earlier than he might have done. Memnon loudly admired how well he was taking care of the imperial messengers, which made him grind his teeth. Magiovinium was a small town, but the posting inn was again large and fine. It had a bathhouse, which the auxiliaries were allowed to use after the gentlemen and the legionaries were done with it. It was a pleasure to be able to steam away the day's riding, to hang wet cloaks up to dry in a warm changing room, to sleep comfortably on clean straw listening to the rain on the roof. It was a pleasure to hear a cook singing as she worked in the kitchen next morning, while her children played noisily in the courtyard. He decided that posting inns were by far the best way to travel.

He envied the imperial freedman Castor his licence to use the post. It meant he always got the best room in the inn, and everyone else had to make way for him.

On the other hand, the chamberlain was likeable. Sharp, but likeable. He knew perfectly well that Memnon was baiting the tribune, but he never said anything about it. Sometimes he'd even set the tribune up for a barb, or make some soothing comment to ensure that no retribution followed one. Memnon returned the favour by rubbing the tribune's face in Castor's status whenever he could. He was sure the chamberlain enjoyed that, though he was too diplomatic to say so. The lady secretary enjoyed it too: she would smile behind her hand, and her dark eyes danced.

The lady secretary, he and the other auxiliaries noted, was under Castor's protection. Fraomarius, one of the Germans, thought that the chamberlain must be her father, or at least her uncle, but the others all plumped for a more remote kinship or a relationship of patronage. They weren't lovers, anyway: the secretary never shared a room with her colleague, but had private quarters of her own. Memnon couldn't help feeling pleased about that, though he knew it was stupid.

Athenais, her name was; he'd heard the chamberlain use it. He had no illusions that a member of the Empress's personal staff was going to sleep with a barbarian auxiliary, but it was enjoyable to be travelling with a beautiful young woman, it was fun to make her smile. He liked to see her leaning out of the carriage window, her eyes bright and her hair, disordered by the jolting of the wheels, falling out of its knot; he liked to watch her get out at the rest halts to stretch the cramps of the journey from her long limbs. He'd been living in an army camp for ten years now, and it often seemed much too long. Oh, he'd had girlfriends, not all of them whores – but it had been a matter of snatching a day here, or a few hours there. He missed the simple pleasure of having women around routinely, women who were working and talking and not paying any attention to their men. It reminded him of a world he'd lost, where war was something that happened only occasionally and far away. This journey was a holiday from a harsher world, and he suspected that it would end much too soon.

Magiovinium to Tripontium: thirty-nine Roman miles, the tribune pushing the pace hard, now that the sun was shining again. Tripontium to Vernemetum, thirty-four miles; Vernemetum to Lindum, forty miles, a splendid long run in the clear autumn sunshine.

The first auxiliary left them at their next stop, Danum. The fort there was the assigned destination of Sita, the Thracian cavalryman. He did not copy the legionary despatch rider who'd left them earlier, and say goodbye at the gates: instead, he spent one more night with the rest of the company at the posting inn. The auxiliaries all bought him a drink and swore to look him up if he was still in Danum when they passed this way again, and he told them that they were 'good fellows, *nai*, very good!'

In the morning they rode on, with a melancholy sense of having almost reached the end of their common journey. If they could maintain the fast pace of the last few days, they would reach Eboracum that evening. The imperial envoys and the tribune would stop there, and the rest of the party would scatter, riding to their own destinations by separate roads.

The landscape changed as they headed north from Danum. There were fewer fields and more forest; the settlements were smaller and more scattered. To their west, above the wooded valley, hills rose steeply, open and wild, empty except for flocks of sheep. They had apparently passed from the territory of the more Romanized southern British tribes into that of the Brigantes, a less civilized people.

Looking at all those sheep made Memnon think of barbarian raiders, and he began to wonder if they needed to worry about them. The enemy they'd come to fight was in the north, and they'd now ridden north a long way. There was a wall across the island, he knew, which was supposed to keep the northern barbarians out. He was vaguely aware that it was supposed to be another three days' ride north of Eboracum – but that didn't mean it was entirely out of reach. The barbarians had been regularly crossing the wall to raid Roman lands; that, after all, was why there was going to be a war. The Aurelian Moors certainly could have slipped a scouting party south through such open and empty country-side. Indeed, they'd once conducted a reconnaisance in force five days into enemy territory, and across a river, too, not just a wall.

As he thought about it, it also seemed to him that *now* was exactly the sort of time he'd expect the barbarians to send out a long-range scouting party. They must have heard rumours about the Emperor's arrival in Britain, and if they had any sense, they'd be trying to learn more. If they wanted to combine their scouting with some plundering, this would be the best time of year for it, too. The harvest was in, but the winter had yet to arrive. The fine dry weather of the past few days had made travelling easy. He was sure in these circumstances old Rogatus would have put their party on the alert, and have sent out a screen of scouts.

Flavius Panthera, however, did not seem to think there was any danger: he did not send anyone ahead as a scout, and the men rode relaxed, their weapons strapped to their horses or even, in some cases, packed away in the baggage wagon. Memnon supposed the tribune had good reason to believe that the barbarians never came so far south, but he was still uneasy. He dared not say anything, however – he had by now goaded Panthera so hard that if he didn't keep his mouth shut for a while he was going to collect a beating.

He consoled himself that they would reach Eboracum that evening. There probably wasn't much risk to start with, and what there was would soon be over.

They made good time during the morning of their last day on the road, stopping for lunch at the posting inn of Lagentium, sixteen miles from Danum. From there the carriage rolled through a ford and up a hill on to the final twenty miles or so of the journey.

Eight miles from Lagentium, however, one of the carriage wheels cracked. The driver felt the vehicle stagger, and pulled over to the side of the road. The two baggage wagons pulled up behind it, and everyone dismounted and came over to look. One of the spokes of the right rear wheel had broken and fallen out, and the wooden hub where it had been seated had cracked right through to the axle.

'It's no good,' the carriage driver announced gloomily. 'That'll have to come off.'

'Can we fix it here?' asked Castor. 'Or do we have to go to a wheelwright?'

The driver could replace the wheel on the spot; apparently the carriage had a spare. The envoy's vehicle was accordingly propped up with stones, and the broken wheel was removed. The spare wheel, however, was then found not to fit the axle. The legionaries clustered around trying to assist, while the tribune fumed at the delay. Most of the auxiliaries dismounted and let their horses graze.

Memnon, still worrying about barbarian raiders, started Dozy up the nearest hill to have a look around. Panthera called out to him sharply to come back.

'I was just going to have a look out from the top, sir!' Memnon objected.

'Well, you can miss the view and stay with the rest of us!' snapped Panthera, adding angrily, 'Gods destroy you, you unlucky half-wit!'

Memnon shrugged, released his horse, and sat down with his comrades.

One of the legionaries – resourceful as legionaries generally were – knew how to adapt a wheel to an axle. He worked on the mismatched socket with a lump of lead, a spare strip of armour, and the driver's hammer and tongs. The others stood round him, chatting and offering advice – and that was how the raiders found them.

Three

M emnon, still uneasy, was the first to spot the raiding party. He looked up and saw the horsemen descending the hill toward them – small, shaggy ponies cantering down the open pasture, with a horde of men in drab cloaks on their backs. They had spears in their hands. He gave a long ululating yell of alarm.

There was a rush by the cavalrymen for their horses. Panthera stared in disbelief, then bellowed, 'Legionaries! To arms!'

Castor grabbed his young colleague Athenais by the arm, then stood looking about helplessly for somewhere to run.

Memnon started Dozy up the hill at a hard gallop, on a diagonal to the intruders, a javelin in his hand. 'Get back here!' yelled Panthera, and he glanced round, and saw that he'd set out entirely on his own. He'd been following the usual tactic of a cavalry skirmisher, to strike fast on the enemy's flank, forgetting that none of the others were skirmishers. 'Back! Back!' shouted Panthera. 'Form up!' Memnon obediently slunk back into line with the others, between the approaching barbarians and the carriage. Melisus gave him a toothy grin and an ironic salute with his spear.

Castor, apparently giving up on anywhere better, bundled Athenais back into the carriage. The slaves had likewise concluded that there was no use running from horsemen in such open country: they were crawling under the luggage wagons – apart from one, a boy, who was waving the driver's whip, his eyes wild.

The enemy spurred their horses to the gallop. They outnumbered the Romans at least two to one.

Memnon gritted his teeth, aching for the order to charge. He hated battles, and this one looked particularly bad. Unarmoured, and armed only with light javelins, he was the weakest point in the line – and the enemy had noticed: three of them were driving straight at him. They would spit him for certain, if he didn't move.

Still Panthera didn't give the order to charge. Memnon realized that the tribune meant to receive the charge standing – standard practice for a legion, but poor tactics for cavalry, and disastrous ones for a skirmisher.

He had no intention of dying because his commander was a fool. He struck Dozy with the riding rod, on the right shoulder so that the little horse jumped left, and yelled the horse into a gallop, trying again for the flanking move. One of the advancing riders turned to cut him off; the other two continued straight on.

He galloped diagonally across the hillside, crouching low over Dozy's neck, listening to the hooves thundering on his right. He slowed, planning exactly what he would do: stop suddenly, use his first javelin on his attacker, then circle round to attack the enemy in the rear. From behind him came shouts; a scream – then Panthera's voice, loud and shrill, yelling, 'Fall back! Fall back!' He jerked hard on the neck-rope, hauling Dozy to a stop and sliding off as he did so: he was better with the javelin when he was on foot.

The barbarian who'd come after him, however, had turned around and was galloping back down the hill to join his fellows. Memnon hurled the javelin at his departing back, but the distance was too great, and he missed. Following his opponent's course with his eyes, he saw that the raiders had got through to the luggage wagons and were swarming around them: his pursuer didn't want to miss a share of the loot. Memnon looked for his comrades, saw them galloping off up the road, and remembered that Panthera had given the order to fall back. Trembling a little, with rage and with the usual reaction to battle, he urged Dozy along the hillside towards his comrades, pausing only to wrench his javelin out of the muddy ground.

He caught up with the others when they slowed to a trot, about half a mile up the road. Flavius Panthera paused to look over his shoulder, then let out an unsteady breath. 'They've stopped to loot the wagons,' he said in relief. He glanced round at his command, then kicked his horse back into a trot.

Memnon glanced round, too – and noticed the missing faces. Fraomarius the German was gone, along with a legionary called Crescens. He had not known either man well, but their absence still brought a stab of loss.

Castor and the beautiful Athenais – they were back there, too, but they were probably alive. The girl, certainly, would be alive, for a while. He glanced back, but the carriage and wagons were now out of sight around a bend.

They hadn't really had any choice but to abandon the people they were supposed to be escorting: if they'd stayed and fought it out, outnumbered and unprepared as they were, they would have died, and left the two imperial envoys with no help at all. They would have to do something now, though.

Panthera slowed his horse and fell in beside Memnon, glaring. 'You!' he spat. 'I'll see you flogged, you coward! You broke and ran!'

Memnon shook his head vigorously. 'No, sir! I tried to attack on the flank, sir!' He held out his javelin so that the tribune could see the mud on it, and know that it had at least been thrown. 'It's how we fight in my unit, sir! We're not equipped, sir, to meet a charge head-on.'

Panthera hesitated: he did know, really, that a cavalry skirmisher couldn't meet a charge head-on. He grimaced, unwilling to admit it.

'Sir,' Memnon said hastily, before the tribune could move off, 'will we circle round, sir, and follow them once they've moved off? I can track them for you, sir. I—'

The officer's attention snapped back to him. 'What, by the infernal gods, are you talking about? There must be thirty of them! No, we ride off, fast as we can, and fetch help.'

Memnon frowned. They could get help at Eboracum. That, however, was twelve miles away, and it was past the middle of the afternoon already. There was no way they could bring the help *back* before nightfall, and it would be impossible to track the raiders after dark. By morning, however, the enemy would have taken their captives far away.

'Sir,' he said, as respectfully as he could, 'certainly you're

right we should send for help, but if we're going to rescue
the imperial envoys, we—'

'You idiot!' exploded Panthera. 'You stupid barbarian!
Didn't you hear me? We can't possibly rescue the slaves.
There are eleven of us, and thirty of the enemy! We need to
fetch reinforcements!'

Memnon was silent a moment. It was true that their
numbers, unequal to begin with, had been reduced even
further by that ignominious scuffle. He could see the logic
of a retreat – but he was sure that old Rogatus would've
mounted a rescue mission, at night, when the barbarians
thought they'd got clean away. Yes: send the scouts in to
murder the sentries, then attack the enemy in their sleep.

Probably that wasn't how they did things in the legions,
though. 'Sir,' he said at last, 'somebody should at least follow
the barbarians and mark their trail.'

'Shut up!' yelled Panthera, turning crimson.

'But, sir, if we don't keep contact with them, we'll—'

'Shut up!' bellowed the tribune again. 'I've had enough
of you, black face! Shut up! Another word, and I'll flog you
myself, right here at the roadside! We're riding for Eboracum,
now!' He kicked his horse back into a gallop.

It was impossible to talk at a gallop. Memnon rode with
his head down, moving easily to the rhythm of his horse.
The muddy javelin was smooth and solid in his damp palm;
the other bumped against his back. There was a mysterious
knot of pain in his throat.

He remembered finding his sister's body in the desert: her
small thin limbs, her face contorted in its final expression
of fear; the blood on her thighs, the thickly clotted blood on
her severed throat, and the dry tracks of tears on her face.

He checked Dozy, fell behind the others. He glanced over
his shoulder. The barbarians weren't following. He let his
gelding slow further. None of his comrades glanced back.
The road crossed a small stream, and he turned the horse
aside into a patch of woodland and tugged him to a halt.

Silence. The birds that had been disturbed by the horsemen's
passage began to call again, and the stream burbled in the
stillness. Memnon drew deep breaths, shaking, the image of
his sister's body still burning behind his eyes. He tried to

banish it – and found himself imagining the body of the beautiful Athenais instead, dead on a British hillside, her throat
cut.

Dozy was tired of this standing about. He tossed his head
decisively and walked down to the stream.

Memnon dismounted and let his horse drink, but not too
much, then led him up alongside the brook and sat down.
He gathered up a handful of moss and began cleaning the
mud off his javelin. Well, so he was going to follow the
barbarians and try to rescue the imperial secretaries on his
own. Probably it was a stupid thing to do, and if he failed
he'd be in trouble with Panthera even if he somehow survived
– but he was going to do it, so there was no use arguing
with himself about it. Perhaps it would ease his sister's spirit;
perhaps it would ease his own. The thing to do was to lie
low until the barbarians had moved off, and then follow their
trail. If nothing else, he could mark that trail, so that when
the search parties from Eboracum finally got there, they
wouldn't lose it.

The barbarians hadn't pursued the Roman troops along
the road – no surprise there: he wouldn't have pursued either,
this far into enemy territory and close to a fort, and anyway,
why bother? What they wanted was in the carriage, and
there'd been a bonus of wagons to loot. They would want
to get away quickly, though. They'd probably kill the slaves
who'd ridden on the wagons, then take the two imperial
envoys off into the hills, travelling fast and trying to muddle
their trail. There were three or four hours of daylight left:
they could be twenty miles away by nightfall.

What would they do with their prisoners? What would
they do with Athenais? Would they consider her worth questioning, or would they just assume that a woman knew nothing
of value? Would they rape her, or offer her for ransom? He
realized he knew next to nothing about these British barbarians. Maeatae, that was what they were called. Maeatae and
Caledones: one group lived north of the other, but he couldn't
remember which.

The questions were no use, anyway: what he needed to
do was follow. He put his clean javelin back into its harness
on his back, then slipped to the edge of the woodland and

looked out. No barbarians in sight. He drew his knife, checking that it slid out of the sheath easily, its passage greased by the mixture of lamp-black and fat he used to protect it and dull its gleam. The edge, when he tested it on his thumb, was sharp enough to shave with. He sheathed it again, then carefully removed the earring from his right ear and stowed it in his purse – a prelude to a scouting mission that had become almost a ritual.

He whistled for Dozy. The little horse, tame as African cavalry mounts had to be, trotted over. Memnon patted him, scratched his jaw, then led him back toward where they'd left the carriage, walking through the trees as much as he could and keeping off the road.

The carriage was still there, still propped on its pile of stones. The mules were missing, not just from the carriage, but from the luggage wagons as well. The slaves who'd ridden on the wagons, then hidden under them, were all dead. The boy who'd tried to defend himself with the whip was alive, but only just: his belly was spilling its torn guts into the road. The doctors said that if a man's guts were intact, you could stitch him up and hope, but when the guts were torn there was no point. Memnon knelt beside him, and the tormented eyes fixed on him.

'Hurts,' the boy whimpered. He was about fourteen.

Memnon gently brushed back the lank hair. 'I'll make it stop,' he promised, and drew his knife.

He closed the child's eyes afterward, and whispered a prayer to the boy's ancestors, asking them to receive him with pride, because he had fought bravely. Then he continued his inspection.

The luggage had all been scattered and opened, valuables removed and bulky items left behind. Memnon went over and checked the carriage. It was empty, and there were no bloodstains, though the mess made of the blankets and cushions and official papers provided evidence of a struggle.

Memnon began casting about for tracks.

He found the bodies of Fraomarius and the legionary, a little up the hill, both stripped of armour and weapons. He didn't touch them: the rescue party from Eboracum could give them burial, when it arrived. By the look of things, there'd been a dead barbarian keeping them company briefly, but his comrades had removed his body, leaving only a blood-soaked patch of grass and some footprints.

He widened his circle, and found the trail left by the raider's departure: it headed off along the west side of the hill across a sheep pasture. He marked it with a rag from the wagon tied to a stick, scratched a trail-mark next to it, mounted Dozy and followed.

The trail was clear at first: a large party of horsemen, leading a few lightly-burdened pack animals and travelling fast. After a couple of miles, though, the trail split, with clear tracks going downhill while a fainter trace led along the crest of the hill on rocky ground. Memnon, dismounting to study them, quickly concluded that the clear markings were only a small detachment, sent out to confuse pursuit. He marked the main trail, and continued along the ridge after it. He had to be careful, though, to ride below the crest of the hill, so that the detachment, somewhere in the valley to his left, would not spot him outlined against the sky and know that he was following. It was a tedious business; he had to keep dismounting and going up to the ridge to check that the raiders hadn't descended on the far side of the hill. The continual delays gnawed at him. Night would conceal the trail. He needed to catch up to the enemy by then.

He kept remembering the time he'd followed the Gaetulians who'd taken his little sister: the running in the heat, the thirst, the exhaustion; the desert shadows growing longer. He had been too slow, and come too late.

He hadn't had a horse then, he told himself, and the Gaetulians had had a longer lead. This time, *this* time, he would be in time.

After another mile he went up to check the trail, and couldn't find it. Gritting his teeth, he followed the ridge back until he found it again, descending the opposite side of the hill. He marked it once more – with an arrangement of stones, since the ground was too hard to take a trail mark – then followed on. The afternoon sun was lowering now, and he pushed Dozy hard. At least the raiders seemed to have slowed down: they were walking their horses now.

Dusk fell, and still he followed, straining his eyes for the trace of hoofprints in the mud. At last the trail became invisible; the rising half-moon did not provide enough light even to him. He turned and rode up the nearest hill to get a view of the land ahead, hoping. The raiders would need to stop and rest their horses, and they must be confident that there would be no pursuit until dawn.

A patch of woodland distant along the brook held one orange gleam: a fire. He sat for several minutes, staring at that glow, then rode toward it along the side of the hill.

He stopped Dozy when he came upon a stone sheep pen, well before he reached the patch of woodland: there would be sentries. If they waited under the eaves of the wood, they would be able to spot a rider crossing the open sheep pasture long before he could spot them. He drove a javelin into the ground and tethered his tired horse. Dozy promptly lay down, well-content to rest. Memnon patted him and praised him, then stood a moment, staring down the slope into the darkness, preparing himself.

There was a demon that had been born within him when he crossed the desert, a creature without pity and without fear – on nights like this he unbarred the door that kept it apart from him. Somewhere down there were sentries; somewhere down there were the raiders who'd killed Fraomarius and Crescens and the boy with the whip; somewhere down there the beautiful Athenais might be suffering the fate of his sister Iyangura.

He drove his remaining javelin into the ground by the sheep pen. He would need silence, and it was impossible to kill a man silently with a javelin.

He heard the sentry before he saw him. He was approaching the edge of the wood, and had dropped to a crouch, drifting in along a line of brambles and heather, when he heard a movement ahead and froze. There, by the trees, the smudge of an upright shape. Memnon flattened himself to the ground and drew his knife.

The sentry must have seen *something*. It wasn't enough to make him raise the alarm, but it was enough to bring him forward, spear in hand, to investigate. Memnon waited for him. His heart was beating hard, but it was not from fear: he *knew* the man would not see him. The demon possessed him, and he knew that no one would see him, unless he chose to let them.

The sentry came closer, closer still; he was slightly uphill from Memnon's position; he took another step . . .

Memnon leapt up, got a hand over the sentry's mouth before the man could raise his spear. He drew his knife over the straining throat, hard, stifling the Briton's last gasp with the heel of his hand. Blood spurted over his knife hand, hot and sticky.

He let the body fall to the ground and wiped his hand on its cloak. He considered it a moment before deciding that there was no need to conceal it: no one would see it in the darkness. He glided silently down the slope and into the dark wood.

He was close enough to the fire to hear the voices of the men around it, still muffled and unclear, when another sound closer to hand on his left caught his attention: a blow and a girl's half-stifled cry of pain.

He froze. So, they'd taken her aside to enjoy her? This would be *easy*!

Beneath that practical, murderous thought lay a dizzying gulf of joy: he was in time.

There was only one man. The girl was lying on the ground, her skin showing pale in the darkness; she was still half-clothed. The man was straddling her, hands moving at the level of his belt. When more pale skin showed, Memnon saw that the man had been unfastening the belt, not doing it up. The fact that he hadn't yet raped her saved his life. A hostage would be useful for holding off pursuit, and this man was probably important: it seemed he'd been allowed to go first. If he'd already forced the girl, his usefulness wouldn't have mattered; as it was, he could be permitted to survive.

The Briton noticed nothing, not until Memnon had a hand over his mouth and a knife at his throat. Then he gave a strangled gasp and went still. The voices around the fire continued on, oblivious.

'Don't move,' Memnon whispered. 'Don't speak. Do you understand me?'

The Briton lifted both hands silently. He was young: the beard under Memnon's hand was still soft. Memnon glanced down; the girl was sitting up, her staring eyes just visible in her pale face. Her hands were bound. Keeping the knife at his captive's throat, Memnon felt for and found the belt, then a knife. He pulled it from its sheath and tossed it down by the girl's hands. 'Stand,' he ordered the man.

The man stood, and Memnon pulled him back. As he staggered off the girl, his unbelted breeches slid down, baring more skin. Good: he couldn't hope to run with his trousers round his knees.

'Lady Athenais,' Memnon whispered, 'can you cut yourself free?'

She said nothing, but she pulled herself on to her knees. She'd lost her cloak, and her tunic was torn at both shoulders, leaving half her body naked to the cold autumn night. She fumbled in the dark for the knife, found it, and sawed awkwardly at the ropes that bound her hands. It was difficult: she could apply little pressure to the rope. Memnon did not offer to help, but waited patiently, holding the Briton motionless. Athenais managed to twist one wrist and hack at the rope more forcefully. It began to give, and she cut more swiftly. Her hands came free. She set down the knife and tried to tie up the torn edges of her tunic.

The hostage drew a deep breath. Memnon at once seized him by the throat, hooked his foot out from under him, and downed him. He pressed the Briton's face into the mossy ground; the young man gave a smothered whimper. 'I said, don't speak!' Memnon whispered to him. 'Try that again, and I'll smash your voice box.'

The Briton struggled, clawing at the damp ground.

'I want a hostage,' Memnon whispered in his ear. 'I want a hostage until we're away. If I didn't, you'd be dead already, understand? So keep quiet and you'll live.'

The Briton stopped struggling. Athenais groped for and found her cloak and pulled it round herself. 'He's the chieftain's nephew,' she whispered to Memnon.

It was the first she'd spoken, and the words gave him a stab of pleasure: no hysterics, no tears; an instant grasp of the situation and a helpful contribution. 'Good,' he replied, with deep satisfaction. 'We need to gag him and tie his hands. Cut some good strips off his clothing.'

Hesitantly, Athenais came forward. She fumbled at their captive's clothes, then caught the collar of his tunic and ripped it open with the knife right down to the hem. The hostage flinched. She cut another slash through the coarse woollen fabric, then another. Memnon took the first strip and shoved it into the man's mouth, and used the second to bind it in place. The third strip went to bind the hostage's arms. The Briton's tunic was reduced to a cape by the time he was secured. His breeches had now descended below his knees, and he was shivering.

'Now,' whispered Memnon triumphantly, 'we leave.'

'No!' whispered Athenais, quiet but forceful.

Memnon hesitated, startled, trying to make out her face.

'They have Castor,' she told him urgently. 'They're torturing him. He's much more important than I am, he knows all the Emperor's secrets! We have to save him!'

Memnon stood still another moment. He realized that the girl couldn't know he was on his own: she must think that the whole escort had come. He let out his breath slowly. 'I'm here alone,' he whispered. 'The others went to Eboracum for help.'

She was silent a moment, taking this in. Then she whispered, pleadingly now, 'Can't we do anything? They . . . they were burning him with fire brands, and . . . no, please, is there *nothing* we can do? He's chamberlain and *a memoria*, it's much more important to save him than me!'

Memnon was silent. He could still hear the voices of the men around the fire. How many of them? Too many to fight. He had a hostage, but a war-like chief would probably at least *try* to rescue his nephew instead of giving in, and the trouble with a hostage was, once you'd killed him, what did you do next?

If he could take the *chief* hostage – that might be different. He would not have considered it, if he'd been himself. The demon, though, knew that it was invincible.

'This chief,' he said, 'he's at the fire? He's a strong chief, his men obey him?'

'Yes.' She was taken aback, but the answer held conviction. 'Yes, he – his men obeyed.'

'Have you ever killed anyone?'

'No,' she replied, shaken. 'But . . . but if it helped us save Castor . . .'

He let go of the hostage, taking the small risk that the man would try to make a dash for it, bound and gagged as he was, but the captive merely swayed. He caught Athenais by the wrist, pulled her into place behind her young attacker, and set her hand on the softly bearded chin. 'Could you kill this man?'

The Briton jerked and Memnon caught him by the hair and brought his knife up under the young man's throat. 'Still!' he ordered softly.

'I thought you wanted him alive,' she whispered, horrified. 'As a hostage.'

'Yes,' he agreed. 'But if we're to get the chamberlain, *you* have to take charge of the hostage. I'll need my hands free. If you let him struggle and make a noise, we are dead, do you understand? You have to be willing to kill him, and he has to know it.'

She swallowed – then steadied suddenly, and brought the stolen knife up against the Briton's throat. Her hand touched his, and there was no tremor in it. 'Yes,' she declared, with conviction. 'For Castor, yes. If he struggles, I *will* kill him.'

'Good.' Memnon let go and stepped back. The girl seemed resolute – but he doubted that she knew anything about fighting. 'If you must strike, remember to use all your strength,' he advised her. 'A man's throat is tougher than you think. It might be better if you don't go for the throat, stab him hard in the kidneys or the stomach. It won't kill him outright, but he will die of it all the same. If you have to stab him, and he makes a noise, run. I'll try and find you before the enemy does. Now, I am going to fetch something from the sentry.'

'There's a sentry?' asked Athenais, shocked.

'There was,' replied Memnon, and vanished into the darkness.

He ran back the way he'd come, and found the body without any difficulty. He crouched beside it and hacked through the neck, then picked the severed head up by its long hair. If he was to take the chief hostage in the middle of his men, he had to have something else to hold their attention long enough for him to get close – this ought to do.

Athenais and the captive were still where he'd left them. The brave girl had not allowed the young lout to escape, good! He wondered, though, looking at her slim pale arms, if a severed head would be enough. She might be brave and resolute, but did the raiders know that? It seemed likely that they would believe she lacked the nerve to kill a man, and try to snatch the hostage away from her. He needed something more.

He set the head down. 'Lie down,' he ordered the prisoner. 'Athenais, he's to lie down on his back.'

Pressed by the girl's knife, the barbarian reluctantly folded on to his knees, then lay down. His bound hands made it impossible for him to lie on his back, but he rolled halfway over on to his side. Memnon caught one of his boots and pulled it off. 'You say his uncle is the leader of these men?' he asked.

'Yes,' agreed Athenais in bewilderment. 'The chief's name is Fortrenn. What are you doing?'

Memnon pulled off the other boot. 'We want to get Castor, we'll have to take him from the middle of them. We need to shock them so much that they don't think of killing us until it's too late.'

He pulled the Briton's breeches off and tossed them to Athenais. 'Put those over his head and hold him so he can't scream,' he ordered, and moved forward to sit on the young man's legs. The captive began to struggle. 'Be still!' Memnon said contemptuously. 'If you move, you're going to get hurt.' He put his hand between the barbarian's legs, ignoring the muffled noise of protest and fear. His knife came forward. Athenais stifled the Briton's shriek of pain and terror.

'What are you doing?' she asked again, in horror this time.

'Circumcizing him,' replied Memnon matter-of-factly. 'Now every woman he goes with will want to know what happened to his prick, and he'll have to tell them he tried to rape a Roman. Still, you idiot! Lie still! There!' He tossed the foreskin over his shoulder. 'They see him bleeding down there, it'll shock them like nothing else.'

He got up. The young man was now crying into his gag and struggling to breathe. 'Is there some way I can tell which one is Fortrenn?' Memnon asked Athenais.

'He's . . . he's wearing a gold torque,' she replied shakily, 'and he's dark-haired, with red and blue lines on his cheeks.'

'Good,' Memnon said vehemently. 'What we're going to do is walk up to their fire. The hostage goes first, and you keep good hold of him and stab him if he causes trouble. I'm trusting you, lady, to be brave, because if you let this idiot get loose, we're dead. I'll be beside you. I'm going to go for the chieftain while they're staring, and I'm going to take him hostage. If his men don't care for him, well, we're dead. If they do, we agree an exchange for the chamberlain and leave. Do you understand?'

'Yes,' she whispered.

'Good.'

He picked up the sentry's head and helped her drag the hostage to his feet. They started through the trees toward the blurred glow of the fire.

As they approached it, somebody called out, 'Cirech?' adding something humourous in British. They stumbled forward more rapidly.

Several voices cried out as they entered the ring of men about the fire, but as they emerged into the light, there was an appalled silence. Memnon saw in a glance that Castor was lying beside the fire, bound hand and foot, but that the barbarians had stopped the interrogation for dinner: their hands were full of mutton. Their horrified faces were all turned toward the naked, weeping, bloody figure of the hostage. On the far side of the fire sat a narrow-faced, dark-haired man with a gold torque, his tattooed face aghast.

Memnon tossed the sentry's head at the fire. It rolled on to an ember, and the hair began to burn. Somebody screamed. Memnon was already running through the midst of the assembled Maeatae, his knife in his hand. He reached the chieftain, Fortrenn, and grabbed him by the hair, dragging his head back and holding the blackened knife at his throat. 'No one move,' he ordered.

There was a wail, and then a terrified babble. The barbarians stared with wild eyes, their hands flashing in gestures to ward off evil.

'One of you cut the chamberlain loose,' Memnon commanded.

Fortrenn gasped out an order in British. One of his followers ran to Castor and began cutting his bonds.

'Get up,' Memnon ordered Fortrenn, tugging at his hair.

The Maeatae chieftain rose. He was tall, a full head above Memnon – much good it did him. Glancing down, Memnon saw that the barbarian had a sword, not a knife; it lay unsheathed on the ground by his feet. He kicked it aside.

Castor, freed, crawled on to hands and knees, then stood, wobbling a little, looking utterly amazed. His face was battered and swollen, and there were burns on his bare arms. Memnon doubted that he could walk very far – but at least he didn't have to be carried.

'This is what happens now,' said Memnon. 'We leave here – me, the imperial secretaries, the chieftain and his nephew. No one follows us. If anyone does or interferes with us, the chieftain and his nephew die, but if you do as I say, we will release our prisoners as soon as we are clear of you.'

'Do you swear this?' asked Fortrenn hoarsely. 'Do you swear that you will release us, without more harm, if we let you take the witch and her father?'

'I swear it,' agreed Memnon.

Fortrenn spoke quickly in British. His men groaned and repeated the gestures against evil, but they did not move.

'Good,' said Memnon, smiling. 'Let's go.'

They walked back through the trees. Castor was stumbling, and the chieftain's nephew was staggering and shaking: Athenais's grip on him was now more support than control. Memnon kept hold of Fortrenn, but the chieftain made no effort to escape.

The trees ended. They continued on up the hill and along its side, and still there was no sound of pursuit, and still the captives did not resist. It was as though they knew that the night was Memnon's, that any struggle would be doomed.

Dozy was still lying down in the stone sheep pen, but when Memnon whistled, the little horse picked up his head, then whickered and climbed to his feet.

'Athenais,' said Memnon, 'tie the chieftain's hands.'

'You swore to release me!' exclaimed Fortrenn in alarm.

'I'm releasing you. But not with your hands free, ah?'

Athenais let go of the nephew, who promptly collapsed.

She sliced some cloth from the hem of Fortrenn's tunic, and Memnon unfastened Fortrenn's cloak and tossed it to Castor: he'd noticed that the chamberlain was shivering. He tied the Briton's hands behind his back. The gold torque caught his eye again: a big thick thing, with terminals in the shape of human heads. It had to weigh a couple of pounds.

He took it from the chieftain's neck and put it around his own. Fortrenn caught his breath in an angry hiss, but when Memnon met his eyes, the British chief looked away, quite cowed, quite tame. It was as though he knew about the demon.

Memnon grinned. 'Now, we will leave,' he announced. 'But if you're thinking of chasing after us, think better of it. The path you took here has been marked, and the Romans are looking for you – follow us, and you may find them. And –' he brought his face close to Fortrenn's – 'even if they didn't catch you, and even if you succeeded in recapturing the imperial envoys, I promise you, you would regret it. You would not catch *me,* and I would come after you, chieftain. I would follow you all the way to your own land. Every night I would come to your camp, and I would kill some of you. There is not one man among you who would return to his home and his own people.'

'Leave my people alone, you black evil!' Fortrenn returned in a low voice. 'Take your own, and go! We will not follow you.'

'Good,' said Memnon. He turned away, pulled his javelins out of the ground and replaced them in their harness. Then he went over to his horse. 'You ride,' he told Castor.

Four

In the small hours of the morning, when it became clear that the two he'd rescued could go no further, Memnon found them a place to rest. It was only a hollow under a clump of gorse bushes, but he cut some bracken to cushion the hard ground, and Castor and Athenais collapsed on it and fell into an exhausted sleep, huddled together under their two shared cloaks.

Memnon tethered Dozy and sat down in front of the bushes, wrapping his arms around his knees; though he was very tired, he did not want to sleep. He had accomplished an impossible task, and he felt triumphant; he had saved Athenais from his sister's fate, and he felt elated. He had also, however, released his demon from its confinement. It was a thing of the desert – fierce, cruel, inhuman – and he was afraid of it. He knew he would not sleep well for some time, and that his dreams would be of flight from a faceless enemy, through burning deserts littered with the bodies of those he'd loved.

The moon had set behind the hills, and the sky was bright with stars. They were dimmer here than in the desert, and their light was less steady. He remembered lying beside his sister Iyangura on hot nights, outside the palm-leaf hut, looking up at those stars and telling stories. He had tried to make her giggle.

'Are you content, little sister?' he whispered, in a language no one on this cold dark island could understand. 'Did it ease your spirit?'

There was no answer, of course, but something like peace brushed the old ache inside him. He sighed and rested his chin on his knees. 'I wish I could have saved you,' he told the night. 'I wish I could have done for you what I did for the Roman girl.'

When the birds began to sing, just before dawn, Memnon
heard Castor groan, toss and then fall silent. As the light
brightened, the imperial chamberlain crawled out from under
the gorse bush and stood, wrapping himself tightly in
Fortrenn's stolen cloak. Memnon turned to face him, and
saw what he expected in the other's gaze: doubt and disquiet.
His comrades in the Moors looked at him the same way, the
first time they saw what he was capable of.

'Good health to you, sir,' said Memnon.

'Good health to you,' replied Castor. The chamberlain's
face was a mess: badly bruised, with one eye swollen shut
and blood staining the stubbled jaw. The remaining eye,
however, was clear and alert. After another moment's hesitation, he sat down beside Memnon. He said quietly, 'I am
indebted to you, soldier. I owe you my life. Thank you.'

Memnon grinned, a trifle insincerely. It would be a little
while before he could again feel confident of himself as the
well-known joker, the popular scout from the Aurelian Moors.
At the moment his identity felt like a mask. 'Glad I succeeded,
sir,' he said – and that, at least, was sincere.

'I noticed that you were alone last night,' said Castor neutrally,
after a silence. 'What happened to the rest of our escort?'

'Two men were killed,' said Memnon matter-of-factly. 'The
tribune took the rest to Eboracum to fetch help.' He paused,
forced another grin, and added, 'One reason I'm glad I got
you out, sir, is that I would've been in trouble with him if
I hadn't. He didn't exactly order me to stay with the others
– but he definitely didn't give me permission to leave them.'

'I see,' said Castor. He sounded bitterly angry.

Memnon was silent a moment, reflecting on that anger.
He liked Castor, but he did not want to be caught in a struggle
between the imperial secretariat and the Alban Legion.
'Second Parthica's been based in Italy for a few years now,
hasn't it, sir?' he ventured tentatively. 'And the tribune, well,
he's not all that old.'

Castor snorted. 'You are entirely correct. The tribune didn't
join the legion until *after* its great victories in the east. That
was his first experience of combat.'

'I should've wondered about that earlier,' Memnon said
thoughtfully. 'It bothered me, the way we were just riding along

yesterday as though we owned the road, no scouts out, everyone easy. But I thought, well, maybe he knows it's safe . . . and, I admit it, sir, I'd pretty much made sure that he wouldn't listen to any warning from *me*. He didn't actually do that badly. We couldn't have held them off, sir. Those bastards outnumbered us three to one *and* they caught us unprepared: there was no way we could've taken them.' He broke off a grass stem and twisted it between his fingers. 'If we hadn't run, we would all have died, and then there wouldn't've been anybody to go for help.'

'I suppose not,' said Castor. He still sounded angry. 'But he could've sent a *messenger* to Eboracum, and followed the barbarians with the rest of the men.'

'Well,' said Memnon, 'that's what *my* prefect would've done. On the other hand, if old Rogatus had been in charge, he would've waited until they were asleep, and that might've been too late, for Athenais, anyway.'

Castor glanced back at the hollow under the bushes where Athenais was still asleep. He looked deeply unhappy, but said nothing.

'That is a brave girl,' Memnon told him warmly. 'She wouldn't leave without you.'

Castor glanced back again, made an indistinct noise – then buried his face in his hands. Memnon stared at him in surprise.

'I'm sorry,' Castor said, struggling to regain control of himself. 'She . . .' He paused, drew a ragged breath, then wiped his face. 'I . . . told the barbarians that she was my daughter. I hoped they'd think she didn't know any secrets and wouldn't torture her. But when they . . . when they started to question me, she shouted at them, and then they threatened her. They told me they would rape her, one after the other, unless I told them what they wanted to know. I was going to let them do it.'

Memnon had no idea what to say to this.

'It was *stupid*!' Castor continued fiercely. 'I should've just *told* them.'

'But – if you told the enemy . . . *she* said you knew all the Emperor's secrets. Sir, if that includes everything about our troops and our plans for the campaign, I'm just as glad you didn't tell them!'

'That's what I told myself: that I should die keeping my master's secrets, like a good slave. The truth, though, is that nothing I know would have done those savages any good. The Emperor intends to conquer them, and they have no more power to prevent him than a . . . a *child* with a wooden sword has of defeating an armed legionary!'

'Speaking as a man who'll have to fight them next summer, sir, I'm still glad you didn't tell them anything. Anyway, it turned out right. You're both out safely.'

The chamberlain looked at him intently, his battered face very earnest. 'Did you . . . that is, were you in time to . . .'

'If that bastard had raped her, sir, he'd be dead now.'

Profound relief. Memnon began to wonder again: what *was* the relationship between the two imperial staff members? 'Do you know the young lady well, sir?' he asked carefully.

Castor shook his head. 'I'd never met her before this journey. I know her father slightly – he's in the Household, too. Finance, in Rome.' He saw Memnon's look of disquiet and added, very softly, 'Yes. I think she is the freshest, loveliest thing I've ever seen – but don't worry, she has no interest in *me*. I don't think she even suspects I . . . feel anything for her but goodwill. We discussed administrative business all the way from Londinium.'

Again, Memnon didn't know how to respond. Castor had clearly detected his own interest in the girl, but was he saying that he was standing aside, or declaring himself a rival? 'Are you married, then, sir?'

'A widower, for four years now.' The chamberlain's eyes probed his. 'You must understand this: Athenais is a slave of the Household of Caesar, and not free to make her own choices. Her mistress, Julia Augusta, strongly dislikes any interference with her personal staff. She is a very great lady, and she was obliged to suffer the spies of Fulvius Plautianus in silence when he was in the ascendant. Since his downfall, she has kept her staff strictly segregated even from other members of the Household. Athenais is loyal, and greatly admires her mistress: she will not disobey her. It's true, what you've heard, that we in the Household have considerable wealth and power – but only over others. We have no power over ourselves.'

Not standing aside; not declaring rivalry: saying that there couldn't be a contest, because the girl already belonged to somebody else. Memnon wasn't sure he believed that: slaves generally seemed able to find ways to sleep with someone when they wanted to. He wouldn't say that, though, not to this powerful man who was himself a freed slave. 'Must've been hard, riding in the carriage with her all that way,' he said instead, 'knowing that and feeling like you do.'

The chamberlain gave a snort of acknowledgement. 'Yes. She *admires* me. I have a reputation, you see: I don't take bribes, or sell favours, or intrigue to further the interests of my protégés by damaging their rivals, or indulge in the other games played among the staff. She admires that, and she wants to emulate it. So, of course, I had to live up to my reputation.' He gave Memnon a wry smile. 'Sometimes I wish I weren't such an honest man.'

Memnon suddenly liked him. He grinned back. 'We probably should wake her up and start moving, sir,' he said after a pause. 'I don't *think* those bastards are going to come after us now, but I don't want to bet all our lives on it.'

'You said you'd marked their trail, didn't you? Surely by now they'll either have fled, or they'll have been killed.'

'I did mark their trail,' Memnon admitted, 'but, well, following even a marked trail at night, over rough country, on horseback – it's not easy to do. If you miss a marker, you can ride for hours in the wrong direction. If the men from Eboracum tried it, they'll have had to go very slow, and I wouldn't say they'd be wrong if they just decided to wait for daylight. So, no, sir, I don't think the Maeatae will have been caught. They may have fled – it's what I'd do in their place: strike camp right away and ride till moonset, then on again at dawn. On the other hand, we may have annoyed them so much that they're out looking for us, now that they have light to track us by.'

Castor regarded Memnon incredulously. 'Would *you* go chasing after a bloodthirsty ghost that steals men's genitals?'

'A what?' asked Memnon, startled and guilty. 'All I did was circumcize the bastard! Gods, if I'd done anything more, he wouldn't've been able to walk up to that fire, would he?'

'You *circumcized* him? It looked worse. There was blood

dripping from . . . I don't think you realize how terrified those men were. They didn't think you were human: they thought you were something Athenais summoned from the dark underworld. I don't think they'd ever seen an Ethiopian before.'

'There are Ethiopians all over the Empire!' Memnon protested. Never many of them, it was true, but always a few – in the cities, anyway: horse-grooms and gladiators, courtesans and cleaners, merchant sailors and market gardeners and domestic slaves. The black faces stood out among the shades of Mediterranean bronze, noticeable but not extraordinary.

'The Maeatae live *outside* the Empire,' Castor pointed out. 'And I think you'd find very few of your nation even in southern Britain, and none at all in the north.'

'I've never found any of *my* nation since I left Africa,' Memnon told him. 'But . . . well.' He let out his breath slowly. He remembered how shocked he'd been the first time he'd seen a northern barbarian – the leprous skin, the hair bleached like that of a dead animal, the blind-seeming pale eyes. If his first encounter with such an apparition had been to have it walk up to his fire and toss in a comrade's severed head, he might have believed he was meeting an evil spirit, too. 'Well,' he said again, 'I *was* trying to scare them.'

Castor was silent for a moment. Then he laughed weakly. 'You succeeded. You scared *me*, and you were on my side. Circumcision. Do your people practice it?'

'Yes,' Memnon admitted. It was a solemn rite of passage, done when a boy became a man. He remembered the feast after his own circumcision, when he had sat down among the men for the first time, sore but proud. He felt a twinge of conscience at the way he'd profaned something that had once been sacred to him.

'I really don't think they're going to come looking for us,' Castor repeated. 'They're more likely to pray to the gods that they never meet you again.' He sighed and added, 'Just as well, because I don't think I could manage any more Numidian-style riding, glad as I was of your horse last night.'

Memnon smiled. 'We call it "Moorish-style" riding in Mauretania, sir.'

There was a stir behind them, and they both glanced back to find that Athenais had woken and crawled to the edge of the hollow. She held her long hair twisted up around one hand so that it wouldn't catch under her palms or in the gorse. Her look of relief as she saw Castor became one of cold horror as her gaze fell on Memnon.

It *hurt*. He had imagined . . . oh, well, gratitude, at least. He knew, somewhere in the back of his mind, that he had been combining two sweet fantasies: one in which he had found and rescued his sister before the Gaetulians killed her; one in which he saved a princess and got the hero's traditional reward. Daydreams both, he acknowledged now – but as that look of horror killed them, his very soul seemed to convulse. He couldn't endure it; he got to his feet looking back at her in disbelief.

The expression didn't change. He'd saved her life, and become a monster to her. Protesting was no use: if you had to ask for praise and gratitude, neither was worth a copper. He had no choice but to bear it – to pretend that it didn't matter.

'Well, then,' he said tightly, 'if you think you'll be safe here, stay and rest. I'll go see if I can find the men from Eboracum.'

He went over to Dozy, who was lying down, and tugged at his nose and his neck-rope to get him up. The gelding groaned and climbed to his feet, surly and reproachful, and Memnon swung on to his back and trotted off without a backward glance. His heart seemed to be seared inside him. He imagined his sister Iyangura looking at him like that. Wajjaj, she whispered in his mind, what has happened to you? You are not my brother; I don't know this man you are now.

Daylight let him identify the ridge along which he'd tracked the raiders the previous afternoon. He rode across to it, ascertained that nobody had been along it since, and sat down to wait. The rescue party from Eboracum would come this way, and going on to meet them would not bring them any faster. Besides, Dozy was tired. The gelding was a hardy animal, but the previous night's work had come on top of a long journey, and the little horse had had every justification for his reluctance to get up that morning.

About midmorning, the official rescue party appeared: two squadrons of heavy cavalry – tall men in scale armour, mounted upon powerful chargers – along with a man in the mail and transverse-crested helmet of a legionary centurion. Memnon got up when he saw them coming, and saluted as the centurion drew rein in front of him.

'Memnon, sir!' he declared. 'Scout, First Squadron, *Numerus* of Aurelian Moors! Sir, I got the imperial chamberlain Castor and the imperial secretary Athenais away from the barbarians, and they're waiting for you to come and help them.'

The centurion's jaw dropped. 'You say you've *already* rescued the Emperor's chamberlain? Where is he?'

'Ah, sir, I came here so I could guide you to them. The chamberlain was tortured, and he and the young secretary are pretty worn out. I left them resting. I'm sure they'll be very happy to see you, sir.'

There was a silence. Everyone stared. 'Your name is Memnon?' asked the centurion at last. 'You the one the Alban tribune said deserted?'

He was too tired to come up with the evasions and half-truths that would make what he'd done fit in with the chain of command. 'Yes, sir. He was mistaken, sir.'

They all continued to stare. 'What's that round your neck?' the centurion asked abruptly.

Memnon put his hand to the gold torque – the weighty evidence of what he had done. 'Took it off the barbarian chief, sir. I managed to take him hostage, sir, and got his people to give me the chamberlain in exchange.'

'Jupiter!' murmured the centurion. 'Jupiter Optimus Maximus!'

The men, it emerged, were two squadrons of the First Sarmatian Horse, a British-based unit currently attached to the Sixth Legion for patrol duties. The centurion, a reliable senior man from the Sixth, had been sent out with them the previous evening, in response to Panthera's report. They had galloped hard down the road to the place where the carriage was attacked – but, as Memnon had expected, had waited for daylight to follow the trail.

The centurion now sent one of the squadrons on after the Maeatae, and took the other to collect Castor and Athenais. The Sarmatians had set out in haste, but they had brought a few remounts. Castor was helped up into one of the high saddles, while Athenais, who had never ridden, was provided with straps to help her stay on.

It was more than twenty miles to Eboracum. Memnon was finding the company increasingly hard on his strained nerves, and he was worried about Dozy. The little horse now walked with his head hanging and the early signs of sore hooves in his halting gait. As they prepared to set out back to the fortress, he approached the centurion. 'Sir!' he said, saluting. 'My horse is exhausted. Permission to fall out, sir, and follow in my own time!'

The centurion regarded him with bewilderment. 'If your horse can't carry you, soldier, you're welcome to borrow one from the Sarmatians.'

Memnon glanced at the nearest of the cavalrymen. The man – a tall, fair-haired fellow in scale-armour – looked less than enthusiastic at the prospect of loaning his precious horse to a bloodstained and very dirty Moor. Memnon wasn't charmed by the Sarmatian, either. He had encountered Sarmatians before, but only as enemies, on the other side of the Danube: he did not feel comfortable with this British unit. 'I think my poor horse really needs to rest, sir,' he said piously. 'If I push him any further, sir, I risk losing him, and it takes a long time to train a horse Moorish-fashion. If your men can leave me some food, I'll just turn him loose to graze right here, and follow on in the morning.'

The centurion stared. Memnon knew what he was thinking: *You fool, you arrive in Eboracum with us, you'll be publicly acknowledged as a hero. You slip in quietly tomorrow, and nobody's going to pay any attention to you.* Memnon stared back, smiling like a stupid barbarian. Being nobody was much less complicated, just at the minute, and he had an urgent need to be alone. If Castor remembered him and got him a bonus, good: if he didn't, to hell with him.

'Very well,' said the centurion at last. 'If that's what you want.'

*   *   *

Memnon watched the party ride away with a deep sense of relief. He held Dozy firmly until the other horses were out of sight, then released him. The little horse tossed his head, then settled down to graze. Memnon sat down on the short, sheep-cropped grass and watched him. It was another sunny day, and the afternoon was comfortably warm. The air smelled of grass and heather, and a lark was singing overhead. Memnon lay down on his back and squinted up at the sun. As a boy, he had always searched for shade; now he welcomed the touch of the sun. In these northern countries the sun seemed another being entirely from the fierce killing power that ruled the desert: a friendly, gentle god, a giver of life.

Lying there, alone on the hillside, he once again remembered the previous night. He began to shake, and he pressed his palms against the grass. What if that would-be rapist had broken away from the girl, and the whole mob had risen to attack the intruders? What if somebody had tripped Memnon when he made his dash round the fire to take the chief hostage? What if the chief – a big, tall, powerful man – had gone for that sword he had at his feet? Gods, gods, it had been such a *stupid* trick; it really hadn't deserved to work. By rights he should be dead now.

Even the memory of the sentry frightened him now. He remembered the man coming closer and closer . . . remembered the hot spurt of blood over his hand. Every time he was assigned sentry duty now, he would remember that, one more death in a lengthening list. Odd to think the Maeatae had never seen a black man before. It seemed shameful: the first Ethiopian those Britons met came out of the dark to kill them.

If he hadn't, though, he'd likely be dead himself. His trick had certainly been stupid, but it had, however undeservedly, worked. They were all alive, and the emperor's chamberlain thought he was a hero.

The girl he'd done it for, however, thought he was a monster.

Was that really so surprising, though? What else was a nice girl going to think about a man who gave her a knife and told her to kill a captive, who enlisted her help to mutilate a prisoner? He should never have expected her to think anything else. What he *really* shouldn't do, though, was conclude that Iyangura would've reacted the same way. To her he had been big brother and protector. If he had somehow managed to get to her in time to rescue her, she would have clung to him and cried, the way she had that time he'd pulled her out of the well. To the Roman girl he'd been almost a stranger: of course she didn't trust him; of course she was horrified by what he'd done. It had been stupid to muddle the two very different things in his mind.

He drew a deep breath, forgiving Athenais and letting his daydream of her gratitude go. He'd saved her, and she was alive and whole and beautiful because of him. Let her life be an offering to Iyangura's spirit. He'd killed men for his sister before, but she'd always hated killing when she was alive, so probably she didn't like it any better now she was dead. Giving her this life – a young woman's life, like her own – would be better. He imagined Iyangura smiling and nodding at him as he offered her the Roman girl's life, and he smiled back.

Athenais might feel more friendly toward him, too, in a few days, once she'd had time to think about things. She didn't have to go to bed with him, though. Probably Castor was right, and clever secretary girls who attended an empress weren't allowed to go to bed with auxiliary soldiers even if they wanted to. If Athenais looked at him warmly and thanked him – it would be enough.

At least Castor seemed grateful. An imperial chamberlain, and he owed Memnon his life! It was like the story about the man who saved the king of snakes, and was granted a wish. Memnon wondered uneasily what he should wish for. He had few wants: he was accustomed to living in the present and finding as much pleasure there as he could. When he first joined the Roman army, it had seemed to hold everything he wanted: he belonged to the most powerful force in the world and he spent his time preventing what had happened to his family from happening to others. For years that had been enough for him. Recently, though, he'd noticed in himself an increasing dissatisfaction, a sense that friends and jokes weren't enough, and violence hurt, somewhere deep down, even if you came through it unscathed. It must be his age, he supposed. After so much fighting and killing, a man just wanted to live. He wasn't sure of his own age – south of the desert nobody counted the years – but he thought he must be a bit short of thirty.

It was time to marry, and get a brood of children whose fortunes he could follow once he'd gone to join his ancestors. That was hard to do just now, though. He'd sworn to fight for the Empire for twenty-five years; only ten had passed since his oath. Severus, in his generosity to the army, had repealed the law that said serving soldiers couldn't marry . . . but still, it wouldn't be much of a marriage, with a husband in barracks or off campaigning up and down the land while the wife struggled to bring up his children in a hut in some lawless settlement next to a fort. No, it would be better to have a discharge from the army, with the veteran's gift of citizenship. An imperial chamberlain ought to be able to ensure that an auxiliary was discharged early . . . after this present campaign, of course: nobody would be discharged from the army until it ended. Then, however, it might be a favour worth asking.

The thought of leaving the Moors, however, filled him with a sense of panicky disorientation. He wasn't Wajjaj any more, and once he stopped being Memnon, who was left? Maybe an early discharge from the Moors wasn't a good idea; maybe if he got it, he'd regret it. He'd think hard before asking Castor for anything.

He wondered what he'd tell the Moors about this escapade – or if he'd tell them anything. If he told them, circumcizing that barbarian would become a joke – and he didn't want to make a joke of it. No, he wouldn't talk about it. He wished he were back in his own tent, though, with Honoratus and Himilis and Victor and the others, telling them inconsequential stories about the journey, making them laugh . . . but that was wrong, because he knew very well that if he were with them, he'd hate himself for laughing, and want to be alone as he was now, on this green hillside, watching his horse graze.

He saw no one for the rest of that day, and spent the night under the gorse bush. In the morning, tired but more settled in his mind, he started on for Eboracum.

*   *   *

Eboracum was a fair-sized city, and it was full to overflowing. A remote provincial settlement was about to become the seat of government of the whole Roman Empire, and it simply did not have enough rooms. As Memnon rode into the town that afternoon, it seemed to him that every building was covered in scaffolding and that the entire population was shouting.

The legionary fortress, the command base for the army, was the other side of the river from the main civilian settlement. When Memnon rode across the bridge to the gate he was almost turned away. 'No space here, black face: you go to the temporary camp, on the north side'.

As he was turning away, though, another of the legionaries on guard called out, 'Wait a moment, Ethiopian! What's your name and unit?'

He told them, and they stared. '*You* took Fortrenn of the Votadini hostage?' one asked incredulously.

'Votadini?' Memnon repeated, bewildered. 'I thought he was a Maeatae.'

'The Votadini *are* Maeatae,' the legionary explained, confusingly. 'Did you really castrate his nephew?'

'*Circumsized*. Not castrated. I had to give them something to look at instead of me.'

The legionary whistled. '*Deae Matres*! Well done, soldier! Don't bother with the temporary camp – the Sixth Legion can always accommodate a hero.'

They gave him a chit entitling him to lodging for himself and his horse, then informed him that, once he'd got himself settled, he had an invitation to the palace. It seemed that Castor had not forgotten him.

The palace was back across the bridge, in the civilian settlement. It had, apparently, been the residence of the commander of the Sixth Legion, but it was in the process of being turned into a palace for the Emperor of Rome. It too was covered in scaffolding, though the workmen were in the process of dismantling it.

Memnon had never set foot in a palace before, and he was thoroughly intimidated the moment he stepped through the gate. Everything was magnificent and spotlessly clean, and everywhere the tall and splendid men of the Praetorian Guard seemed to be looking down their noses at this short black auxiliary in his travel-stained tunic and muddy boots.

One of the superior guardsmen, however, escorted him to Castor's rooms, and Castor welcomed him warmly. Memnon was impressed that the chamberlain actually *lived* in the palace. The suite of rooms looked fit for the Emperor himself – they had mosaic floors, and frescoed walls painted with fruit and flowers; even the ceiling was decorated with birds and trees. The rooms did not, however, have anywhere to sit. Castor apologized for the disorder.

'The slaves who came with me were to have seen to everything,' he explained, 'but they . . .' He broke off abruptly, pinching his nose.

The slaves who came with him were dead. Memnon noticed that the chamberlain's eyes were red and swollen, and his liking for the man increased. 'Had they been with you long, sir?'

'Years. In one case, all his life. What I will say to that poor child's mother, I do not know. But, come, I didn't mean to talk to you about this, but to see if there is any way I can properly express my gratitude. We can use one of the smaller public reception rooms; they're all free, since the Emperor's not in residence. I'll send someone for wine.'

The 'smaller public reception room' was the size of a praetorium's main hall, and much grander: the walls were faced with polished marble, and the dome was painted blue as the sky, with gods and goddesses lounging in it. The couches were of cedarwood, upholstered in a blue so vivid that Memnon, guessing the cost of the dye, was almost ashamed to sit on them. A slave mixed wine and brought it to them in delicate cups of clear glass. Memnon held his nervously. What if he broke the fragile thing and spilled wine on the Emperor's upholstery? Would that be treason?

'I expected you to return to Eboracum with us,' Castor said, with a touch of reproach. 'It wasn't until we were on our way that I noticed you weren't one of the party.'

'My horse was very tired, sir.'

'So the centurion informed me. I'd intended to present you to the legate as my deliverer, and ask him to see to it that you were honoured for your courage. Well, I have told him what you did, and I've written out an account of it. I gather from the soldiers here that this man Fortrenn is well known, and is judged to be a most formidable war-leader – the British troops, at any rate, are deeply impressed by your achievement.'

'Thank you, sir. I sort of gathered that when I arrived at the fortress. Sir, they said there that Fortrenn was chief of the Gotadini or something. I thought the enemy were called Maeatae?'

'The Maeatae are a confederacy of several different tribes,' Castor explained at once, 'the largest and most powerful of whom are the Votadini. They seem to be well known to our people here – they traded with us extensively before the current difficulties began.'

Memnon nodded: that made sense. It was always the biggest and most Romanized tribes of barbarians who made the most trouble.

'Unfortunately, however,' the chamberlain continued, 'while the British troops honour you, there may be some trouble from the Alban Legion. Tribune Flavius Panthera made his own report of the matter, seeking to justify his conduct, and in it he named you as a deserter. This absurd charge has already been dropped, but the fact that it could be raised at all may be enough to allow the Albans to deny you honours. They do not like it that one of their tribunes has been put to shame by a common auxiliary.'

That side of things had barely occurred to Memnon. He snorted. No, the Albans certainly wouldn't like that! He hoped they didn't find out who was responsible for the drunkard banner. Maybe it would be good to get out of Eboracum quickly.

'I will press your cause, of course,' Castor continued, 'but I must warn you, I have little influence in the army. I'm sorry.'

Memnon shrugged. 'I wasn't thinking of honours, sir, when I did it.'

There was a moment of silence, and then Castor said, cautiously, 'What you did was undertaken at great risk to your life and in defiance of your orders. Why *did* you do it, if I may ask?'

Memnon shrugged again. Meeting the chamberlain's reddened eyes, he decided that he liked the man well enough to tell him the truth. 'My sister was carried off by some Gaetulian raiders, sir. I tried to save her, but I was too late. What happened – it was like a second chance. I tried again, and I was in time.'

Castor's mouth formed a silent 'Oh', and he lowered his eyes. 'I see.' After a moment he went on. 'Athenais, too, was sorry that you did not escort us home. She told me that she very much regretted her failure to thank you.' He raised his eyes again. 'I was intending to send her a note asking her to come now.'

Memnon thought about that. 'She wants to see me? She didn't seem to like the look of me yesterday.'

'She was frightened . . .'

'I worked that one out.'

'But she is well aware how much she owes you. We would both have died, slowly and in great pain, if you hadn't come for us. Yes, she was very shaken yesterday morning: what woman wouldn't have been? But she truly does want to thank you, and I think it would ease her distress if she does. I'll send her that note.'

He sent the slave for a notebook, wrote the note, and despatched the slave 'to Athenais, the assistant secretary for Latin letters in the household of Julia Augusta'. After the boy had left to deliver it, he poured Memnon some more wine.

'Now,' he said brightly, 'can I be of any assistance to you? I do not, of course, believe that I can *pay* you for saving my life, but it would certainly be proper for me to compensate you for anything you've lost to the barbarians. You had property on the luggage wagons, didn't you? Valuables?'

Memnon almost responded with a surprised 'no', then realized that the chamberlain was giving him an excuse to take money, as if he might refuse it without one. 'Umm . . .' he said, taken aback by this strange notion.

'Or is there some legal assistance I could render you?'

He thought again about discharge from the army – and again decided, *Not yet*. 'I . . . not at the moment, sir. When the war is over, maybe. Sir, I've been wondering, what does someone who's *a memoria* do?'

Castor smiled. 'Arrange the schedule and keep the appointments list for my patron, Septimius Severus Augustus.'

'Ah.' It was immediately apparent, even to someone
with as little knowledge of administration as Memnon,
that the man who got people appointments with the
Emperor was a very powerful man, and that the Emperor
must trust him.

'Do you want an appointment with my patron?'

He imagined meeting the man whose portrait had adorned
the Moors' standard since he joined the unit; imagined that
man looking at him and asking testily, *Who, by all the gods,
is this?* 'Ah, no, sir.'

'Compensation for your valuables, then?'

It sounded as though he could ask for a fortune! On the
other hand, he had no idea what to do with a fortune, and
if he accepted it, Castor might think he'd been amply
rewarded, and decline to give any further help. 'There wasn't
anything really valuable on the wagon, sir.'

Castor looked disappointed. 'Well – I will see that you
receive some compensation for what there was. You're staying
at the fortress?'

The door opened, and Athenais came in.

Memnon immediately doubted Castor's assertion that she
wanted to see him. She recoiled, then stood with her hand
on the door, her beautiful eyes huge and black. He got uncomfortably to his feet.

'As you can see, our deliverer has arrived in Eboracum,'
Castor explained quietly. 'I told him you'd wanted to thank
him, that you much regretted not having done so before.'

'Yes.' She managed a sick smile. 'Yes, I did.' She did not
meet his eyes.

What could he say to reassure her? *I'm not really a piti-
less killer?* She wouldn't believe that: it was patently untrue.
'I did it for my sister.'

That startled her into looking at him squarely.

'She was taken by some Gaetulian raiders. They did to
her what the Maeatae meant to do to you. I found her body
in the desert.'

'Oh,' she said, and swallowed. 'Oh, I'm so sorry.'

'They'd killed the rest of my family already. They raid

the southern tribes all the time. I was out herding goats when it happened; I came back and everyone was dead – everyone except my sister, who was missing. So I went after them, hoping I could save her – but I was too late. When I saved you, it was a little like I'd been faster then. Do you understand that?'

'Yes,' she whispered. Her face had gone red. 'I . . . I'm sorry. I'm sorry I didn't . . . didn't thank you at first. It was because it was so . . . so horrible, all of it; because . . .'

'I know,' he said matter-of-factly. 'I made you help me hurt a man and agree to kill him, and you hated that.'

'I'm sorry!' she exclaimed again, blinking back some tears now. 'I know you only asked it because I'd begged you to get Castor out, any way you could, and . . . and, it was incredibly clever, what you did, and incredibly brave. I know that . . . and I am grateful, really I am. And I know what would have happened to me if you hadn't come. I'm very, very glad you did come.'

He nodded and smiled at her. 'I'm glad I came, too, ah? Ah, don't cry!'

She had burst into tears, and turned away from him, covering her face. He took a step toward her – then stopped. She might be grateful, but it was perfectly clear that she was still afraid of him.

'Hush, child!' Castor said gently. He took her arm and steered her to the couch. She sat down on it with a thump and tossed a corner of her cloak over her head to shield herself from their eyes. Castor patted her on the back. 'She needed this,' he explained to Memnon. 'I've been worried about her. I expected her to cry, after we escaped, and she didn't. Oh, child, there's nothing to be ashamed of! *I* cried – I've wept tears enough to fill a basin!'

'Well,' said Memnon. He sat down and poured himself some more wine. Athenais sobbed, and blew her nose, and sobbed some more.

Castor eventually refilled his cup and offered it to Athenais. She had to pull her cloak aside to take a gulp, and it helped her to stop sobbing. She looked at Memnon, her nose streaming and her face wet. 'I'm sorry!' she choked again, and went on, her eyes suddenly shining with emotion, 'and

I'm so, so grateful! Thank you, thank you for coming to fetch me away from there!'

It was not exactly what he'd wanted, but it was enough. He smiled, basking in that warmth. 'I'm glad when I look at you, alive and pretty, and Lord Castor –' he acknowledged with a nod at the chamberlain – 'alive and . . .'

'Not so pretty,' put in Castor quickly, smiling.

Memnon grinned at him. 'I was going to say, "rich and distinguished", sir.'

Castor laughed. 'A condition I will do my utmost to extend to you, soldier! It will be easier to do, if you remain here in Eboracum a bit longer.'

'My prefect sent me to Aballava, sir,' replied Memnon dutifully. 'He and the rest of my unit will be on their way to Eboracum now; if I'm to report back the way I was supposed to, I need to be on my way fairly soon.'

'I'm sure your prefect would understand why you were delayed. I would be happy to explain it to him myself.'

Memnon hesitated – then grinned. 'Maybe, sir, but there's a commissary investigation into what happened to Second Parthica's banner, and I don't want it to catch up with me.'

Athenais gulped in surprise, and Castor stared. 'Jupiter!' he exclaimed. 'That was you?'

'Of course not, sir!' replied Memnon, with a look of wide-eyed innocence. 'Second Parthica's sentries swore that nobody could've slipped into their camp, so it must have been one of their own legionaries. But there was a rumour that someone in the Aurelian Moors was responsible, and my prefect thought it would be better to send me on an errand.' He sobered slightly, and went on, 'I really don't want to hand Flavius Panthera an excuse to have me arrested.'

'He wouldn't *dare*,' said Castor, frowning. 'The tribune should be worrying about his own career, not yours. My report will give him cause.'

'Maybe so, sir – but I still think it would be simpler if I were out of Eboracum when the commissary investigation gets here.' He got to his feet, grinning. 'I'd best be going, sir. Thank you, sir, for the wine, and the money, and your goodwill.'

Castor got to his own feet. 'Thank *you*, soldier, for my life. I am ashamed at how little you've accepted from me in return; if you think of something else I could do for you, I would count it a favour.' He pulled a ring from his finger and offered it. 'If you ever have any need, either of money or of a friend at court, send this to me, and I will do my utmost for you.'

Memnon took the ring and slipped it into his purse, then offered Castor his hand. Castor shook it firmly. He went over to Athenais and offered the hand to her as well.

She clasped it in both of hers, still sniffing. 'I . . . that goes for me, too. If I can ever do anything to help you, I would be very glad to. Thank you very much.'

'There is one thing I would like you to do for me,' he said seriously.

She drew back a little, nervous again, questioning him with her eyes.

'Go to a temple, of whatever god you prefer, and make an offering for my sister's spirit. Her name was Iyangura, the daughter of Lianja and Agonadi. She was thirteen when she died.'

'Oh!' she said, relieved. 'Yes. I would be very glad to do that. Ian . . . Iangoura, the daughter of . . . of . . .'

'Ah, that's good enough! I never met a Roman who could pronounce "Lianja". If the gods aren't smart enough to know who you mean, then they'd be no use anyway.' He smiled, and, leaning forward, kissed her very gently on the cheek. Her skin was wet, salt with tears, and smooth as polished ivory.

'I'll see you to the gate,' offered Castor.

As they were walking down the corridor, the chamberlain said softly, 'These Gaetulians who murdered your family – you followed them, didn't you? You followed them all the way to their own land, and every night you came and killed some of them. Not one returned to his home and his own people.'

Memnon looked at him in surprise and disquiet – then realized that the words were his own, spoken to the British chieftain. He nodded, not liking to speak of it.

'It was Rome's gain.' The chamberlain stopped: they were in the entrance hall of the palace. 'It brought you north, to us. Thank you again. If there is any favour I can grant, you have only to ask.'

Five

When Memnon returned to the fortress, he found a message from Melisus the Gaul, inviting him out for a drink.

The meeting was not a complete success: Memnon was not eager to talk about What Happened, which was what Melisus and everyone at the tavern seemed to want to know. However, it emerged that Melisus also wanted company on the road: his route and Memnon's lay together almost all the way to their respective forts. Memnon was relieved to have a travelling companion; he still wasn't sure of his itinerary. They set out together the following afternoon.

They rode at a moderate pace. Their travelling funds were running low, but Castor had provided a purse with a year's pay, so they continued to stay in posting inns and live well. The first night in an inn, Memnon asked his companion not to mention What Happened and, because Memnon had the purse, Melisus complied. The rest of the journey was soothingly uneventful.

They arrived at the northern town of Luguvalium in the evening four days after leaving Eboracum. Melisus was bound for a fort called Uxelodunum, which turned out to be less than a mile from Luguvalium: they rode the last short distance together in the morning, and parted at the fort gate. Aballava wasn't much further – a matter of five miles or so on the military road which ran next to the famous wall.

It was impressive, the wall, Memnon had to admit: three times as tall as a man, built of crenellated stone above a deep ditch, with a fortlet for the guards every mile and a watch-tower every three hundred paces. There was another, even deeper, ditch and a bank to the south which marked the edge of the military zone – and incidentally enclosed some good grazing for cavalry horses.

Dozy ambled along at an easy pace, wall to the right, fields and woods to the left. It was a land of wide skies, the country rolling only a little, rich and full of life. The apple harvest was over now, but pigs had been set to forage in the orchards, and sheep and cattle grazed the mown fields; in the patches of woodland he glimpsed deer and wild swine, and birds sang from every perch.

Of the land to the north, though, he could see nothing: the great bulk of the wall blocked it out entirely. The gates of the first two fortlets he passed were bolted shut, though there were hobbled horses grazing the land around them. At the third fortlet, however, the gate stood open. Memnon checked Dozy and stared through it with some interest. The walls enclosed two small stone barracks, one on either side of a grassy aisle. Beyond them was another gate, also open, and giving a view north. He touched Dozy forward, stopping again just outside the outer gate, and saw that on the other side of the wall the land dropped sharply. Beyond the drop he could see a stretch of vividly green marshland, with hills rising in the distance. There was nobody in sight, though he could hear voices from beyond the gate. He dismounted and silently walked through to the north gate. There was a river at the bottom of the hill, and a couple of men were fishing in it. They were blond and shaggy and dressed in the German fashion, in tunics and breeches, and the spears they had ready to hand appeared to be the typical short, narrow-bladed German *frameae*.

Memnon studied their backs curiously. His destination was garrisoned by a unit called the Formation of Frisians of Aballava, and he suspected that these men belonged to it. The fact that the unit was a formation rather than an *ala* undoubtedly meant that it consisted of irregular cavalry, and probably of men from outside the Empire. He *thought* that Frisians were Germans of some kind, though they weren't a tribe he'd ever encountered. The fishermen certainly *looked* German. He wondered how they felt about having to share their fort with a company that had been fighting Germans only the year before. They would probably be annoyed if they looked up and found him trespassing. He went back to Dozy, remounted, and rode on.

The wall snaked along the riverbank, then turned toward a rise which was crowned by the stone walls of a fort. As he rode up, the combination of the rise of the land and the turn of the wall at last gave him another view to the north-west, and he stopped Dozy and stared in surprise. The marshes he'd glimpsed through the gates ended in golden sands, and beyond them was sea, vividly blue in the noonday sun. The hills to the north rose beyond the water for a distance, then ended in a limitless horizon. The Western Ocean, the edge of the world – he hadn't realized it was so close.

He remembered the first time he'd ever seen the sea, when he came to Caesarea with Saturninus, a new recruit. He had never imagined that there was so much water in all the world – and yet it had seemed familiar, too. A blue desert, open and empty and light-drenched as the Great Sea of Sand, its waves ruffled by the same hot winds. The winds here, though, were cool and moist, smelling of rain. It was a long way to Africa.

He started Dozy on again, now inspecting the fort where the Aurelian Moors would spend the winter. It was stone-built, like the wall and, by the look of the bright roof-tiles, it had been recently renovated and repaired. A thriving civilian settlement of the sort that grew up around every fort trailed its southern flank. Memnon knew that it would contain plenty of taverns and brothels eager to relieve soldiers of their money. Most of the establishments would be run by ex-soldiers, and most of those narrow little timber houses would contain soldiers' wives and families. It didn't seem a bad place at all.

The east gate of the fortress had once had an imposing double gate, but the southern gate of the pair had been bricked up. A couple of auxiliaries guarded the remaining entrance, leaning idly on their spears; they were blond and bearded, like their comrades in the fortlet. They watched Memnon's approach casually at first, then straightened as they noticed his colour, and made the now-familiar gesture to avert ill-fortune: Ethiopians really were unknown in the north. Memnon waved back cheerfully.

'Stop there!' shouted one of the auxiliaries, when he was still some distance away. His accent was quite different from the familiar Quadic German, flatter and more nasal.

Memnon obediently halted Dozy. He slid off the gelding's back, put his riding rod through his pack, and stood easily with both hands visible. 'Greetings!' he called back. 'Is this Aballava?'

'What are you that wants to know?' replied the auxiliary, staring at him in amazement and suspicion.

'He's one of the Moors!' exclaimed his comrade excitedly. 'You know we're supposed to be getting Moors. Alaisiagae! I didn't know they were *that* black!'

'*Are* you a Moor?' asked the first auxiliary.

'A messenger from the *Numerus* of Aurelian Moors, yes,' agreed Memnon. 'I'm called Memnon. I have a letter for your commander from Valerius Rogatus, our prefect.'

The auxiliary hesitated – then beckoned him to come forward. Memnon led Dozy up to the gate, halted and dug the letter out of his pack. The Frisians, he noted ruefully, were both huge, as Germans tended to be. They towered over him, and their expressions were not friendly.

The Frisian took the letter, glanced at the seal – the eight-pointed star – then grimaced and handed it back; Memnon at once guessed that he couldn't read either. 'All right!' he said. 'The chief's probably in his house, this time of day. Verritus, you take him there.'

The second, younger, guard, opened the gate and escorted Memnon through. The buildings inside looked much like those in any fort along the Danube: stone-built barracks in rows, with the taller and more imposing facade of the headquarters building visible down the street between them. What was unlike any Danube fort Memnon had ever seen were the women. There were several of them washing clothing in the water-tank beside the gatehouse, and a group of blond, half-naked children were running about the street, playing with some shaggy gray dogs. Chickens scratched in the open aisle that flanked the fort wall. Men were lounging by the barracks' walls, tending to their weapons or just chatting. The fort smelled of beer and roast meat and offal, of dung and straw and dirt, a complex scent that

nevertheless was immediately recognizable as German.
Memnon was surprised and disquieted. It was quite common
for the Roman army to hire barbarian warbands, but usually
they were attached to a regular cohort, which would prohibit
them from anything as flagrant as moving their families
into a Roman fort.

One of the children noticed Memnon and shrieked, and
everyone turned and stared. The men stood up. The women
began gabbling to one another in their own language. A
couple of dogs came over wagging their tails.

Verritus ignored them and led the visitor on to the nearest
building, a stable. Several of the men followed, looming in
the entrance way behind them. 'You can leave your horse
here,' the guard said, then watched in fascination as Memnon
slipped Dozy into the nearest empty stall without doing
anything more than taking his pack off the gelding's shoulders and slinging it across his own. He had no intention of
leaving that pack unattended. It had Fortrenn's gold torque
inside, and Castor's purse of money.

'How can you ride without a bridle?' the young Frisian
asked incredulously.

'You can train horses lots of ways. That's how Moors train
them. The training takes longer, but you never have to clean
any tack.'

Verritus shook his head disapprovingly. He glanced over
his shoulder and informed the several onlookers, 'He's one
of the Moors. He says his name's Memnon.'

'Sounds Greek,' replied an onlooker, a burly older man.

Memnon grinned at him; he'd be sharing the fort with
these men all winter, so he might as well try to make friends
of them. He could already see that it wouldn't be easy.
Rogatus would never stand for women in the fort, and when
he turned them out, the Frisians were bound to resent it. 'It
is Greek. Romans could never say the name my mother gave
me, so they started calling me Memnon, after an Ethiopian
hero in a Greek poem.'

No smile, just a look of bovine astonishment. 'And you're
a Moor?' asked the onlooker. 'Are they all as black as you?'

Memnon hesitated, sorely tempted. Then he sighed, remembering the lecture Saturninus had given him before he set out:

'And if I get to Aballava and find that the troopers there, our future comrades-in-arms, expect us to eat dogs, or paint ourselves purple on holidays, or be anything we're not – *you* will be on latrine duty all winter, understand?' He was pretty sure that telling the Frisians that all the Moors were black, except for the red ones with dogs' teeth, would fall in the category of 'things we're not'.

'No,' he admitted reluctantly. 'Most of us are only brown. Ha! And you people, you're Germans?'

'Frisians!' the onlooker corrected him.

'That's not a German tribe? You've got *frameae.*'

'You've never heard of Frisians in Mauretania?'

'No. Nor on the Danube, where we were until this summer. Met a lot of Germans there, but they were all Quadi and Marcomanni.'

This was received with a chorus of grunts; the Frisians knew little about Africa, but they had heard about the wars on the Danube frontier. Memnon was aware, without glancing around, that his audience had grown.

'We're Germans,' explained Verritus, 'but from the western lowlands, on the edge of the ocean.' He glanced at the audience and added, 'He has a letter for Lord Farabert. From his prefect . . . I'd better take him.'

Farabert, the chief of the Frisian Formation, was, as the guards had thought, in his house. The commandant's house had obviously been built with the fort, a traditional two-story building with a colonnaded courtyard and a private bathhouse. The interior now held an odd mixture of Roman and German furnishings – painted wall panels and drinking horns; mosaic floors and wolf-skin rugs. Farabert himself was a thickset man with a hideous scar that left one side of his face misshapen and half his nose missing. He was in the dining room, playing a board game with a fair-haired child, almost certainly his son. He glanced up when Verritus led Memnon in, then stared and stood up. The child exclaimed in Frisian and bolted behind his father.

Memnon saluted smartly and held out his letter. 'A message, sir! From Valerius Rogatus, prefect of the *Numerus* of Aurelian Moors!'

'Oh!' said Farabert, staring at the letter without touching

it. The child said something excited in Frisian, to which
Farabert replied. The child ran off.

'He will fetch my clerk,' explained Farabert. He frowned
at Memnon: the scar made the expression intimidating. 'So,
you're a Moor.'

'Yes and no, sir,' replied Memnon easily. As the frown
deepened, he went on, 'I'm a Moor by membership of the
numerus, sir, but by tribe I'm a Tebu. Our officers recruit
anybody with the right skills.'

Farabert's expression changed to one of uneasiness.
Numerus was a vague term: it could mean a group of barbarians under their own native commander, or it could mean a
specialist company with a more Romanized command structure. Farabert must have hoped the Moors fell into the first
category: he now knew they fell into the second, and would
be unlikely to tolerate the way he'd been running his fort.
'And your prefect sent you here to inform us that your
numerus is coming . . . when?' he asked irritably.

'I left them in Londinium sixteen days ago, sir. They were
planning to set out the day after I did. They wouldn't travel
as fast, but I had a bit of a delay in Eboracum, so I don't
suppose they're more than three days' journey away now.
I'm to report back to my prefect, sir, after I've seen you
here.'

Farabert grunted, and his eyes narrowed assessingly. 'How
many in your unit?'

'Three hundred and two at present, sir. We're a little under
strength.' Memnon was sure that Farabert must have received
that information along with the news that the *numerus* was
coming; if he was pretending not to know, that probably meant
he was going to cause trouble about sharing facilities.

That was an entirely foreseeable problem. The Frisians
were well established in the fort, and it was only human
nature to resent an intrusion – even if you hadn't brought
some of your womenfolk into the fort with you, contrary to
the regulations. The army usually made some effort to billet
similar units together – Melisus the Gaul had been sent to
a fort which was garrisoned by a Gaulish cavalry unit, for
example – but there weren't any other units of African light
cavalry in Britain. The high command probably thought that

shoving them in with another unit of barbarian irregular cavalry was good enough. Memnon hoped the Frisians' discipline was better than it seemed, because in cramped quarters tension between two such dissimilar groups of men was inevitable. Even Farabert was in for a difficult time. As commander, he was entitled to keep his family in the *praetorium* with him, but Rogatus was entitled to share the house – and Rogatus didn't like children.

'Three hundred and two!' objected Farabert at once. 'We did not know there were so many of you. Skirmishers, I am told, and cavalry scouts. Maybe a hundred I was told. I have said to my men there is no need to make space for more.'

'We're accustomed to the standard cavalry arrangement, sir,' offered Memnon helpfully. 'Six to a room, two squadrons to each barrack block.'

'There are only eight barracks in the fort,' said Farabert coldly. 'We . . .'

Memnon beamed at him. 'Well, there you are, sir! We get four, and you get four. It'll be a bit cramped, but not bad.'

'We use *all* the barracks,' Farabert told him, narrowing his eyes. 'I have told my men, they must clear two.'

Memnon allowed himself to look anxious. 'How many in your formation, sir?'

Farabert glowered. 'Three hundred and twenty.' He obviously couldn't mention the women: he knew as well as Memnon that they shouldn't be in the fort at all.

There was a silence, and then Memnon said brightly, 'Well, sir, I'm sure that if you explain to your men that you didn't know we were going to be so many, they'll understand why they have to move.'

Farabert scowled menacingly.

'Just as well I came ahead, isn't it, sir?' Memnon went on happily. 'You can shift your men, and I'll go back and meet Rogatus so he'll know he has to assign some of our people to double up, and then when we move in everything can go smoothly.'

Farabert scowled harder. 'It is *our* fort.'

'Ah, no, sir, I'm sure that's wrong. It belongs to the Emperors, sir. They sent you here, and now they've sent us.'

Farabert grimaced.

'I'm sure the imperial staff will be pleased to know our move here has gone well,' Memnon continued significantly. He dug Castor's ring out of his purse and held it out so that Farabert could see the seal. 'This belongs to Septimius Castor, the Emperor's secretary and chamberlain. Rogatus said I could use it if there was any trouble.'

Farabert gazed at the ring in surprise and misgiving, then looked up suspiciously at Memnon's face. Memnon held the gaze. He doubted Farabert would recognize the seal any more than he had – it was certainly a private seal, not an official one. It was, however, the same general size and style as more familiar seals that routinely stamped official military documents, and the ring – gold with an oval of chalcedony – unquestionably looked official and important.

He had no desire to call in Castor's favour over a minor problem like this, but if he'd judged right it wouldn't be necessary. Farabert was, unmistakeably, a barbarian chieftain who had hired himself and his personal following out to the Romans, probably because he'd lost some argument in Frisian tribal politics. He was unlikely to have friends or patrons at the imperial court. If he thought that Rogatus did, then the Moors' life at the fort would be much easier.

Farabert grimaced again. 'Four barracks for you, and four for us,' he agreed.

'That sounds fair to me, sir,' Memnon said cheerfully, and put the ring away.

When Memnon left the fort the following morning, the four barracks on the north side were being cleared, and the women and children were moving out – not without a great deal of screaming and shouting. Everyone involved gave him filthy looks, and many of them spat at him and made the signs to avert evil. He was glad to get away.

He met up with his *numerus* two days later, back on the road to Eboracum. He was braced for questions about What Happened, but Rogatus only asked about the situation at Aballava. Memnon told him; the prefect nodded with satisfaction and sent him to rejoin his tent-mates. They were pleased to see him, and asked if he'd had a good time on the journey.

'Ahhh . . .' He hesitated. He still didn't want to talk about
What Happened. It was too raw, too unwieldy. 'Didn't you
. . . stop in Eboracum?'

They shook their heads. 'We reached it about midday, and
rode right past,' explained Honoratus. 'Camped in a field ten
miles away. What's interesting about it?'

'Scaffolding,' Memnon replied, relieved. 'If I sold scaffolding I could make a fortune. They're rebuilding the whole
place all at once!'

He supposed that he would have to make a full report at
some point, but . . . not yet. Let the horror fade, let the demon
go back to sleep. He wanted a chance to become himself
again.

The Moors moved into Aballava to a sullen silence from the
Frisians. The civil settlement, however, was more welcoming:
most of its establishments predated the arrival of the Frisians,
and were pleased to get new customers. The Aurelians, as a
small, flexible unit, were accustomed to being moved around,
and they settled down for the winter happily enough.

Memnon found no occasion to make a full report on his
journey; by the time he felt able to, it was too late to do so
without embarrassment. It was halfway through October
before he was summoned by the prefect.

He was in his room in the barracks, planning a joke, when
Saturninus threw open the door and glared thunderously at
him and his assembled tent-mates. Memnon's first thought
was that the decurion had somehow found out about the
intended prank, which involved one of the Frisians' dogs and
some blue dye. He began to run through possible extenua-
tions: *We didn't hurt the dog, sir! We thought it would make
both units laugh, sir, and improve relations between them,
sir!*

'You,' said Saturninus, focussing the glare. 'You're to
report to Rogatus. Now.'

'Yes, sir!' Memnon slid off his bunk and saluted smartly.
His tent-mates gave him looks of anxious sympathy as he
followed the decurion out of the small room.

The fort had changed since he first saw it. The women
and children had all been moved out into huts in the village,

and the Frisian men were now confined to the southern half
of the fort. The narrow verandah which flanked each northern
barrack block was now cluttered with the small pottery
hearths and sacks of charcoal the men used to cook their
meals, and a scent of asafoetida and cumin lingered in the
porch, the smell of North African cooking. Charms against
the evil eye dangled over every doorway, along with a few
damp tunics and breeches hung hopefully in the damp sea
air. It was raining – the fine, steady drizzle off the sea which
seemed normal weather for October in the northwest of
Britain. Memnon hadn't picked up his cape, and he hunched
his shoulders unhappily as Saturninus led him along the duck-
boarded aisle between his barrack and the neighbouring one.

'What's it about, sir?' he asked, as they approached the
praetorium, which Farabert and his family were now obliged
to share with Rogatus.

'I think you should tell us, scout,' said Saturninus tightly.
'*We* have no idea.'

Memnon received the first inkling that maybe this wasn't
to do with a dog, after all. He swallowed uncomfortably, and
wished that he'd forced himself to explain things to Rogatus
before.

The *praetorium* was warmer than the unheated barrack
block, and when Saturninus led him into the dining room,
he flexed his toes luxuriously at the heat seeping up through
the floor from the hypocaust below – for a moment. Then
he registered the number of visitors facing him, and decided
that he would rather be on sentry duty in the rain.

'This is the man,' Rogatus told the visitors. Memnon reckoned that there were three principals, though one of them had
brought a clerk, who stood behind his master with a notebook. There was a beefy red-faced man in the silvered mail
of a centurion; a reserved thin man in the purple-striped tunic
of the equestrian order and a short military cloak; and a well-
dressed civilian of middle age. They sat in a row on one of
the dining-room couches, rain-damp clothes steaming slightly
in the warmth, cups of hot spiced wine in their hands. Rogatus
was leaning against the table by the window, arms crossed,
and Farabert – who surely had no right to be present at all –
was sitting quietly in a chair by the door.

Memnon saluted smartly and stood to attention. 'Sir!' he said to Rogatus, ignoring the others. 'You sent for me?'

'Yes,' agreed Rogatus, with a dark look. 'These gentlemen wished to inquire into some details of what happened on your journey to Eboracum. This –' he indicated the centurion – 'is Varius Marcellinus, *hastatus* of the First Cohort of the Alban Legion. This –' the civilian – 'is Julius Salutaris, freedman of Augusta, and *this* –' the thin equestrian – 'is Oclatinius Adventus, *princeps peregrinorum.*'

Memnon caught his breath. *Princeps peregrinorum* was the title bestowed upon the head of the Castra Peregrina, the Rome base of the Grain Commissary. This ordinary-looking man was the head of the Emperor's spies, and one of the most feared individuals in the Empire.

'At ease, soldier,' Adventus said, in dry amusement. 'Your conduct is not in question: indeed, everyone agrees it to have been entirely praiseworthy. My investigation, such as it is, is being undertaken at the request of the Praetorian Prefect, in order to ascertain whether a certain tribune of the Alban Legion should be dismissed, hence the presence of the legion's representative.' He nodded at the centurion, Marcellinus, then smiled indulgently and added, 'My own presence here is not entirely on your account, either. Ordinarily, I would assign a matter like this to one of my men, but –' he shrugged – 'I was making a tour of the wall anyway.'

'Yes, sir,' whispered Memnon queasily, wishing more than ever that he'd explained the situation to Rogatus. He cast an uncertain glance toward the prefect, but Rogatus was at his most impassive. Saturninus, who'd taken up station behind him, was no better. Farabert was gaping in amazement, but that was no help. Memnon thought fleetingly that at least this would do away with any doubts the Frisian might have had about the Aurelians' powerful connections at court.

'Just explain to us what happened when the barbarians attacked your party,' coaxed the spymaster. 'In your own words.'

'Yes, sir,' Memnon whispered again, and cleared his throat. With an apologetic glance at Rogatus, he began to recount what had happened.

Marcellinus the centurion stopped him almost at once. 'Our tribune says that when the barbarians attacked, you ran,' he declared harshly.

Rogatus stirred irritably. 'No, sir,' said Memnon, with another anxious glance at the prefect. 'I tried to attack the enemy on the flank as they advanced. I'm not trained or equipped, sir, to stand a charge head-on.'

'You *ran,* soldier, and as for what you did afterward, you did it because the tribune had threatened to have you flogged for cowardice!'

'Cowardice!' exploded Rogatus angrily. 'Not this man! Not any of my men, but certainly not this one!'

Adventus shook his head. 'The tribune ordered you to fall in line, is that correct?' he asked Memnon.

'Yes, sir. And I did, but—'

'But, being a cavalry skirmisher – unequipped, as you say, to stand a charge head-on – you naturally assumed that you were at liberty to attack the enemy when you saw opportunity, in the way you knew best?'

It was precisely the dodge Memnon had been about to produce. 'Yes, sir.'

'*Assumed*?' repeated the centurion. 'A soldier's job is to follow orders!'

'Of course.' Adventus smiled. 'But, according to his own account, the tribune *gave* no orders, apart from the one to line up – and the one to retreat. An experienced skirmisher doesn't expect his commander to stand at his shoulder, pointing out opportunities, isn't that correct, prefect? He's expected to use his own judgement as to the best time and place to strike. Now, it's perfectly clear that this scout did exactly that – but the tribune, unfamiliar with cavalry tactics, misunderstood it when he left the line of battle.'

'If he expected a skirmisher to stand a charge, he's guilty of worse than "misunderstanding",' Rogatus said resentfully. 'He could've—'

Adventus shut him up with a single lifted finger and nodded for Memnon to go on. Memnon gabbled his way hastily through his decision to follow the Maeatae, his discovery of their camp, and his rescue. He cast another look at Rogatus, who was now much less impassive – indeed, the prefect

almost seemed impressed. Encouraged, he managed to
confess, 'I, uh, I haven't told anyone in my unit about it, sir.
I should have, but I . . . was a bit shaken, and, well, I didn't
want to talk about it. I thought they'd ask, but they missed
the news, so they didn't. I'm sorry. Sir.'

'Jupiter!' murmured Adventus. He cast an assessing eye
at Rogatus and Saturninus and asked, 'So this was a surprise
to you, gentlemen?'

Rogatus uncrossed his arms. 'The events, yes,' he admitted.
'That the man is capable of such a feat, no.' His lips were
compressed and his eyes were gleaming. Memnon realized
that the prefect was immensely proud. 'We're good,' he told
the room softly. 'We're very good – and Memnon's our best.'
He turned his gaze to the centurion of the Alban Legion and
went on, 'Do I gather that this "investigation" is because the
conduct of Second Parthica's tribune has been questioned?
That it is felt to be disgraceful that an auxiliary scout accomplished something a legionary officer refused even to
attempt?'

Marcellinus flushed. 'Second Parthica's tribune behaved
entirely properly!' he declared angrily. 'No one had any idea
that the barbarians would strike so far south!'

'Oh, I agree,' said Rogatus, now openly smiling. 'And,
being a *legionary* officer, he would necessarily rely on what
he'd been told, rather than make his own judgement as to
whether more caution was needed.' The centurion opened
his mouth, and Rogatus quickly continued, 'The legions are
the backbone of the army, as we all know – and the spine
is entitled to rely upon the eyes for information.'

'Cavalry scouts being the eyes?' asked Adventus, amused.

'That is, sir, how able generals have always used us,'
replied Rogatus. 'If Second Parthica's tribune committed
any errors, it was in failing to make use of the resources he
had to hand. I think, for example, that if the escort had been
composed only of *legionaries*, he would have been entirely
correct to ride to Eboracum for help rather than try to follow
the raiders. Memnon, the trail the barbarians left – was it
clear?'

Memnon shrugged. 'Not too bad, sir. They'd made some
attempt to muddle it – they sent some of their number off,

to confuse things, and they went over stony ground. But they were in a hurry; they didn't have time to do much.'

'How many *legionaries*,' said Rogatus, turning back to the centurion, 'could follow the trail of a party of cavalry which split and traversed stony ground, with enough speed to catch up before night hid the trail – and yet not themselves be seen?'

There was a silence. 'Yes, well,' said the centurion, not sure whether to be pleased or annoyed, 'as you say. The tribune knew he would need help, and he made all speed to fetch it!'

'That was not the point the prefect was making,' Adventus gently pointed out. 'The tribune *had* help, in the person of a man who *was* able to follow such a trail – but because of his contempt for auxiliaries he neglected to make use of it.'

'How was Tribune Flavius Panthera supposed to *know* he had an expert tracker to hand?' snapped the centurion. 'It was surely up to the Moor to tell him!'

Memnon grimaced. 'I did try, sir. Tribune Panthera told me to keep my mouth shut.'

'Told you he'd have you flogged if you said another word, I believe,' put in Adventus smoothly. 'Or so it was reported to me.'

Memnon rubbed his lips uncomfortably and admitted, 'He didn't much like me, sir. I'd, um, managed to get on the wrong side of him on the journey.'

'We'd gathered as much from the tribune himself,' said Adventus, eyes glinting. 'We heard his opinion of you at some length. Tell me, soldier, what's your opinion of him?'

'He's a *tribune*, sir,' Memnon said nervously. He had no intention of giving his honest opinion of Panthera in front of a senior centurion of Panthera's legion: he had no desire to be waylaid by irate Albans next time the army assembled. 'I, uh, I know Septimius Castor was very angry about being deserted by his escort, and, well, I think it's understandable. His slaves were killed – they were riding on the wagon and the Maeatae slaughtered the lot of them. And the young woman, Athenais – she was under his protection, but he couldn't protect her any more than he could protect the members of his household. The raiders tied him up and beat him in front of her, and then they dragged her off into the woods, and he couldn't do a thing about it. If a man isn't angry after something like that, he's not much of a man. The fact that I got them out made him think that Panthera *could* have done more, if he'd tried, so he's angry with Panthera. But, really, the tribune didn't do that badly. There was no way we could've held the bastards off, outnumbered and unprepared the way we were; retreating was the right decision. As for following, well, I hadn't appreciated what the prefect just said, that Panthera assumed we'd need help to track them. If he thought that, he was right to go for help. Honestly, sir, I don't fault him.'

'I see,' said Adventus. 'Tell me, though, what would you have expected to happen, if your own prefect had been in charge of that escort?'

'Oh, well,' said Memnon, 'that's different. We would have spotted those bastards a mile off, and if they'd been stupid enough to attack us, well . . .' He glanced at Rogatus. 'Probably we would still've had to let them take the imperial envoys, though we would've made them pay for it. But they wouldn't have got home alive, sir. Not one of them. We're irregulars, we're used to hitting and running and slipping in and out under cover of darkness. It's what we do. Legions go about things differently.'

'So you see, centurion,' put in Rogatus, almost, but not quite smirking, 'there's no disgrace to your legion's tribune. It was impossible for him to rescue the imperial ministers by legionary methods. Why, even ordinary auxiliaries might have found the task too hard!'

'Your lot aren't of much damned use in the line of battle!' exclaimed the centurion angrily. 'A lot of half-naked horsemen with a couple of javelins apiece! Send you up against armoured infantry, let alone cavalry, and all you can do is turn and run!'

'Which is why our great armies contain both legions and auxiliaries,' said Adventus soothingly, before Rogatus could reply. 'Prefect Rogatus, with respect – we are considering a *tribune*, not a general. While a general may be culpable if he fails to make proper use of all the troops at his disposal, a legionary tribune is permitted to think in terms of the capabilities of his own men. I tend to agree with the scout: Flavius Panthera did nothing that merits dismissal.'

Rogatus bowed. 'I accept your judgement, sir.'

'Well,' said the centurion, grudgingly, 'there we are, then.'

'The scout, on the other hand,' Adventus went on, 'clearly acted with exceptional courage and resourcefulness. My colleague here –' indicating the civilian, who had listened with interest but said nothing – 'has been sent by our Empress, Julia Augusta, to convey her personal thanks to him.'

The freedman, Salutaris, inclined his head in acknowledgement. 'I have a small token of her gratitude,' he announced. From a fold in his cloak he extracted a rosewood box; he opened it to display a beautifully crafted medallion. On an oval of ivory, framed by gold, lay a portrait of the Empress, her dark eyes brilliant and her skin glowing, her smiling lips seemingly caught in mid-breath. Rogatus drew in his breath in admiration.

'There is also a gift of some money,' said Salutaris. 'I do not know whether you wish me to present it in private, or whether you'd prefer to hold some sort of ceremony.' He smiled and added apologetically, 'I'm sorry it isn't a civic crown. That may come in due course, in respect of my esteemed colleague Septimius Castor – but, as you are no doubt aware, the civic crown is awarded to a soldier who saves the life of a *citizen*, and my patroness's young secretary is presently of servile status. Julia Augusta, is, nonetheless, glad that her slave was preserved from harm, and wishes to reward the courage and loyalty of the man who delivered her.'

'If it would be convenient to you, sir,' Rogatus said at once, 'I would prefer to hold a ceremony tomorrow, and have all the men attend to witness.' Memnon winced, and the prefect gave him a glinting smile. 'If you're going to be a hero, scout, you're going to have to take the consequences! The gratitude of our Empress should, surely, be received as what it is: a great honour for the whole *numerus*.'

Salutaris smiled and closed the box. 'I will be happy to present it at such a ceremony, sir, and I will tell the Empress of your loyal words.'

'So, that completes our business,' said Adventus mildly. 'And, I think I may say, completes it to everyone's satisfaction.' He sipped his wine. 'The *Numerus* of Aurelian Moors is clearly an excellent unit, prefect. You seem justly proud of your command.'

'Yes, sir,' agreed Rogatus at once. 'We have been of service to the Empire.'

'You were called to this war from the Danube, were you not? How long had you been stationed there?'

'Thirty-seven years, sir,' Rogatus answered proudly. 'We were founded in the reign of the deified Marcus.'

'Thirty-seven years!' exclaimed Adventus, surprised. 'But, prefect, you must have recruited in Mauretania since then. This excellent scout is obviously not from Pannonia.'

'We send officers back to Mauretania regularly, to recruit men and to buy horses,' agreed Rogatus. 'We've never been able to follow the usual practice of recruiting locally. The African style of riding is foreign to that of other nations, and we've found that European breeds of horse are not amenable to the training. We've been moved regularly as well – posted at every fort between Castra Regina and Singidunum, I suppose, and never for long enough to raise either bastards or colts to resupply our losses.'

'You were much in demand, I see,' remarked Adventus, looking at him with interest. 'And if your scout is anything to go by, it's easy to see why.' He smiled. 'I am certain that we can find good use for the *numerus* here in Britain, too.'

Memnon, looking at that smile, suddenly wished that Rogatus had kept his mouth shut about the Moors' excellence, and that he himself had done nothing to attract the attention of the high command. The Emperors' use for the Aurelian Moors was unlikely to be either safe or pleasant.

Six

The Aurelian Moors received orders to reconnoitre the northwest in December, just after the Saturnalia festival. They were resignedly preparing a winter expedition when a letter came from Eboracum, this one privately. Saturninus brought it from headquarters to the stables where the men were packing and delivered it to Memnon with a scowl.

'For me?' asked Memnon, surprised, taking the missive gingerly. It was a small set of wax tablets, folded shut, tied round with a complicated web of cord and sealed with two seals. Both were unbroken. Rogatus was extremely scrupulous where his men were concerned: he never violated their property or privacy, and he never permitted any of his officers to do so. Saturninus, by his expression, would have been more ruthless.

'So it says,' agreed Saturninus, pointing at the superscription on the tablet's wooden back.

Memnon squinted at the incomprehensible squiggles of ink. Honoratus came over and took the letter. 'It says it's from Septimius Castor,' he informed his tent-mate. 'Do you want me to read it to you?'

Memnon had a bad feeling. He could imagine why he might want to write to Castor, but why would Castor write to him? He glanced at Saturninus, who was still scowling, then round at the audience of curious fellow packers.

'I think old Rogatus will want to know what's in it,' he told Honoratus, and took the letter back. 'Might as well let him break the seals.' Saturninus looked a bit happier, and nodded.

Rogatus was in the *principia*, working his way through the stacks of provisioning orders, when Memnon slipped in, trailing both Saturninus and Honoratus. The prefect's face brightened and he set down the list he'd been inspecting. 'This is about your letter from the Emperor's chamberlain?'

'Yes, sir,' said Memnon, holding it out. 'If there's some reason he wrote to me just now, it might be something that would hit the whole *numerus*, but he sent it to me, privately, so maybe it's something the whole *numerus* shouldn't know. That's why I've brought it to you, sir.'

This analysis obviously troubled Rogatus, but he took the letter. He cut the cord with his knife and broke the seals.

'Lucius Septimius Castor,' he read, slowly and clearly, 'freedman of Augustus, greets Memnon, of the *Numerus* of Aurelian Moors.' The letter continued:

My friend, I hesitate to write, doubting whether or not I might be troubling you without good cause, but the great debt I owe you, coupled with my faith in your discretion, compel me to issue this warning, which I implore you to share only with those who most need to hear it.

Chance brought to my ears the rumour of a plot against the good order of the state, many details of which are still obscure to me, but which, by what little I have been able to ascertain, seems to touch upon some operations beyond the wall. When I learned that your unit was to be committed to an expedition beyond the wall, I feared that you might be exposed to the malice of the enemy. I therefore urge you, most strenuously, to show this letter to your esteemed prefect, and to urge him to take great care in the expedition proposed to him. I recommend, most fervently, that he alter his itinerary from that which was agreed with the authorities in Eboracum. He should also carefully search among his own papers and those of his officers before your departure from Aballava, and he should be sure that his archive is secure and sealed when you go. If he should find anything strange, he should send it to me, if he can do so safely by a messenger he trusts.

I hope that in recommending this I am suffering from an excess of caution – and it may well be so. I beg you, do not make public this warning or preserve this

letter, but use it only for your protection and to ensure
the safety of your fellow soldiers. Farewell.

Rogatus's voice had grown strained as he read, and when he
finished he sat a moment, staring at the scratches on the little
wax tablet.

'Jupiter Optimus Maximus!' exclaimed Honoratus softly.
'Is he serious?'

Rogatus looked up at him sharply, and Honoratus flinched.
The prefect got to his feet and went over to the charcoal
brazier that heated the office – the *principia* lacked the
hypocaust that kept the *praetorium* so comfortably warm.
He tucked the letter under his arm and warmed his hands
over the glowing coals. 'Memnon?' he asked at last.

Memnon shifted uneasily. 'I don't know anything about
this, sir. I don't think, though . . .'

'What?'

'It's not a joke,' he said flatly.

'No,' said Rogatus bleakly. 'I didn't think so.' He took the
wax tablets out from under his arm and dropped them into
the brazier. The coals beneath them darkened, and the wooden
edges began to char. Then a trickle of melting wax ran out
of a corner of the tablet and caught. The flames curled up
brightly, licking around the wood, releasing a summery scent
of beeswax.

Rogatus looked up sternly at his shocked witnesses.
'Decurion. *Optio*. You are not to mention this to anyone. If
anyone asks, say that the letter contained nothing more than
good wishes from a man who has cause to wish Memnon
well. Do you understand?'

'Yes, sir,' they murmured together. Then Honoratus burst
out, 'No, sir – that is, I'll keep my mouth shut, but I don't
understand why! What is it that the Emperor's freedman
thinks could happen to us?'

'The chamberlain didn't make that clear, did he?' asked
Rogatus mildly. 'Nor did he say what this "plot against the
good order of the state" might be, or who it is that's plot-
ting. A man like that, though, a high official, he's not going
to spill secrets to the likes of us. From the sound of it, he
was in two minds whether to tell us anything – but, thank

the gods, he owes his life to Memnon, and decided to risk it.' He held out his hands to the brazier again and continued softly, 'Maybe there isn't a plot at all. Generals sometimes decide to sacrifice men, *optio* – to distract the enemy, or mislead him, or buy time for another operation. If there really is some plot against the state, well, a plotter, too, might want to distract or mislead an enemy. A small unit, composed mainly of men who aren't citizens, whose officers aren't wealthy or noble or in with the high command – that's an easy unit to sacrifice, because nobody's going to make too much fuss about it. What that letter says, soldier, is "Look out! Someone wants a sacrificial goat, and you're available!".'

'How do we know we can trust this Castor, though?' asked Saturninus quietly.

'Memnon?' asked Rogatus. 'Is the man trustworthy?'

'Yes, sir,' Memnon replied at once. 'I liked him. If he were forced to lie to somebody, I don't think he'd choose us, either. When I saved his life he admitted the debt right away, and he gave me his own ring in case I ever wanted a favour in return. And he's sharp, too, sir, very sharp. He's not some fool who sees plots everywhere, or starts screaming fire for every wisp of smoke. Besides, he's not actually asking us to do anything much: change the route, take care with the office-work. No harm in that for us, and no advantage for him.' He shrugged. 'I'd be surprised, though, if you ever told anybody in Eboracum which way we're going, sir, since you never even tell *us* until we ride.'

Rogatus favoured him with a sour smile. 'I have *orders*, scout, telling me which way to ride. What do you think is our danger? What will you be watching for, when I send you out ahead?'

Memnon grimaced. 'I'll be watching to see whether anybody told the enemy we were coming, sir.'

'Yes,' said Rogatus harshly. He looked at Honoratus. 'Satisfied?'

Honoratus looked mulish. 'Not really, sir. I still don't understand. Why would any Roman tell the enemies of Rome that we're coming? Why *waste* good men?'

'To buy a favour from the enemy, perhaps?' Rogatus replied

at once. 'I'm sure that the chieftain of the Votadini, at least, would pay well to be able to revenge himself on the man who humiliated him. To distract the enemy from operations elsewhere? Or perhaps – since the chamberlain is worrying about planted documents – to convey false information to a domestic enemy, or incriminate him, with a charge of taking bribes, or incompetence leading to the disastrous loss of Roman lives? I don't know, soldier. I think the chamberlain knows, but didn't see fit to tell us. I, however, am prepared to trust the warning without knowing any more, and to thank the gods that it was sent.' He gave Honoratus a grim, dark look. 'You'll end up a decurion before long. You know that, don't you?'

Honoratus shifted uneasily, then nodded. Obviously he knew he was officer material: he held the citizenship and he could read and write.

'When you're an officer,' Rogatus told him softly, 'you'll need to remember that lives like ours are cheap. It'll be up to *you* to guard them like rubies, because to the high command we're small change. Honoratus, Saturninus: dismissed. Memnon, stay here.'

Honoratus and Saturninus shuffled out. Memnon remained, uneasy at parade rest.

Rogatus held out his hands over the brazier, where the flames from the burning tablet were beginning to die down. 'So,' he said, 'the chamberlain gave you his ring, did he? You showed it to Farabert?'

'Yes, sir,' Memnon admitted. After a pause he added, 'I did tell you, sir, that he thought you had friends at court.'

'You did,' agreed Rogatus. 'I'd wondered how you'd persuaded him it was true. It made our lives a lot easier: that barbarian doesn't want us here, but doesn't dare do anything about it.' He looked up from the flames. 'I want you to learn to read and write,' Rogatus told him abruptly. 'I'll arrange for you to have lessons, once we get back from this expedition.'

Memnon stared at the prefect in surprise. 'Why, sir?'

'Because officers need to be able to read and write.'

'But I don't want to be an officer, sir!'

Rogatus scowled at him. 'You've the intelligence *and* the skill with men. I sent Honoratus to your tent to keep an eye

on you, and you simply enlisted him and made him part of
every mad scheme you've come up with since. You understood *exactly* what that letter implied, while Citizen
Honoratus had to have it all explained to him. I'd be an idiot
to promote him and not you.'

'But I don't want to be an officer!' Memnon protested,
alarmed now. 'I like it where I am!'

'You like it wherever you are,' Rogatus pointed out. 'You
like having a good time, and taking it easy, and thinking up
jokes to entertain your friends. Fine. You'll just have to think
up more officer-like jokes in future.'

'But, sir, I—'

'You've got friends at court, scout, and I don't. You got
this warning, which may save all our lives: I didn't. This
unit, scout, this unit is my *life*, and I'm not going to waste
its assets, you understand? *We* enrolled you, you took oath
to *us*, and you're damned well going to serve us to the best
of your considerable abilities. Understood?'

'Yes, sir,' said Memnon resignedly, and wondered again
about asking for an early discharge.

The Moors set out on the reconnaissance at the beginning
of January. Only about two thirds of the men rode north,
however: the rest remained behind in the fort, under the
command of Saturninus, ostensibly because their horses were
unfit for the journey. Though the problems with the horses
were real enough, Memnon was quite certain that most of
the men would have come – on borrowed mounts, if need
be – if it hadn't been for Castor's warning. Rogatus wanted
a force of his own people in their base, to guard their backs.

The African horses were suffering from the British climate.
The cold weather didn't bother them – they'd become accustomed to bitter winters on the Danube – but the persistent
wetness and mud did. Their hooves weren't used to it: they
softened and split, and the tender frogs of the feet within
them developed infections. The Moors had done what they
could, treating the lame horses with poultices and painting
the hooves of the rest with pitch, but there were still too
many horses with weakened hooves. There was no sense in
taking a horse with a bad hoof on a long hard journey.

Dozy was one of the horses deemed weak-hoofed, but Rogatus had no intention of leaving his best scout behind, and Memnon found himself setting out from Aballava on Saturninus's horse Ghibli. The animal had been called after the desert wind, and was a bay stallion, fiery as its name. Saturninus prized it highly and loaned it only with reluctance – though not as much reluctance as Memnon felt taking charge of it. By the Moors' exacting standards he was a poor horseman. He'd only learned to ride after he came north to Mauretania, while most of the others had been on and off horses since their infancy; hitherto he'd been assigned well-behaved older mounts. After ten years in the cavalry, he could cope with Ghibli's capers, but he didn't like or trust the stallion, and he was privately determined to swap it for a quieter horse as soon as he could.

It was a chill dark morning when they set off, with sleet driving in from the sea. Two hundred and eleven men assembled on the military way at the fort's east gate, most of them leading horses or mules laden with supplies and tents. The standard was furled and covered with an oilskin casing, and the men, all hooded and cloaked, huddled anonymously beside their horses. Farabert and some of the Frisians watched from the shelter of Aballava's gate, but Saturninus, as the ranking officer left behind, came out into the sleet to say goodbye. He and Rogatus stood together for some time, speaking in low voices, while the rest of the unit stamped their feet and tried to fasten their javelins in such a way that the wind couldn't take their hoods off. At last Saturninus nodded, shook the prefect's hand and stamped off back towards the gate.

He paused at his own squadron, though, first to slap the shoulder of his temporary deputy, Honoratus, and wish him luck, and then to say goodbye to Ghibli. The stallion butted him with its nose, and he scratched its jaw affectionately.

'Look after him for me,' he told Memnon gruffly, and Memnon nodded.

The order to mount up came. When Memnon climbed on to his back, Ghibli realized that not only was he supposed to leave the shelter of the fort and trot off into the sleet, he was also supposed to take Memnon instead of his master.

He laid back his ears and refused to budge. Memnon, who would have swatted Dozy with the riding rod for such a trick, didn't want to hit Saturninus's horse with Saturninus watching. He kicked the animal instead, and yelled. Ghibli started forward, then sidestepped and twisted his head round to bite; Memnon had to use the riding rod to fend him off. The horse squealed angrily and kicked, and Memnon wrestled him with the neck rope. They turned around and around in tight circles, like a dog chasing its tail, while Saturninus stood and watched with a smirk of amused superiority. Only when the rest of the squadron had moved off and Ghibli found himself left behind did the stallion at last break into a pounding gallop, rolling his eyes and snorting indignantly. Memnon's tent-mates yelled facetious advice as he caught up with them, and Memnon laughed.

It was the only thing he found to laugh about for several days. He was hauled out from among his companions at the first halt, and sent ahead to scout while they huddled in the shelter of a wood to rest. It was lonely, dangerous work, in the nastiest weather he'd ever experienced. He thought he'd prepared for the climate: he'd spent some of the Empress's gift on a thick cloak of unwashed wool and some fleece-lined boots and mittens, greased on the outside to keep them dry. The cloak was a dirty gray and stank of sheep, but the seller had assured him that the natural grease in the wool would keep the rain out. Perhaps it would, for an hour or so – but the sleet that pelted the western hills was another matter. The countryside wasn't pleasant, either: it seemed to have bogs everywhere – not only the places he expected them, like river valleys, but in every available hollow, and sometimes even at the tops of hills. There were streams running down every dip in the ground, and it was impossible to avoid crossing several in an hour. Memnon was thoroughly soaked with freezing water and black mud before he'd ridden ten miles. His comrades, who had to splash along in each other's wake and became even muddier, complained bitterly about his failure to find them a drier path. He'd never been so cold and miserable in his life.

The expedition was of a type the Moors were intimately familiar with: the reconnaissance in force. The task was to inspect the enemy's territory, checking for signs of activity, identifying strongpoints, estimating numbers, and seeking out the best route for an invasion. The high command already had some idea of all these things, of course – the territory beyond the wall was chequered with Roman outposts and crossed by Roman roads – but the army needed to update its information and check the reliability of its informants. Two hundred horsemen constituted a strong enough force that the Britons couldn't oppose them without raising a call to arms over a wide area, and by the time the call had gone out and a sufficiently large militia had been assembled, the Moors would be long gone – or so they hoped. If someone really had warned the Britons they were coming, they could be crushed.

Rogatus's technique for dealing with the possibility that the enemy had been warned became apparent almost at once. The Moors had been ordered to go first to Castra Exploratorum, an outpost fort half a day's ride northeast of Aballava along a good military road. There they were to collect some guides from a unit of regular border scouts. Instead, as soon as they'd crossed the wall – which they did at Uxelodunum – Rogatus detached a squadron with orders to fetch the guides and bring them to a rendezvous, then led the rest of the men almost due west, into the hills on the far side of the estuary from Aballava.

The land was owned by a tribe called the Novantae, who were members of the confederacy of the Maeatae. It was an area of wooded valleys and high, bare hills, of small shaggy cattle and tiny settlements surrounded by fields. The Moors made their way across country into the hills above the sea, then followed the coast westward, riding as fast as the unfamiliar country and atrocious weather allowed.

The days were short, that was the only mercy, the hours of light compressed by the northern winter. The sleet turned to snow and then back to sleet again, and the world seemed to consist of ice and mud. They never saw the sun: gray dawns gave way to days of lowering clouds and wind, then faded into black nights. They camped in valleys, because the trees gave some shelter, and piled branches on the tent floors to keep themselves out of the mud when they slept. Tents regularly fell down in the night, blown over by the wind when the tent pegs pulled out of the muddy ground. The men looked wistfully at the settlements they passed – small groups of round wattle-and-daub houses where smoke drifted from the warm hearths, with barns and outbuildings where they might all sleep dry. Rogatus ignored them: taking and securing a settlement would delay them, and draw too much attention to their passage. The great advantage of the miserable weather was that few of the Britons ventured out into it, and their expedition could travel almost unremarked through the heart of the enemy's territory.

They took prisoners for questioning regularly: here a woodcutter, there an unlucky shepherd out seeing to his flock even in the bad weather, here a wretched traveller on his way to a neighbour's to borrow salt. None of them spoke Latin, but the Moors had brought along a couple of hirelings from the civilian settlement at Aballava, to translate for them. Whose is this land? Rogatus would ask. How many men in your clan? How armed? Who is the lord? Is there a stronghold? What are the roads? Answer me truthfully and you will live.

All the prisoners did answer – they didn't know any secrets, and had no qualms about sharing what was common knowledge – and they were duly released alive, though usually after being carried miles from wherever they'd been taken. Rogatus disliked letting them go, since he knew they would raise the alarm – but killing every Briton he laid hands on would discourage future prisoners from cooperating.

It was a relief to Memnon, who found himself feeling sorry for the men. When he'd been young, he'd been eager to beat and humiliate Gaetulians, but he found it impossible to hate Britons in the same way: none of them had ever done him any harm. He was aware, too, that if his luck went bad, he could be taken prisoner himself, and would be forced to answer similar questions from British interrogators. He tried to show the prisoners kindness. He'd been learning British – knowing the local language made a scout much more effective – and, though his grasp of the tongue was still only rudimentary, he tried to talk to the captives. Mostly they didn't reply, only stared at him, terror all over their tattooed faces. They accepted his offered small favours – a cup of hot broth, an old blanket – with muttered invocations to the gods to protect them. It emerged that they'd heard the story of what had happened to the nephew of the chieftain of the Votadini, and that Rogatus and the translators had specifically identified Memnon as the man responsible and threatened to hand the captives over to him if they proved uncooperative. The other Moors thought it very funny, and began to make jokes about Memnon's 'collection of foreskins'. Memnon was indignant, but knew better than to complain. Nobody gets less sympathy than a practical joker when the joke's on him.

After five interminable days, they met up with their comrades and the guides from Castra Exploratorum. They had by then swung first north and then east, and they reached the pre-arranged rendezvous in the early afternoon. It was a well-known halting place for Roman troops, and the guides had been waiting there for three days. There were half a dozen of them. Their unit was officially named the Aelian Cohort of Spaniards, but it was apparent at a glance that none of the guides were Spanish:, some of them even had British tattoos. That was to be expected: a unit raised under the emperor Aelius Hadrian was eighty or ninety years old, and for four generations its members had been recruited locally.

As soon as the main body of the Moors appeared, the Aelians hurried over to Rogatus with complaints. Why, they asked, hadn't the Moors collected them at the start, as arranged? And why had Rogatus gone west? The imperial army was never going to go west: it would certainly follow the main road north – the track they were on now!

Rogatus responded blandly that he'd supposed the high command wanted information which the Aelians *hadn't* already collected. He declined to stop in the well-known halting place, and insisted that the guides strike their tent, mount up, and ride on while there was still light. They were quite horrified.

Rogatus summoned Memnon and the other Moorish scouts and introduced them to the six Aelians. 'You're to ride with my scouts,' he told the guides, who were staring curiously at the damp, mud-covered Moors. 'Advise them on the route.

I want to do a loop to the northeast, to complement the one we've just done to the northwest. We'll go across country and avoid notice as much as possible. Memnon, you're to find and mark the route. Senorix –' he nodded to the senior Aelian – 'you go with him. Let your friends finish your packing. Go now.'

Memnon saluted and climbed wearily back on to Ghibli. He had not succeeded in getting rid of the stallion, but the days of hard riding had taken the edge off the animal's temper. He and Senorix trotted up the main road past the descending tents, eying one another with wary curiosity. Memnon saw a thin man a bit older than himself, blue-eyed and brown-bearded, his cheeks tattoed with blue swirls and his nose red with cold. He was wrapped in a heavy hooded cape much like Memnon's own and riding a shaggy horse no larger than Dozy. Memnon grinned to himself at the thought that Senorix undoubtedly saw a mud-man on a moving mud-horse.

Senorix coughed. 'If all your prefect wants is a loop to the northeast, we should follow the road,' he said. 'It turns northeast here.'

'I think he wants us to stay off the road,' replied Memnon.

Senorix grunted. 'Any reason why?' he asked, after a moment.

'He's worried somebody might've talked about which way we were planning to ride,' Memnon answered. There was nothing peculiar about the worry, if you didn't know Rogatus and his habit of keeping his plans secret. Taverns in fort settlements were frequented by locals as well as by auxiliaries, and gossip flowed freely over the wall.

'Thought it might be that way,' said Senorix, with gloomy satisfaction. 'Bastards!'

Memnon gave him another sideways look.

'They told you not to trust us, didn't they?' asked Senorix.

Memnon considered a moment. 'Who do you think told us that?' he inquired cautiously.

'The generals,' replied Senorix at once.

That was surprising. 'Why don't they trust you?'

'We've gone native,' Senorix answered bitterly. 'Or so they believe.' He clicked his tongue to his horse and turned it to the left, up a hillside. 'If we're going to stay off the road, we want to go north a bit. South of the road you have to cross the uplands, and it's a harder ride.'

Memnon slid down, left a marker for the main force, then followed Senorix, wondering if he *could* trust him. Troops did go native: it was an inevitable consequence of local recruitment. He had never heard of any that betrayed their fellow Romans, though – the problem usually manifested itself in favours or warnings to relatives. He couldn't believe that Senorix would betray a Roman force he was actually accompanying. He rather liked the Aelian's blunt admission of the problem.

He quickly decided that the Aelian scout was worth more than diamonds, precisely *because* he was a native. Senorix had been born on the wall, and had been riding about north of it all his life: he knew how to avoid bogs! He also knew the hills, the valleys, the strong points, how to find people or avoid them. He knew all the history and law and customs of the Maeatae, too, and was able to answer some of Memnon's questions as they slipped along over the empty hills. Yes, he said, the Maeatae were a confederacy of different tribes, and the name meant 'Warriors'. They'd first come together about thirty years before, but the current troubles had started when Roman troops were withdrawn from the wall to fight for the pretender Clodius Albinus against the Emperor Severus. With the Roman defenders gone, the greedier tribesmen had been tempted to raid. Once the first raid was successful, the remaining warlords had found it impossible to resist joining the spree of looting and pillage. 'I never expected this, though,' Senorix said wearily. 'Not that the Emperor himself would come to conquer the North. I thought there'd be a punitive expedition, and maybe a few extra units for the wall.' He lowered his voice and added, 'That's what the tribes expected, too, the wiser ones.'

He had some questions of his own, as well. 'One of your comrades told me,' he said, when they'd been riding about an hour, 'that you're the "black ghost" who castrated the nephew of Fortrenn son of Talorgen.'

Memnon rolled his eyes. 'Gods and spirits! I did not *castrate* him, I *circumcized* him. His prick should be just fine by now – more's the pity. As for ghosts . . .' He spat, to avert the omen. 'Is it my fault people here have never seen an Ethiopian before?'

Senorix was silent a moment. He looked sideways at Memnon and asked apologetically, 'Do all your people look like you?'

'No,' Memnon said firmly. 'Ethiopian women are *much* prettier.'

Senorix snorted in acknowledgement of the point. 'Well. No reason men shouldn't come in different colours, I suppose. The first time I heard about you, though, was a ghost story.'

'Ha. You hear about things like that, do you? From people *this* side of the wall?'

Senorix nodded. 'Fortrenn's chief of the Votadini, and the bards sing of his deeds. When I first heard the story, I thought it was just a song a bard had invented. Then I heard the story from the *other* side of the wall, that the "ghost" was a Roman soldier who'd fooled Fortrenn and his warband and stolen away their captives.' He paused, then added significantly, 'Fortrenn heard that story, too.'

'I wasn't trying to *fool* them!' Memnon protested. 'I wanted to scare them, sure – I needed them to keep still – but I never expected them to believe I was some kind of *iblis*!'

'Some kind of what?'

Memnon grimaced. 'An *iblis*. A . . . spirit, a ghost that drinks blood. People say they live in the desert.' He spat again, and made his own gesture to avert evil. He was mildly shocked that he'd even mentioned the belief to a stranger. When he crossed the desert, following the Gaetulians who'd murdered his family, he believed at times that he was indeed such a creature. A vivid, hallucinatory memory struck him, of crouching beside a dying raider and drinking blood from his slit throat. He had never confessed that to anyone, and he told himself again that he had been out of his mind at the time, from the heat, the thirst and the unbearable grief.

The heat alone seemed impossible, here in this world of cold and mud, but the memory persisted, nightmarish, unreal. Sometimes when he lay awake in the small hours of night, he became afraid that when he died he would find himself trapped in the desert, to haunt the steps of lost caravans and

drink the blood of unwary travellers. Sometimes he thought
that his whole life since had been an effort to escape that
fate. He had fled across the Middle Sea, across a thousand
miles of fertile land, across the streams of Ocean; he had
taken another name and another life. Surely it couldn't trap
him now?

'Well,' said Senorix, 'Fortrenn son of Talorgen thinks you
tricked him. He's said that he'll cut your prick off and feed
it to his dogs, then put your head on a spike above his gate,
because of what you did to his heir.'

Memnon made himself grin. 'Thanks for the warning. Has
he said how he intends to catch me?'

Senorix smiled and shook his head, and Memnon grinned
again, this time with feeling. They neared the crest of a hill
and, without a word spoken, turned their horses before the
top, so as not to show up against the skyline. 'His heir?'
Memnon resumed. 'I thought the lout was his nephew.
Doesn't he have any sons?'

'Yes,' agreed Senorix, 'two of 'em. Among the Maeatae,
though, a man's heirs are his sister's sons, not his own. They
trace descent through the female line.' He hesitated a moment,
then added, 'They're not *ruled* by women, understand! They
just trace descent that way.'

Memnon wondered whether Senorix's mother had come
from the tribes, and how the Aelian scout reckoned his own
descent. 'The Garamantes do that,' he observed neutrally.
'And some of the Gaetulians.'

'Are they African?' asked Senorix, making Memnon blink
in surprise. He supposed, though, that for Senorix to know
nothing about the Gaetulians was no stranger than for a Moor
to know nothing of the Maeatae. 'They're African,' he agreed.
'Bad neighbours. They raid my people to the south, and the
Romans to the north.'

Rounding the slope, they saw below them a sheltered dell
full of pine trees. 'Camping place?' suggested Senorix, abandoning the topic of Gaetulians.

Memnon glanced at the the sky. There might be another
hour of light left. Rogatus would be reluctant to stop before
it was fully dark, but they were unlikely to find another sheltered camping place in just an hour. He was still pondering

whether Rogatus could be persuaded to call a halt early when Senorix let out a soft exclamation. A little way down the slope was a trail – a place where the turf had been churned into mud by the hooves of many horses. The Briton trotted over to it, then jumped down from his horse, tossing the reins to the ground, and began to examine it. Memnon followed him.

The prints, he saw, led from the pinewood; they'd been made by small horses, trotting, carrying riders; they were half full of water. 'Old,' he observed.

Senorix nodded. 'At least four days.' He blew out a breath slowly, white in the cold air. 'Lots of them, though. Sixty, eighty men? And heading south.'

They both looked south, toward the wall and the road which the Moors had been expected to ride. Senorix blew out his breath again. 'O, *deae Matres*!'

'Do the Maeatae often set out on raids in the winter?' Memnon asked.

Senorix shook his head. 'Almost never.' He scratched his beard and added unhappily, 'Maybe the generals were right. But, I don't . . . I can't believe any of *us* would . . .'

'No reason to assume it was one of yours,' Memnon told him sympathetically. 'Maybe there was a leak in Eboracum. Maybe there was a spy. Maybe this wasn't left by a raiding party at all, but by a hunting party or wedding party!'

Senorix relaxed a little. 'They probably camped there,' he remarked, indicating the wood. 'They may have left some trace of who they were.'

They walked cautiously back along the trail into the pine woods, leading the horses so as not to miss any marking on the ground. The woods were empty of people, but full of signs that a substantial body of men had camped there several days before. Senorix picked up a broken belt buckle from beside a fire pit, examined it a moment, then inspected some markings on a stone. 'Selgovae,' he stated. 'Brude's clan, probably. They live north of here.' He glanced round and added unhappily, 'They weren't hunting. No sign of dogs. And they weren't on their way to a wedding or a feast, either.'

The camp had been sober and austere, with no sign of either the high spirits or the comfort that would have attended a group on its way to a festival. Memnon took the belt buckle and looked at the curving lines incised into the bronze. They bore some resemblance to the tattoos on Senorix's face – but he had no doubt at all that the scout's surprise and dismay were genuine. 'We're in the territory of the Selgovae now, right?' he asked. 'And you think this was a waycamp of just one clan? How many men in the tribe as a whole?'

'If all the clans rose, several thousand,' replied Senorix. 'I doubt that they could get so many, though, not in winter. They wouldn't need to, either, if what they wanted was your lot. Five hundred would be plenty, particularly if they took you by surprise.' He met Memnon's eyes, his gaze now anxious. 'The real question is, where are they now?'

That question was one which Memnon and Senorix were required to answer. Rogatus, informed of what they'd found, merely snorted and ordered the two scouts to track the Selgovae. The rest of the unit spent that night camped in the wood; Memnon and Senorix followed the trail as long as they could see it, then made a bivouac in the dark, shivered away the night hours, and continued on at first light.

Even a novice scout would have spotted the encampment they found. Neither of them was a novice, and they skirted the camp cautiously without being detected, fixing its number – just over five hundred men – and its composition – predominantly Selgovae, with a sprinkling of Novantae and and a large and solid clump of Votadini.

'The chief's warband,' Senorix whispered, pointing it out. 'See the shields? Thunderbolts, red on white?'

'Fortrenn come for my head?' Memnon whispered back.

'That's what I'd guess.'

The Maeatae encampment was perched in the hills above the rutted track that was the main road north, and it had been there for at least five days.

'They were waiting for you,' Senorix admitted unhappily.

Memnon sniggered, and the British scout looked at him in surprise.

'Well, they've been sitting here in this miserable weather *five days*,' Memnon pointed out. 'It's *freezing*! And here they've sat, teeth chattering, toes numb, not daring to light a fire because the smoke would give them away, nothing to eat but cold bread, wet ground to sleep on, mud everywhere, while we . . . well, we've ridden up one side of their lands and we're about to go back down the other. That Fortrenn, he's going to have to go home and explain *that* to his people. If I were them, I'd be pretty damned mad at whoever betrayed us to them.'

Seven

The trap that had been set for the Moors might have its humourous side, but escaping it was nerve-racking. Memnon and Senorix reported back to Rogatus – who was already well east of the wood where they'd left him – and were instantly sent out again, to find a Maeatae-free route back to the wall.

By this time, however, the Maeatae had appreciated that their enemies would *not* ride obligingly up the road into their ambush, and had sent out scouts of their own. Over the next few days Roman and British scouting parties tracked one another, and occasionally dodged one another, over the cold damp hills. Long afterwards Memnon treasured the occasion on which he and Senorix had tried to hide in the same sheltering clump of fir trees which already hid a pair of Selgovans: both sets of scouts stared, yelled, and ran away as fast as their horses could gallop. It had not been funny at the time: he and Senorix had galloped back to the main body of the Moors sick with dread, convinced that the Maeatae would now be able to block their escape. The British scouts, however, must either have been far from their base, or have been doing their scouting for a small detachment, because there was no pursuit.

Senorix proved his value again and again: finding secluded valleys to lead them around a point of danger; locating safe places to stop for the night; leading them to isolated settlements from which they could steal cattle when their supplies ran short. The Moors were very glad of him.

Seven days after finding the tracks of the Selgovae, and twelve after leaving Aballava, the Aurelian Moors limped back across the wall at the fort of Condercum, cold, wet, hungry, exhausted, and well to the east of anywhere they should have been. Apart from that ludicrous meeting in the fir wood, however, they had not encountered their enemies face to face, and not a man had been lost.

Rogatus wrote a preliminary report on their mission the evening they arrived at Condercum, and presented it to Memnon the following morning. 'Take this to headquarters,' he ordered, 'and then see if you can arrange a private meeting with your friend the chamberlain. Do you still have his ring?'

Memnon nodded: it had lived in his purse ever since he was given it.

'Send it to him, then. Find out what's going on. The high command is going to want to know how the enemy knew we were coming, and it's my guess that your friend would prefer it if we kept his name out of it. Go learn what you can, and then report back to me at Aballava.'

The ride south to Eboracum took him three days; when he arrived in the city, late in the evening, it was to find that his mission from Rogatus wasn't enough to get him accommodation in the fortress, which was still overcrowded. The events of the previous September were now so long ago that they might have belonged to another generation: people vaguely remembered him, but they weren't prepared to grant him special privileges. He ended up sleeping in a stable in the fortress annexe, next to Ghibli. The stallion had lost all his fire: he was drooping and sore-footed, as bone-weary as his rider.

Next morning, after presenting the preliminary report at headquarters, Memnon went down to the city marketplace, where he got a writer to draft him a note to Castor, asking for a meeting. He enclosed the ring and handed it to the guards at the palace gate. To his relief, the chamberlain replied the same day, not merely agreeing to a meeting, but inviting him to dinner at the city's posting inn.

He arrived at the inn early, largely because he was hungry: the past weeks of hard riding had left him with chilblains and an insatiable appetite. The innkeeper showed him to a small private dining room on the upper floor, its walls painted a dark red that the evening and the single lamp rendered gloomy. The furniture consisted of a small scarred table and a single couch. There was a basket on the table which held a loaf of bread. He sat down and fell upon it.

He was chewing the heel of the loaf, a little while later, when the innkeeper returned, escorting not Castor, but the beautiful Athenais. Memnon set his bread down and stared, not knowing whether to be delighted or angry. The innkeeper smirked and left them.

'Oh!' exclaimed Athenais, looking as though she very much regretted coming. 'Castor isn't here yet?'

'No,' he replied, wondering what *she* was doing here. Castor had told Memnon none of the reasons behind his warning; had he told Athenais? Maybe Castor *hadn't* told her. Maybe this was some kind of palace intrigue, and Athenais was spying.

She came round the table and perched primly on the end of the couch. 'Castor told me he'd sent you a warning. He said he hadn't actually told you much, though. Just enough to let you guard yourself, if the danger was real.'

'How much has he told *you*?' Memnon asked warily.

She shook her head slightly. 'It's the other way round. *I* told *him*.'

Looking at her calm, composed face he suddenly saw that he'd underestimated her all along. He'd assumed that being an assistant secretary to the Empress wasn't a *real* job. The Empress, however, was an extremely wealthy and influential woman: she undoubtedly controlled property and patronage on a grand scale. To be on her staff at such a young age, Athenais had to be both capable and ambitious.

He'd valued Castor's promise of favours, but dismissed Athenais's, once he'd understood that the favour he'd hoped for was one she wouldn't grant. It was Athenais, though, who'd succeeded in moving her imperial patron on his behalf. He'd been quite wrong to think of this woman as just a pretty girl. She was that major asset, a 'friend at court'.

Memnon drew in his breath, then let it out again. 'Well . . .' He met those sober dark eyes. 'Is this . . . that is, was it your lady, the Empress, who . . . ?'

Athenais was already shaking her head. 'She doesn't know. Not yet. Castor and I will tell them when . . . when we've got all the evidence.'

Tell them. Who was 'them'? It sounded as though she meant the Emperor and Empress: that was disquieting in the extreme. He frowned down at the table. 'Any use my asking you what the whole story is?'

'I'd rather wait for Castor,' she replied, and he nodded. *No, she wasn't spying.*

The bread was all gone. Memnon glanced about for something else to eat, but apparently the innkeeper, too, was waiting for Castor, and the table was bare, apart from the lamp.

'How much do you actually know?' Athenais asked him.

He grinned. 'I don't know anything, lady, anything at all. An ignorant auxiliary, that's me.'

'Was there any . . . *trouble* during your trip north?'

He cocked his head slightly. 'You mean, like a couple of tribes of the Maeatae setting up an ambush for us?'

'Yes, or . . .' She abruptly stopped, her mask of calm slipping. 'They *didn't*, did they?'

'They sat in the hills above the main road north for five days, waiting for us. Five or six hundred of them, freezing their toes off in the snow and sleet. Our friend Fortrenn was one of 'em, we think.'

'Oh!' said Athenais, and swallowed. She'd clearly thought that the warning would turn out to have been unnecessary, a precaution only.

'We hadn't taken that road, thanks to Castor's letter. We'd circled round to the west, and finished up to the north of them. We had a mucky time getting home, though: we were dodging parties of Selgovae and Votadini all the way from the Bodotria Estuary to the wall.' He told her about the Selgovans in the fir wood, making a joke of it. She didn't laugh.

'You were betrayed,' she said, with real anger. 'You were *shamefully* betrayed. I'm very glad you escaped safely.'

He grinned at her again. 'So am I!' He leaned back, then looked at the table again and said, 'You think that innkeeper would fetch more bread if I asked?'

'I'm sure he would,' Athenais murmured, 'and you're certainly entitled to it!'

When Memnon opened the door, however, it was to find

Castor paused on the landing at the top of the stairs. There were exclamations and handshakes, and then the chamberlain came in and sat down on the couch beside Athenais. The innkeeper, who'd accompanied his illustrious guest, bowed and recited the contents of his wine cellar and larder.

'Hot spiced wine,' Castor said decisively. 'It's a miserable night. To eat – whatever's hot and filling. The best the house can manage, eh?'

'And more bread!' Memnon put in. 'Right away!'

'Yes, sir,' agreed the innkeeper, and bowed himself out the door.

Memnon raised his eyebrows. 'Sirred by an innkeeper, ha!' he observed. 'What it is to be a friend of the rich and powerful!' He seated himself beside Castor, at the other end of the couch from Athenais.

'What it is to be a friend of a freedman of the rich and powerful,' Castor corrected him, smiling. 'My friend, I'm glad to see you. You look like you've had a rough month.'

Memnon waved that aside. 'I've had worse – but not often. Thank you for your warning. It saved our lives.'

Castor looked at him with shocked attention, and Memnon repeated what he'd told Athenais.

'When we finally made it back to the wall,' he finished, 'my prefect asked me to come here to find out if there's things he shouldn't put in his report.'

'He sounds a sensible man, your prefect,' said Castor.

'He's *good*,' Memnon said warmly. 'Not like some you hear about.'

'Does he have friends at court?'

'You, I hope, sir, and the lady secretary.'

Castor sighed. 'Well, that simplifies matters. He might have had friends in the wrong faction. Can he keep his mouth shut?'

To anyone who knew Rogatus, the question was almost funny. 'Yes.'

Castor regarded him quizzically. 'Yes, without qualifications?'

'Yes, *sir*,' replied Memnon.

'I didn't mean . . .' began Castor, then shook his head. 'I'm not Panthera!' he protested. 'You don't have to "sir" me with every other word!'

'No, sir,' agreed Memnon contritely. 'Sorry, sir. In answer to your question, sir – Valerius Rogatus, our prefect, isn't Panthera, either. He's sharp, he's honest, and he's tight-lipped. He's never liked to say anything that gossip might carry across the river – across the wall, I mean, here in Britain. If you let me know what's going on, he'll see to it that it doesn't get any further. I swear that by the spirits of my ancestors. Sir, you *need* to tell us. The high command is going to be asking questions about how the enemy knew we were coming, and they're going want to know how Rogatus suspected that they might. It's our guess that telling them you warned us would be a very bad idea.'

'Yes,' agreed Castor earnestly. 'Please don't. For both our sakes.'

A pause was enforced by the appearance of a servant with a laden tray containing the wine, cups, bread and a dish of stewed beans as a starter. Memnon dipped some bread in beans, and began eating before the servant had finished pouring the wine.

''Scuse me,' he said, around a mouthful. 'It was a long, cold ride.'

Castor flipped a hand in dismissal of the very notion of taking offence. When the servant had gone again, Castor said softly, 'Are you aware of the conflict between Our Lord, the Emperor Aurelius Antoninus, and his brother, the Caesar, Septimius Geta?'

Memnon looked up in bewilderment. He knew that the imperial couple had two sons, though only the elder, Antoninus, had been made Augustus. Geta, the younger brother, held the lesser title of Caesar, though there was a vague expectation that he would become an Augustus even-tually. On the Danube he'd heard very little about Geta; in Britain, however, there had been some animated discussions in taverns.

He swallowed his mouthful of beans. 'I've heard rumours.'

'Oh? What sort of rumours?'

Memnon grimaced. 'That Antoninus Augustus thinks Our Lord the Emperor has given too many favours to the army – that he might try to take some of 'em back. Cut our wages, or rescind our privileges or something. They say that the

Caesar disagrees with him, that he favours soldiers, the way his father does. I don't know if it's true.'

'Ah.' Castor took a sip of wine. 'Well, as far as I know, Antoninus Augustus agrees with his father's policy on the army and has every intention of continuing it. On that subject the brothers are in complete agreement. Unfortunately, they seem to disagree on practically everything else.'

'They *hate* one another,' Athenais put in, very, very quietly. 'They've hated one another since they were children. There was an incident in Rome, before we set out, an accident in a chariot race. Cara . . . that is, Antoninus, broke his leg. He accused Geta of arranging the accident, of trying to kill him. It might be true.'

Memnon frowned, feeling queasy and out of his depth. This wasn't the sort of thing an auxiliary usually heard. It wasn't the sort of thing he *wanted* to hear. Emperors ought to be living gods, powerful and wise, not boys who hated their brothers.

'Geta Caesar has been courting the legions *assiduously*,' continued Castor, in a low voice. 'I have no doubt the rumour you've heard originated with his supporters. His brother fears that this attention to your fellow soldiers is the prelude to an attempt to supplant him.'

This was getting more and more frightening. This sounded like civil war in the making.

'Antoninus has therefore embarked on a conspiracy to discredit his brother in the eyes of the army,' Castor whispered. 'It has two main planks. The first is to disrupt the supply of food and fodder. Forged letters, purporting to be from Geta Caesar, have been inserted in the offices of the fleet responsible for shipping corn and oil to troops. Since Septimius Geta will be in charge of supplying the army once the campaign begins, these will be accepted without question. The letters contain orders diverting supplies to Gaul, where they will be sold. When the troops start to go hungry, any investigation will conclude that Geta stole their food to enrich himself.'

When the troops start to go hungry . . . that would be in the summer. In the middle of the campaign, among those barren hills from which he had just returned. Disrupt the army's supplies, and there would be real hardship, very quickly – and scores of deaths, as disease attacked the men hunger had weakened.

'That's the part of the plan we know about,' Castor continued. 'Chance led Athenais to overhear a fragment of it, and we've investigated together. These things leave a trail, you understand, a trail of documents, which those who know about such things can track. I think we've grasped all its essential details. The second part of the plan we were less sure of – until you confirmed it just now. Our only knowledge came from . . . another fragment overheard.'

'They spoke of a "reconnaissance mission north",' Athenais put in, in a low voice, 'and of leaving letters in somebody's office, and about somebody who'd be "glad to do it". I wasn't sure what it meant. All I could think of to do was ask Castor to check if there were any reconnaissance missions about to set out. When we found out that the next one was yours, we decided that we had to warn you, even though we weren't sure whether we'd understood what the conspirators intended.'

'Now we are,' Castor concluded.

Memnon looked from one of them to the other. 'I don't see how it would've discredited Geta if a unit of cavalry scouts got ambushed!'

Castor sighed. 'There would have been planted documents linking Geta to a breach of security about your mission. Whether Antoninus intended this, too, to look like the result of greed, or whether it was to appear as simple incompetence, I don't know. It would have turned the troops against him either way. I am extremely glad that you and your comrades managed to escape.'

Memnon sat silent for a long moment. It was hard to take in: the Moors had been betrayed by an *emperor*, condemned to death at the hands of the enemies of Rome, simply in order to make that emperor's brother look bad.

He shook his head and took a swallow of wine from his cup. Then he set the cup down and returned his attention to the bread and beans. He'd be able to think better if he wasn't so hungry.

'Don't you have anything to say?' Athenais demanded indignantly.

'I need to think about this,' Memnon returned evenly. 'What about the Emperor? About Severus Augustus, I mean?'

'He doesn't know,' Castor replied. 'Not yet. This news will shock and grieve him deeply and I . . . you must understand: Antoninus is his son. I can't approach him with this news without *abundant* evidence.'

'Antoninus hates Castor already,' Athenais elaborated. 'He'd say it was a plot.'

The chamberlain nodded shamefacedly. 'I tried to reconcile the two brothers once. The result is that each thinks I'm the partisan of the other, and both hate me.'

'So – who else *does* know about this?'

Castor leaned back on the couch – then swung his legs round behind Athenais and reclined. 'You,' he said quietly. 'And, for the moment, that is all I can tell you.'

For a few minutes they ate in silence. Athenais sat straight, sipping the wine but only nibbling at the food. Memnon wiped out the dish of beans with the last of the bread and picked up his cup of wine. 'So,' he resumed, 'you say that it was Antoninus Augustus who told the Maeatae we were on our way north, but that it will look like the work of Geta Caesar if anybody investigates.'

'That was the plan, so far as we understood it,' agreed Castor. 'I assure you, neither I nor Athenais is a partisan of either prince. My master is the Emperor and hers is the Empress, both of whom grieve at the enmity between their children, and long to see them reconciled.'

Memnon grimaced. 'You're saying that *Aurelius Antoninus Augustus* told the Maeatae where to find us on the road north. That he intends us to starve in the campaign this summer.'

Castor flinched. 'Yes.'

'Doesn't he . . . doesn't he even care about the *war*? In the name of all the gods, he'll be on the campaign himself!'

'He won't be going hungry himself,' Athenais put in sourly. 'Believe me, he cares about defeating his brother much, much more than he cares about beating the Maeatae.'

Memnon was silent a moment longer, then burst out, 'We treat this man as a *god*! We burn incense to his image! We hang his ancestor's portrait on our standard, and call ourselves by his name!'

Castor sighed. 'Antoninus is no relation of the deified Marcus Aurelius. He simply bears the same name.'

'It isn't even his original name,' Athenais added. 'He was born Lucius Septimius Bassianus – his mother still calls him Lucius. His father changed the name because Marcus Aurelius was a wise and great emperor, and he wanted Caracalla to be revered the same way.' She made a face. 'That's what most people call him in Rome: Caracalla. You know, like that kind of long cloak with a hood? He likes to wear one, and slink about with his bunch of bodyguards, keeping the hood over his face, spying on ordinary people and beating them up for fun. The Hood, that's who he really is!'

'Shh,' said Castor uneasily.

'I hate him,' Athenais declared, lowering her voice, but speaking with bitter vehemence. 'He's disgusting. And Geta is almost as bad.'

'Shh! Shh!' repeated Castor, giving her a very worried look. 'You must not say such things – *especially* when they're true.'

'This . . .' began Memnon – and stopped himself before he uttered anything treasonous. After a moment he asked in a low, fierce voice, 'Why should I serve him?'

'Because apart from him is only chaos,' replied Castor immediately. 'The war of tribe on tribe. You probably know more about that than I do.'

Memnon was silent again, struggling with rage and, worse, with *disappointment*. Was this how his Emperors behaved?

Not Severus, he reminded himself; not the *real* Emperor. And not the Empress, either. Just their worthless sons.

'You were born outside the Empire,' Castor insisted. 'What does it seem like to you, the Roman state?'

'Miraculous,' Memnon answered truthfully, after a long silence. 'When I first came north, and discovered what was there, I couldn't believe my eyes. So many different tribes and nations, so much wealth and knowledge. Such wide peace.'

'Yes!' agreed Castor, his eyes brightening. 'Such wide peace. I'm sure you know, though, what happened at the death of Commodus Augustus. Were you with the troops which marched on Rome then?'

Memnon shook his head quickly. 'That was a long time ago, before I even came north. Nobody in my unit went; it was just the legions. I heard about it, though.'

'It was not much of a campaign,' Castor told him. 'Afterwards, though . . .'

There was a heavy stillness, full of memories. The inn's serving man came back into the room with a second laden tray. He set out mutton stew, carrots in coriander, cabbage in fish sauce, a dish of spiced quails and more bread, then collected the empty bowl of beans and departed. Memnon at once began eating again.

'My point in mentioning old wars,' said Castor, 'was to demonstrate that, whatever we may think of an Augustus, to reject him is to open the gates of Hades.'

Memnon thought about what Senorix had said, that the trouble in Britain had begun when the troops on the wall were withdrawn to fight for Severus's rival, Clodius Albinus. Yes, it was certainly true that rejecting an Augustus opened the gates of Hades. If there were two Augusti, however, and they were at odds – what were you supposed to do?

'It is possible to serve the *Empire*, despite the failings of a particular emperor,' the chamberlain went on. 'It is what we in the Household of Caesar were born to do – and what some of you in the army do by choice. The Empire is always greater than the man who heads it, and always worthy of our loyalty.'

Memnon chewed a mouthful, then swallowed. 'All right,' he said. 'I'll serve the Empire and keep my mouth shut. What are you planning to do about this plot, then?'

'When we have enough evidence, I will present it to my patron,' replied Castor quietly. 'I cannot say for certain what he will do, but my best guess is that he will correct all his son's errors, and then have a private word with him.'

'What? His son does *that*, and goes right on being Emperor?'

'Do you expect Our Lord Severus to kill his own son?'

'No, but why can't he just, well, *demote* him? To Caesar or something?'

Castor looked at him wearily. 'What do you think a demoted Augustus might do – or what might his brother do, in a province packed full of troops and preparing for a war? And what do you think would eventually happen to Antoninus if my patron promoted someone *else* to the position of Augustus?'

Memnon had no answer to that.

'If I'm right, and it's settled in secret, you and your prefect should be very careful not to allow anyone to find out how much you know.'

Memnon looked at him intently. 'What would happen to us?'

'Probably you'd simply be found dead. I doubt Antoninus would want to draw attention to the matter with a treason charge – though you ought to bear in mind that he could fabricate one, easily. You *could* try to ask for protection from Septimius Geta – but it is never wise to stand between princes.'

'I said I'd keep my mouth shut.'

'It really is the best course; I'm sorry. For my part, I hope – I *very much* hope – that Severus Augustus will not allow Antoninus to learn of my role in his embarrassment: this secret is one that is dangerous to all who know it. Please believe that I don't intend to allow matters to run until things become critical. At the moment there are no ships sailing anywhere, so those letters about the grain shipments won't matter until the spring. I expect to approach my patron long before then.'

Memnon nodded. 'All right. What should Rogatus say to the high command, then? I'm particularly worried about this because of my friend Senorix, who's in the Aelian Cohort of Castra Exploratorum. He says that the high command think his lot have gone native and don't trust them. He thinks that when the generals hear that the Maeatae knew we were coming, they'll immediately blame the Aelians. I don't want to see them suffer for it.'

'I can arrange for a copy of your written orders to go missing,' offered Castor. 'That should distract the investigators into a spy hunt. Perhaps your prefect could say that he'd heard that there were rumours about your expedition in the taverns and, though he couldn't track them down, he nonetheless decided to change his route as a precaution?'

Memnon nodded. 'That would work. All right, then. That should hold everything until the spring'

He set out back for Aballava the following morning, on a borrowed horse to give poor Ghibli a chance to recover. It was snowing, and he huddled miserably in his cloak as he clopped along the dark, empty road. He kept remembering the young man he'd seen sitting on the throne at the troop inspection: the gilded armour, the purple cloak, the proud young face watching as the Moors rode past in the rain. He would not think of that man as Aurelius Antoninus; he would not profane the name of the Moors' founder. He'd call him Caracalla, the Hood.

'*I hate him,*' Athenais had said. '*He's disgusting.*'

He didn't think such an outburst was typical of her. He could imagine one thing Caracalla might have done, though, that would've provoked it. The fact that she'd overheard private things the young emperor had said to his staff, tended to confirm the suspicion. Maybe Caracalla, too, had regarded her as nothing more than a pretty girl, and had spoken freely in front of her. It wouldn't have been rape, exactly. She was a slave in the imperial household: she would've obeyed an Emperor's orders.

He wondered again what her relationship was with Castor. The two had seemed very close during that dinner party . . . but they were fellow conspirators. Had Castor really watched and done nothing as a woman he loved was forced into the bed of a man she detested?

Castor, too, had been born a slave of the imperial house. Maybe if you were Household of Caesar you just regarded abuse by an emperor as a natural hazard, like an earthquake or a flood, to be endured because it could not be contested.

He supposed he must be a slave, too, in a way, since Caracalla had tried to get him and every man in his *numerus* killed – and he, too, could do nothing but endure. If Athenais had turned to him and begged him to rescue her again – would he have tried to do so? Or would he have told her no, sorry, I can't, not against an emperor?

He didn't know. He'd sworn an oath of loyalty to that emperor, which complicated matters. He supposed, though, it didn't matter: Athenais had not turned to him. He suspected that she might have turned to Castor – but for comfort, not for help.

Was he jealous? Yes, he admitted silently. When he thought of how Castor had assured him that Athenais belonged to the Empress, not to any man, he felt that he'd been cheated. But that, he told himself, was unfair. Castor had not robbed him of anything he was likely to gain. Athenais was willing to be his friend at court, but nothing more.

If she had turned to Castor, it was understandable. Harrassed and oppressed by a cruel young man, it would be natural to look for comfort from the older colleague she admired, someone fatherly and kind. If Castor's feelings *weren't* fatherly – well, Memnon couldn't blame him. At any rate, jealousy, as the saying went, might heat the heart, but wouldn't warm the bed.

Memnon rode through the gates of Aballava, three days after leaving Eboracum, chilled through and weary to the bone. He wanted, more than anything else, to curl up in his bed underneath every cloak and blanket he possessed, and sleep the month out. Instead he found himself directed straight to the *praetorium* for an urgent consultation with Rogatus.

Saturninus hurried in while he was still trying to put his thoughts in order. He glared at Memnon indignantly and demanded, 'Where's my horse?'

'He's in Eboracum, sir,' Memnon replied virtuously. 'He was worn out, and starting to go lame on the off fore, so I didn't think I should take him on. The stable-hands at the fortress annexe said they'd look after him until somebody came to fetch him.'

Saturninus grunted and sat down on the edge of Rogatus' desk. Memnon slumped in a variant of parade rest, too tired to keep his back straight.

'So,' said Rogatus, 'was the man willing to see you?'

'Yes, sir,' agreed Memnon. 'I sent him the ring, and he sent it back with an invitation to supper. He answered my questions – but he begged me to see that it went no further than you, sir. I swore by my ancestors that it wouldn't.' He thought of adding 'the girl was part of it, too', but decided against it: Rogatus distrusted women on principle. Noisy, troublesome creatures he considered them, always causing quarrels and sapping men's morale, good for nothing but producing babies. Memnon wondered what he'd make of Athenais. He wasn't quite sure what he made of her himself. His usual strategy with women was to try to make them laugh, but he wasn't sure whether such a cool, elegant, educated creature ever laughed out loud.

Rogatus and Saturninus were both regarding him in uneasy silence. 'Do you object to Saturninus being here?' asked Rogatus.

'No, sir!' exclaimed Memnon in astonishment. He glanced nervously at the decurion, who snorted in satisfaction but didn't seem to find it outrageous that a soldier under his orders should be able to send him out. 'Of course not – just that the man made it clear that it could kill him and us both if anybody found out that we know about this.' He took a deep breath and recounted what he'd learned.

His superiors took it much as he'd expected: with shock, outrage and grief. They began debating what to do in low voices. Memnon drooped. The floor of the *praetorium* was warm under his feet, and he wondered if he could just lie down on it, spread wide his arms and bask, as though in the heat of some underground sun.

'Scout!' snapped Rogatus, and he picked his head up, then blinked in surprise: the prefect was giving him a look of affection.

'You've done well,' said Rogatus softly. 'The furnace here at the *praetorium* is running, and the bathhouse is hot: go use it, and then get some rest.'

Most of the servants who looked after the *praetorium* were Farabert's; Rogatus, however, had a couple of old men who'd followed him from one fort to another up and down the Danube, and one of these showed Memnon to the fort commandant's private bathhouse. He stripped off in the changing room and walked through the three-room suite, marvelling at the blue-frescoed walls, the tiled pools, the gilded dolphins and, most of all, at the delicious heat. The furnace that heated the house was indeed roaring at full blast, and the bathhouse stood right next to it: the floor and walls radiated heat like the sands of the desert.

He rinsed the mud off himself in the warm room, carefully using a ladle over the drain so as not to spoil the beautiful clean pool, then went into the hot room and sat down slowly in the hot plunge bath, luxuriating in the glorious sensation of being warm all over.

He was inspecting his feet, wondering if all the peeling skin on his toes meant he'd had a touch of frostbite or whether it was just from the wet, when there was the sound of someone arriving in the changing room. He was not consciously aware of feeling any alarm, but he put his foot down, climbed out of the pool, and moved over to just beside the door, ready to slide out. Farabert came in, glanced quickly round, and grunted in satisfaction when he noticed the room's occupant.

'Rogatus said I could use the baths here, sir,' Memnon explained politely. 'But this is your house, I know. I'll be happy to leave if you like.'

'No, no!' protested the Frisian chief quickly. 'There's room enough for both of us.' He came into the room and settled himself on the edge of the pool, dangling his feet in the water. He was spectacularly hideous naked: a thickset body, hairy as a pig's, red with blotches and criss-crossed white with old scars. He spread out his thighs on the wooden floor slats and rested his elbows on his knees.

Memnon sat down opposite, wondering what the man wanted. While it was, of course, possible that Farabert normally took a bath at about supper-time, it seemed more likely that he'd come to see if he could dig some information out of Rogatus's messenger. His servants had probably told him Memnon would be here.

Although neither Rogatus nor Farabert ever commented on it in public, everyone in the fort was aware that relations between the two commanders were bad. It was inevitable that they should be: Farabert had been living comfortably and noisily in the *praetorium* with his wife and four children for years, and now he was required to share the house with a severe old Mauretanian bachelor. Rogatus had slapped one of Farabert's sons when the boy had intruded into his office, and nearly provoked violence from the child's father. Farabert, moreover, was a nobleman among his own people, and had arrived in Britain with a small fortune; Rogatus was a poor farmer's son, without any of the manners or money expected of a prefect. Farabert's wife Ahteha – who was pregnant – was known to have berated her husband for 'letting this stranger, this commoner into *our house!*' and questioned his manhood for submitting so tamely to the intrusion. The two men's respective units were equally uncomfortable with one another, though so far there'd been no trouble apart from a few tavern brawls.

'You're just back from Eboracum,' observed Farabert, after a silence.

'Yes, sir,' agreed Memnon.

'Rogatus sent you straight there, didn't he, soon as you crossed back over the wall? You weren't with the others when they got back here six days ago.'

'Yes, sir.' Memnon gave him an earnest look and added, 'Rogatus wanted to send a message to his friends at court. You know we almost got ambushed? Our guides from the Aelian Cohort were afraid they'd get the blame for that, and they begged us to make sure the inquiry was fair.'

Farabert grunted. He looked as though he didn't entirely believe the explanation, which surprised Memnon: he'd thought it quite convincing. 'Rogatus prizes you, doesn't he?' the Frisian asked, after a moment. 'He uses you for all the delicate, secret stuff.'

Memnon stared incredulously. His career in the Aurelian Moors had been punctuated by spells on latrine duty in penalty for some joke or other, and Rogatus had frequently informed him that he was a damned fool, a disgrace to the standard, and that he ought to leave the army and get a job as a clown. While his abilities as a scout were highly regarded, he had certainly never been a prefect's pet. 'I don't know about that, sir,' he said doubtfully. 'He has no sense of humour.'

'Oh,' said Farabert dismissively. 'Yes. Jokes.'

There was a silence. The big barbarian studied Memnon resentfully. 'You've never been wounded in battle,' he observed at last, his voice low.

Memnon glanced down at his own unscarred black skin. 'No, sir,' he agreed cheerfully. 'I'm not much good at battles. I try to stay out of 'em.'

'You're good with a knife in the dark,' whispered Farabert. 'That's what I've heard.'

Memnon suspected that he was being insulted, but he saw no reason to be offended by the truth. 'That's right,' he acknowledged, with a smile.

There was another silence. 'In Eboracum,' Farabert said at last, 'did you speak to Oclatinius Adventus?'

'No, sir!' Memnon replied instantly. 'In my opinion, a man shouldn't speak to the Commissary unless he has to.'

Farabert grunted, but Memnon thought he looked relieved.

He excused himself as soon as he decently could, pulled on his wet, muddy clothes and went to his room in the barracks. His tent-mates were delighted to see him, and disappointed when he turned down their offer to take him out for a drink. He got into bed with a half loaf of bread and fell asleep still eating it.

He was woken the next morning, much earlier than he would have liked, by another summons from Rogatus. He stumbled over to the *praetorium* wearing an assortment of out-sized borrowed clothes: his tent-mates had stripped him while he slept and sent all his own clothes to a laundress in the fort village. They told him he'd woken up, agreed, and even thanked them, but he had no recollection of any of it. Rogatus and Saturninus were in the prefect's office, just as he'd left them the evening before. He wondered if they'd been there all night.

'Farabert tried to question you yesterday,' Rogatus said, without preamble, as soon as he staggered in. 'What did he want to know?'

Memnon smothered a yawn. 'What I did in Eboracum mostly, sir.'

Saturninus scowled. Memnon's sleep-heavy wits began to wake, and he wondered what had been going on in Aballava while the Moors were reconnoitering the north. 'He asked if I spoke to Oclatinius Adventus,' he added. 'I told him no. I also told him that you sent me to Eboracum because the Aelians begged you to do what you could to ensure that the inquiry was fair.'

'Oh, very good!' said Rogatus, with satisfaction. 'It's even true.'

'He's worried,' said Saturninus. 'He thinks the Grain Commissary will be after him.'

Rogatus smiled. Seeing Memnon's inquisitive look, he explained, 'It seems that Lord Farabert tried to get into my office while we were away.'

Saturninus snorted agreement. 'When he found it was locked and sealed, he asked me for the key. He said he just wanted to check an inventory. I told him I didn't have the key. When the *numerus* got back, I asked him whether he still needed the key, but he said he'd settled the matter.'

'It could be true,' said Rogatus. He could be relied upon to take particular care never to be unfair to anyone he disliked.

'He's up to *something*, tent-mate,' replied Saturninus. 'Always creeping about and trying to stick his thick fingers into our business – the pale-eyed grunter! You can't trust a German.'

Rogatus shrugged. 'It was his fort. He was used to running everything that happened in it. Naturally he wants to know at least what's going on. If he's worried about the Commissary, that doesn't mean he's guilty. Plenty of innocent men worry about the Commissary.'

'He knew we were supposed to go to Castra Exploratorum first,' objected Saturninus. 'He's been in Britain, on the wall, for years. He would have a much better idea of how to get information to the enemy than someone higher up who's only just arrived in the province. Somebody who wants to leak still needs to pick a suitable channel, and it makes sense to pick a man like Farabert, rather than somebody closer to the top: it'd be harder to trace if something goes wrong.'

'It's supposed to be *easy* to trace,' Rogatus pointed out. 'With a clear false trail.'

'Which is probably what Farabert was trying to plant in your archive!' snapped Saturninus. 'I don't like him. That barbarian is sharper than he looks. He hates having us here, and he'd be delighted to get rid of us.'

'I don't like him, either,' said Rogatus, 'but we don't need to *like* our fellow soldiers, old friend. I agree that we have cause to be careful with him, but I don't think we should jump to conclusions.'

Memnon cleared his throat. 'We could ask Castor to watch

out for him on the headquarters' side, sir,' he suggested diffi-
dently. 'I think he could probably get some of his friends to
do that without making any noise about it.'

Rogatus frowned. 'Would he be willing? His goodwill is
precious, and I don't want to wear it out.'

'This was *his* investigation, sir,' Memnon pointed out. 'He
was working on it before he knew it had any bearing on us.
He'd probably be pleased to have another thread to follow.'

The prefect smiled. 'In that case, it's an excellent suggestion, scout.'

Memnon abruptly realized who Rogatus was most likely
to send as a messenger to Castor, and cursed his own stupidity.
Gods and spirits, not *another* journey on that cold, wet road!

Rogatus noticed his dismay. His eyes glinted. 'I'll write
a letter to your friend this very morning.'

Saturninus frowned. 'Rogatus,' he said unexpectedly, 'the
man needs a rest.'

'I agree,' said Rogatus. 'Which is why I'll let *you* take the
letter, Saturninus, along with the full report from our mission.
While you're in Eboracum, you can collect your beloved horse.'

Saturninus winced, but said resignedly, 'Yes, sir.'

Memnon smirked at him, and Rogatus turned the glint on
him. 'As for you, scout, you need some quiet indoor work
for a while. You're to report to your tent-mate Honoratus,
and tell him he has orders to teach you to read.'

Honoratus accepted the assignment with interest but without
surprise. 'Oh?' he asked, eying Memnon speculatively. 'He
wants to fix you up with a red sash.'

Memnon glowered at him. 'I don't want one.'

'Why not?' asked Honoratus in surprise. 'Decurions get
paid ten times what we do. More than that.'

Memnon grimaced and shrugged, unable to put his feelings into words. For ten years all important decisions had
been made for him by somebody else. He had been free as
a child, playing pranks and snatching at pleasures, evading
or enduring the discipline of his stern fathers. He did not
want to grow up. He had done so once, and had become not
a man, but a demon; he was afraid to try again.

Honoratus studied him with a frown. 'Look,' he said, 'if

you're afraid you'd be standing in my light, don't worry.
There's no rule that says you can't promote two men from
the same squadron. I'd *like* it if we both got the red sash. It
would be much . . . much *friendlier* to become a decurion
along with one of my tent-mates.'

'That's not it,' muttered Memnon, ashamed that his tent-
mate believed him so noble. 'It's just . . . can you imagine
me trying to be Saturninus?'

Honoratus grinned. 'You're good enough at mimicking
him. You've got that trick he has of crossing his arms dead
to rights.'

'Ha, ha,' Memnon said gloomily. 'Honoratus, I don't want
to be an officer! I'm . . . just the wrong sort for it.'

'Don't be an old woman!' Honoratus exclaimed, rolling
his eyes. 'You're *exactly* the sort for it. You can make people
do what you want them to, even when they know better. You
remember that trick you played at the Temple of Augustus
in Carnuntum? I still don't know why I agreed to help you
with it.'

'Because it was funny,' Memnon reminded him, grinning
at the memory. 'You remember the look on the priest's face
when he found the tablet in the cow's stomach? A special
message for *him*, from the gods themselves!'

Honoratus struggled not to laugh. 'It was *sacrilege*,
Memnon; if we'd been caught . . . that damned tablet was in
my handwriting!'

'"O thou most unworthy of mortals",' quoted Memnon,
'"this the gods send thee, by bovine instrument . . ."'

Honoratus did laugh, then stopped himself. 'You changed
the subject on me!' he complained. 'The point was, I didn't
want to do that, and I did, because you made me. You'll be
a *good* officer, once you know how to read.'

Memnon grimaced. 'Maybe I won't be able to learn,' he
said hopefully. 'Maybe it's something you have to learn when
you're a child, or not at all.'

'I shouldn't think *you'll* have any trouble,' returned
Honoratus sourly, 'the rate you pick things up. You should
count yourself lucky; I had *my* letters beaten into me by the
most wicked old schoolmaster in Caesarea. Hah, do you
think I'd be allowed to . . .'

'Try it, and see,' said Memnon darkly.

'No, thanks. Here, don't look so gloomy! It may all come to nothing: we may all be dead this time next year. I'll get us some wax tablets.'

Eight

In April the war began in earnest.

The Maeatae and Caledones had sent embassies to the Emperor during the course of the winter, offering hostages and tribute in exchange for a peace treaty. They had been sent away unheard: Severus had not come all the way to Britain in order to discuss terms. Besides, the barbarians had broken treaties in the past.

The invasion of the north began with the army divided into two main groups. The larger group, commanded by the two Emperors, was to march up the east of the island, while a smaller, but still very powerful, force took a parallel route through the west. The two armies would meet at the Bodotria Estuary, then divide again to continue the invasion through the Caledonian Highlands.

The western force was commanded by Junius Faustinus Postumianus, the governor of Britain, and by Julius Avitus Alexianus, the brother-in-law of Empress Julia Domna. It consisted of two of the British legions, detachments from an assortment of Danube legions, and a large and varied collection of auxiliaries – including the Frisian Formation of Aballava and the Aurelian Moors. They were to proceed slowly through the territory of the Maeatae, establishing a series of large base camps from which the troops could fan out to subdue the surrounding territory.

The campaign was a disaster from the start. The army crossed the wall in pouring rain, and the baggage train promptly got stuck in a bog; it took nearly two days for it to dig itself out again. The two western commanders did not get on, and their respective staffs were jealous and resentful; orders contradicted one another, or were duplicated, or were lost altogether. Worst of all, the enemy were nowhere to be found. The settlements were deserted, the people all fled into the hills; what was more, they'd taken their flocks, herds and provisions with them. The Romans had expected to be able to live off the land, at least to some extent, and the rations they'd brought with them were consumed much faster than anyone had anticipated. After five fruitless days marching, the commanders, alarmed at the rate at which their supplies were dwindling, decided to reduce the men's rations. Thus the men who fanned out to forage and to subdue the abandoned countryside were hungry and short-tempered.

At this point, the Maeatae began to show up again. Many of the foraging parties found sheep grazing in lush patches of open ground. They rushed in eagerly to seize them – and found themselves plunging into bogs. While they were struggling to extricate themselves and the sheep, the Maeatae finally appeared. More lightly armed than legionaries or most auxiliaries, mounted on their small, tough horses, they galloped rapidly about the mud and slaughtered the Romans before they could form up in line of battle.

Some men surrendered. These were found by their comrades over the next several days – hung from trees with their bellies slit open and their entrails hanging down around their ankles, or bound and hurled face-down into bogs, or blinded, castrated and left to bleed to death in the hills. After that, men cut the throats of wounded comrades rather than allow them to fall into enemy hands.

Auxiliaries and skirmishers were sent to comb the hills for the elusive Maeatae. Sometimes they found them by springing an ambush in some deeply wooded valley or muddy swamp. By the time the Roman forces could regroup and defend themselves, the barbarians had usually vanished again. Reports were soon circulating, though, that the ambushes weren't just by the local tribes, but that the Maeatae and the Caledones were working together. The ambushes grew larger, the losses heavier, day by day.

Oh, there were some successes: here a group of women and children discovered in hiding with provisions; there an ambush sprung too early, and cut down to the last man. But Roman successes were few, and Roman losses were appalling – and still it rained, and rained, and kept on raining.

'I've never known such a wet spring,' Senorix told Memnon, as they headed off on another scouting mission, Senorix on his shaggy bay and Memnon once again on Dozy, whose hoof had recovered.

Memnon just grunted. The Aurelian Moors had been sent out with the other skirmishers – except that their reputation as crack troops meant they always got the dirtiest and most difficult tasks. So far they had not suffered heavy losses. Good scouting and a wary commander had done much to keep them safe, but they also owed something to the guides from the Aelian Cohort, whom Rogatus had specifically requested. Memnon liked working with Senorix, and relied on his local knowledge, but the rain and short rations oppressed even his easy temperament. He was worried, too. The whole army, from the commanders on down, was blaming the campaign's troubles on poor scouting. Rogatus had been subjected to a dressing-down by General Postumianus, and he in turn had torn strips off Memnon. 'Find the enemy!' he'd ordered. 'You're supposed to be good; why can't you locate the bastards?'

Memnon didn't know why he couldn't locate them. He was trying. The land, however, was a wilderness of dank forest and barren hillside, and the enemy slipped about from one place to another, appearing always where least expected. Waking, he was constantly anxious that he had missed some vital trace of the enemy; sleeping, he dreamed of returning from a scouting mission to find all his comrades dead.

'It's not usually this bad,' Senorix told him apologetically. 'We often get beautiful weather in April and May.'

'The gods hate us,' Memnon declared bitterly. 'They want the Britons to keep this country – and as far as I'm concerned, the Britons are welcome to it!'

'It's true, we'd have an easier time if we left the frontier at the wall,' Senorix commented. 'This is, what, the third time Romans have tried to conquer the north?'

This Memnon hadn't heard before. He stared at Senorix, peering from under his mud-splashed hood. 'What happened the other two times?'

'Oh, they succeeded,' replied Senorix. 'You saw the northern wall at Bodotria, didn't you? All the tribes of the Maeatae were officially part of the Empire when that was built. There are even a couple of forts beyond it. One of them, the Winged Fortress, is huge – built for a whole legion, but abandoned before it was ever finished. I went there once. It's a strange place – foundations of walls, all covered over with moss, and streets overgrown with trees. The Caledones say it's haunted.'

'Is that why it was abandoned?'

'No.' There was a silence broken only by the plopping of their horses' hooves in the mud.

'The Romans can conquer the north,' Senorix said at last, very softly, 'but they can never hold it. The men and the silver they pour into these hills slip away like water, and always the cost is more than the return. After a while, they get tired of it, and pull back.'

Memnon noticed the use of 'they' rather than 'we', but made no comment on it. He already knew that Senorix had divided loyalties. The British scout could, he felt, be trusted to help the Moors avoid the ambushes which had cost other units so many lives, and that was the main thing. He suspected that Senorix was also trying to steer him away from anywhere Maeatae women and children might be hiding, but he was happy to collude in that: he hated rape.

All Roman troops would rape and abuse enemy women and children who fell into their hands: the Aurelian Moors were no exception. It was allowed; it was even expected. For Memnon, though, the screams and tears always violently recalled the bodies of his family, mauled and murdered and cast aside. He couldn't bear it, and when his comrades indulged in it, he was filled with a murderous hatred for them. The very presence of captives was so uncomfortable and disturbing that he'd actively try to prevent the unit from taking any.

Finding the men, the warriors, was another matter. He wanted to throw the whole army at them, and get the awful war over with as quickly as possible. The trouble was, the men probably shared the women's camps at least some of the time. Perhaps he should push Senorix . . . only what if they did find a camp full of women?

He'd thought he knew what a war was: he'd been fighting the enemies of Rome for ten years, after all. He saw now that what he'd known on the Danube had been nothing but raids and counter-raids, and that this vast enterprise was something quite different. He hated it: the rain, the mud, the bodies hung from trees, the tears of captive women and children, the endless angry orders. He wanted to go home – wherever home was. He wanted, anyway, to get back to the sort of life he knew – and instead he scouted the hills, day after day, looking for enemies who dissolved like mist. They had no intention of meeting the Romans in battle: they knew that they would lose. Instead they harried, and ambushed, and retreated north.

It was the end of May before they reached the Bodotria Estuary and rejoined the rest of the army. Memnon was fairly sure that those months of effort to subdue the lands of the Maeatae had been wasted: the Maeatae weren't there. The Romans couldn't even burn their deserted settlements and new-planted crops: everything was much too wet. They had trampled and torn down as much as they could, but what was left was still salvageable. A hundred thousand men had struck the Maeatae as hard as they could – and the blow wasn't fatal.

At least there were fresh supplies stockpiled at the estuary, newly shipped from the main depot at Arbeia. Memnon had heard nothing more from Castor and Athenais, but it seemed that they must have delivered their dossier of evidence to the Emperor Severus, because the troops weren't threatened with anything worse than the short rations they'd endured since the campaign began.

The weary men who arrived at the estuary were told they would be allowed eight days' rest before setting out again. The two sections of the great army compared their experiences; the eastern force, too, had suffered heavy losses – and had the additional disturbing news that the Emperor was ill. Severus had apparently been unable to ride at the head of his men; he had instead made the journey carried in a litter. Memnon wondered if Castor was with him, and contemplated going to ask the chamberlain how ill the Emperor really was. He was still contemplating it when the Moors were ordered north again, for another reconnaissance in force before the rest of the army set out.

He was unhappy about it, and doubly unhappy when

Senorix came and told him that the Aelian scouts were being reassigned to one of the detachments from a Danube legion. 'Sorry,' Senorix told him miserably. 'I'd rather stay with your lot – but orders are orders.'

Memnon shrugged resignedly. 'It was bound to happen. We got off more lightly than most, largely thanks to you – and as soon as a legion noticed that, they were bound to steal you.'

'You scarcely need us any more,' Senorix said, trying to reassure them both. 'And I don't know the Caledonian lands the way I know the Maeatae ones. You'll manage as well as I would.' He hesitated, staring at Memnon, his blue eyes anxious. 'If . . .' he began – then paused.

'If?' asked Memnon.

'You don't hate my mother's people,' Senorix whispered. 'You fight them as though they were your kinsmen, too.'

Memnon nodded, relieved that now it was out in the open. 'I don't like to make war on women and children.'

Senorix sighed in relief. 'My mother's people are Selgovae; my cousins belong to Fotlaig's clan. They're in the north, somewhere. My aunt's with them, and . . . others I care for. If you should come across them, I would be forever grateful for any mercy you might show them.'

Memnon raised his right hand. 'Any kindness I can do them inside my oath to the Emperor, I will do. I swear by my ancestors.'

Senorix took the hand and shook it. 'Thank you.'

The engineers were constructing a pontoon bridge to the Caledonian lands on the far side of the estuary, but it hadn't been finished, and the Moors were ferried over the river in boats. Assembled on the northern bank, they followed a rough track northwest into the hills. Memnon had questioned Senorix at length about the Caledonian confederacy, but he was far from confident. With only his instincts to guide him in unfamiliar country, he worried more than ever.

They were three days northwest of the estuary when he ran into trouble. He was riding about an hour ahead of the main body of men, on his own. The track they were following lay to his left, glimpsed now and then at the bottom of a hill;

he made his way carefully along the slope above, choosing the best vantage points, picking a route to them that made the most of the scant cover, trying to replicate the actions of an enemy scout so that he would spot any traces left by one. The countryside was rough pasture, steep and wild, though there were no cattle or sheep to be seen – only mountains in the distance, and a narrow lake in a wooded valley ahead. The rain had finally stopped, and the sun glittered on the wet slopes. He spread out his cloak widely so that it would dry a little.

When he found the first hoofprints, pressed into a patch of open turf, he dismounted to examine them. A single horse, unshod and carrying a rider; recent. He rode a wide circle about the trail, but found no sign that anyone else had been nearby. It could be a solitary herdsman or messenger – but it could be a scout or look-out. He tracked it a little further, saw that the rider had followed cover to a vantage point from which the road was visible, dismounted, and spent some time there. A scout, certainly; an enemy scout.

He rode down to the track and left a warning marker, then took Dozy back up the slope and followed the trail, heart beating hard with eagerness: maybe at last he could find the Moors somebody to fight!

The trail led him across open mountainside to a small stream, half-hidden by undergrowth, then up alongside it into a narrow gully. He was following it warily, beginning to wonder if he should tether Dozy and continue on foot, when an arrow came hissing out of the bracken on the slope above him.

It caught Dozy in the chest, and the little horse screamed, shied and staggered. Memnon leapt from his back and rolled into the cover of the gorse that flanked the stream, and somebody on the slope above him shouted. Dozy, squealing and coughing in pain and distress, tried to follow his master.

Memnon caught the horse's neck-rope, and Dozy fell, almost on top of him. The arrow was buried almost to the fletching in the little gelding's body, and blood had already soaked him to the hooves. Memnon set his teeth, pulled out his knife, and slashed the animal's throat, then crawled away, blinking back stupid tears of pity for his poor innocent horse.

Another arrow thunked in the undergrowth behind him, and there was a shout – from the *other* side of the stream.

Memnon froze, crouched on his belly, and listened intently. The man on his own side of the stream called a query to his fellow; the voice was close, which he should have guessed anyway. The British bows were not very powerful, and only at short range would an arrow from one strike that deep. The other voice, replying, was further away: a second sentry, Memnon guessed, posted within hailing distance of the first. He bit his lip, convulsed inwardly with shame: he must have ridden right to the perimeter of the barbarian camp, as though he were some half-blind *legionary*!

He began to crawl onwards on his belly, trying not to disturb the undergrowth, listening to the footsteps of the first sentry rustling in the gorse behind him. One of the javelins strapped to his back snagged, and there was a shout, very close. His knife was still in his hand, sticky with Dozy's blood. He set it down, took hold of the javelin, then rose to his feet and hurled it at the speaker in one motion. He barely had time to see the man, let alone aim, but at least the arrow the Briton had on the string flew off wildly as the man shrieked in alarm. Memnon turned, snatched up his knife again, and plunged through the gorse into the stream. He splashed along the stony bed, bent double to keep under cover as much as possible; another arrow followed him.

He reached a place where there was a dip in the ground to his right, with a trail where sheep or deer had descended to the stream to drink. At once he turned up it, crawling so that the searchers would see nothing but the fronds of bracken above him, trying not to touch them and make them move. He heard the two sentries babbling excitedly behind him: it didn't sound as though his javelin had hurt anyone. To his disgust, one of the men sounded a horn. So, more searchers would now come running.

He reached the top of the gully without attracting any more arrows. The bracken stopped there; beyond was open hillside, covered with heather. Too exposed; he turned and half-ran, half-crawled along the edge of the fern brake, hoping that the sentries would think he'd followed the stream.

They didn't: he heard one of them come charging up the

slope behind him. He slid into the bracken and lay still, hidden by the fronds. The hilt of his knife was damp in his hand. If the Briton came this way, he would slide out and kill the man.

The Briton stopped, close enough that Memnon could hear his quick breathing. He called over his shoulder; Memnon understood the British words: 'I don't see him!' though the accent was strange. He waited, but the man didn't come any closer.

Memnon groped and found a stone, tossed it skittering through the bracken behind the searcher, then slid quickly back down the slope through the concealing greenery. The searcher was shouting and following long before he reached the stream again.

The other man's answering calls came from downstream, in the direction of safety. Memnon cursed and began hurrying upstream, in the direction of the expected reinforcements, hoping he could find a way out of the gully again once he'd put some distance between himself and his pursuers.

There were no more sheep-trails; instead, the sides of the gully grew steeper and stonier. The sentries' shouts receded, however: apparently they hadn't seen him turn upstream. He was beginning to think he might get away after all when he heard the sound of horses ahead. The stream was wider at that point, providing little cover, so he threw himself up on to the bank on the opposite slope from the trail. The cover was thin there, too, however, and an excited shout ahead let him know he'd been seen. He cursed and ran directly up the slope. It was too steep for horses, and if none of the new arrivals had bows he might escape.

What he hadn't realized, in his head-down course through the undergrowth, was that the slope now rose into a sheer cliff. He dashed desperately along its foot, still running bent over, now more from shortness of breath than from any hope of escaping notice; the yells were close behind him, and his shoulders hunched in terrified anticipation of an arrow or a javelin.

Then he saw a cleft in the cliff ahead of him, a cross between a fissure and a cave. He plunged in and scrambled up its slick wet floor, going deeper into the rock, bracing his elbows and knees against the granite to keep from falling – until the cleft ended, narrowing into nothing before his face. He turned, panting, and looked back.

Beyond the narrow opening of the cleft he could see half a dozen riders at the base of the slope staring up, and the two sentries running up the gully to join them. He let out his breath slowly. So, this was it. He would join his ancestors today. The terror which had filled him an instant before vanished, leaving only a great calm clarity. The gully was green and beautiful, full of shade and the sound of running water – a paradise, for a child of the desert. Here he could die, and trust that the deadly sands would never claim his spirit.

No need to make things easy for the enemy, though: he would die like a man. He pulled out his last javelin, then unfastened his cloak and wrapped it about his left arm as a shield. He set his back against the stone, and waited.

The sentry with the bow fired an arrow as soon as he joined the others – but the cleft was at an angle to him, and the arrow rattled harmlessly off the stone. He moved back, found another angle, and tried again, but again missed. Another man threw a stone and shouted, 'Come out of there!'

'You come in!' Memnon shouted back, in his rudimentary British.

There was a silence. Then another of the men yelled something Memnon couldn't understand, apart from the words 'Roman' and 'up'. Somebody else laughed, and made a sound like a cat.

Cat up a tree, was it? Memnon replied by imitating a sound he hadn't heard since his youth: the deep, barking roar of a leopard.

There was another silence, this one surprised. Unable to resist it, Memnon imitated the whimpering of frightened hounds.

That brought a chorus of yells and a volley of stones, along with another arrow. One of the stones struck Memnon's improvised shield. He tossed it back. 'Bad aim!' he shouted, in Latin since he didn't know the British. 'Try again!'

They did; he shrank into the cleft, covering his head with his cloaked forearm, while the stones rattled about him. A

few struck him, hard enough to bruise but without enough
force to do real damage. The archer seemed to have given
up; presumably he'd run out of arrows.

Some more horsemen rode up, one of them evidently some
kind of chieftain or officer, since he wore a gold torque. The
stone-throwing stopped while the two groups conferred. Then
a couple of the men, including the officer, dismounted and
started toward the cliff.

'First man,' Memnon shouted in British, 'has the javelin.
Second, third, fourth man, he has the knife.' It was bravado,
he knew. He might be able to get one of them with the
javelin, but the knife would be useless against their long
spears.

'You up there!' replied the officer, in Latin. He set his feet
squarely and stared up into the dimness of the cleft, hefting
his spear. He was about Memnon's age, brown-haired and
bearded. 'You can't kill all of us. Hand over this javelin and
knife of yours, and come down!'

'No, thank you!' Memnon replied, relieved to find someone
who knew Latin. 'I don't like the sort of fruit that grows
hereabouts, on the entrail trees. I'm quite comfortable where
I am. You come up!'

There was a flash of teeth as the man grinned. 'What are
you doing up there, Roman?'

'Just sitting and admiring the view, Briton, just admiring
the view. What are you doing down there?'

'Us? We're hunting.'

'Oh? Well, your men will tell you, you've treed a leopard.'

'A leopard, is it? What sort of beast is that?'

'A very fierce and dangerous beast, Briton!'

'Yet when it's chased, it runs and hides in a hole in the
rock?'

The other men had been whispering among themselves,
explaining to one another what was being said; at this they
laughed. Memnon laughed, too, which seemed to surprise
them. 'You've never met any leopards, obviously,' he told
the Briton. 'They climb up to high places to store their kill,
or to get a bit of peace, and it's not good to disturb them.'

'It's true I've never met any leopards,' admitted the Briton.
'Indeed, I've no good notion where such beasts come from,

still less what one should be doing in my country . . . admiring the view.'

'To tell the truth,' Memnon answered, 'I've no good notion what I'm doing in your country, either – but it's a fine view.'

'Are your friends down on the road?'

'Why don't you go and see? I'll wait.'

At this the Briton laughed. 'What's your name, Roman, and your unit? If I can, I will let your people know you died bravely.'

'A kind thought. My friends in the *Numerus* of Aurelian Moors call me Memnon.'

'Come down, then, Memnon of the Aurelian Moors, and I will fight you in single combat. Such a brave warrior shouldn't die like a fox in a den!'

Memnon considered that a moment. He had never had much of a lust for glory, but to die in single combat with a British chief sounded better than being stabbed to death in a hole. 'I'll come down,' he agreed. 'Who am I to fight, Briton?'

'I am Argentocoxus,' the leader told him, 'son of Aenbecan, a chieftain among the Caledones! I will fight you.'

'Oh, indeed!' said Memnon. He'd never heard of him. 'You're not Maeatae, then?'

The men hooted in derision and made rude comments about the Maeatae.

Memnon crept and slid his way out of the cleft in the rock and picked his way down the slope, javelin in his right hand and knife in his left, to the stream where the Britons were waiting for him. They were not much taller than him, which was a relief – wiry men, brown- or red-haired, all bearded, with tattooed cheeks and forearms. He was aware, as they stared, that he was soaking wet and muddy, still spattered with poor Dozy's blood. He thought they were staring because of that – until they began making the familiar gestures against evil, and he realized that it was because they hadn't had a good look at him before, and, like the rest of the north, were shocked by their first sight of an Ethiopian. They backed away, except for Argentocoxus, who surveyed him with deep interest.

'Now, this I have never seen before!' he exclaimed. 'Did you paint yourself that colour?'

Memnon grinned. 'In my country, people sometimes paint themselves white, but never black. We don't cover ourselves with blue the way you do, either. I've never fought a Briton in single combat before; how are we supposed to go about it?'

'Ai!' exclaimed the Caleldonian, eyes narrowed. 'Are many Romans that colour?'

'Some,' Memnon said cautiously. 'Not many. Here in the north, very few, and most of those in my unit.'

'I heard a tale of a Roman soldier something like you,' Argentocoxus told him. 'It was said he made a eunuch of the nephew of Fortrenn of the Votadini.'

Memnon rolled his eyes. 'I didn't make a eunuch of the young lout, I just trimmed his prick a bit! And that wasn't all I did, either. I also took Fortrenn hostage, stole his captives out of the middle of his camp, took the gold collar from around his neck, and left him tied up with his own tunic. I've heard he wants my head on a spike before his gates, but if you want to give it to him, you'll have to fight for it.'

'So that was you?'

'That was me.'

The Caledonian laughed. 'I am honoured to meet such a warrior!' Then his eyes narrowed again and he studied Memnon speculatively. 'A thing has occurred to me. We are to meet together soon, the leaders of the Caledones and of the Maeatae. It would please me, Roman, if, instead of fighting me, you would come to that meeting as my guest.'

Memnon frowned. 'So that you can hand me over to Fortrenn?'

'No!' cried Argentocoxus indignantly, and spat. 'I am no friend of Fortrenn son of Talorgen – his arrogance has brought us nothing but trouble and grief. I swear the oath of my people, if you agree to come with me to that meeting, I will not hand you over to any man. I also swear that until the meeting ends you will be treated as my guest, and that if any man raises his hand against you, he raises it against me and my house, and I will avenge it.'

Memnon cocked his head slightly. His heart was beginning to speed up as the calm certainty of death ebbed away from him. It would probably take some time to get to this meeting or council, and if he was being treated as a guest, he would have opportunities to escape. It took an effort to keep his voice steady when he said, 'Fortrenn is a rival, and you want to embarrass him in front of your council, is that it?'

Argentocoxus grinned. 'And if I do?'

Memnon took a deep breath. 'I have no objection. I agree.'

'Then give me your javelin and your knife,' said Argentocoxus, his eyes very bright, 'and swear by whatever gods your people worship that you will come to the council with me, and not try to escape.'

Ah. Argentocoxus was no fool. Slowly Memnon took the javelin and rammed it point down in the earth before the Caledonian chieftain, then offered the black-bladed knife, hilt first. 'I swear by my ancestors,' he said solemnly, 'and by all the gods and spirits, that I will go with you to this council, Argentocoxus, and that I will make no attempt to escape until it is over.'

The Caledonian took the knife, grinning. 'And then?'

Memnon shrugged. 'You didn't say what would happen then, either.'

The grin widened. 'I like you, Roman. If I have to kill you, I'll make it quick.'

They did not tie him up, which helped ease the juddery feeling in his stomach – if they'd bound him, he would have been sure they meant to kill him slowly. Instead, Argentocoxus treated him very politely, even dismounting from his own horse to walk beside him on the way back into the Caledonian camp, since with poor Dozy dead he had no horse to ride. The Caledonian chief sent a number of mounted men down the gully, though, before escorting Memnon up it: scouts, undoubtedly, off to discover the location and the numbers of the Aurelian Moors. Memnon wondered how many of the Caledonians were assembled up that gully, and hoped Rogatus had taken good note of his warning marker.

The camp was a huge one: a ramshackle collection of huts and tents at the head of a glen, damp and dirty. A large clan, obviously: Argentocoxus was evidently an important man among the Caledones. The first sound Memnon heard on entering the camp, though, was the crying of children, and he noticed the old men and women lying exhausted on a sunny bank, coughing and whispering to one another, soaking up the rare warmth. Like the Maeatae, the Caledones had abandoned their settlements to hide in the hills, and it was clearly causing hardship.

This was nothing, of course, compared to what the Britons would suffer during the winter if the war continued. They had planted crops early in the spring; if they couldn't return to their settlements and harvest them at the end of summer, they would starve.

Still, most of the people seemed cheerful enough. Barefoot children ran alongside the chief's party, screaming in excitement, and when the group stopped, most of the camp's inhabitants thronged about them, grinning and jostling and exclaiming. All of them were staring and pointing at Memnon, amazed by their first sight of a black man. Argentocoxus made a short speech, most of which Memnon couldn't understand, though he did recognize Fortrenn's name and his own. To his relief, the Caledonians looked more impressed than indignant.

Despite his status as a guest, and despite his oath not to escape, he was assigned guards – two sullen young men, one with a leg wound, the other with an arm in a sling. Argentocoxus wasn't wasting able-bodied warriors on guard duty, but it was obvious from the pair's expressions that they meant to take their duties seriously. The chieftain escorted Memnon and his new keepers to a large hut in the middle of the camp, lifted the blanket which hung over the door, and led him inside.

There were two young women sitting there spinning, one redhaired, the other chestnut-brown, both tattooed. 'My wife, Drustocce,' Argentocoxus informed him, indicating the redhead. ' And my sister, Sulicena.' He motioned to the brunette. 'This is Memnon, a Roman; he is the man who shamed Fortrenn of the Votadini. Because of his courage I have spared his life, and he will be our guest until the meeting of the tribes. Fidach and Ivomagus will attend him.' He went over to his wife and kissed her, adding something in British – then departed. They could hear his voice outside, shouting orders, and the sound of men gathering weapons.

Memnon stood uncomfortably by the entrance of the hut, damp and muddy, looking at the two Caledonian noble-women and wondering how on earth a man was supposed to behave in a situation like this. He imagined telling the story to his tent-mates, then sent up a prayer to Juno Caelestis that his tent-mates would survive the day.

'So,' said Drustocce, after a long silence, 'my husband goes now to fight your people.' She spoke excellent Latin.

'So he does, lady,' Memnon agreed. 'Believe me, I'm as worried about it as you are.' He had concluded that while the Caledones in this encampment had enough men to try an attack on the Aurelian Moors, they didn't have enough to triumph; he was, nonetheless, very anxious.

Both the women snorted. Fidach, the guard with the leg wound, sat down stiffly. He drew out his belt knife and a whetstone, and began to sharpen the blade ostentatiously, glowering at Memnon as he did. Ivomagus, the one with the broken arm, also seated himself, in the middle of the doorway, arranging his spear across his lap.

Well, that seemed clear enough: they would spend the battle sitting here in Argentocoxus' hut. Memnon sat down on the floor between his guards, and glanced around. The place was plain enough: a circular framework of poles bound together with reeds and covered with hides, with only a smoke hole in the roof for light. There was a hearth, but no fire, and no furniture except a couple of chests and some bedding, now piled at the sides of the hut. As his eyes adjusted to the dimness, he noticed that there was a baby asleep in the bedding behind the women. The chieftain's nephew, or just his son?

His feet were cold, and he wondered if he could take his wet boots off. He decided that it would probably be consid-ered impolite. He did not want to be rude to a chief's wife, particularly not while his guard held that knife.

'You wear no armour,' the chieftain's wife said, after another silence. 'You're not a legionary.'

She was, he decided, trying to work out what odds her husband faced. 'I'm a scout for a *numerus* of irregular cavalry,' he told her amiably. Then, to reassure her and himself, he continued, 'I think the numbers are nearly even. Your people will attack mine, find that we're tough meat, and pull back. My people will pull back, too, to the south. We're three days north of the estuary, and my prefect's not going to hang about waiting for your allies to turn up.'

Sulicena, a slim woman very similar to her brother in looks, narrowed her eyes in the same thoughtful way. 'A short fight, you think,' she observed, also in good Latin. 'Without many dead on either side?'

'A short fight, certainly,' agreed Memnon. 'As to the losses – that depends on how hard your chief wants to push.'

There was another long silence, filled only by the sound of Fidach's whetstone. The baby began to whimper. Drustocce went over to it, picked it up, and began to rock it: so, a son, then, not a nephew. Or a daughter, he supposed; he couldn't tell.

'I have never seen a black man before,' remarked Sulicena at last. 'Where do you come from?'

He grimaced. 'My people are called the Tebu – but you won't have heard of us. If you cross the narrow sea into Gaul, and then go south a long, long way, through Gaul and Iberia both, and cross the Middle Sea by the Pillars of Hercules, you'll come to the province of Mauretania, which is in Africa. If you go through Mauretania, and cross the mountains of Atlas, you come to the great desert. Cross that – and it's a long, long, hard journey! – and you come to the lands where my people live. There are a lot of different tribes south of the desert, all of them Ethiopian, like me. I never even heard of white people until I came north.'

'What *province* is this, though?' Sulicena asked impatiently.

He laughed and shook his head. 'Lady, where I come from, we hadn't even *heard* of the Roman Empire. I'd heard there were supposed to be many tribes beyond the Sea of Sand, and that they were enemies of the Gaetulians, but I never imagined anything like what I found when I came north.'

Both the women stared. The two guards, who didn't seem to speak Latin, glanced at them uncertainly.

'So you're not a Roman, then?' asked Drustocce at last.

He shrugged. 'I'm a Roman soldier. When I've completed my service, I'll have the citizenship, just like any man born in the Empire.'

'And it's to gain that *citizenship* that you came from

this faraway country to make war on us?' asked Sulicena incredulously.

He shrugged again, ran a thumb over his lips. 'I have no quarrel of my own with the Caledones – but if your people raid the Empire, what do you expect?'

'The Caledones have never attacked *Rome*,' Sulicena pointed out. 'If the Romans come here, and attack us, and try to take our lands and impose their laws on us, do you expect us to treat them as our friends?'

'What is your country like?' asked Drustocce, before he could think of a good answer to that. 'Is it hot there? Is that why your people are black?'

He smiled at her, remembering a girl on the Danube who'd asked him the same question. 'It's very hot there,' he agreed. 'And dry. Not like Britain at all. Lady, would you be offended if I took my boots off? They're wet.'

'So are all your things,' Sulicena remarked. She set down her spindle, went over to one of the chests, and rooted around in it for a minute before pulling out a pair of breeches, a tunic, and a checked cloak. 'These were my husband's,' she said, tossing them to him. 'Your people killed him earlier this year. Change into these, and I will hang your own things up to dry.'

He held the dead man's clothes awkwardly, staring at her in bewilderment. He did not for a moment believe that chief's wives and sisters were supposed to watch enemy soldiers strip naked.

Sulicena's mouth curved in a mischievous smirk. 'What, you're worried that I'll see that your black dye's coming off on to your wet woollens?'

Surprised, he grinned back at her. 'That's *mud*, lady. I would think here in Britain you'd know about mud! I'd prefer it if you took my word for it that I really am black, and let me get changed behind a screen. I wouldn't want the chieftain to get the wrong idea.'

She laughed. 'I'll fix up a curtain for you,' she conceded, 'since you're so modest.'

Nine

The Caledonian men didn't come back to the camp until evening. Memnon, waiting in the dark inside the hut, heard the shouts and discussion that greeted their return, and relaxed slowly: that didn't sound like a victory. To be fair, it didn't sound like a defeat, either – but at least nobody was cheering.

Presently Argentocoxus came into the hut, carrying a lantern. His wife leapt up to embrace him, and he kissed her. Looking round, he saw Memnon sitting over to the side. He recoiled a little, then came forward, holding up the lantern. He was scowling. 'How was it that you warned your friends?' he demanded.

'I left a mark on the road when I found the tracks of your scout,' Memnon replied equably. 'So, they did not ride into your ambush?'

The chieftain looked disgusted. 'We had the better of the encounter. We sent them fleeing back to Bodotria!'

Memnon nodded sagely. 'I was telling your lady wife they'd withdraw without waiting for you to fetch your allies.'

'Tomorrow we will ride in pursuit!'

'They expect nothing else.' He grinned at the Caledonian. 'It wasn't our first reconnaissance mission, you know.'

Argentocoxus gave an abrupt bark of laughter and made a gesture of concession. 'Just as well. There is no glory in fighting children!'

Caledones, Memnon decided, were a strange people.

This opinion was only confirmed in the days that followed. Here they were, hiding in the hills, living in huts and caves for fear of the Romans – and they acted as though they were at a festival. They swaggered about their pitiful camps, clinking in all their jewellery and flashing their tattoos at one another; at night they made music with the harp and the pipes and the drums, and sang songs about Caledonian heroes. They were boastful, brutal and violent, and honoured courage and skill in war above all else – and yet, they revered bards and artists, who were exempt by law from everything to do with the shedding of blood. They loved feasting and, given half a chance, would be drunk every night – yet they also gave themselves tests of endurance, such as standing all day up to their necks in a bog to honour their gods. Whenever they had done something they considered praiseworthy, like performing a ritual for their gods or killing an enemy, they rewarded themselves with a new tattoo, which they then flaunted before all their neighbours. The women were as bold as the men: they laughed and joked with the warriors and, so it seemed to Memnon, slept with anyone they pleased – and yet they considered Romans immodest, and professed horror at the notion of public bathing.

Sulicena had been teasing him, of course, that first day when she suggested he change in front of her. She did tease – sometimes openly, with biting mockery; sometimes straight-faced with a pretense of seriousness. He quickly learned never to believe a word she said, but he liked her. He teased her back; it surprised her the first time, but afterward she fell to sparring with him with relish. It was an unexpected delight, to have found a pretty woman he could laugh with, in the middle of war and this anxious semi-captivity. He was fairly certain that she liked him, too: he noticed her watching him. Of course, she thought he was a much more important person than he actually was. To the Caledones he was the famous warrior who'd overcome the mighty Fortrenn, so they saw nothing wrong with a noblewoman falling a bit in love with him. He was glad they didn't realize just how low the status of an auxiliary cavalryman was. It was very pleasant to be a famous warrior, to have other men treating him with wary deference and women regarding him with admiration. He even wished he could take things a bit further – but Sulicena was his host's sister and, moreover, an enemy. His prospects with her were as hopeless as they'd been with the beautiful Athenais. Still, a man could enjoy his dreams.

He spent most of his time with her and Drustocce – and Fidach and Ivomagus, of course, his two shadows. There were children, too, besides the baby: Drustocce had an eight-year-old daughter, and Sulicena, a six-year-old son. Both were interested in the guest. The girl, Melluna, was beginning to learn Latin – the language was considered to be essential for nobles – and, after some initial nervousness, was delighted to find a Roman to practise it on. Cathluan, the boy, began the acquaintance by declaring that he would cut off the Roman's head, but, on being told that he wasn't allowed to decapitate guests, wanted to hear war stories, and was frustrated by the barrier of language. They were bright, lively children and Memnon enjoyed their company. He taught them a few of the games he'd played when he was a boy, and would have carved a toy leopard for them, except that he was not allowed to have a knife.

His first few nights among the Caledones were spent in the camp at the head of the glen. When the men returned from harrying the Moors back to the estuary, however, the clan packed up their huts and tents and moved further west, to another valley deeper in the mountains. The Romans had found their first site, and it was no longer safe.

Some eight days after the clan had settled in its new hiding place, however, Argentocoxus took his household, a dozen of his finest warriors and his guest, and set out for the meeting of the tribal leaders. Drustocce brought the baby, which was not yet weaned. The two older children were left with their relatives, much to their disappointment.

They travelled first north, then east, and then south again, a roundabout winding path through wild mountains and along the shores of deep, clear lakes: Memnon wondered at first whether the indirect route was chosen to confuse him, but decided that it was dictated instead by the need to avoid the Romans. The Caledones tried not to discuss the war in front of him, but he gathered that the Emperor's forces had begun the move north from the estuary, and that the British were hard-pressed.

The site chosen for the meeting was a hill fort above a lake – a rough place, with a tumbledown palisade rather than a proper wall around it, enclosing a thatched barn which the

Britons called a 'feast hall', and some shabby huts. Memnon thought the place was somewhere in the southeast of Caledonia, which seemed a bit risky to him: the imperial troops were certainly intending to march up the river valleys of the southeast, and if they got wind of a meeting of the chiefs, they would descend on the place like harpies. He supposed, though, that the southern location had been chosen for the convenience of the Maeatae leaders – and he was sure the British chieftains had scouts and sentries out, and would disperse into the hills if there was any danger.

They arrived in the evening of a sunny day in late June. The meeting was being hosted by the chief of the Venicones – a member-tribe of the Caledonian confederacy. He solemnly welcomed Argentocoxus and his household at the fort gates. He cast a wary eye over the Caledonian chief's followers – then noticed Memnon and gasped. Memnon grinned at him.

'This is my guest, Memnon,' Argentocoxus said blandly. 'A Roman who . . .' Memnon couldn't quite follow the rest of what he said, but there was something about 'courage'. He kept grinning at the Veniconian chief, who stared back aghast.

'Fortrenn of the Votadini is here,' the Veniconian chief said, making a gesture to avert evil, 'with his nephew, Cirech. This isn't the man who . . .?'

'Certainly it is!' replied Argentocoxus, grinning. 'He is my guest.'

'He is a Roman!' objected the Veniconian, and added something about spies.

Argentocoxus, however, insisted on his right to bring in any guest he liked, and eventually the Veniconian yielded. The Caledonian party was shown to a hut north of the big barn and offered a ceremonial cup of mead, which Argentocoxus at once drank to indicate that hospitality had been accepted. The women promptly went off to fetch some water for washing.

Argentocoxus grinned at Memnon. 'Tonight there will be a feast,' he informed him, in Latin. 'We are the last to arrive, and tomorrow the council begins. As a Roman you are forbidden to go to the council, but as my guest you are welcome to the feast.'

'Fortrenn will be there?' Memnon asked.

Argentocoxus' grin became a smirk. 'And his nephew, too, it seems. Don't worry! We are here under oath of truce, and we have all accepted hospitality from Nechtan of the Venicones. If Fortrenn tries to draw steel in our host's hall, his own men will cry out and stop him.' He surveyed Memnon critically. 'The women will see to it that you have your own clothes back, but it is a shame that they're so plain. Whatever happened to the gold torque you took from Fortrenn?'

'It's in the strongroom of my unit's base in Aballava,' Memnon told him. 'I don't wear gold to scout.' He hesitated for a moment, then reached down to the purse he still wore at his belt; his guards had searched it and returned it to him intact. He took out the gold earring. 'I have this, though.' He had taken it off when he first rode north from the estuary, and it felt odd to put it on again, here in the very middle of a barbarian stronghold. He felt, though, that he owed Argentocoxus all the show he could manage.

The Caledonian was startled. '*What* is *that*?' he demanded.

'It's an earring,' Memnon replied patiently. 'A gold star, see? That's the emblem of the Aurelian Moors. We all wear one of these. Didn't you notice?'

'I noticed how your friends fought,' Argentocoxus said drily. 'I wasn't paying much attention to their jewellery.' He considered Memnon a moment, uneasily. 'We say that mark is the sign of a goddess.'

'Ah? Well, so do the Moors.'

'Indeed? Of what goddess?'

'Juno Caelestis, the Queen of Heaven. She is patroness of Mauretania, and our protectress.'

'We say it is the sign of Brigida, the Lady of Night, Mother of the Gods. She is much to be feared.'

'So is the Queen of Heaven,' Memnon informed him. 'And they call her Mother of the Gods, too.'

Argentocoxus drew in his breath with a hiss. 'She would seem to be the same goddess. A powerful protectress, to be sure.' He hesitated – then, with a smile, took the brooch off his own cloak. It was a ring-brooch of gilded bronze, worked with sinuous curves of red enamel, and had a garnet set in the pin. 'Wear your emblem, but borrow this as well!' he said. 'A warrior shouldn't enter a strange feast hall with no more display than a single earring!'

Memnon hesitated, then smiled and accepted it.

The women returned with buckets of water, and everyone began to prepare for the feast. It seemed that the Caledonian custom was for the men to sit down first, and for the women to enter the hall after the meal had started: the men's preparations were thus more urgent. Argentocoxus sat down to let his wife trim his hair and beard.

'Here!' said Sulicena, coming over to Memnon with a comb and a razor. 'I'll do you.'

He was startled, and eyed the sharp blade uneasily. 'I, uh, don't . . .' he pointed out, drawing a hand over his smooth chin.

She paused, frowning. She glanced at the razor in her hand, then back at him. Everyone else in the hut was looking too, with the same expression of shocked surprise as they realized he hadn't shaved since he arrived among them.

'You're not a *eunuch*, are you?' Drustocce blurted out.

'No!' he exclaimed indignantly. 'Of course not! Do I *sound* like one? Men of my tribe just don't grow hair on our faces until we're old. Nothing to do with our ability to father children.'

They all considered this, then shook their heads in amazement. Drustocce resumed her work on her husband's hair. Sulicena renewed her critical frown at Memnon. 'Let me trim your hair, then. You look like an unshorn sheep.'

He suspected that he did: he had not had his hair cut since setting out from Aballava. He sat down on the floor of the hut, a bit nervously, and Sulicena knelt behind him, exchanging the razor for a small pair of shears. She touched his hair hesitantly, then drew some of it up between her fingers. 'You *feel* like an unshorn sheep, too!' she protested. 'Your hair isn't like ours at all.'

He sighed. 'That's because I'm an Ethiopian, and you're Celts. If you have a mirror, I could cut it myself.' Maybe he could palm the razor.

'Ha! And leave it in a mess round the back. I can do it.' She drew up some hair with the comb and snipped it off with the shears, working with quick, steady clicks of the blades. He liked the strong, gentle touch of her hands on his head, but didn't dare to say so.

When she finished, she picked up a tuft of cut hair and rolled it between her fingers. Then she set it down, and very gently ran her hand over his shorn head and along his cheek. He twisted his head, and saw her face very close. She had a crescent moon tattooed on her brow; another tattoo at the base of her throat ran down under her tunic, and he wondered where it stopped.

'The world is bigger than I thought it was,' she said, softly, almost sadly. 'Until you came here, I had no idea that there were men with black skin, or that there were countries so far away that the people there had never even heard of the Roman Empire.'

'The world is very big,' he agreed. 'The more I see of it, the bigger it seems to get.'

She stroked his cheek again, then traced the curl of his ear. Her fingers cherished what they touched, and he held his breath, quite dizzy with the desire to reciprocate. 'All I have ever seen of it is Caledonia,' she told him quietly. 'Why did you come here to make war on us, Memnon?'

'I . . . swore to fight for the Empire,' he told her, trying to keep his voice level.

'Why?'

He turned and caught her hand. 'When I came north – when I first did, when I crossed the desert – I had three camels and a handful of gold I'd taken from the Gaetulians. I came out of the desert toward the high country, because I thought there'd be water there, and I'd had no water, not for two days. I came to Auzia, which is a fort that guards the settled lands from the Gaetulians. I'd never seen anything like it – I'd never seen any stone building bigger than a goat-pen before, and there it was, a fort with gates and towers! I was afraid to go near it, but I had to or die of thirst. The soldiers wouldn't let me in, but they gave me water from their well, for myself and the camels, and they bartered with me for food. Yes, they overcharged, they cheated me out-rageously – but, you see, if *they* had come to a Tebu well, complete strangers who didn't speak a word of Tbawi, we would have killed them. That was the first I saw of the

Empire: skill at building, and power, and tolerance. It astonished me – and I didn't even know that Auzia was just one small fort on the fringe of something so vast a single mind can't know it.'

He took a deep breath, wondering how she could possibly understand what he'd told her, when he didn't even understand himself why he'd said it.

She frowned at him. 'You're saying that you fight for the Empire because you love it?'

He released her hand. After a moment he nodded. 'At first I fought for it because it was fighting the Gaetulians, and I hated them. When I swore my oath, though – I was tired of hating.'

'And yet you come here to fight,' said Argentocoxus, standing up in a scatter of trimmings from his own hair. 'Do you hate *us*?'

Memnon had forgotten he was there. He sighed. 'To tell the truth, chieftain, no. I would grieve for the death of any member of your house. I wish you and the Empire could make peace.'

'We tried to make peace,' said Argentocoxus in a low voice. 'The Emperor sent our envoys away unheard.'

'Maybe you should try again,' said Memnon. 'He might listen now.'

Argentocoxus looked at him thoughtfully, then smiled.

A few minutes later Memnon found himself walking beside the chieftain up the hill to the feast, with Argentocoxus's men following behind.

The feast hall had a dirt floor and walls of wattle and daub. Trestle tables had been set up in it, flanked by benches, many of them looking very rickety. There was a fire-pit in the middle of the room, and a raised wooden platform at the far end. At the moment the room was lit by the evening light that slid under the eaves – here in the north the evenings seemed endless – though once night fell the only illumination would be the fire. About a hundred men were milling about the room talking loudly, and nobody had yet sat down.

As they entered the hall several voices hailed Argentocoxus, and he went over and slapped backs and clasped hands; Memnon understood just enough of the conversation to work

out that these were other Caledonian chiefs, allies of
Argentocoxus in some dispute. Fortrenn's name was
mentioned, and Argentocoxus grinned. He waved a hand at
Memnon, and the other Caledonians were amazed. One of
them laughed.

Memnon stood with Fidach and Ivomagus, waiting for
something to happen, but the only event worth mentioning
was that a harpist and a pipe-player turned up on the platform and began playing cheerfully. After a while, some of
the men sat down; Argentocoxus, however, stayed up in
earnest consultation with his fellow chiefs, so Memnon
remained standing as well. Even Fidach stayed on his feet,
though from his expression his leg wound hurt like fury.

Then, at last, there was a sudden disturbance on the other
side of the hall, and a tall man came pushing through the
crowd toward them. As he drew closer, Memnon saw that it
was indeed Fortrenn, son of Talorgen. He had a new gold
torque and his hand was on the hilt of his sword. Memnon
grinned at him and raised a hand in greeting.

Fortrenn halted, his face flushing under its tattoos. All
around them the hall went silent; even the musicians stopped
playing.

'What is *this*?' roared Fortrenn, in British, indicating
Memnon with an outflung hand. 'What have you brought to
our council, Argentocoxus son of Aenbecan?'

'You know my guest already, Fortrenn of the Votadini,'
replied Argentocoxus, smiling maliciously. 'You've met him
before.'

Fortrenn said something furious about 'spies' and 'enemies'.
Argentocoxus replied sharply with words about 'your shame'.
The host of the gathering, Nechtan of the Venicones, hurried
up panting and tried to soothe his guests. Fortrenn glared at
Memnon and spat something about 'lying Romans'.

'No lie,' Memnon said deliberately, in British. 'What lie
I say, ha?'

Fortrenn indignantly roared a reply containing the word
'ghosts'. Memnon held up one hand. 'I never said I was a
ghost,' he said, in Latin. 'I didn't even realize that it was
what you and your men believed, until afterwards. It's not
my fault you never saw an Ethiopian before. Now, if you

say that I killed one of your men, circumcized your nephew, stole your prisoners and your gold necklace and even your cloak, well, that's fair enough, I did – but I told no lies.' He noticed a young man in Fortrenn's entourage who was looking at him with a mixture of terror and fury, and guessed that it was the nephew. He didn't really recognize the boy – he'd barely seen his face on the night – but he nodded to him.

Fortrenn ripped his sword out of his sheath; several men cried out, and Nechtan seized his hand. The chieftain of the Votadini gritted his teeth and lowered the weapon. His eyes were murderous. 'I will kill you, Roman!' he whispered.

'I've heard about it,' Memnon replied. 'You tried last winter, didn't you? You sat there in that camp above the road, waiting for me, while my comrades and I went up through the Selgovae and down through your own lands, just as we pleased. Well, my decurion always told me I'd get caught one day, and he was right, so maybe you will kill me.'

'You did lie,' said the nephew, suddenly pushing forward. 'You said that if we tried to take our prisoners back, none of us would reach home alive.'

'That wasn't a lie,' Memnon replied softly, meeting and holding his eyes. 'That was a promise. I would've kept it, too, Briton; I've done as much before. You weren't the first to think I was a ghost, and perhaps the last men who thought so were right. They died in the desert, every one of them.'

There was an absolute silence. Then Fortrenn turned back to Argentocoxus. 'Why did you bring this here?' he asked in British.

Argentocoxus spat, but didn't answer. Nechtan caught his arm and, with an anxious look at Memnon, drew the Caledonian chief off toward the upper end of the hall. Memnon considered following, but nobody else was, so he remained where he was, facing the chief of the Votadini.

'Why did you come here?' Fortrenn asked in a low voice.

'Argentocoxus invited me.'

'What is he to you?'

'My host, for the present. His men caught me: I was scouting too eagerly. I have you to thank for the fact that he spared my life.'

Fortrenn gave him a look of deep disquiet, made the gesture

to ward off evil, then spat – three times, the repetition ring-
ingly significant. 'I *will* kill you,' he said, 'whatever you are.'
He turned on his heel and strode off after Argentocoxus.

Memnon stayed on his feet, watching the chieftain make
his way to the table on the wooden platform. So, the chiefs
sat up there; the followers sat down here. He supposed he
was a follower. He wondered if he could still have something to eat, now that he'd half-convinced the company that
he was, after all, a ghost.

He did not enjoy the feast, not even after the women came
in, beautiful in their finest gowns, with flowers in their hair.
They didn't sit with the men – they had their own tables,
near the fire – and he still had no one to talk to. Everyone
except Fidach and Ivomagus was afraid of him, and they
couldn't speak Latin.

When the food was cleared away and the serious drinking
started, the women left again. The bard began to sing something sad about a hero. Memnon touched Fidach's arm. 'We
go?' he asked hopefully.

Fidach nodded, looking relieved: he evidently wanted to
rest his leg. Memnon scrambled off the bench, helped his
guard up, and walked out of the hall.

In the Caledonians' hut, the women were preparing for
bed by the light of a tallow candle. They paused when
Memnon and his guards came in. Sulicena was smiling, her
eyes bright under the tattooed moon. 'What happened?' she
asked eagerly. 'We were with the women, and none of them
knew. Did you speak to Fortrenn?'

'Yes,' agreed Memnon. 'He came up and shouted at your
brother about me.' He sat down heavily and fingered his
earring. 'Everyone at the council has been reminded that the
great Fortrenn of the Votadini was once humiliated by a
Roman. Everyone's seen that Argentocoxus of the Caledones
has that same Roman at heel. I imagine your brother's
pleased.'

Drustocce laughed and clapped her hands. Fidach said
something about ghosts and Sulicena frowned.

'Yes,' Memnon said, guessing the news. 'Fortrenn seems
to think I might be a ghost after all.'

She laughed and came over to squat facing him. 'Because

you look so strange? Because you wear the sign of the Lady of Night?'

'Because I scared him again.' He knew that when he spoke about the Gaetulians, everyone around him had sensed what had happened in the desert: it had been in his eyes and in his voice. They had recognized a demon, supernatural or not; they'd been right to recoil. He looked at the pretty face opposite his, and felt comforted by the expression of cynical disbelief.

'Fortrenn's a fool,' said Sulicena. 'He doesn't want to believe any man could get the better of him, so he tries to convince himself you aren't an ordinary man.' She smiled at him and added softly, 'And of course, you aren't. You're a great warrior.'

He ached to kiss her. *My enemy's sister*, he reminded himself, *and the sister of my host.*

A woman whose brother would probably kill him tomorrow. He was instinctively certain that if Argentocoxus had ever been willing simply to release his guest, he wasn't now. Take an enemy scout into your family, let him see the hiding place of your clan, bring him to your council of war, and then *let him go*? It had never been very likely. Now that Argentocoxus knew he had a very dangerous man under his roof – and Memnon was certain that he'd shared that moment of insight in the hall, and did know – it was out of the question.

He met Sulicena's smiling eyes seriously and honestly. 'Tomorrow is the council,' he reminded her. 'What happens to the great warrior – the great *enemy* warrior – when it's over?'

She started back as though he'd struck her, then leapt to her feet, scowling. 'My brother will never harm a guest!' she declared. 'It would be dishonourable.'

Memnon was awake when Argentocoxus came back from the feast, and aware of it when the Caledonian stood over him in the dark. He remained perfectly relaxed, breathing evenly, apparently asleep and ready in every fibre to bolt if the chieftain drew a weapon.

He wasn't surprised, though, when Argentocoxus moved off without disturbing him. The Caledonian had sworn to treat Memnon as his guest until the meeting ended, and he wouldn't break his oath. Most likely he wouldn't personally do anything to harm Memnon even after the council ended. There were plenty of others at the meeting who'd be happy to do the killing for him.

For his part, Memnon was sorely tempted to slip out into the night. The Caledonians had all drunk heavily at the feast. Even Fidach and Ivomagus, who'd left early, had downed enough to keep them snoring until the small hours. There would not be a better opportunity to escape . . . but he had sworn by his ancestors that he wouldn't.

He imagined his ancestors sitting under the date palms where they'd lived, shaking their heads, saying to one another, 'That Wajjaj, what does he think he's doing? He runs off north and neglects us completely – never pours us an offering on feast days, or sings the chants for us, or tends our graves, the impious boy! Who does he think he's fooling, swearing by us and pretending he thinks it's holy?'

He smiled at the image. He was cut off from the world the other side of the desert, in body and in name; the world of spirits, though, was bigger even than the Roman Empire. He would honour his oath by his ancestors, because if he failed it, the patchwork construction that was his new life would lose its last connection with the old, and perhaps begin to unravel. He would not try to escape – until the council was over.

In the morning, Argentocoxus kept looking at him as they ate their breakfast of oatcakes, but said nothing. When the chief had finished, Memnon went to him and offered back the brooch he'd been loaned the evening before. Argentocoxus flushed slightly and shook his head. 'No, no!' he said. 'Keep it.'

Memnon raised his eyebrows, then bowed and pinned the brooch to the breast of his tunic. 'Thank you,' he said. 'I'm honoured.'

Argentocoxus gave him a forced smile. He kissed his wife and baby son, then said a few quiet words to Fidach and Ivomagus before leaving for the council.

Memnon stood a moment, fingering the pin, sure that he'd

just been given a gift for his grave. He sighed, dropping his hand, and found Sulicena staring at him. He smiled at her, but she sniffed, gathered up her skirts and left the hut.

It was a quiet morning, sunny and clear. He tried to persuade his guards to accompany him for a walk, but they refused, and told him that Argentocoxus had given orders that he was to stay in the hut. Time passed, and Sulicena did not come back. Drustocce sat quietly, spinning or playing with her baby. Memnon prowled restlessly about the hut, wondering how he'd know when the council was finished.

Sulicena finally returned to the hut at noon. She had an angry, defiant air, and when she set foot inside the door she glared at Memnon and loudly declared in British that she wanted to 'stop' something-or-other.

Drustocce looked shocked. Fidach and Ivomagus protested. Sulicena snarled at them and marched over to take hold of Memnon's arm. Fidach protested again, this time comprehensibly, 'The chief said he stays here!'

Sulicena said something angry about her brother, then something about a hut. She waved Fidach and Ivomagus back, and led Memnon, surprised but unresisting, into the open air.

'What were you saying?' he asked in bewilderment.

Her face was flushed. 'I said that I want to put an end to my longing, that I've arranged the loan of an empty hut, and that they're to leave us alone.'

'Oh!' he exclaimed, flabbergasted. 'Oh, gods and spirits!'

She caught him in her arms and kissed him fiercely, then rocked back and gazed into his face. There were tears in her eyes. 'Why must you be our enemy?' she demanded.

'I wish I wasn't,' he told her, shaken to the core. 'Lady, I . . .'

'You could stay with us. You could take oath to my brother, to fight for him. We could adopt you into the clan. You weren't born a Roman: why should you die as one?'

He shook his head, unable to speak. 'Come!' she commanded, and tugged him after her around the feast hall and down the hill.

The empty hut was derelict and smelled of damp straw; the bundles of thatch which formed its roof were beginning to slide loose from the rafters. In winter it would be uninhabitable, but on this fine summer day it was merely pleasantly cool. Sulicena spread her cloak on the bare earthern floor, then hurried over to the door. She glanced back up the hill, then closed it firmly.

'They followed us,' said Memnon, beginning to regain his scattered wits.

'Ivomagus did,' she said dismissively, with a toss of the head. 'He will stay outside, though.'

He stood silent a moment, looking at her. She was dishevelled, angry, breath-takingly lovely. 'You've discovered that they mean to kill me.'

She caught her breath and turned her face away. 'I heard some of the men talking about it. My brother will allow you to leave freely when the council ends this afternoon – but there will be twenty men waiting for you outside the fort gate, mounted, with spears and bows, and you will be sent out unarmed and on foot.'

It was about what he'd feared. He looked at her seriously. 'So why have you fetched me here?'

She whirled back and punched his shoulder. 'Why do you *think*?'

He was amazed that she could do this – give herself to an enemy of her clan, and one who was about to die. He was doubly amazed that her household would allow it. He caught her face between his hands. For all the ache of desire, he wanted most of all just to look at her, to see there in her eyes the unmistakable fire of love.

She caught and held his hands, then took them and put them around her waist. She kissed him.

'Isn't . . . isn't this considered shameful?' he asked weakly, when he'd caught his breath. 'Among my people it would be.'

She snorted and narrowed her eyes at him. 'It isn't shameful! Why do you think it's shameful?' She let go of him abruptly. 'You're married!'

'No, no!' he protested. 'I'm not. But my people – and the Romans – we think that for a man to sleep with his host's sister, or any other woman of his host's family, is an abuse of hospitality.'

'Oh,' she said, and shook her head. 'Among *my* people, it's only a breach of hospitality to sleep with your host's wife. Who a sister sleeps with is no business of her brother's.'

'I'm an enemy, though. Doesn't that . . . ?'

'You are a great and famous warrior,' she corrected him. 'A leopard from the south, whom all men fear. Every woman in the clan will know why I chose you, and most of them will envy me.'

He frowned at her, bewildered, not daring to admit the truth about his lowly status. 'But you're the chief's sister; your children are his heirs! How can he . . . ?'

She silenced him with a kiss. 'There is no shame in this,' she said, meeting his eyes. 'There is only honourable love.'

The tattoo ended between her breasts, in a blue spiral. He traced the line of it, after the stunned rapture of their love-making. His heart ached with grief. He had found a treasure, the greatest life had to offer; he could not keep it, beyond this hour.

She kissed his shoulder and he put his arms around her, holding her close. 'I wish we had peace,' he whispered. 'I wish I could stay with you forever.'

'Yes,' she whispered; then, more urgently, 'you *could* stay. If you took oath to my brother . . .'

'If I could forsake my oaths and change my loyalties so easily, what use would they be to your brother – or to me?'

She sighed, as though she'd known that this would be his answer. She rested her chin on his chest and traced the lines of his face. 'What will you do?' she asked, after a long silence.

'When does the council end?'

She winced. 'It is probably over already.'

'Already?'

'There was only one real argument, and I think Fortrenn will have lost it. By now they will be drinking together and making pledges of friendship and support.'

He considered that for a long moment. Then he kissed her passionately. As he did, he felt for and found the long strip of dyed leather she used to girdle her tunic. He caught her hands and began to wind it round them, pulling her wrists together behind her back.

Her eyes flew wide open, but he kept her silent, pressing his mouth against hers in what was no longer a kiss. She started to struggle. He knotted the leather binding, then felt for and found her discarded gown. Breaking away from her at last, he shoved a fold of the gown into her mouth as she drew in a breath to scream.

'I'm sorry,' he told her, 'but if there are going to be twenty men waiting for me outside the gate, I'd prefer to leave by going over the wall.'

She stared at him in shock and indignation and tried to spit out the gag. He straddled her hips, to prevent her from moving, and rearranged the gag, securing it by tying the gown's arms. He pulled the knot away from her nose, so that she wouldn't have trouble breathing, then drew the long skirts down to cover her body and protect her modesty from whoever eventually came into the hut and found her. He spotted the little knife she carried to cut her meat; it had a loop of leather to attach it to her girdle, but it had fallen aside when they undressed. He had to stretch to pick it up without freeing her legs, but he managed. 'I'm going to have to cut the hem off your cloak,' he told her, and slid the sharp little blade out of its sheath. 'Sorry.'

He tied her legs with the strip of wool, then got up. She lay half on her side, half on her back, staring at him with a mixture of fury and relief.

'I swore I wouldn't try to escape until the council was over,' he explained to her. 'If this ends up shaming you, well, I'm sorry. They'll see clearly enough that at least you're no traitor.' He found his clothes and put them on. His hooded riding cape was still in Argentocoxus's hut – well, he would have to hope it didn't start raining. He fastened Sulicena's little knife to his own belt – then went over and knelt beside her. He unhooked his earring and set it down on the ground in front of her. 'That is all I have to give you,' he told her. 'That, and my promise that I will never knowingly do harm to any member of the clan of Argentocoxus. I will not tell the Romans where your clan is hiding or betray any secrets I may have learned while I was your guest.' He grinned. 'Not much of an offer, since I didn't learn any, but there it is.' He kissed the crescent moon on her forehead. 'I pray to the gods that this war ends in peace, and that your life is joyful.'

She sniffed, her eyes bright with tears. He wasn't sure whether they were tears of sorrow or of rage. He kissed her again, then went over to the hut's central roof-pole. Ivomagus was outside watching – but he was watching the door. Memnon leapt, caught hold of a rafter, and swung up. He straddled it and peered out through one of the places where the thatch had come loose. He had a good view of the area behind the hut, where there was nobody in sight; since he couldn't see the front of the hut, presumably nobody waiting there could see him. He climbed out, quietly and carefully, eased down the roof to the ground, and walked swiftly away.

Ten

It took him three days to work his way back to Roman territory. On the first afternoon there were signs of pursuit: the baying of dogs in the distance; a group of horsemen spread out along the crest of a far-off hill; fresh hoofprints by a river. He never felt himself in real danger. He knew all the tricks, and he used them.

When darkness fell he kept walking. When he was a boy he'd been accustomed to walking all day to find pasturage for the goats; for all his time as a cavalryman, he'd not lost that habit of endurance. He walked all night, partly because he wanted to put some distance between himself and his pursuers; partly because without a cloak it was too cold to sleep in the open, even now, in high summer.

Morning found him in a land of steep, heather-covered hills, empty of life, except for the birds. He slept for a few hours curled up in the heather, then continued on. At the next valley he cut a couple of young saplings and whittled them into crude javelins; he tried to bring down game-birds with them, but the birds were wary and the javelins badly balanced. He could've made better, or woven cord and set snares – if he'd had time, if it had been safe to stop. As it was, he went hungry, and pressed on. He kept to wild country, avoiding all tracks and settlements: he couldn't possibly blend in with the natives. He encountered deer, foxes, and once, a wolf, but nothing human.

Late in the afternoon of the second day he reached a river. It was too deep to wade, and he'd never learned to swim, but he was certain it must flow into the estuary of Bodotria; all he had to do was follow it back to the east, and he would reach the Roman pontoon bridge. He celebrated by building a proper bivouac in a pine wood, and sleeping warm, curled under a pile of pine needles and branches.

It began to rain before morning. It was hard to force himself out of his snug nest and start walking again. He managed it by telling himself that before evening he would be back with his friends, eating a hot meal in a dry tent.

It was the middle of the afternoon when he reached the pontoon bridge, and he was soaked through, exhausted, and light-headed with hunger. The armoured legionaries guarding the bridge were one of the most beautiful sights he'd ever seen.

His gladness, however, was not reciprocated. When he walked out of the forest he was greeted with suspicion and surprise; when he told the legionaries that he'd escaped from the Caledones, he was instantly accused of being a liar and a deserter.

'No!' he told them, shocked. 'How can you say that?' He noticed, for the first time, that their standard had the centaur on it, and his heart gave a jolt. This troop didn't seem to know who he was, and they shouldn't have any grudge against him even if they did, since he hadn't spoken out against Panthera and had never been accused over the banner – but you never could tell.

The senior Alban snorted. 'I'm sick of you mongrel auxiliaries! You ran off, black face, didn't you? Only you've found you can't get back south again, because there's a river in the way. You'd take to your heels again as soon as you were across!'

'No!' Memnon repeated, his voice cracking with rage and exhaustion. 'All I want is to rejoin my unit.'

The legionary only shook his head and signalled two of the other men. 'Take him back to the gatehouse. We'll see what his commanding officer has to say about him.'

The two legionaries marched him across the bridge as far as the shelter of the Roman encampment. There they put irons on his legs and left him locked in the rough gatehouse while someone went to find the Aurelian Moors.

He sat on the cold earthern floor and rested his head against his knees. He remembered Sulicena smiling at him and saying, 'You're a great warrior.' What would she think if she saw him now? He rubbed at the shackle around his ankle and felt the tears start to his eyes. Oh, immortal gods, he was so *tired*!

He told himself that everything would be all right once Rogatus knew he was here. His comrades would hurry to fetch him; they would give him food, and he could go to sleep in his own tent, with all his friends around him.

The afternoon passed; the trumpet sounded for the day's end; the smell of cooking drifted in the air. Unable to bear it, Memnon shuffled clanking to the gatehouse door and banged on it.

After a little while, one of the guards came and opened it. 'What do you want?' he snarled.

'I want to rejoin my unit and have supper,' Memnon told him, keeping his temper raggedly under control.

'They're not in camp,' the legionary replied shortly. 'You'll be dealt with by the camp prefect tomorrow.'

The Moors were not in camp? Where were they? Argentocoxus had harried them southward, but by all accounts the casualties had been light. He supposed, though, that that had been . . . how long ago? He'd spent three days in the first Caledonian encampment, eight in the second, and then there was the journey . . .

It had been the better part of a month. It wasn't surprising that the Moors were off on another mission. Probably everyone believed he was dead. The camp prefect would be left to 'deal with' him as he saw fit.

Who was the camp prefect? He had a nasty suspicion that this man, too, would belong to the Alban legion: they were the most prestigious of the forces stationed here. Maybe he should never have touched that banner: it seemed to have brought down a curse.

'If my unit's not here, you can send to the chamberlain Septimius Castor,' he announced loudly. 'He'll vouch for me.'

The legionary stared incredulously. 'The Emperor's chamberlain will vouch for *you*?'

Memnon reached in his purse to fetch out Castor's ring – then remembered that he didn't have it. Rogatus had advised him not to carry it while scouting, so he'd locked it in a strongbox in the base camp.

'I'm a friend of the chamberlain,' he insisted. 'I saved his life. You must have heard about it: it was all over the army last autumn!'

The guard frowned. 'What, you're *that* Ethiopian? The one that castrated the British hostage?'

Memnon gave up on correcting the story. 'Yes. Castor will tell you I'm no deserter. Send to him! You'll see.'

The legionary shrugged. 'Very well, we'll send to him. Don't hold your breath, though. Even if you're telling the truth, Castor the chamberlain may not want to know about your troubles. He has plenty of his own.' He closed the door.

The guard, however, had slandered Castor. It was only a short while later that there was a commotion outside, and then the door was opened. 'It's him,' Castor declared to the legionary behind him; then, as Memnon stood, 'You've put irons on him! How *dare* you? This man has made his way back here against who knows what odds, after being given up for dead! The Empress *herself* has rewarded him for his courage!'

'We thought he was a deserter,' said the guard sullenly. 'His *numerus* is out of the camp, and there was nobody to ask about him.'

'There were plenty of people to ask, if you'd bothered! Release him immediately!'

Released from the leg irons, Memnon followed Castor out in the clear evening. Two scarlet-clad soldiers of the Praetorian Guard were waiting there, their gilt-edged, old-fashioned armour and ridged helmets standing out among the plainer gear of the legionaries.

'My poor friend, I'm overjoyed to see you!' said Castor, looking Memnon over anxiously. 'We'd given up hope of ever seeing you alive.'

The chamberlain had a black eye. It was an old one, green at the edges, but spectacular. There was a dried red scab on one ear, and more bruises on his forearms. Memnon drew a deep breath, shivering. It was hard to think clearly. Fortrenn couldn't have beaten Castor *again*: Fortrenn was away in the north.

'Come back to my quarters,' urged Castor. 'Have you eaten?'

* * *

Castors's quarters consisted of a very large tent in the camp-within-a-camp that was the preserve of the Emperors and the Praetorian Guard. Inside it was almost like a house: it had furniture and carpets, and multiple rooms divided by hangings. Memnon, following his host, stopped inside the entrance, abruptly aware that he was filthy, covered in the debris of three days' worth of bogs, forests, and mountainside.

'Sit down,' Castor ordered. 'I'll have the slaves bring some food. Or do you want to wash first? I'll have them heat water.'

Memnon wolfed down some bread and wine, then washed off the worst of the mud with a bucket of hot water. With indescribable pleasure, he changed into a clean, dry tunic and sat down at a table. The slaves brought him soup, sausages and more bread and wine. Replete, he was almost too sleepy to tell Castor the story of his capture and escape, but the chamberlain pressed him with sharp questions and extracted it.

At last Memnon yawned. 'Thank you, sir, for the food. And thank you for coming to vouch for me. I would have had a hard time of it if you hadn't.'

'It was outrageous behaviour by the Albans,' Castor said seriously. 'Though I suppose they have some justification: there have been problems with desertion. The army's morale is very low. Now, I believe your unit isn't expected back for several days. You must stay here in the meantime.'

'I'd be very grateful for that, sir, tonight, but tomorrow I can . . .'

'No, no you must stay here!' insisted Castor, and touched his arm. 'To tell the truth, I'd be very glad of your presence.'

Memnon stared into his bruised face and finally asked, 'Sir? What happened to you?'

Castor lowered his hand, then locked his fingers together between his knees. 'Antoninus found out that . . . that I was the one who told his father about his plot against Geta.'

Memnon stared. 'So he came round and beat you up?'

'No. No. He . . . I was summoned to his tent, six days ago. It was supposed to be about some imperial appointments, but when I got there he started to talk about supplies. I didn't

know what he meant at first. Then I realized. I pretended I
didn't know what he was talking about, but he just flew into
a rage and started shouting that I was Geta's whore and I
was poisoning his father's mind against him. I was terrified.
I told him he was greatly mistaken and left, but when I got
out of the tent, there were soldiers there, a whole mob of
them, waiting. Antoninus rushed out after me, yelling that
I'd *wronged* him, and the men all came at me with swords
and cudgels. I thought I was going to die. I would have died,
only my patron happened to be nearby and came over to see
what was going on.'

Memnon was appalled; what Castor had just described
wasn't an assault in the heat of the moment, but attempted
murder, cold-bloodedly arranged to look like a spontaneous
attack by loyal soldiers. 'What did your patron do?'

'Oh, they stopped hitting me the moment he appeared.
He's given orders that I'm to have an escort whenever I leave
my own quarters – you may have noticed the Praetorians.'

'But – what did he do to *Caracalla?*'

Castor looked up sharply. 'You shouldn't call him that.
He doesn't like it. I believe his father rebuked him and
ordered him not to interfere with me again.'

'*Rebuked* him? Is that all?'

'What else could he do?'

'Demote him! Send him back to Rome in disgrace! Sir,
you're his father's chamberlain! When you told your patron
what he was up to, you saved thousands of Roman lives and
maybe this whole campaign, and you protected your patron's
younger son from disgrace. You're entitled to more protection than a *rebuke!*'

Castor gave a small snort and reached over to pat
Memnon's arm. 'Thank you. Your support is . . . most appreciated. But . . . no, I'm not entitled to ask for the dismissal
of an Emperor. I am a freedman of the Household of Caesar:
we are here to serve the Emperors, not to dictate to them.
If anyone goes, it should be me: my presence on the staff
will do nothing but inflame the young emperor's feelings. I
offered my patron my resignation, in fact – but he refused
it.' He sighed. 'I wish he'd accepted. It would be much safer
if I could drop out of sight and be forgotten.'

A chilling possibility occurred to Memnon. 'They were saying a month ago that the Emperor's been ill.'

Castor flinched slightly and nodded. 'He's recovered a bit since then, but his health is still poor. I pray the gods he recovers!'

'If he dies, or if he gets worse, what happens . . . ?'

'He will recover. He has always been a strong man. He will live for many years, I hope, and this matter will be forgotten. I *think* that Antoninus will obey his father, and leave me alone. What frightens me is the possibility that someone else might decide that my life would buy him advancement. Everyone in the camp knows what happened. Everyone knows that Antoninus would be very glad of my death.' He gave a weak smile. 'That, my friend, is why I'd be very happy to have you stay here until your unit returns. I have not slept well since that incident, and it would relieve my mind greatly to have such a redoubtable warrior close at hand.'

Memnon looked at him uneasily. 'I'm pleased, sir, if I can be of any help.'

'Thank you.'

There was a silence, and then the chamberlain said, in a vehement whisper, 'I thank all the gods, the young Emperor has no idea that *Athenais* was the one who found out about his conspiracy. When I went to my patron, I never mentioned her. Or your *numerus*, of course.'

There was something chilling about this; it took Memnon a moment to work out what. 'You think that *Severus Augustus* was the one who betrayed you to Caracalla?'

Castor winced. 'Don't, please! And . . . no, I'm sure that my patron didn't *betray* me, only that he may have said enough to let Antoninus work it out. I *begged* him – I was afraid of this from the start – but he . . .' He stopped, then resumed earnestly, 'You have to understand: he disapproves of giving too much power to slaves and freedmen. He wants the offices of the state to be controlled by free men of rank; most noblemen do – and I admit that under his predecessors things were completely out of hand, with chamberlains and procurators wearing purple and demanding bribes from senators. Of course, he can't run the Empire without the

Household, but he . . . likes us to know our place. He . . . faced with the need to discipline his son for an abuse of imperial authority, the security of a Household freedman was not a major concern.'

Memnon gazed stonily on the plump, bruised face of his host. 'It should have been.'

'No, no!' Castor got to his feet. 'Come, we are both tired, and it's late. Rest. In the morning I'll send to Papinian and Adventus. I'm sure that they'll want to question you about this "meeting of the chiefs".'

Memnon stared again, this time in alarm. Being questioned by the Praetorian Prefect and the Princeps Peregrinorum did not sound comfortable at all.

'Don't worry,' said Castor, with another tired smile. 'Your conduct was, as ever, worthy of your hero's name, and I'm certain that my colleagues will be suitably impressed.'

The meeting, in Castor's quarters after breakfast next morning, was not as much a trial as he'd feared. Aemilius Papinian, Praetorian Prefect, managed to look and sound like the eminent lawyer he in fact was: a thin, dark man with a pronounced Syrian accent and a habit of steepling his fingers. Oclatinius Adventus gave Memnon a brief smile of recognition, though he was just as cold and smooth as he'd been at their last meeting.

Memnon described the meeting of the chiefs for them. He had no hesitation about identifying the location. While he had no desire to unleash the imperial cavalry on Sulicena, he was sure that she wouldn't be in the Veniconian stronghold when the Romans arrived. The meeting, after all, was over, and everyone who'd been there would have left – particularly since they must all be aware that Argentocoxus's Roman guest had got away.

He also recounted what he knew about the people who'd been at the meeting. He was careful to praise Argentocoxus as an honourable and honest man, and even went so far as to call him 'pro-Roman' – though he knew that Argentocoxus was merely pro-Caledonian, and wanted a settlement for his own tribe's safety, not because he had any love for Rome. The Caledonian chief had, however, treated him well, and he'd be glad if he could help him with the Roman authorities. Besides, Argentocoxus *was* an honourable man, and the Romans could pick worse to deal with.

He held back only the details of how he'd got away: he did not want Sulicena to become a joke for soldiers to snigger at. He said only that he'd been left in a hut, and had clambered out through the thatch.

When the imperial ministers had gone away to organize a cavalry expedition, Memnon went down to the armoury and got himself a new knife and new set of javelins, so as to be ready to protect Castor if need be – though to him the danger did not seem acute. Whatever his failings, Severus, in providing the chamberlain with an escort from the Praetorian Guard, had given a clear signal that, while the junior Emperor might be pleased by Castor's death, the senior Emperor would not be.

Re-armed, he had nothing to do except drift about the camp and wait for the Aurelian Moors to come back. Castor was busy with his responsibilities to the Emperor, and Memnon wouldn't see him until the evening. He wandered about for a while, first trying to find out what had become of his unit, and then asking about the units of other men he knew. Most of the auxiliary troops and many of the legions were scattered about the north, looking for the elusive Britons, but he found the First Gaulish Horse, the home of his one-time travelling companion Melisus. Further inquiries, however, brought the depressing information that Melisus was dead – had died a month before, in a Selgovan ambush.

The army's mood was, as Castor had said, bad, and nobody wanted to gossip. There was a pervasive sullenness, a widespread sense that the country they'd come to subdue wasn't worth the losses they'd suffered. Nobody seemed to expect a decisive end to the war. Desertions, as Castor had indicated, were a problem, and were causing tensions within the army: auxiliaries, especially British-based ones, formed the bulk of the deserters, so the overseas legions had been assigned to oversee them. Memnon was asked his business so frequently, and in such insulting terms, that eventually he went back to the Emperors' camp-within-a-camp to see if any of Castor's slaves wanted a game of dice.

That evening, after dinner, Castor gave him back the same ring he'd given him before. Memnon stared at it in surprise.

'Your Prefect Rogatus returned it to me,' the chamberlain explained. 'He came here to tell me that you were missing and to thank me for my favours to you.' He smiled. 'He seemed to me a most excellent old man, a model of all the ancient Roman virtues: stern, honest and disciplined. I'm not surprised that you regard him highly.'

Memnon thoughtfully stowed the ring back in his purse. 'I suppose Rogatus thought I was dead.'

'He said there was still some hope, but not much. He was very distressed about the matter. He said he'd driven you to take risks, and that all the way back to Bodotria he'd dreaded what body they might find on the next tree.'

Memnon winced.

'He wanted my help, too,' Castor continued, without resentment. 'There were some scouts from a British unit he wanted reassigned to the Moors – he said they'd been taken away and allocated to a legion, and that they were much missed.'

'That's right. They're very good, and much more familiar with the country than we are. Were you able to help, sir?'

Castor smiled. 'Indirectly. At any rate, when your comrades set out again, they had the scouts from the Aelian Cohort to accompany them.'

'That's very good news,' Memnon said, relieved. He had felt uneasy about how well the Moors would cope, without him or Senorix. 'Thank you, sir!'

Castor made a dismissive gesture. 'It was less my influence than that of Julia Augusta. I had written to Athenais to tell her the sad news that you were missing, and I mentioned your prefect's visit. Julia Augusta at once wrote to her brother-in-law, General Alexianus, and asked him to reassign the scouts.'

Memnon was taken aback. 'The Empress reads all her slaves' letters?'

Castor's look of pleasure vanished. 'No. Not normally But . . .' He stopped, then went on in some embarrassment: 'My liaison with Athenais during our research into the conspiracy was deemed to be improper. As I told you before, Julia Augusta does not like any interference with her personal staff. She is a wise and humane woman, however, and she has allowed us to correspond, on condition that her staff are shown the letters. Apparently the senior secretary found my letters to Athenais interesting. Now, I gather, Athenais is required to read all my letters out to her mistress.'

And Castor wasn't terribly happy about that, Memnon noted – understandably. The chamberlain, too, had engaged in heroics on behalf of the beautiful maiden: he had exposed a conspiracy and protected the Empress's son. His only reward was to be allowed to *correspond* with the object of his desire – and even his letters were being read out to her mistress.

He wondered how improper the 'liaison during our research' had been. He supposed he ought to hope that the chamberlain had had some luck. After all, Memnon had now had a stupendous piece of luck of his own, with Sulicena – even if he'd lost her again.

'Sir . . .' he said, impulsively – then stopped.

Castor gave him a look of inquiry.

'When I met you and the lady secretary last in Eboracum,' he said, in a low voice, 'it seemed to me that Lady Athenais was very unhappy about Emperor Caracalla – and maybe I'm wrong, but I thought probably he'd forced himself on her.'

There was a silence. Then Castor said, 'You were not wrong. But . . . that's over now, I thank fortune. Our Lady Julia Augusta put a stop to it. She insisted that her son respect the sanctity of his mother's roof, and said that, if he would not, she could no longer welcome him.'

'Ah? Good for the Empress, then!'

'She is the best of that house,' Castor declared, with some force.

Memnon noted silently that Castor had just rated her above his own patron. He saw suddenly that, for all his refusal to criticize his patron, the chamberlain knew that he had been owed at least as much protection as the Empress had given Athenais. He would make excuses for Severus, and continue to serve him with the same loyalty, because he had no other choice – but he knew that he had been betrayed.

*   *   *

The following day there was a great commotion in the camp: the Maeatae and the Caledones had sent envoys, who'd begged for an audience with the Emperors. The sullen mood vanished into eager hope: the barbarians were going to surrender! The war was over! Castor excitedly told Memnon about it that evening.

'They bowed down the moment they were admitted, and begged Our Lord Severus Augustus to offer them terms for peace. He said that if their chieftains would accept the supremacy of the Roman state, obey Roman laws, yield up some territories, accept garrisons, and pay tribute and taxes to Rome, he would allow them to conduct their own affairs. They weren't happy, but they didn't reject the terms outright, and they've gone off to report them to their tribes. This might be the end of the war!'

Castor went on to say, more anxiously, that Antoninus had wanted to offer more lenient peace terms. The younger Emperor was fed up with the war, and had openly said that Rome would be well rid of the country; he was also – and less admissably – anxious about his brother. Geta had been left in charge back in Eboracum, and it seemed that he was receiving embassies and issuing imperial rescripts, as though he were an Augustus, and not just a Caesar. Antoninus wanted to return south as quickly as possible and put a stop to it.

'He and his father argued about it, after the envoys left,' Castor said. 'Antoninus lost his temper and used very offensive language. His father had to shout at him to be quiet.'

'Severus Augustus thinks we should keep fighting this war?' He must, Memnon thought, be the only man in the camp who did.

'He thinks it's worth persevering. If the Britons reject our terms, they'll lose the harvest. They've suffered already in this war, but it's nothing to what they'd endure this winter without supplies. They know that.'

The Aurelian Moors returned to Bodotria a couple of days later, before the British envoys came back. Memnon had been asking about his unit every morning at the office of the camp prefect, and had received no news. That evening, however, as he and Castor shared a cup of wine after supper, one of the chamberlain's slaves came in and whispered in his master's ear.

'Send him in!' replied Castor, smiling.

The slave went out, then returned, escorting Rogatus.

The old man looked worn to the bone and had an expression of dread – an expression that changed instantly to amazement as he saw Memnon. Memnon got to his feet and started to salute, but Rogatus ran over, embraced him, and burst into tears.

Memnon was quite horrified. He was afraid to imagine what could have made the old man break down in this unprecedented way. He patted Rogatus gingerly on the back.

'My lad!' exclaimed Rogatus, standing back and staring into his face. 'Oh, Juno, I'm so glad! I thought you were dead!' He let go and turned to Castor, smiling now. 'When I got your message, sir, I thought you were calling me to identify his body!'

Castor, too, was on his feet, smiling widely. 'Forgive me. It was an indulgence, wishing to witness this reunion.'

'You're well? Unharmed?' Rogatus peered at Memnon anxiously and patted his arm. 'I thank the gods! What happened?'

'I was taken prisoner, sir. I escaped.'

'I thank the gods! Oh, my lad, we've missed you! We've had a hard, hard time since you were lost. Saturninus is dead, my poor old tent-mate! We buried him in the hills, as well as we could. We lost others, too – too many others. I can't say how glad it makes me to see you safe and sound!'

Memnon took his leave of Castor that evening, with thanks and apologies, and went back to the Moors with the prefect. Everyone was very glad to see him: they clustered round, shouting his name, slapping him on the back and shaking his hand, laughing at the news that he'd *escaped*; he'd been captured, but the Britons hadn't hurt him, and he'd *escaped!* He found, though, just as Rogatus had indicated, that the *numerus* had suffered while he was absent.

Saturninus had taken a javelin in the stomach during the Moors' skirmish with Argentocoxus's clan, and Rogatus had cut his throat to ease his passage, knowing that his wound doomed him to a slow and agonizing death. Honoratus was severely injured, his right arm broken in three places when he was thrown from his dying horse; infection had set in, and it was uncertain whether he would survive. Forty others of the *numerus* were dead, and another fifty-two were injured. The skirmish with Argentocoxus's clan accounted for twelve of the dead and fifteen of the injured; the other casualties had occurred on the Moors' last reconnaissance, when they'd been cut off from the main army by a much larger force of enemy cavalry, and had had to fight their way back through the hills.

'We got off lightly,' Rogatus said grimly. 'Things would've been much worse if your friend the chamberlain hadn't got us our guides back. It was your friend Senorix who found us a way around the barbarians.'

Memnon said nothing. Logically he knew that if he had been with his comrades, he couldn't have changed anything – but he had once again come home and discovered that something dreadful had happened in his absence. He fingered the brooch Argentocoxus had given him and wondered whose javelin had killed Saturninus.

The decurion's death was frightening, disorienting. For ten years Saturninus had ordered his life. He had relied on Saturninus to tell him what to do during all the bewilderments he had encountered when he first left Africa. Now Saturninus was gone. His body had been hastily buried in a makeshift grave in the hills; his meager property went to his old friend Rogatus – apart from Ghibli. Rogatus formally presented the stallion to Memnon. Saturninus's office . . . also went to Memnon.

It was only an 'acting' rank, but there was every reason to expect that the generals would confirm it, particularly since there was apparently some talk of honours for conspicuous valour as well. Memnon would have protested, only with Saturninus dead and Honoratus wounded, the rest of his squadron naturally assumed that he was now their leader. They expected him to arrange things for them, to judge their quarrels, to tell them what to do. He didn't want to in the least; he would infinitely prefer to rely on somebody himself – but who was there? It seemed he was stuck with the rank, at least temporarily. He wondered how soon he could get rid of it, and thought again about an early discharge.

He suddenly found himself imagining taking his discharge and going back to Sulicena – no longer an enemy, a friend of the clan in a land newly joined to the Empire. It wasn't impossible, was it? Admittedly, the circumstances of his departure from the Caledones might leave Argentocoxus more inclined to skewer him than welcome him – but perhaps he could do something to win the chief over? He was a great warrior, after all – and he even had a bit of money, with the various sums he'd been given by Castor and by the Empress. He'd be a full citizen, too, a Roman citizen, once he had that discharge – surely the Caledones would find that useful?

The prospect was fascinating, enticing. He struggled to put it from his mind. It was very likely that Sulicena hated him for having shamed her, and that the Caledones would kill him on sight. Even if they didn't, his happy daydream depended on the conclusion of a peace. Everything depended on peace.

Eleven

The British envoys returned to the Roman camp two days later, saying that the tribes had agreed to a truce to negotiate on the terms proposed. The army cheered loudly as this news spread through the camp, and Memnon cheered as wholeheartedly as any man there.

It was agreed that the Emperor and the British chiefs would meet on the north side of the pontoon bridge and swear to the truce. The army's numerous units of cavalry scouts, including the Moors, were sent out first; all reported that there were no signs of planned treachery. Accordingly, the two Emperors set out across the bridge, accompanied by the whole of the Praetorian Guard and the Alban Legion.

Memnon did not witness the meeting: he and his squadron were posted away on the flank of the army, watching, from a distance, a group of British scouts who were watching them. It was only afterward, riding back into the camp, that he knew that something had gone wrong: the troops were nervous, whispering to one another, rather than loud and exuberant.

He rode over to one knot of auxiliaries and asked anxiously, 'Didn't the barbarians swear to the truce?'

'They swore, all right,' replied the auxiliary, frowning. 'There was trouble, though, between our own Emperors.'

Memnon called on Castor that evening to get the whole story.

'The Emperors were in a good mood when they set out,' Castor told him. 'They're both pleased at the progress toward peace, and they rode out side by side. Antoninus, though – well, he started to urge his father to make concessions, to get a settlement more quickly, and Our Lord Severus Augustus was annoyed. He was tired and in pain anyway. He suffers from gout – I don't know if you're aware of that. His feet give him so much pain that on the way north he couldn't ride. He should really have used a litter again today, but he was embarrassed to, in front of the barbarians. He started to snap at his son, and his son snarled back.

'When we'd arrived within sight of the British chieftains, Severus lost his temper and ordered his son to be quiet. Antoninus shouted back that he was an Augustus, and didn't take orders from anyone. Then Severus said, "It's easy to make an Augustus. Your brother will get that title as soon as we're back in Eboracum."'

Memnon winced.

'It was like goading a mad ox,' Castor said ruefully. 'Antoninus drew his sword as though he was going to stab his father – in the back, since Severus at that point had turned away from him and was riding toward the British leaders. Everyone in the entourage shouted, of course, and Severus looked round and saw the sword. He didn't say anything, just continued forward, and met the chiefs and arranged the details of the truce. Afterwards, though . . .'

'He's going to demote him?' Memnon asked eagerly, when the chamberlain fell silent.

Castor looked at him and shook his head. 'He can't: I've explained that. No, he had Antoninus summoned to his quarters. He summoned me, as well, and Papinian, and he put a sword on the table in front of Antoninus. Then he gave him the most savage dressing-down I've ever heard, first for drawing a weapon against his lord and father, and second for doing so in front of so many thousands of witnesses, Roman and barbarian.

'Antoninus just listened, patiently at first. Then he started to get angry – by the end he was in a terrible rage – but still, he didn't dare say a word. At last Severus said, "If you want to kill me, there's a sword! I'm an old man, you can do it easily – and if you don't want to, tell Castor to, or Papinian! They have to obey you, don't they? After all, you're an Augustus: everyone has to do what you say, and nobody can give you orders!"'

'And what did Caracalla do?'

'Nothing. Apologized for his "rash passion", and denied

that drawing the sword had been anything more than an angry gesture – which is probably true.'

Castor was silent another moment, then said, in a whisper, 'It was a lesson in the limits of command – but I doubt that Antoninus will draw the moral. What he will remember is that Papinian and I heard everything his father said. I wish my patron had called on someone else.'

It was the last time Memnon spoke to the chamberlain for several months. It had been agreed that the British chiefs would go to Eboracum for the peace negotiations, and shortly after the truce was declared, Severus marched south with his entourage, the Alban Legion, the Praetorian Guard and five thousand select cavalry. The rest of his forces were dispersed about the north to police the truce.

Memnon did not even have time to say goodbye. He was much too busy struggling to cope with the duties of a decurion.

Since that scene in Castor's tent, Rogatus had reverted to his usual grim sardonic self, but the facade no longer served to cover the affection and pride beneath. His feelings toward his men had always been vaguely paternal, and Memnon, who had won the unit some of the recognition Rogatus had always craved, had clearly become the favourite son. That was ... disconcerting. Memnon respected the prefect, and liked him, too, as far as it went, but had never felt any emotional closeness to him. He wasn't sure he wanted to now. It seemed too binding. It made him a responsible equal instead of a carefree subordinate.

Rogatus wanted the favourite son to grow up, that was the problem: to leave behind the childish pranks and jokes and take on a man's responsibilities. He wanted, Memnon thought grimly, another Saturninus. *I'm not him!* he wanted to protest – but what would be the use? Rogatus mourned his old friend deeply; he was the last man in the world who would feel that Saturninus could be in any way replaced. What he wanted now was somebody to do Saturninus's work – and he was determined that that 'somebody' would be Memnon.

They set out westward in mid-July, two hundred and fifty-eight men, including twenty injured, carried in horse-litters.

They travelled with the detachment of the British legion –
the Twentieth, Valeria Victrix – at comparatively easy pace,
and halted seven days later at the site of a marching camp,
which the legions had used on the way north. The tents
were pitched inside the already-constructed earthworks, and
the Moors settled down for the rest of the summer. Eight
of the twenty wounded had died on the journey; Honoratus
was one of them.

The news that a peace treaty had been concluded was brought
to the scattered troops early in August; in issuing it, Severus
took the title Britannicus, Conquerer of Britain. With the
news came a donative of half a year's pay to reward the
soldiers for the victory: the coins were freshly minted, and
stamped with images of bridges over northern rivers and
barbarians kneeling in submission. There was, however, no
additonal order sending the troops back to their bases.
Memnon hoped it would come soon, and that they wouldn't
have to overwinter in the temporary camp. He wasn't sure
how things were in other areas, but if the Twentieth Legion
and the Moors remained much longer among the Selgovae,
war was going to break out all over again.

The Roman troops' first task had been to police the truce
– to make sure that the Britons weren't taking advantage of
the pause in hostilities to regroup for war. Once a treaty was
concluded, they were required to act as garrisons, enforcing
the Roman peace in the newly conquered territories. In practice there was no difference between the two roles, and in
neither were they supposed to interfere with tribespeople
who'd returned to their settlements and were working to
salvage the harvest. There was, however, a great deal of anger
and bitterness over Roman losses, and the troops wanted
some of their own back. The British, in the soldiers' view,
were now a conquered people. In the opinion of most of the
men and many of the officers, it was perfectly all right to
steal British sheep and cattle, to demand goods and services
without payment, to rough up any man or rape any woman
you and your friends might meet in the hills. The Maeatae
had earned it, and a conquered people had no right to object.
Rogatus and his counterpart in the Twentieth Legion were

well aware that the British were not so much a conquered people as a people who'd been forced to accept unfavourable terms for peace: pushed too hard they could still decide to reject the settlement – particularly after they had the harvest safely in. The commanders knew they had to restrain their troops, at least enough to avoid immediate trouble with an armed and hostile populace. This meant that the war-sick and angry soldiers had to be curbed by the full strength of Roman discipline. The men were confined to camp or given forced marches to keep them busy, and even minor transgressions were awarded punishments ranging from latrine duty to flogging. The few officers who could be trusted not to share their men's feelings were put in charge of all the difficult patrols, and soon found themselves exhausted and very unpopular. In spite of all this, however, there were still incidents, and relations with the local population were very tense.

At last, however, when the treaty was signed and sworn, the harvest in, and the campaigning season at an end, the Roman troops received the orders sending them back to winter quarters in their own forts. It was issued in the name of *three* emperors, and it arrived with another donative of a quarter's wages for each man, to celebrate the elevation of Septimius Geta to the rank of Augustus. The troops cheered the new emperor heartily. Memnon was more relieved than any other man in his *numerus*.

He had, of course, been one of the trustworthy officers – and he'd hated it. He had always been easy-going, and he'd had to become a petty tyrant; he had always been well-liked, and now his old friends looked sourly at him and muttered among themselves that his promotion had ruined him. He missed Saturninus; he grieved for Honoratus; he ached to go home . . . wherever that was. A time, he thought, not a place. A time before he'd been to war. Aballava, though, would do for a start.

The Aurelian Moors rode back into the fort early in October. The Frisians, whom they'd barely seen since the campaign began, were already in residence. They greeted the Moors sullenly, with eyes that took note of their losses. The Moors' official strength was three hundred and ten; with deaths and discharged wounded they could now muster only two hundred and thirty-eight.

The Frisians, however, had losses of their own. Although the high command had not used them nearly as intensively as it had the Moors, they'd suffered severely in an ambush early in the war, and nearly a quarter of their number were dead. The two reduced units now fitted into the barracks blocks without crowding.

The confirmation of Memnon's acting rank was waiting for him at the fort. He was allotted a room of his own – the first time he'd had a private room in his entire life. It had been Saturninus's room, and most of the decurion's gear still occupied it. Memnon tried to persuade Rogatus, Saturninus's legal heir, to take the things, but Rogatus claimed only a silver ewer and cups and told Memnon he might as well use the rest.

He supposed he should: he had virtually nothing of his own. For years he had slept on army bunks under army-issue blankets. He had supplemented his army uniform only with clothing useful for his work or for keeping warm. When he piled his own things in Saturninus's clothes chest, he had completed his move in, and made no difference to the room. It was strangely unsatisfactory, and he felt that he ought to go out and buy something to set his own stamp on the place. He went down to the fort village and wandered round the shops a few times – but he could think of nothing he wanted to buy, except a new earring and a better knife.

He had expected to abandon himself with relief to the routine of camp life, familiar for ten – no, eleven! – years now. He found that that routine, and everything else, had changed. In the strange, stressed world of the camp among the Selgovae the fact that he no longer shared a tent and routine duties with the other men had been only one change among many; here, in a familiar setting, it was jarring. He was cut off from all the things he'd enjoyed about army life – the jokes, the close friendships and easy cameraderie, the assurance that somebody else was in charge. The silence of his room at night disturbed him, and he kept waking up and straining his ears for the sound of breathing. His new duties continued to bewilder him; he decided that he preferred even latrine duty to accounts.

At one of the daily morning meetings in the middle of October, Rogatus advised him to get a servant. 'You can afford it,' the prefect pointed out. 'You can pay an enlisted man's wage, and still have ten times as much as you used to get. Or you could buy yourself a slave. You still have all that money from the Empress. You could buy several slaves with that.'

Rogatus knew exactly how much was in the fat purse Memnon had been presented by the Empress's freedman. He'd carefully placed it in a locked box in the fort strongroom, with Memnon's name written on the lid and an account ledger inside saying exactly how much was there, so that nobody could pilfer it. Memnon hunched his shoulders and muttered, 'Sir.'

'You should get someone,' Rogatus told him bluntly. 'You don't have time to do your own cleaning and mending any more. I expect you to fulfill all your duties as an officer, *and* to keep up with your reading and writing.'

Memnon looked at him sharply. 'Honoratus is *dead*, sir!'

Rogatus drew in a long breath and let it out again. 'I know. I am sorry for it, too. But he was not the only literate man in the *numerus*. I'll arrange for my clerk to give you lessons – or you can buy yourself a clerk of your own.'

Memnon grimaced. His whole situation in the fort suddenly seemed unbearable. He was among familiar people, but forced to live as a stranger, to them and to himself – and all at once he wanted to run away. 'Sir!' he exclaimed. 'I . . . I'd like to make a journey first. Before the weather turns completely.'

Rogatus frowned. 'A journey where, decurion?'

'Ah . . .' Inspiration struck: 'Eboracum, sir! If Castor ever found out anything about Farabert, he didn't tell us. I should have asked about it when I saw him up north, but I didn't, and I've been kicking myself since.'

Rogatus's frown didn't ease. Relations between the Moors and the Frisians had not improved since the war ended.

'If Farabert really did try to get rid of us, sir,' Memnon coaxed, 'we ought to know about it'

Rogatus considered it. 'I think I'd prefer not to know – but I suppose you're right, we ought to. Whatever your reasons for coming up with the suggestion, you have a point.

Very well, you have leave to travel to Eboracum. I'll give you some letters which I need to send to the fortress commissariat. I want you back, though, within ten days.'

'Yes, sir!' Memnon said happily. 'Of course.'

Preparations for the journey weren't complicated. He bought a new hooded riding cape – he'd been using a dead man's since he got back from the Caledones, and it had made him a bit uncomfortable every time he put it on – packed a few things into saddlebags which he slung across Ghibli's withers, said goodbye to his . . . men; they weren't tent-mates and mess-mates any more – and set out.

It was with immense relief that he left the fort behind, and he played with the idea of never going back to it. He could cross the Wall, ride north to the Caledones. He could swear loyalty to Argentocoxus – there was no moral obstacle, now that the war was over and northern Britain had officially been added to the Empire. He imagined Sulicena welcoming him back, and smiled.

Daydreams, of course: he still didn't know how he'd be welcomed among the Caledones, given the circumstances of his departure. The Romans would regard him as a deserter, too, unless he first got himself a discharge.

He more or less intended to ask Castor to arrange that discharge, maybe this visit, maybe the next – but the thought started him worrying about Castor. The chamberlain's situation was precarious – dependent on the negligent favour of an emperor who was aging and ill, and caught between the distrust of one son and the active malice of another. It seemed to him quite monstrous that a man who had served the Empire so faithfully should be rewarded with the threat of assault and murder.

The Aurelian Moors now burned incense to all three Emperors. Memnon wondered how Rogatus felt, pouring the precious frankincense into the saucer of coals before the portrait of Antoninus Caracalla, the man who would have betrayed the whole *numerus* to their deaths. For his own part, his hands clenched into fists just watching it.

He sighed, remembering what he'd told Sulicena about the Empire's skill, power and tolerance; remembering also a hundred examples of its cruelty, greed and injustice. What else was there, though? The world outside the Empire wasn't one where peace and justice ruled, that was certain! From all he'd seen it was tribe-on-tribe everywhere: Tebu and Gaetulians, Sarmatians and Quadi – and, he had no doubt at all, Maeatae and Caledones, if they hadn't had a common enemy in Rome. The Empire offered its citizens a chance to live in peace. He still wanted that citizenship.

He rode easily through the afternoon, stopping at evening at a posting inn at Voreda. He didn't have a licence for the post, of course, but the innkeeper was willing to let him pay for accommodation, and disappointed that he chose the cheaper option of sleeping in the stable.

In the morning he rode on, feeling happier. The war had been horrible, but the war was over. As for being a decurion, well, maybe he'd adapt to it in the end and maybe he wouldn't. If he did, well and good; if he didn't, he could do something so outrageous that Rogatus would be forced to give up and demote him – or he could ask Castor for that favour. He thought again of Sulicena smiling at him, and he smiled back – maybe he'd ask it this very visit. In the meantime, it was a sunny day in mid-October, he was riding a good horse along a good road, through a land at peace, and he would see some friends at the end of his journey. What more could a man want?

Twelve

The rank of a decurion and Rogatus's letters to the commissariat still weren't enough to get Memnon a bed in the legionary fortress at Eboracum: once again he found himself assigned a bunk in the annexe – though at least it *was* a bunk, this time, and not a place in the stall with his horse. He dumped his saddlebags, went down to the market, and got a letter-writer to draft him a note to Castor. He no longer felt any need to send the ring as a reminder.

One of the legionary adjutants woke him early the following morning, coming into the room in the barracks and knocking on the wall beside his head. He sat up groggily; his temporary room-mate, another messenger, swore. The adjutant, subdued and respectful, offered him a slip of vermilion parchment; Memnon took and inspected it. Honoratus had taught him the rudiments of reading before the war started, and he'd had more lessons over the summer from Rogatus's clerk: he could just about make out the words. He stared at the lines on the parchment, unable to credit them, then looked up at the adjutant, who was hovering, fascinated. '*What* does it say?'

The adjutant took the parchment back. He cleared his throat. '"The sovereign Augusta Julia Domna, to Memnon, of the *Numerus* of Aurelian Moors. Our Lady the Empress invites you to dinner this evening at the eighth hour. This letter will suffice to gain you admission."'

'That's what I thought it said.' Memnon stared at the parchment, wondering how on earth his note to Castor had ended up bringing *this* as a reply. Dinner with the *Empress*! 'Is it a joke?' he asked the adjutant helplessly.

The man turned the parchment and showed him the seal, a seated woman holding a horn of plenty. 'No. Could I ask . . . ?'

'I once rescued one of her slaves. Oh, Juno! Do you happen to know what a man's supposed to wear to a dinner with the Empress of Rome?'

He ended up buying himself a brand-new tunic and a good cloak – a nice blue one, not one of the sheep-coloured garments he'd used in the past. He had to borrow money from a bank to do so, as he didn't have anywhere near enough cash to hand, but he was pleased with his purchases. He tied on his new decurion's sash, and he pinned the new cloak with the brooch given him by Argentocoxus. He felt very splendid when he walked out of the fort annexe in his new finery.

He felt small and tawdry, though, by the time he'd been passed through three Praetorian Guardsmen at the palace, each one of them escorting him deeper into an overpowering magnificence. At last he was led into a marble atrium where there was a fountain, and there was Athenais, graceful in a long cloak of midnight blue, her beautiful face set in an expression of serene composure. He smiled in relief.

Athenais dismissed his escort and gestured for him to go into a room on the right, but he baulked. 'Why am I here?' he demanded in an anxious whisper. 'What does the Empress want?'

She smiled in amusement. 'She's curious. She heard about you from me, and from Castor, and from the wife of one of the Caledonian chieftains. When Castor sent me a note saying you were in Eboracum, she decided she wanted to meet you.'

'The wife of one of the Caledonians?' he repeated, aghast. Of course, he'd known that Argentocoxus would be part of the peace negotiations, and he'd known that the negotiations had been held in Eboracum – but still! 'Drustocce? She was *here*? What did she say about me?'

Athenais smiled again, and the glint in her dark eyes told him that, yes, she'd heard the full story of his escape. 'My mistress entertained all the chieftains' wives while their husbands were discussing the peace. Don't worry! The wife of Argentocoxus had nothing but admiration for you.'

He gazed at her incredulously.

'She told us the story about her sister-in-law,' Athenais admitted. 'She didn't seem to think you'd behaved dishonourably, though.'

'She didn't?' Memnon was shocked. 'But . . .'

'Caledonian women seem to have a completely different attitude to these things. My mistress twitted her about it, and she replied that, "British women openly sleep with the bravest and best men, but Roman women allow themselves to be seduced by scoundrels in secret." My mistress thought it was funny. Come along! We can't stand here in the atrium.'

She turned toward the room on the right, but he stayed where he was, feeling like a landed fish. She turned back, delicate brows arched in inquiry.

'I've never *met* an Empress before!' he whispered. 'Is there anything I'm supposed to do?'

'Bow. Wait until she speaks before you do. Oh, you know she doesn't speak much Latin, don't you?'

'No, I didn't! What does she . . . ?'

'Greek. And Aramaic, but you don't have to worry about that.'

'I don't speak Greek!'

Her eyes sparkled. 'Don't worry, I'll translate for you. Oh, and don't worry because no one else is here yet: you aren't going to be the only guest! Castor should be here soon, and two of my mistress's freedmen. It will be an informal dinner, too, of course – you understand, she couldn't invite a common soldier and freedmen to any other sort. Oh, but –' she laid a hand against his chest and looked into his face with sober warning – 'nothing about her son. Remember, you don't know any of that.'

He drew in a long breath and nodded.

The room on the right was full of gold: ceiling, panel surrounds and lampstands all glowed warmly in the light of the multitude of lamps. The lamp oil was scented with attar of roses, and filled the October air with a summery perfume. The floor was decorated with a black and white mosaic and spread with sumptuous carpets; exquisite paintings hung upon the walls. In the centre of the room, the Empress reclined on a couch of ivory. She was a handsome woman in her forties, dark-eyed, her elaborately dressed hair still jet black. She wore purple silk, and she gleamed with jewels. When Memnon's eyes met hers, she smiled.

Memnon looked desperately at Athenais, then began to

bow; Athenais surreptitiously jerked a thumb, indicating that he should go further down, and he knelt hastily.

The Empress said something in Greek; apparently it was an order to fetch a chair, because Athenais brought one over. Memnon scrambled to his feet and folded into it, wondering if he would survive the evening.

Julia Domna spoke genially.

Athenais leaned forward to whisper in his ear. 'She says, "So you are the brave hero who rescued my slave."'

Memnon bowed, as well as he could sitting. 'I am deeply honoured to be here, My Lady. When I go back to Aballava, my whole *numerus* will be very excited to hear about this great honour. My prefect will be overjoyed.' That was certainly true.

Athenais translated. 'Your prefect Rogatus sounds a loyal man,' Domna stated.

He was amazed: she not only knew who Rogatus was, she'd even remembered his name! 'Yes,' he agreed, and licked his lips. 'The portrait you sent before, My Lady – Rogatus in particular was moved by it.' The prefect, was, in fact, inordinately proud of it. 'We keep it in our chapel of the standards, and on parade days we take it out and fix it on the signum, so that everyone can see how you've honoured us. Rogatus has spent his whole life fighting for the Empire, but it was the first time anyone in the imperial house ever noticed us.'

Domna smiled, looking pleased. 'Tell him I am glad of his loyalty. Tell him that the divine powers notice our steadfastness in honour and virtue, even if the eyes of men overlook it.'

Memnon bowed his head. 'He will be very glad of your words, My Lady. He'll treasure them. Thank you.'

The Empress smiled complacently.

At this point the other guests arrived: the freedman Salutaris, who'd run the Empress's errand to Aballava, together with his wife, who did something or other on the staff; with them was Castor. He bowed to the Empress, then smiled warmly at Memnon and shook hands. Things became less tense. Julia Domna asked Memnon about his capture by the Caledones; he began to reply stiffly, but

Castor interrupted with an injunction to 'tell her the leopard story!'

Well, if that was what they wanted! He told the Empress how he'd been treed by the Caledones, complete with animal noises, and Julia Domna laughed, just like a real woman. Her attendants brought in the first courses – stuffed dates, and eggs in fish sauce – and set them out on small folding tables of cedarwood and silver. Athenais filled the guest's cups with sweetened wine. Memnon noted that he and the other guests sat, while the Empress reclined, and Athenais stood. Athenais didn't eat or drink, either. Presumably Empresses didn't recline with freedmen and common soldiers, and slaves didn't eat with their masters – but the distinction wasn't too oppressive. Athenais stood behind Memnon's chair, smiling and murmuring translations.

The meal continued pleasantly, the conversation winding from dates – a crop which Memnon's family had grown from time immemorial – to the problems of irrigation in Africa and in Syria. Second courses of mussels and halibut arrived, and they talked about fish, about the Roman passion for it and about how the British tribes strangely ate so little of it; about saltwater fish and freshwater fish, and about the hazards encountered by fishermen.

They were settling to the third course – fried cream and apples – when another attendant suddenly hurried in and whispered into Domna's ear.

The Empress straightened, pulling her legs off the couch and asking a sharp question. Even as she spoke, her son Caracalla came in.

He was smiling as he entered, but as he saw the guests his expression changed to an angry scowl. He wore one of the long hooded cloaks which had given him his nickname, but had it tossed back, revealing a purple tunic. All the guests scrambled to their feet and bowed low, Memnon a little later than the others as he had to copy them.

'What's *he* doing here?' Caracalla demanded, pointing accusingly at Castor.

Julia Domna sighed, and spoke in an exasperated tone; Memnon noticed that she really did call her son 'Lucius' – the forsaken name of his birth.

Caracalla replied in the Greek his mother had used, flapping a hand dismissively at the guests – then paused. His eyes, dark and ferocious, fixed on Memnon. The Emperor was no taller than he was, Memnon noted distantly; it seemed odd that an Emperor should be short. He bowed again, trying to look awestruck.

'You're the one who escaped from a meeting of the British chiefs, aren't you?' Caracalla asked him.

Memnon didn't for a moment believe he'd been recognized: this must have been information Caracalla's mother had provided in Greek. He bowed a third time. 'Yes, My Lord Augustus.'

'You stay, then. The rest of you, out!'

The freedmen glanced nervously at the Empress. Domna, sitting very straight, her eyes blazing with anger and her lips pressed tightly together, gave them a small nod. They fled.

Caracalla relaxed and said something in Greek; his mother replied with something quietly reproachful. Caracalla responded with scorn. He sat down in one of the just-vacated places and pushed the scarcely-touched pudding aside.

That brought a sharper reproach, and was answered with something defensive: Memnon caught Castor's name, and shot Athenais a helpless look. Caracalla remembered him and snapped his fingers. 'You,' he said, in Latin now. 'Soldier. What's your name?'

He snapped to attention and gave his best parade-ground salute. 'Memnon, My Lord! Decurion, First Squadron of the *Numerus* of Aurelian Moors, My Lord!'

'This meeting of the British chiefs – did you hear any of the discussions?'

'No, My Lord!' declared Memnon, doing the wide-eyed barbarian act. 'I was not allowed to attend, My Lord!'

Caracalla made an impatient gesture. 'You overheard nothing?'

'No, My Lord! I was kept in a hut, under guard, My Lord, while they met in their feast hall. And I don't speak British, My Lord.'

'Idiot,' remarked Caracalla. 'So you know *nothing* about what factions there were, and who led them?'

Memnon hesitated. 'My Lord? What I told the Princeps

Peregrinorum and Papinian the Prefect was that I thought Fortrenn of the Votadini was part of one faction, and that it might be the war faction, and that Argentocoxus of the Caledones was head of another, which might be the pro-Roman one. But that's just a guess, My Lord. I am very sorry, My Lord Augustus, that I didn't have the opportunity to learn more; I am ashamed that I can't serve you better in this.'

'Yes,' agreed Caracalla irritably. 'Very well, you may go.'

Memnon bowed to the Empress. 'Thank you again, My Lady, for the great honour of your invitation.' He bowed to the Emperor. 'My Lord, I am doubly honoured to have seen your glory with my own eyes.' He saluted again and marched to the door. Athenais hurriedly slipped out after him.

They passed Caracalla's guards, who were now standing at attention by the entrance to the Empress's quarters, and crossed the atrium into the next section of the palace. There Memnon stopped. His heart was beating hard, with outrage as much as fear; he was glad that he'd managed to escape without betraying his feelings toward that vicious young weasel. He let out a long unsteady breath and rubbed the back of his neck, then caught Athenais' worried eyes and rolled his own.

She smiled at him. 'You handled that well,' she whispered. 'Any more abject and he would have had you punished for incompetence; any less, and he would have had you flogged for disrespect.'

'Gods and spirits!' he whispered back. 'Save me from the court! Would it be possible for me to see Castor before I leave? There was something I really needed to ask him.'

Athenais hesitated, then said, eagerly, 'Yes!'

Castor's quarters were in the same location as before, but that section of the palace was much more heavily guarded, now that the Emperor was in residence. Athenais, however, was able to breeze past the guards with a murmur of: 'Guest of the Augusta . . . wants to take leave of his friend Septimius Castor.'

Castor opened the door himself, looking worn and anxious – but his face lit up when he saw Athenais. 'My darling!' he exclaimed breathlessly – then, anxious again, 'should you be here?'

'Memnon wanted to talk to you,' she explained, and the chamberlain noticed the additional presence for the first time.

Well. *That* answered the question about how improper the 'liaison' had been. He made no comment, however, merely accepted Castor's offer of a cup of wine.

The chamberlain had replaced his furniture. There was a painting of a landscape on one wall, two couches, a book-rack and a lampstand. A slave brought them wine in some fine Samian-ware cups, then accepted his dismissal in silence. The three of them sat down together with the wine, Castor on one couch and his guests on the other.

'Are you hungry?' Castor asked Athenais softly.

'I had something before you arrived,' Athenais assured him.

He sighed. 'I hated to see you standing while I sat.'

Memnon cleared his throat. 'The two of you are . . . you said before you were "permitted to correspond"?'

Castor glanced at him bitterly. 'We are, however, forbidden to associate.'

'This will be all right,' Athenais said earnestly. 'Memnon wanted to take leave of you, and I'm sure she'd approve of me guiding him here. She was very angry about Caracalla dismissing her guests.'

'It's probably for the best that we stay away from one another,' said Castor heavily. 'If you were my wife, Caracalla would hate you, too.' He took a swallow of wine, and added, looking at her, 'My dearest girl, you should find yourself someone else.'

'I don't want anyone else,' Athenais told him determinedly.

'Sweet girl,' said Castor. 'My lovely, loyal Athenais – don't make me face what's coming with the knowledge that I've destroyed the person I love best in all the world. If Caracalla ever suspected your part in his embarrassment, he would hate you even more than he hates me.'

Memnon wondered when Castor had given up his insistence on calling the young emperor 'Antoninus'.

Athenais looked at Memnon, and her face coloured as she explained what he'd guessed long before. 'Caracalla made me sleep with him. I never, ever wanted to, but he'd still feel that I've betrayed him. I thank the gods, my mistress put a stop to that, too.'

Memnon was silent a moment, trying to think of something to say that would help that wound to heal. 'What you overheard saved my life and the life of everyone in my unit. I'm glad you heard it, though I'm sorry for the circumstances . . . and I'm sorry, for both of you.'

It was the right thing to say. She smiled at him, then reached over and patted his wrist.

'What did the Augustus ask you just now?' Castor wanted to know.

'What were the factions among the Britons at that meeting of the chiefs and who led them. I don't know why he bothered to ask me about it: I already told everybody everything I know, and your friend the Praetorian Prefect had it all written down.'

'He doesn't trust Papinian,' said Castor. 'Or Adventus, for that matter. They're his father's men. I wonder why he's interested in that?'

'That surprised me, too,' Athenais commented. 'He's been to visit his mother a lot recently, but it's always about the same thing.'

Castor grimaced; seeing Memnon's look of puzzlement, he explained, 'As I'm sure you're aware, Septimius Geta has been proclaimed Augustus. Cara . . . Antoninus Augustus has been going to everyone the Emperor might listen to, complaining about his brother's conduct and trying to persuade them to persuade his father to revoke the proclamation.'

Memnon asked hopefully, 'But your patron won't? Won't it help you, sir, that Caracalla won't be the only Augustus?'

The chamberlain sighed and shook his head. 'Geta doesn't like me, either.' He met Memnon's eyes and added, very, very quietly, 'Don't put any faith in Geta Augustus. He may be less impulsive and violent than his brother, but he's just as treacherous and ruthless. Neither can be relied on, and anyone who tries to use one against the other is likely to be crushed between them.'

There was a silence. Castor's bluntness was worrying, given his usual habit of making excuses for the imperial house – it seemed to Memnon a counsel of despair. 'If that's so,' he said slowly, 'then what's going to happen when your patron dies?'

Castor looked away. Then he set his wine down abruptly and covered his face. Athenais put her own wine down, jumped up, and went over to sit beside him and wrap an arm around his shoulders. He turned and hugged her tightly a moment, then let her go; dutifully, she drew back.

'I'm sorry,' Castor said, wiping his face. 'That's a subject that haunts me sleeping and waking.'

'No, I'm sorry,' said Memnon. 'I shouldn't have asked.'

They were all silent. Castor picked up his wine again, his hand trembling.

'I had a reason for coming to Eboracum, sir, if you don't mind,' Memnon said at last. 'You never told us what you'd found out about Farabert, and when I saw you last, I forgot to ask.'

'Farabert?' asked Castor, puzzled.

'The leader of the Frisians at Aballava,' Athenais reminded him. 'The one who was corresponding with Euodus.'

'Oh, him!' Castor looked uneasy.

'Who's Euodus?' Memnon asked quickly.

'He's on Caracalla's staff,' Athenais told him grimly. 'He was the one who made the arrangements for the whole business. Does this Farabert have a grudge against your unit?'

'Yes. He's never liked having us in what used to be his fort. You say he was corresponding with this man Euodus?'

Athenais nodded. 'We didn't see the letters, just the record of their delivery. I can't think, though, of any other reason your Farabert would've been writing to Caracalla's staff. And Euodus told Caracalla that the man he'd found was "happy to do it" because he had a grudge.'

'I hope you and your prefect won't do anything rash,' Castor said urgently.

Memnon raised his eyebrows. 'Like cut Farabert's ugly throat? We're not fools, sir. If Farabert died suddenly, this Euodus might wonder why. He and his master must've been surprised when we escaped that ambush, and you said that if they realized we knew about their plot, we were likely to turn up dead. Now that I think of it – should I be worried that Caracalla saw you and me together tonight?'

'I doubt that Antoninus even remembers your unit's name,' replied Castor.

Athenais made a noise of disgust. '*I* doubt he noticed it in the first place!'

Castor nodded. 'He left all the details to Euodus. Euodus is the one we need to worry about. I went to school with him, and he's sharp – a slimy little hanger-on of the school's chief bully, but sharp. He may already suspect that I warned you – so I'm glad you understand the need to leave this Farabert untouched and convinced that you suspect nothing.' He smiled weakly. 'No, you aren't fools, are you? I shouldn't have worried. Incidentally –' he smiled – 'congratulations on your promotion.'

Memnon grimaced. 'That was something else I wanted to ask you about, sir. To be honest, I don't like being a decurion.'

Castor was taken aback.

'Whyever not?' Athenais asked, equally startled. 'I'm sure you're an excellent officer, and you certainly *deserve* to be one!'

'I deserve to lose all my friends and spend my time staring at accounts I can't read? Thanks!'

'You haven't lost *all* your friends,' Castor said quietly.

Memnon sighed. 'No offence intended, sir. It's just that I've lost all the friends I had in my squadron – because you can like and respect your decurion, but you can't be *friends* with him. Rogatus . . . expects me to be something I don't want to be. And there are all the rosters and requisition sheets and accounts. I'm a barbarian, sir: I only learned to *read* last year!' He ran a hand over his head and added, 'To tell you the truth, sir, I'd like it if you could arrange for me to get a discharge, as the favour you once promised me. I've served eleven years now, and if I really deserve well of the army, they should let me go.'

Castor stared at him in consternation. 'But I thought . . . I *know* that your excellent prefect has the highest opinion of your abilities, that he hopes you will follow in his footsteps!'

Memnon stared. The idea that Rogatus wanted him to become prefect of the Moors was horrifying. 'Did he tell you that?'

Castor nodded.

'Sir, I . . . I *respect* Rogatus, but I *don't* want to follow in his footsteps. He and Saturninus fought all their lives, and what do they have to show for it? The Emperors never even noticed their loyalty, let alone rewarded or deserved it. And from everything you've told me, there's real trouble coming. No. No, I'm sure of it now: I want out. The war's over; there are going to be lots of men discharged early. I would be very grateful, sir, if you could get my name down as one of them.'

Castor continued to stare at him, very pale now. He, too, had served all his life, with a loyalty which had never been rewarded or deserved.

'Does this have anything to do with that Caledonian woman?' Athenais asked suspiciously. 'Because if it did – well, a prefect is a good match for a noblewoman, but a discharged decurion isn't. I don't mean to talk you out of anything – but if she's why you want to leave the army, you're making a mistake.'

Of course, it had quite a lot to do with 'that Caledonian woman'. 'Was Drustocce actually talking as though I could *marry* Sulicena?' he asked eagerly.

Athenais opened her mouth, then closed it. 'I . . . don't think she mentioned marriage, no. But when she found out who I was she tried to see if I was jealous, and she was very pleased when the Empress praised you. I'd say she knew that her sister-in-law's feelings were serious. She also said that you'd given the woman your earring, so I thought you must have . . . really liked her, too.'

Sulicena's feelings were serious; Sulicena had kept his earring, showed it to her sister, valued it: this was very good news! Memnon drew in a breath slowly and let it out, reminding himself that it didn't mean that Sulicena would *marry* him. 'I did like her. I liked her a lot.'

Castor shook his head. 'I really, truly don't want to get you a discharge, my friend,' he said slowly. 'Rome needs men like you.'

Memnon's brows drew down, and the chamberlain raised a hand defensively. 'I'll get your name down for it, if that's what you really want – but can I ask you just to think about it a little longer? Think about your prefect, and about your men. Think about what will happen to your unit if it's led by a greedy fool or a violent brute; think about the lives of

the people you protect. So much of the army is already brutal-
ized, and the Empire is suffering for it: what will we do if
all the good men leave? Think about it, please, just for another
month or two! The Emperor won't present any discharge
diplomas until the troops are ready to leave next summer,
so it won't affect the timing of your release.'

Memnon sighed: that was true enough. 'If you like, I'll
wait until after the Saturnalia. I don't think I'm going to
change my mind, though – not if you're right about what's
coming. That's a war I don't want to fight.'

Thirteen

Memnon started back for Aballava in a very thoughtful mood. He tried to imagine being in Castor's position, threatened by a malevolent young tyrant while your only protector was in ill health – and, at the same time, forbidden to 'associate' with the woman you loved. He was quite certain that he would never stand for it. If that lovely Athenais had looked at him the way she'd looked at Castor, he would have stolen her out of the palace and run off with her. Part of him kept trying to despise Castor for spinelessness – only he was aware that the chamberlain wasn't spineless. The man had withstood torture, after all; he had dared to investigate the misconduct of a prince and report on it honestly; he had lived for months in the fear of sudden death, and had kept on quietly with his normal duties despite it. No, he wasn't spineless – but passive, yes, he certainly was that.

So was Athenais, for that matter. Surely a woman that clever could have found some way round her mistress's ban if she'd tried? It said something for her honesty and loyalty that she was so obedient to the Empress, but Memnon wasn't at all sure that so much obedience was admirable. He supposed, though, that if you grew up in this Household of theirs you found it simply inconceivable to disobey an imperial order.

He wondered whether Castor really would do anything about getting him his discharge. It was obviously something the chamberlain didn't want to do; he seemed to think it undutiful, that it would deprive the Empire of something valuable. That was flattering, but Memnon very much doubted the Empire saw things the same way. He knew himself to be an uneducated barbarian from a tribe no Roman had ever heard of. Rogatus might hope to make him prefect one day – but it wasn't Rogatus who was in charge of appointments. Rogatus himself had only got the job because nobody more exalted wanted it, and now that the Moors had been noticed by the high command, it was very likely that their next prefect would be an outsider – probably some junior equestrian hoping to make his mark. That wouldn't necessarily be a bad thing: a junior equestrian probably had more of the skills needed for running a *numerus* than Memnon did. Even if Memnon's friends at court pulled strings, though, so that he did end up a prefect, and even if he somehow learned how to do the job properly, it still wouldn't mean much. The Aurelian Moors were only a small, unimportant unit of irregular cavalry, and had no control over anything of significance. No, the Empire wouldn't lose much if Memnon left its service.

Now that he'd committed himself, he had no more doubts. It was more than just the unwanted promotion; more even than the dreadful prospect of involvement in a civil war. In the end, he was simply tired of being a soldier. He wanted peace; he wanted to marry some cheerful, bright-eyed woman, and settle down to raise children with her. Now that he'd finally admitted it to himself, he wanted it fiercely. It would hurt to disappoint Rogatus, but Rogatus's footsteps led only to a sterile and lonely end: he wasn't going to follow them.

He kept thinking about Sulicena. He wished he could have asked Athenais more about what Drustocce had said. It was clear that Athenais had understood it to be sympathetic – but it was also clear that Athenais had no idea how things worked among barbarians. Drustocce might well be pleased to hear that her sister-in-law's lover had been praised by the Empress, and that his love had been honourable and sincere – but that didn't mean Argentocoxus wouldn't kill him if they ever saw him again. It certainly didn't mean the clan would let him *marry* Sulicena, the mother of the next clan chief. Sulicena must have other suitors, men who'd bring her clan allies or riches, and in such a war-like tribe, some of them would necessarily be famous warriors as well.

He remembered the glint in her eyes as she advised him to strip, and her fierce solemn gaze when she told him she offered honourable love, and knew, with a certainty that went through to his gut that, yes, he did want to marry her.

It occurred to him that Senorix could tell him more about the way the tribes were likely to view the matter. He decided to call in at Castra Exploratorum on his way back. The outpost fort was only half a day's ride from Aballava, and he had plenty of time in hand.

He arrived at the outpost early in the evening of the sixth of November. The guards at the gate were nervous, and told him to halt while he was still some distance away. He obeyed, and answered their shouted questions with his name and errand. At this they relaxed and opened the gate. The two men stared at him hard as he rode in, and one made the gesture against evil. The other, however, asked him if he was 'Fortrenn's black ghost'.

'That's me,' Memnon agreed. 'Is my friend Senorix in?'

Yes, the sentries told him; if Memnon waited, one of them would fetch him.

Senorix, when he turned up a few minutes later, seemed genuinely pleased to see his visitor. He shook hands warmly and, discovering that Memnon hadn't eaten, at once offered to get him something from the Aelians' stores.

They stabled Ghibli and went to the fort stores. Memnon was disconcerted when the attendant supplied him with field rations of hard biscuit, bacon and beer; normally troops resident in a fort bought food locally and ate a richer and more varied diet. Senorix noticed his surprise.

'Things have been tense,' he explained. 'Our prefect's refusing the tribesmen permission to approach the fort, and he's keeping us confined to it.'

Memnon frowned at him. 'Things got tense where we were, too, by the end of the summer, but I thought they'd be getting better again by now.'

The British soldier snorted. 'You'd think so – though I don't think your lot know about "tense". Your officers managed to keep their men under control, from what I heard: others weren't so strict. My kinsmen have told me that . . . well, never mind. A lot of the Maeatae feel that they were cheated. The Emperor promised that if they recognized his authority, they would be allowed to govern themselves – and then he set up garrisons all over their territory and oppressed them cruelly.'

'But they agreed to garrisons.'

Senorix shrugged. 'They didn't know what to expect from them. The Maeatae were pushed into this settlement by the Caledones, too: they think they could've got a better bargain if they'd held out just a little longer. There's a rumour going round that they could still get a better bargain – if they were willing to fight for it.'

Memnon stared in horror. That sounded like a rebellion in the offing. Gods and spirits, not a second act of that horrible war!

'That's wrong,' he said worriedly. 'I'm sure that's wrong. If they break the treaty, they'll be punished for it. It'll be worse than last summer.'

'I know,' said Senorix grimly, 'but that's what they're saying among the tribes.' He hesitated, then added softly, 'They even say that they heard it from somebody at the imperial court last summer – that somebody high up drank too much and let it slip. The story is that we wouldn't be willing to fight another war, that if the Maeatae rebelled, we'd agree an easier treaty. I pray to the Mothers that the talk dies down over the winter!' He grimaced. 'What *really* worries me is what would happen if the Maeatae wait until the troops from overseas have left, and then rebel.'

The Emperor was planning to leave Britain early in the summer, as soon as predictably calm seas assured an easy voyage. Most of the imported troops would leave with him, though a few units would be left in Britain, to assist the province's regular troops in controlling the new northern territories. The Moors had yet to receive any information about their own next assignment.

'You should tell your friend the chamberlain about this,' Senorix went on, now watching Memnon intently. 'We've reported it to our prefect, but I don't know how much the high command listens to him. Nobody ever wants to deliver bad news, either. I'm worried that by the time our message got all the way to the Emperor, it was so watered down by other people's boasts about how well they're doing that it was meaningless. Your friend the chamberlain can give the Emperor the truth – and from what I've heard about him, he wouldn't be afraid to, either.'

'I'll tell him,' Memnon promised. 'Soon as I can.'

Even as he said it, he realized that Rogatus was unlikely to allow him to make another trip to Eboracum any time soon: if he wanted to pass this news on to Castor, he would have to send a letter. He could get Rogatus's clerk to write it for him – but he had an uncomfortable feeling that this might have some connection with the question Caracalla had asked him in Eboracum. If it did, then it was definitely something that ought to be kept quiet. Rogatus's clerk gossiped: the whole *numerus* knew that you could pump him for information if you bought him a drink. Rogatus always handled any sensitive letters himself.

He could ask Rogatus to write the letter – but then he couldn't mention the favour he'd asked of Castor, not unless he wanted a bitter argument with the prefect. He would have to try to write the letter himself.

He'd never written a letter. He had labouriously scrawled any number of individual words, but he'd never tried to string them together. It was likely to be a complete shambles. He hoped Castor would be able to decipher it.

Senorix brought him back to his barracks and introduced his tent-mates, an assortment of more-or-less Romanized Britons. They'd heard about Memnon and were pleased to meet him – pleased and, to his dismay, a little awed. They asked for the stories of his encounters with Fortrenn and Argentocoxus, and they listened reverently. They didn't even laugh at the leopard imitation: they probably thought it would be disrespectful. It was irritating.

He discovered, though, that they'd heard about Sulicena – a story Memnon had scrupulously kept from his Roman colleagues. Senorix asked about her, which gave Memnon the opening he needed for his own question.

'You liked her that much?' asked Senorix, raising his eyebrows.

Memnon nodded.

The British scout thought about it. 'I'm sorry' he said at last unhappily, 'I don't think it's possible. The tribes expect women to sleep with famous warriors, there's no disgrace in it, they won't resent you for that. But marriage . . . that's another matter. Argentocoxus's clan was always powerful and important, and it's come out of the war even more powerful and important. There will be plenty of other clans who want to supply Argentocoxus's sister with a new husband. If she turned them down in favour of a Roman, they'd be insulted. I don't think Argentocoxus would welcome you if you turned up there again, and he'd welcome you even less if it pleased his sister. The clan wouldn't be happy to see half-Roman heirs to the chieftainship, either – particularly ones who . . . your children would look like you, wouldn't they?'

'If they didn't, I'd have something to say to their mother! Though probably they'd take after her, too. Brown instead of black.' The thought of a pack of giggling brown children made him smile.

Senorix did not smile back. 'That wouldn't be good. They'd be marked as Children of Night.'

Memnon raised his eyebrows incredulously, and Senorix went on seriously, 'You're favoured by Brigida, the Lady of Night, the Mother of the Gods. The British are half-convinced that you have supernatural powers. I heard one story that said you were only captured because your powers weaken as the sun grows strong, and you were taken at noon. It said you're strongest during the hours of darkness.'

Memnon grimaced. 'Who tells you these stories?'

'Travelling bards, mostly. In ordinary circumstances we offer them hospitality in exchange for their songs. It's a good way to get information about what's happening among the tribes. We entertained several bards before things got tense. You ought to do the same: you'd be amazed what they say about you.'

'I think I'd prefer not to know!' He returned to the much more interesting subject of Sulicena. 'She has a son by her first husband. If she had one by me, he wouldn't inherit. Wouldn't that make a difference?'

'Some, I suppose – but nobody likes to rely on a single life. The eldest son gets a fever, or has a riding accident, and then what? And anyway, it's *daughters* who pass on the inheritance. Does she have a daughter?'

Memnon winced and shook his head.

'Of course, the clans *elect* their chiefs from among the members of the chief's mother's family,' Senorix said thoughtfully. 'They don't have to pick the first-born son; they can choose a younger child, or an uncle or cousin, if they feel he'd do a better job. But your daughter's children would certainly be the first line of succession. It would be bad enough if you were Italian, but at least then the Roman blood would be invisible by the second generation; in your case it would still show, wouldn't it? Everyone would see at a glance that they were the grandchildren of the Black Ghost, unnatural. It could divide the clan.

'Women among the tribes pick their own husbands, of course, and if the lady decided that she wanted you, regardless, presumably her brother would have to make the best of it – or see to it that you met with an accident. But if she's a sensible woman she'll be aware that it would be bad for her clan, and choose someone else. Besides, how could you even get up there to ask her? You'd have to travel for days among hostile tribes. I know you're good at sliding through without attracting any notice, but you'd still have to ask directions. With feelings among the tribes running as high as they are now, a Roman soldier travelling alone into the Highlands would simply disappear. And you don't even speak British, do you?'

'I can speak a little!' Memnon objected, but his heart sank. Sulicena was a sensible woman, and an honourable one. She would not pick a husband who was bad for her clan, or raise children who might divide it. A honourable man, come to that, wouldn't ask her to.

'My advice is, give her up,' said Senorix gently. 'It's no use wanting what you can't have.'

Memnon nodded heavily. It was certainly true that wanting what you couldn't have was a sure way to be unhappy. He'd fallen in love twice since he arrived in Britain, and in both cases the result had been frustration and pain. He supposed it was his own fault, for allowing his eyes to fix on princesses and imperial attendants, when he should have been looking out for some smiling cook or farmgirl . . . not that a man had much choice about which woman caught his eye.

Give her up. Silently, he relinquished the hope of seeing Sulicena again, and wished her a long and happy life.

He sighed, realizing even as he surrendered one hope, that it had concealed another one which was still firmly hooked. Gods, he thought he'd given up any expectations of Athenais a year ago! He supposed it was because he knew her better now: she'd become warm and friendly, no longer afraid of him. He told himself firmly that his hopes there were even more misplaced than they had been in regard to Sulicena – the Empress wouldn't give Athenais to him, and Athenais herself loved Castor. Give her up, Memnon told himself in disgust; you'll get nothing from it but grief.

Memnon, Decurion, *Numerus* of Aurelian Moors, to L. Septimius Castor, Chamberlain to Our Lord Severus Augustus.

SIR, SORRI I RITE THIS BAD. I AM LURNING, I DO NOT TRUST THE CLARC.
SIR, MI FRENND SENORIX OF THE AELIAN COHORT SEZ THERE IS A RUMORR AMOG THE MAEATAE THAT THEY WOOD GET BETTER TERMZ OF PEECE IF THEY FITE FOR THEM. HE SEZ THEY SAY SUMWON HI UP AT COURT TOLED THEM WE WOODUNT FITE ANUTHER WAR. THIGS ARE VERI TENS, AND HE IZ WORIED. HE ASKED ME TO TELL YU THIS. HE SEZ THE MAEATAE THINK THEY WERE CHEETED BEECOZ OF THE GARISONZ, AND HE DOZ NOT NO WAT WIL HAPEN WEN THE OTHER TROOPS GO HOME. I DONT NO IF THIS HAZ ANITHIG TO DO WITH WAT I WAZ ASKED LAST TAIM I WAZ IN EBORACUM. I THIGK MAYBI.
I HAVN CHAGED MI MINED ABOUT WAT I ASKED YU.

Memnon inspected his missive with resignation. It didn't look much like a letter from Castor: the large, clumsy letters had been made with so much force that in some spots the wax had come right off the tablet, leaving the letters scored into the wood beneath. Only the superscription, on the back, looked neat: it had been written by Rogatus's clerk. He hoped that Castor would consider the contents, and not the form.

He sealed the letter with the Moors' star and Castor's own ring and gave it to the next messenger bound for Eboracum. Then he returned his attention to the affairs of his squadron, and settled down to wait.

Septimius Castor, freedman of Augustus, greets Memnon.

First, let me assure you that I have passed on your friend's concerns to those most able to deal with the matter. I agree that it may be significant that Antoninus Augustus was inquiring about factions among the British tribes, though whether this was because of his own interests or because he had noticed his brother doing so, I cannot be certain. Thank you for your efforts to bring effective attention to the problem.

A most joyous and unexpected result has been that our beloved Empress, impressed by the devotion Athenais and I both have shown to the welfare of the Empire, has, in her infinite kindness, rescinded her ban on our association. I fear it may be improper for me to reveal this news, since we are still compelled to discretion, but I am so overjoyed that I find it difficult to keep silent, and you were good enough to express your sympathy for our former predicament. Discretion, however, is indeed required, if Athenais is to avoid the odium that now sadly attaches to me.

As regards your request, there is no hurry. Please, discuss it with your friends. If you have not changed your mind after the Saturnalia, I will do as you ask.

I wish you good fortune in all things.

'What did your friend the chamberlain have to say?' Rogatus asked.

Memnon kept his eyes firmly on the duty roster. The letter had arrived the day before, and he'd spent most of the afternoon puzzling over it. It was full of words Honoratus had never taught him, but he'd managed to get the gist of it in the end; by the time he'd got all of it, he'd even managed to master the sting the central piece of news had caused him. He knew that Rogatus had expected to be allowed to see the letter, but he had no intention of letting him do so. It would be hard enough to face the prefect when his application for early discharge was approved; to give the man a hope of talking him out of it would make life miserable for months.

'He says he passed on what Senorix said to the people who can deal with it,' he said. Then he looked up, and added a cast-iron excuse for keeping the letter to himself, 'And he said he's got a girlfriend, but I have to be discreet about it. He told me because it's Athenais, the secretary to the Empress that I rescued along with him.'

'Oh!' said Rogatus, startled.

'Did you ever see her, sir? Beautiful girl, eyes like a gazelle and fabulous long legs. Brave, too, and smart – can write as fast as you can talk, and rattles away in Greek like a philosopher. Wouldn't think a man like Castor could get himself a girl like that, would you? I don't mean to be disrespectful, but you have to admit he looks like a marmot. *She* looked at him, though, like he was the most wonderful man she ever set eyes on. Lucky marmot! Not surprising he couldn't resist telling me about it.'

Rogatus had no use for women, apart from the occasional whore in a discreet brothel. He gave an embarrassed grunt.

'He asked me not to talk about it, though,' Memnon admitted resignedly. 'In case it gets her into the same trouble Castor's in himself.'

'Then you should keep quiet,' said Rogatus firmly.

They went over the rosters and discussed the latest efforts to protect the hooves of the unit's mounts. They were still in the middle of this when there was a knock on the door, and Memnon opened it to find Farabert.

The tension between the Moors and the Frisians, never absent, had recently become dramatically worse: a rumour had started that the Moors were going to be assigned to stay in Britain – and would keep Aballava while the Frisians were posted somewhere else. Rogatus had had the troops assembled the moment he heard the rumour, and had truthfully sworn that the Moors had not received *any* orders for the summer, and that as far as he knew they would leave Britain

when the Emperor did – but it hadn't been enough to calm
the eruption of bitter rivalry. The two units could not be
trusted to share a watch, let alone be allowed into the fort
village at the same time. The fort was effectively divided in
two, with no trespassing allowed, and even the fort baths
were used on separate days.

'Lord Farabert,' said Memnon warily, and saluted.

Farabert grunted; Rogatus hurried forward, frowning
anxiously.

'Prefect Rogatus,' said Farabert, and cleared his throat
unhappily.

'Has there been trouble?' asked Rogatus sharply.

Farabert blinked in surprise. 'Ah, no. I come here to talk
to you about what more we could do to avoid trouble.' He
made an uncertain gesture. 'I am thinking, it does not look
so good, that we divide the fort in two.'

Rogatus gazed at him impassively for a moment; Memnon
knew him well enough to see that he was pleased. While
Farabert had punished his men when they were involved in
fights with the Moors, he had not been particularly forward in
agreeing more positive measures. Presumably he'd just woken
up to how his lack of activity would look to the high command.

'You're quite right,' said Rogatus. 'It looks bad. Come in,
and we can discuss what to do about it. Memnon, dismissed.'

'Ah, let him stay!' exclaimed Farabert. 'He is your right
hand, yes, now that Saturninus is gone?'

Rogatus reacted to the sound of his old friend's name on
Farabert's lips with a cold glare, but he indicated with a
gesture that Memnon was to stay.

What Farabert proposed was the usual army remedy for
disputatious soldiers: exercises. Specifically, a competition
which would require Moors and Frisians to cooperate to
win a prize; Farabert offered to provide the prizes at his
own expense. Rogatus endorsed the proposal heartily,
though he suggested a few refinements to make sure the
members of the inter-unit teams didn't start fighting one
another.

When Farabert had left the office again, Memnon closed
the door with a frown. 'At the risk of sounding like Saturninus,
sir,' he remarked, 'I wonder what he's up to?'

Rogatus gave him a startled look – then smiled. 'He's worried that the rumour will prove to be correct,' he declared confidently. 'He's trying to establish that there's no need to move his people out of Aballava, that they can get along with us here if they have to.' He smiled again, this time in satisfaction. 'I think . . . I think he's finally giving in. He realizes that he can't get rid of us. We've won!'

'I suppose so, sir,' said Memnon. 'But let's be careful of him, ha? We know he tried to get rid of us once.'

The proposed contest was a version of the popular cavalry game 'Greeks and Amazons', in which teams took turns to charge each other with dummy javelins. In regular cavalry wings, the game was played in specially designed armour, but neither the Moors nor the Frisians possessed anything so luxurious. Instead, they prevented injury by using javelins which were little more than twigs, and stationing the defending team behind straw targets. It was agreed that there would be four teams, the winners of the first two matches to play each other in the final; each team would be composed of six Moors and six Frisians. Farabert supplied three barrels of beer, one for the winning team from each match, and a purse of money for the overall winners.

The men were doubtful at first about cooperating with their rivals, but the lure of beer and money, together with the practical wish to ease the restrictions provoked by their quarreling, proved strong enough. For several days the squadrons competed for places on the teams; then the mixed-unit teams were assembled and allowed to practise together. At last, on a cold bright day on the twenty-fifth of November, the contest was held – and proved a huge success.

Memnon did not have a place on any of the teams – he still lacked the consummate horsemanship of the Moors' best riders – but he was nonetheless compelled to attend the practices as well as the final: relations between the units were still so tense that a reliable officer from each side had to be on hand at all times to keep order. The practice sessions nearly all took place in cold, wet, windy weather. Memnon huddled miserably in the rain, crouched on Ghibli's damp back, watching as his comrades galloped up and down the muddy practice field hurling javelins, and he cursed Farabert and his good idea.

He had to admit, though, it did seem to be worthwhile. Each unit had strengths which were valuable for the game: the Moors were faster and more agile in the attack; the Frisians stronger and more forceful in the defence. Men from each unit were willing to seek out the best riders from the other for 'their' team, and on the day of the contest itself, Moors and Frisians united in cheering for their own. A couple of enterprising innkeepers from the fort village turned up with charcoal braziers and sold chestnuts and spiced wine; the Frisians built a bonfire and roasted an ox while the Moors made flatbread on a polished iron skillet set in the coals, and everyone enjoyed himself.

Farabert and Rogatus watched the contest side by side from the tribunal, and when the last match was done, they invited the officers of both units to a feast in the praetorium.

When Memnon arrived in the dining room, he saw at once that the feast had been provided by Farabert: it was a very Germanic meal of roast pork, cabbage and beer, to which Rogatus had contributed only a few flasks of wine. Memnon felt a bit embarrassed: it was true that Rogatus wasn't wealthy, but on his large salary he could have done a bit better than that. Neither of the commanders, however, remarked on it, and it was very clear that Farabert was putting himself out to be agreeable. As the meal wore on, he kept refilling Rogatus's cup, until the prefect became almost genial, beaming and nodding at the company. 'Enjoying the spoils of victory, eh?' he said to Memnon later, in private.

The talk was mostly of hunting: dogs, and horses, and dangerous game. Farabert and his cousin and deputy, Trupo, recounted the story of a boar they had hunted, not ten miles from Aballava, which had killed three dogs, a horse and a man. Rogatus countered with a story of a lion-hunt.

'Ah, lions!' exclaimed Farabert. 'I saw one of these beasts once, in the arena. What an animal! Do you hunt them much in Africa?'

At this all the Moorish officers began talking at once about lion hunts they had taken part in or heard about. The Frisians

listened with jealousy, and tried to turn the conversation back
to boar.

'But you say nothing,' Farabert pointed out to Memnon,
ignoring his own officers. 'You never hunt a lion?'

'There never were any lions around where I lived when I
was growing up,' Memnon replied. 'We heard about them,
but never saw any.'

'Ah? A pity.'

Memnon grinned. 'We didn't think so. The less we saw
of them, the better we liked it.'

This declaration was met with a baffled silence. A Frisian
might occasionally be glad to have missed an encounter with
danger – but he would never publicly admit as much.

'We got leopards sometimes, though,' Memnon went on,
pouring himself some more wine.

'I've never hunted leopard,' said Rogatus, with a smile. 'I
believe they're very dangerous. They climb well, and their
bite is deadly.'

'Tricky animals,' agreed Donatus, the senior Aurelian decurion, also smiling. 'They kill more men than lions do. You
never know where they are, until they pounce.'

The other Aurelian officers sniggered: everyone knew the
leopard story. Memnon sighed, wishing he'd never told it.
'They used to kill our goats,' he informed the company. 'You
have to go after an animal if it's killing your livestock.'

'Poor leopards!' murmured Donatus. 'They picked the
wrong goats.'

'You ever hunt boar?' asked Farabert. He was smiling in
what was probably intended to be an ingratiating fashion,
though his scar twisted the expression.

Memnon shook his head: he had never seen the point of
going after dangerous animals unless you had to. Obviously
if you were a farmer and wild swine were damaging your
crops, you had to hunt them, but why *soldiers* would go after
the animals was a mystery to him. Most of his comrades,
however, had hunted boar on the Danube, and now they
eagerly recounted their stories. The Frisian officers at once
praised the hunting to be found in the neighbourhood of
Aballava. Memnon became bored with the discussion, and
stopped listening; he only started paying attention again when

he realized that a boar-hunt was being arranged for the near future – and that he was expected to attend.

'But I don't want to!' he protested, startled. 'I'll stay home and mind the fort.'

Rogatus turned a disapproving look on him. 'Donatus will do that,' he ordered. 'He's senior. This is a generous and peaceable offer from our colleagues, and we will certainly accept it.'

Fourteen

The boar-hunt was arranged for the end of November, in a forest to the southwest of Aballava. Memnon was unhappy about it on several counts. First, and most simply, he hated the thought of getting up well before dawn in order to spend a cold winter's day riding about a miserable patch of swampy woodland, probably in the rain. Secondly, however, he was worried about the safety of the enterprise. In order to determine where to find a good-sized boar, the Frisians made enquiries among the local farmers – which was as good as announcing where they intended to mount the hunt. If the Maeatae really were serious about rebelling, they would have an opportunity to remove two unit commanders with one ambush. Thirdly, there was Farabert; it might seem to him that a hunting accident would be a good way to rid himself of Rogatus and his 'friends at court'.

Rogatus, however, dismissed Memnon's concerns. Farabert, he said confidently, was trying to conciliate the Moors, not get rid of them. There would be five other Aurelian decurions on the hunt as well as Memnon: the Frisians couldn't possibly expect to murder Rogatus without someone noticing. As for the Maeatae, the hunt would take place *south* of the wall, on Roman land – but Memnon could go and scout the area the day before, if he insisted.

Memnon cursed himself for having opened his mouth – but he did go and scout the area the day before. He found no signs of enemy activity, and it snowed.

He was silent and disgruntled when the hunting party mounted up before dawn next morning. One of the Frisians had loaned him a boar spear, which he'd fastened to the harness he used for his javelins. It was far and away the heaviest weapon he'd ever carried, and the crosspiece dug uncomfortably into his shoulder blades. He had no idea how to use the ugly great thing, and he hoped fervently he wouldn't have to try.

The snow had stopped, but it lay thick on the ground, creating a wash of pale gray light in which the figures of men and horses loomed large and black. The Frisians' dogs rushed back and forth barking, and the Frisians cuffed them and secured them on leads. There were, Memnon noted unhappily, roughly twice as many Frisians in the party as Moors. Rogatus, however, was cheerful, looking forward to the day's sport.

They rode along the military way for about five miles, then turned south on a smaller track, crossing out of the military zone around the wall. The sun was up, blood-red in a clear sky, casting long blue shadows over the snow. It showed tracks printed in the cleared fields: fox and hare, fallow deer and wild cat. Then the narrow cartway led them into forest – old forest of scrub oak, birch and alder, all leafless now and gray. Memnon had discovered on his scouting expedition the day before that it was full of patches of bog, now hidden beneath a thick covering of snow, but otherwise it was possible to ride through it, at least now, in the winter. The Frisians said there should be plenty of wild swine there. Memnon slitted his eyes against the light and tucked his cold hands under his armpits.

After another mile, they found what they were looking for: the tracks of a pig crossing the road, printed freshly in the snow – a large and solitary pig, almost certainly a boar. The Frisians released their dogs, which ran back and forth, sniffing and barking, before charging into the forest. The riders followed them.

Memnon had hunted as a boy in Africa, and had learned most of his scouting skills from it; on the Danube he'd regularly gone after small game and wildfowl, and occasionally joined his friends in hunting deer. He'd always believed that hunting required silence, careful observation, forethought and patience and a quick sure strike. He had never experienced anything like this noisy chase through a snow-bound forest, with twenty men on horseback pelting after a pack of a dozen baying hounds, and he was disgusted and amazed.

Ghibli, however, had evidently joined in similar enterprises before, presumably with Saturninus. Snorting with excitement, he plunged through the undergrowth and leapt over fallen trees, racing Farabert's ferocious black stallion in a struggle to be first. Memnon hung on to his mount's neckrope with both hands, flattened himself to his neck, and longed for the hunt to end. Rogatus, close beside them, actually gave a whoop of excitement.

After an endless pounding race, the hounds finally checked and Memnon straightened again. Most of the hunting party was nowhere to be seen. The dogs milled about, snarling and barking, and after a moment a pig screamed. He saw that what he'd taken to be another dog was in fact a wild pig, black and hairy, surrounded by the Frisian hounds. Farabert urged his horse into the midst of them, lowering his boar spear; Rogatus and one of the Frisian officers followed him. The boar, however, charged into the dogs, leaving one of them whimpering on the ground behind it, and plunged off through a dense thicket.

Memnon, reluctant to take his thin-skinned horse through the brambles, fought to stop Ghibli from following, twisting the neck-rope until the stallion snorted and coughed. The other hunters thundered away into the snowy woods – Frisians, all of them, except for Rogatus. One of the gallopers, however, turned his mount back to Memnon, grinning widely; it was Trupo, Farabert's deputy. 'Come on!' he yelled. 'We catch him!'

'Where are the others?' Memnon yelled back.

'Too slow!' the Frisian replied cheerfully. 'Come on!'

Memnon almost did – but he suddenly thought to wonder why, if Trupo was so unconcerned about leaving the others behind, he was so eager for Memnon to keep up. 'My horse is favouring his off fore,' he said. 'I need to check his feet.'

As soon as Memnon swung a leg over Ghibli's back, Trupo did the same. Memnon's blood ran cold. He touched Ghibli's shoulder with the riding rod and elbowed him sharply on the right, and the stallion exploded left, tossing his head and neighing loudly. Trupo swore; Memnon, flat to his stallion's back again, twisted his neck and saw from the corner of his eye that the Frisian was pulling himself back into the saddle and driving hard after him, and that he had lowered his boar spear.

Ghibli galloped into the woods, dodging trees, leaping brambles, head down and snorting as his rider urged him faster. Trupo fell behind: his larger and heavier mount couldn't keep up in such rough country. Then there was a sharp *thwack* of a branch hitting something, and a loud and anguished curse: sitting up to hold a boar-spear was a bad idea while galloping through trees. Memnon kept his own head down.

After a few minutes Ghibli slowed to a canter. Memnon sat up on his back, listening intently. He could no longer hear Trupo – but Ghibli's own passage was making so much noise that it didn't mean much. His trail, at any rate, was clear enough for an ignorant child to follow: a dark path of upflung leaf-mould and hoofprints dug into the snow.

He let Ghibli slow again, though, to a trot, while he tried to think. It was hard to do: there was a hot hard knot of emotion in his throat which threatened to choke him. He wanted to find Rogatus; he feared he would already be too late.

If he circled round, found the trail of the hunt and rode up it – what would happen? How many of the Frisians were party to this? Farabert and Trupo, obviously – and presumably there had been others among the hunters in the rest of the party who had been instructed to delay or mislead the other Moorish officers, so that there would be no hostile witnesses to what their chief had planned. There must be half a dozen ways to explain a dead body after a confrontation with a boar. Two dead bodies would be a little harder, but still possible: 'his horse slipped and crashed into the prefect's, and they both fell', 'he tried to save the prefect, and the boar got him, too', 'he stabbed at the boar, but the other man got in the way, and he killed himself from remorse when he saw what he'd done'. The high command would believe it, and even the Moors wouldn't be completely sure it was false.

Whatever excuses were planned, it was clear that the other Frisians at the front of the party had to be part of the plot. Three of them, Memnon thought, reviewing that moment of thundering hooves. Three of them, armed with boar spears and knives . . . as well as Farabert himself, of course, and Trupo, too, somewhere back there in the forest. All strong men and experienced fighters; the smallest of them was half a head taller than Memnon. Five to two: not good odds, particularly when one was old and unsuspecting. Desperately he pushed aside the fear that already the odds were five to one.

Maybe *all* the Frisians were part of it. Maybe that rumour had them believing that they would lose Aballava, the fort which was their home, unless they could get rid of the two Moors who had those important friends at court.

No. No, the Frisians who'd joined in that contest of Greeks and Amazon had certainly not been aware that their leader intended to murder his rival: their resentment and uncertainty and hard-won respect had been genuine. They'd believed, as Rogatus had, that Farabert was trying to conciliate the Aurelians. This boar-hunt had been arranged by Farabert with a small group of his most trusted officers.

Had Farabert noticed that Memnon was no longer at the front of the hunt? Would he go ahead with what he'd planned, relying on Trupo to deal with the missing man – or would he decide it was too risky to undertake the murder when an influential witness had escaped?

Farabert, Memnon realized sickly, couldn't know that Memnon had witnessed anything. For all the Frisian chief knew, Memnon's horse had gone lame, and Trupo, unsuspected, was waiting for a convenient moment to spit him. There was no reason for him to cancel any plans.

Memnon drew in a deep breath, then another; the cold air seared his throat. Ghibli flicked an ear back, and Memnon, straining his own ears, heard it too: hoofbeats behind them. Trupo was still following. He had to deal with that – and make up his mind what to do to protect Rogatus.

He patted Ghibli's neck gently, touched him to a canter again, then glanced around until he spotted a forked tree to the left. He guided the horse over, caught the trunk, then gave Ghibli a kick and yelled loudly. The stallion snorted and shied off; Memnon swung himself up into the fork of the tree and flattened himself against the bark. He stripped off his mittens, tucked them into his belt, and drew his knife. The boar spear had a much longer reach, of course, but he far preferred to rely on the weapon he knew best.

Trupo appeared, trotting swiftly, his head bent low over Ghibli's trail, the boar spear wedged under his arm. He glanced up, though, as he approached the tree – and caught a glimpse of Ghibli's bay hide ahead. He spurred past.

Memnon had hoped he would come close enough that he could be taken by a leopard-like leap from the tree – but never mind. He dropped to the ground and hurried silently after Trupo.

Ghibli had stopped, of course: he was tired and had no rider to urge him on. Trupo reined in beside him and glanced around wildly, looking for the footprints of the man who'd been on that horse only minutes before. Memnon flattened himself behind a tree and waited. He shielded his mouth with his left hand, so that the white smoke of his breath would not drift out and betray him; his right hand held his knife.

He heard Trupo dismount; heard the crunching of leaves as the man cast about on foot, still looking for footprints. Finding none, he paused, and there was a long minute of silence. Then the footsteps began again, crunching back along the trail; he was leading his horse now. Memnon tensed, waiting. The steps drew level, moved past . . .

He shot out from behind his tree, adjusting his rush mid-step as his eyes finally saw his target: Trupo, bent to scan the ground, but already straightening and trying to bring his spear into line. He had just dropped his horse's bridle, and the animal was rearing in alarm.

Memnon tackled the Frisian before the spear was halfway round, brought him down on to the snow with a thud, caught his hair and dragged his head back to expose his throat to the knife. Trupo heaved, still trying to bring up the spear, and Memnon nicked him and shouted, 'Don't move!'

The Frisian went still, lying on his belly with Memnon kneeling on top of him. His breath smoked, and he watched Memnon from a corner of his eye. A red weal from the branch he'd hit marked his cheek, and the blood from the cut on his throat was warm over Memnon's hand, and red, red, red on the snow.

'What I want you to do,' Memnon told him breathlessly, 'is go to Farabert, *now*, and tell him not to do it. If Rogatus lives, nothing will come of this. If Rogatus comes home unharmed, I swear by my ancestors that I will say nothing about this to anyone. Do you understand?'

'Yes,' croaked Trupo.

'Drop the spear.'

Trupo let go of the spear. Memnon reached over and picked it up, then stood, levelling the weapon at Trupo. The Frisian sat up, lifting his hands.

'Swear that you'll go straight to Farabert and tell him not to do it,' Memnon ordered.

'I swear it!' exclaimed Trupo. 'I swear it by all the gods! What else *would* I tell him, with you alive to bear witness?'

'Go, then,' commanded Memnon, with a jerk of his head.

Trupo scrambled to his feet. He took a few uncertain steps backward, then turned and ran for his horse, which had bolted back along the trail. He tried to catch its bridle; it shied. He shot a frightened look at Memnon, drew a deep breath, spoke the horse's name and tried again, more slowly. This time the horse allowed it, and Trupo quickly pulled himself up into the saddle.

Memnon slid noiselessly back into the forest as the Frisian turned his mount and galloped back up their trail. He waited until the other was gone, then whistled for Ghibli.

He wanted, desperately, to ride after Trupo. Instead he turned Ghibli in the opposite direction and rode for the wall. The best protection he could offer Rogatus was Farabert's certainty that the planned murder could not be passed off as an accident. To ride up and offer Farabert the hope of getting both his targets would be stupid. If Trupo came too late, and Rogatus was already dead . . . then it would still be stupid. There was no sense in assaulting a stronger force head-on. Rogatus had always known that.

Back at Aballava, he stabled Ghibli and retired to his room, glad for the first time of its privacy.

It was night when the hunting party returned. He knew what it brought as soon as it entered the gate: the fort was suddenly alive with shouting and the sound of men running.

He picked up his javelins and walked silently down to see the worst.

The body lay on a litter improvised from branches and slung between two horses, and already it was surrounded by a mob. The men on the gate had fetched torches, which cast a red light over Rogatus's still face and haloed his white hair; the gold earring in his right ear was a pinpoint of light. Everyone was shouting wildly, but when Memnon appeared, they stopped. He walked up to the litter through a gradually deepening silence, and gazed down into Rogatus's face. At first he couldn't see how the old man had died – but then he noticed the blood on the right side of the back of the head, and realized that the skull there was crumpled inward. Struck down from behind, he thought remotely, probably with the iron-clad haft of a boar spear. He looked up and found Farabert with his eyes.

The Frisian chief's face was red with the cold. His blue eyes were wary.

'You will pay for his life with your own,' Memnon told him flatly.

Farabert's mouth twisted. 'His horse fell, and he was thrown against a tree. Why not threaten the horse, or the tree?'

Memnon stared at him. Martialis, one of the Moorish decurions who'd been at the back of the hunting party, asked urgently, 'What happened? Did you see?'

'No,' said Memnon quietly. 'I did not see it.' He glanced around and found Trupo, who flinched. Had Trupo come too late, or had Farabert simply decided to commit his murder anyway, and rely on denials to bluff his way through?

Memnon's own threat to bear witness was, he saw now and too late, itself a bluff. If he accused Farabert of murder his fellow-Moors would certainly believe him. The night was thick with their outrage; they would rise against the Frisians at a word. But what then? It would effectively start a war inside the fort. The high command would never overlook that: they would come down on both units, hard. He could make his accusation openly only if he didn't care how many others died as a result.

'Lives like ours are cheap,' Rogatus had said once. *'It'll*

*be up to you to guard them like rubies, because to the high
command we're small change.'* He'd been speaking to
Honoratus, of course – but Honoratus and now Rogatus were
gone, and these lives were in Memnon's charge now, whether
he liked it or not.

What if he kept quiet now, and rode to Eboracum to lay
charges there? No, that was no good either: it would give
the Frisians plenty of time to prepare counter-charges.
Investigations by the army or the Commissary tended to be
brutal, particularly when the men questioned weren't citizens. Men in both units could expect to be tortured; Memnon
would have to be prepared to endure that himself – and in
the end there was no certainty as to who the investigators
would choose to believe. Castor might be a valuable ally,
but he had little influence with the army, as he'd demon-
strated with his vain attempts to get Memnon honoured and
Panthera dismissed.

Farabert would pay: that was not in doubt. Memnon's best
course, though, was to exact the price privately, and guard
the lives of his comrades.

'I did not see it,' Memnon repeated. 'I got separated from
the others during the chase, so I came home.' He caught the
satisfaction in Farabert's eyes and threw down a challenge
of his own. 'Swear that this was an accident. Swear it by
your own gods, and by Juno Caelestis, and by the heads of
the Emperors.'

There was an profound silence. Every eye rested on
Farabert.

'I will swear it,' said the Frisian chief at last. Torchlight
and the scar rendered his face monstrous as he raised his
hands, palms outward. 'I am innocent of this man's blood.
I swear it by Thincsus and the Alaisiagae, I swear it by Juno
Caelestis, and I swear it by Our Lords the Emperors Severus,
Antoninus and Geta.'

'The gods hear you,' Memnon told him, now sure of his
own alibi. 'I leave vengeance to them.'

The next few days were inordinately difficult.

Farabert ordered Rogatus's servants out of the praetorium
the same night the hunt returned. The two old men went in

tears to the decurion*s*, who'd been meeting together in the chapel of the standards to discuss the funeral. The decurions, hot with indignation, marched to the praetorium in a body and demanded that the servants be allowed to remain long enough to secure Rogatus's property. Farabert yielded, but sullenly. It was the first of many confrontations, and Memnon found himself in the middle of all of them.

When Rogatus's will was read, Memnon was the principal heir. He was the one who ended up delivering the funeral oration, lighting the pyre, distributing the prefect's legacies and sending letters to notify the few distant relatives of the death. He had the assistance of Rogatus's clerk, the old gossip Verinus, who had immediately transferred his loyalties to the designated heir; he also had the support of Rogatus's two old servants, who now expected to serve their master's appointed successor. Donatus, the senior decurion, should have been the one in charge of the Moors, but he, like everyone else, deferred to Memnon – the heir, the hero, the Man with Friends at Court. He hated the role, but it was impossible to withstand it.

As regarding those Friends at Court, Memnon decided that he ought to let them know what had happened. Quite apart from the fact that Castor had seemed to like Rogatus, both he and Athenais had warned Memnon not to touch Farabert, for fear of revealing that the Moors knew they'd been betrayed. Now that he was determined to kill Farabert, he owed his friends some explanation. There was also the possibility that Farabert would kill Memnon instead, in which case he hoped his friends would see to it that his killer was punished.

Memnon had no doubt whatsoever that Farabert would kill him, given half a chance; fortunately, denying him that chance wasn't difficult. He was never alone; during the day he was always busy with his squadron or with the other decurions, and at night the two old servants made up their beds in his room, which was in the middle of the Moors' half of the camp to begin with. Farabert tried, rather half-heartedly, to order him to take a message to Eboracum, then tried to post him to one of the fortlets manned from Aballava. Memnon refused both orders on the grounds that Farabert had no right to command Moors, and Farabert backed down. Memnon was aware of Farabert's friends watching him, but he ignored them: they were not going to do anything in front of witnesses.

The Frisian chief was both aggressive and nervous, continually trying to seize authority over the whole of the fort, but yielding swiftly when confronted. He was persistent, though: Memnon and Donatus had to face him down repeatedly, often on the same subjects, until Memnon wondered if Farabert hoped to win simply by exhausting his opponents. He found it exasperating. He would have far preferred to fade into the background, and allow Donatus to run the Moors – but Donatus, too, was nervous, and wanted support. It was assumed that a unit's decurions were capable of running that unit in the absence of the prefect – but they did not usually have to cope with the commander of a rival unit in the same fort.

The Frisian chief's authority was such that Memnon wasn't even confident that he could send his letter to Eboracum without someone interfering with it. Eventually he enlisted the help of the clerk Verinus and drafted a missive that he hoped sounded innocuous, but which ought to give the two very clever recipients enough clues to let them know what was going on.

Twelve days after the boar hunt he received evidence that his friends had understood perhaps too well: orders arrived from the Praetorian Prefect Papinian summoning him to Eboracum for 'detached duties'.

Fifteen

His first reaction on receiving the orders was dismay. How could he leave Aballava with Farabert in charge? His friends were trying to keep *him* safe, but who was going to look after the men of the *numerus*? He cursed himself for sending the chamberlain his news.

Then, however, he had an idea.

He made a great show of his departure from the fort. He met with Farabert and uttered veiled threats about what he would say to his friends in Eboracum; he met with Donatus and the other decurions; he made up a pack with some good clothing and some camp comforts – and, at last, in the afternoon of the twelfth of December, he set off from Aballava, riding Ghibli and leading a mule with the pack of luggage. The whole *numerus* saw him off, most of them looking very worried.

He trotted and cantered as far as Luguvalium, a mere six miles away, then stopped at the posting inn. He indulged himself by taking a private room, as befitted a decurion with friends in high places, though he committed his valuables to the innkeeper and got a receipt for them. As the early winter dark closed in, he ordered a good supper, and ate it with pleasure in the inn's common room. Then he retired to bed, barring the door behind him.

He lay quietly on the bed, listening as the sounds of voices from the common room faded, waiting until the last clunk and gurgle of the inn staff cleaning up gave way to silence. Then he got up and opened the window.

His room was on the first floor, but the inn's ceilings weren't high: the drop wasn't bad, and there was a window on the ground floor just below which would provide a foothold for climbing back in again. He straddled the sill a moment, wedging a piece of straw into the lower edge of the window-shutters, to hold them closed, then dropped down into the cold damp night outside. There he paused, looking around. The night was overcast, with a gusting wind from the east. He pulled up the hood of his cloak and set out for Aballava, walking at a good swinging pace. This walk was nothing at all compared to the escape from the Caledones.

He arrived at Aballava at the fifth hour of the night. He circled the fort to the west gate, then sat down in the shelter of a tree and waited while the watch changed. When the torches had gone out and the last sound of voices had died away, he slid through the darkness to the wall by the first guard turret.

He had often noticed the rough patch in the angle of the tower, where the masonry had been repaired clumsily, and thought that the protruding stones would be easy to climb. So they proved: he'd been prepared to take his boots off, but there was no need. He scrambled up on to the wall, then descended silently on the far side.

The *praetorium* was dark and silent, its doors locked. The dogs did not bark. Farabert had been careful about what he himself ate and drank since the prefect's death – but he hadn't worried about who fed his dogs, and it had been an easy matter for one of Rogatus's servants to slip them some drugged meat. The window of the furnace stoke-room was ajar, just as Rogatus's servants had promised: apparently it helped the furnace to draw. Memnon opened it fully and climbed through.

He was perfectly familiar with the layout of the building from many visits there; he knew the habits of Farabert's household, both from his own observation and from talking to Rogatus's men. Farabert's wife had given birth to his third son the year before, and she would not share her husband's bed until the child was weaned: the Frisian chief slept alone. Memnon glided noiselessly along the dark corridors of the house until he reached the chieftain's bedroom. The door opened easily under his hand.

He slipped in and closed it gently, then stood silent a moment. Farabert grunted and stirred on the bed, and Memnon flattened himself against the door. This would have to be done quietly: he'd known that from the start. If the household woke, he would die.

The Frisian chief was merely a shadowy bulk in the darkness of an unlit room. His breath whistled, snorted, whistled again. Memnon stood silent, waiting, until he was confident that the sounds were merely those of a man asleep.

He edged away from the door, straining his eyes to make out the details of that black shape. Head *there*, arm trailing *thus*, legs curled. Silently, he removed his decurion's sash and readied it in his hands.

Farabert didn't wake until the sash was wrapped around his neck and his arms were pinned by Memnon's legs straddling him. Then he struggled desperately. He was a big, strong man; he nearly managed to tip the bed over. He thrashed, heaved himself up and down, lashed out wildly with his legs, trying to jar that choking grip free. Memnon clung on grimly, wrapping his legs round bed and victim and riding them like a bucking horse, making no more sound than the occasional grunt. He drew the sash tighter. Farabert's desperate struggles weakened. He stopped heaving. His thrashing grew feeble, then stopped altogether. Memnon kept up his deadly grasp on the sash, however, long after the body beneath him was still. In the darkness behind his eyes he could still see Rogatus's face, motionless in the torchlight – and somewhere behind it was the face of his own father, with the flies drinking from its dry mouth, and the scent of flesh left too long in the African sun.

Several interminable minutes after Farabert's struggles ended, Memnon let go of the sash. He climbed off the bed and looked down at the body. In the darkness he could not make out the face. There was no sound from the rest of the house: Farabert's death throes had not been loud enough to wake his family from their sleep. He unwound his sash from Farabert's throat and wrapped it around his own waist, then squatted beside the body and gently massaged the dent left in the still-warm flesh. It was not the sort of deep ridge which would have been left by a cord: in the morning it should be barely noticeable. He moved silently to the door and stood there for a little while. The sound of his own breath, hard and fast, was the only sound in the room; the silence of the night-time house was undisturbed.

He opened the door and slipped noiselessly out, then retraced his steps to the furnace stoke-room. No one moved in the house, no one spoke; there was no disturbance. He turned his mind from what Farabert's wife would feel when she came to kiss her husband awake, and from what would become of the chieftain's children. Farabert had murdered Rogatus. Memnon had never returned the old man's love – but that didn't alter his obligation, or his duty to avenge his patron's death. Farabert had stolen a life and repaid one, and that was justice.

He arrived back at the inn in Luguvalium at about the tenth hour of the night, and curled up in the hayloft above his horse to rest for about an hour. When the eastern sky was gray, he got up, and climbed back into his expensive private room. He was not surprised to find that the door had been forced during the night: it was entirely to be expected that Farabert had sent men to kill him as soon as he was away from his comrades' protection. It was what he'd hoped for: it would've been much harder to murder Farabert while he had his trusted aides around him. He quietly removed the broken bolt from the door, bound it back together with cord, and replaced it again.

When the house began to stir, he went to the kitchen and bought himself some breakfast, then paid the reckoning and set out.

He rode hard during the short hours of daylight; when darkness fell he stopped at the nearest farmhouse, showed the householder his order to report to Eboracum, with its official seal, and asked permission to sleep in the barn. Early next morning, he paid for some bread for himself and grain for his horses, and set out again, confident that no pursuit would find him until he had reached his destination.

On the fifteenth he stopped early, so that he would be able to arrive in Eboracum in the morning rather than the evening, and on the sixteenth rode directly to the legionary fortress, saluted the guards, and presented them with his orders.

The army was not at its most efficient: it was the day

before the Saturnalia festival began, and everyone was already in a holiday mood. After much shuttling between offices in the legionary headquarters, however, he was at last informed that he had been seconded to the guard of the procurator of Britain, Sextus Varius Marcellus, and was ordered to report to the *cornicularius* Claudius Proculus, who commanded that guard.

He was surprised and puzzled. The procurator was the chief financial officer of the province, second only to the governor; *cornicularius* was the title of the head of one of the provincial departments. Like all the provincial posts it was a military rank, so it wasn't surprising to find a *cornicularius* in charge of troops – but the Consular Guard was an elite force, far superior to auxiliary *numeri*. He couldn't guess what it wanted with the services of a barbarian cavalryman, but he dutifully went to report to Claudius Proculus.

Proculus was a man of middle age in shiny armour and a spotless uniform. When Memnon appeared in his quarters he gazed in amazement. 'You're filthy, soldier!' he snapped. Memnon noticed that, for all the fastidious neatness, the man's teeth were black.

'Yes, sir!' replied Memnon, saluting. 'I've just ridden from Aballava, sir, and I've had no chance to change or wash up, sir!' He offered Proculus his orders.

The officer took them and glanced over them. 'Oh,' he said, with distaste. 'You're the one who castrated Lord Fortrenn's nephew.' He surveyed Memnon a moment. 'Very well, decurion. The Lord Procurator will be visiting the chiefs of the Maeatae, who, it seems, are restless. We have been gifted with you because it was thought the sight of you might settle them a bit.' He snorted. 'You certainly look villainous enough. What in the name of the infernal gods have you been doing with that sash, using it to tie a yoke on an ox?' He pulled out a beechwood writing tablet without waiting for a response, and scribbled on it. 'Show this to the prefect of the camp, and he'll allot you your quarters. Then go clean up. While you're under my orders you'll keep yourself spotless, like a proper soldier.'

'Yes, sir!' said Memnon, saluting again. 'Sir, I have friends in Eboracum. May I have permission to visit them, sir?'

Proculus grimaced. 'It's the Saturnalia tomorrow, decurion, and for the next seven days, Liberty rules. Please yourself – but try to look like a soldier when you next report to me!'

'Yes, sir!' Memnon took his authorization and departed.

He was interested to see that an assignment to the Consular Guard was a threshhold of some sort: he was actually allotted quarters *inside* the legionary fortress of Eboracum, rather than in the annexe. He had time to inspect the room, stow his gear safely, send a note to Castor, and have a bath before they came to arrest him.

The legionary lock-up was next to the guardroom on the south gate of the fortress. It was a narrow stone box of a room, windowless and, in this season, very cold. When Memnon was escorted to it, it contained a couple of sorry drunk-and-disorderlies sitting miserably on the straw-covered floor, but they were released that evening.

'The Saturnalia start tomorrow,' one of the guards explained. 'We'll need the space.'

Memnon had loved the Saturnalia festival from the first time he encountered it. 'When's my hearing?' he asked. 'I don't want to miss the whole festival!'

The guard snorted. 'You're charged with murder, black face: that will need the attention of the legate. He's over at his daughter's house for the holiday, and you couldn't pry him away with a lever. You won't be out of here until the festival's over.'

The guard, however, was mistaken. The following afternoon – the first day of the Saturnalia – there was a sudden clatter at the door, and two men of the Sixth legion appeared, flustered and resentful, to escort him to the court for a hearing.

The person in charge of hearing serious cases involving soldiers on the wall was the legate of the Sixth Legion, Antonius Gargilianus, who, in normal circumstances, was commander-in-chief of the Roman forces in the north of Britain. When Memnon was escorted into the *praetorium* of the Sixth, the legate was seated at the tribunal in the great hall. The huge room was largely empty, and the few officials required to be there were all out of uniform, dishevelled and resentful; one of the court ushers was evidently drunk. Seated on the benches to the legate's left were the reason the hearing was being heard even in the holiday: Castor and Athenais. Next to them, to Memnon's surprise, sat his current superior, Claudius Proculus, resplendent in the full dress uniform of a *cornicularius* of the Consular Guard.

To the legate's right sat the accusers: Trupo and two of his Frisian colleagues, looking nervous and out of place in their rusty chain mail. When Memnon came in, Trupo gave him a look of fear and hatred, dropping his eyes when Memnon grinned back.

The legate Gargilianus eyed Memnon resentfully, then declared, 'This is a preliminary hearing to determine whether there is a valid case against the prisoner Memnon, a decurion of the *Numerus* of Aurelian Moors, currently seconded to the Consular Guard. You are Memnon?'

'Yes, sir, My Lord Legate!' said Memnon, standing to attention.

'That's your real name?' the legate asked doubtfully.

'Not originally, sir!' Memnon admitted. 'My mother named me Wajjaj – but a lot of people find that hard to say. Memnon's the name I've gone by ever since I joined the army, sir, and it's what's written down on the rolls of my unit.'

Gargilianus mouthed 'Ouadhadh' silently and made a face. 'Very well. Who brings the charges?'

Trupo stood up. 'I do, My Lord! Trupo, sir, senior officer of the Formation of Frisians of Aballava.' He drew a deep breath. 'I accuse Memnon of the murder of our lord and chieftain, Farabert, son of Hariobaudes, Lord of the Frisians of Aballava.'

'Sir?' Memnon promptly interjected. 'Sir, am I allowed to say something, or should I keep my mouth shut unless you tell me I'm allowed to speak?'

Gargilianus scowled at him. 'If you have something to say, you may ask my permission to say it. You have something to say now?'

'Yes, sir. When I set out for Eboracum, Lord Farabert was very much alive. Can I just ask Trupo when and how he's supposed to have died?'

There was a silence. Trupo's face flushed, and he glared.

'Answer the question!' ordered the legate.

'He was found dead on the morning of the thirteenth of December,' Trupo admitted reluctantly.

'I left Aballava on the twelfth,' Memnon stated. 'The whole fort knows it.'

'You went back during the night!' exclaimed Trupo, with sudden cold vehemence.

'Lord Legate,' said Memnon respectfully, 'I left Aballava on the afternoon of the twelfth; I rode as far as Luguvalium, and took a room at the posting inn there. I stabled my horse and my pack animal, and the grooms at the inn can surely testify that I did not take them out again until the morning. I had supper and went to bed, and in the morning I set out early. All of this is true, I swear it by my ancestors, and the staff of the posting inn will certainly be able to confirm it.'

There was a silence. 'You went back during the night,' Trupo insisted. 'On foot.'

'Permission to reply, Lord Legate?' asked Memnon. 'The gates of the fort are guarded at all times, and locked at night! How am I supposed to have got in? Farabert kept dogs, half a dozen of them in the *praetorium*: how am I supposed to have entered the building without raising any alarm? I swear by my ancestors, if somebody cut Farabert's throat, it wasn't me!'

'You killed him!' snarled Trupo. 'Everyone heard you threaten him!' He turned to the legate. 'Lord Legate, he *did* threaten Farabert. When that bastard Rogatus died, Memnon told Lord Farabert, "You will pay for his life with your own." Everyone heard it!'

'Lord Legate? He's talking about Valerius Rogatus, who was prefect of my unit. Farabert invited him on a boar hunt, and brought him back to the fort dead. It's true, when I first saw the body I did believe that he'd been murdered. We all did – all of us in the Aurelian Moors, I mean. There'd been ill-feeling between us and the Frisians ever since we arrived in Aballava. They never wanted to share the fort with us, and there'd been a rumour that we're going to be posted to Britain when the other troops from the Danube leave. The Frisians are afraid they'll lose the fort. Farabert and Rogatus

in particular had been on bad terms, until Farabert suddenly
became very friendly and suggested the boar hunt. You have
to admit, sir, it looked suspicious! Farabert swore, though –
publicly, by his people's gods, and by our goddess Juno
Caelestis and by the heads of the emperors – that Rogatus
was killed when his horse fell and threw him into a tree. Sir,
I didn't see what happened, so I felt I had to accept Farabert's
oath. Men do die in falls when they're hunting, and if Farabert
was willing to swear by such great divinities, I had to take
his word. I told him that I trusted that the gods heard him,
and that I left it to them. Everyone in the fort knows it.'

'Is this true?' the legate asked Trupo.

'It was a trick!' the Frisian exclaimed angrily. 'He only
pretended to accept that oath! Really he was already planning how to murder Farabert – yes, and blame it on the
gods!'

The legate grunted, looking at Trupo with disapproval and
disbelief.

'Sir?' Memnon said again, respectfully.'If Trupo's honest,
he'll admit that since Rogatus died, I've worked hard to try
to calm things down. Rogatus appointed me his heir, and I
gave his funeral oration: I could've called for vengeance, but
I didn't. Instead I reminded everyone how Rogatus always
insisted on discipline and obedience to the laws of Rome, and
I urged them to make him proud of them. I met with Farabert
almost every day, along with the other decurions, and whatever problem came up, I always urged everyone to respect our
discipline and wait for orders from the high command. Is
Trupo going to claim that that was a trick, too? Sir, I asked
him this before, but he didn't answer: how did Farabert die?
I swear by my ancestors and by all the gods that I never even
took my knife out of its sheath in his presence!'

Another silence. 'Answer the question!' snapped Gargilianus.

Trupo, trapped, muttered something inaudible.

'Speak up!' snarled Gargilianus.

'He was found lying in his bed,' said Trupo unhappily,
'cold and dead, his face swollen with blood.' He glared at
Memnon. 'He must have been strangled or bewitched.'

'There were no wounds?' asked Gargilianus. 'No signs of
violence?'

'There was a . . . a bruise on his neck,' said Trupo. 'He must have been strangled with something soft which didn't leave much of a mark. Or bewitched.'

'A *bruise*?' Gargilianus asked incredulously. 'That was all? A man is found dead in his own bed, in a house full of dogs, inside a fort which was locked at night, and you accuse a man who wasn't even in the fort at the time – because of a *bruise*? How old was this Farabert?'

'Forty, and in excellent health!' protested Trupo. 'This man –' he pointed at Memnon, his hand shaking with anger – 'this man – he's a witch, a sorceror. He can make himself invisible. He has secret African arts which he used to charm the dogs to silence. He's an unnatural creature: look at him! Black as night, and devoted to the gods of darkness!'

Everyone looked at Memnon. He suddenly remembered the desert – the taste of blood in his mouth and the horror in the eyes of the dying Gaetulian. The memory was so vivid that for a moment it seemed as though everyone in the room must see it, must *know* what he had done, and believe that Trupo spoke nothing but the truth.

'My Lord Legate,' he managed to protest, 'that's *stupid*.'

'He looks to me like an ordinary Ethiopian,' the legate agreed, disgusted. 'No more unnatural than a German.' He turned his attention back to Memnon. 'Are you a sorceror, decurion?'

Memnon shook his head emphatically. 'My Lord Legate – no, of course not! I never—'

'Of course he doesn't *admit* it!' snarled Trupo.

'I don't even know what you *mean*!' protested Memnon. 'What sort of sorcery am I supposed to have worked? What's a god of darkness? Do you mean Juno Caelestis?'

'Juno Caelestis is Queen of Heaven!' objected the legate, shocked. 'Of course he doesn't mean her!' He made the fisted warding-off gesture.

'Well, the British call her Lady of Night, and I do worship her,' said Memnon. 'All of us in the Moors do. If he doesn't mean her, I don't know what he does mean. I've never heard of these "gods of darkness" before. I've certainly never worshipped them!'

'Have you any evidence that the man you accuse is a

practitioner of magic?' the legate asked Trupo impatiently.
'That, for example, he has broken into tombs, or pronounced
curses, or sold charms or cast horoscopes?'

Trupo, baffled, muttered, 'Not that *sort* of witch!'

'Not *any* sort of witch!' protested Memnon. 'What is it
that Trupo *thinks* I did to Farabert?'

The legate looked at Trupo, who set his jaw obstinately
and muttered something including the words, 'Dead and
cold.'

Memnon shook his head. 'When I set out from Aballava,
Lord Farabert was alive. I don't pretend that I grieve for his
death, but what evidence do these men have to connect me
with it? What evidence do they have that he even died by
murder? It sounds to me like he could have drunk too much
and choked in his sleep. He was in a very angry and uneasy
frame of mind after Rogatus's death, and he was drinking a
lot every night. Or, maybe the gods punished him. He swore
that Rogatus's death was an accident, but Trupo knows better
than I do if that was true.'

'Have you any reply to that?' Gargilianus asked Trupo.

The Frisian was silent for a long moment. Then he drew
himself up. 'Memnon did not sleep in Luguvalium on the
night my lord Farabert died,' he stated quietly. 'I and these
with me broke into the room he'd taken in Luguvalium, and
found it empty. We waited there until almost dawn, but he
did not come back.'

'Sir!' Memnon exclaimed urgently. 'Sir, listen to what the
man says: he and these two others broke into my room in
the posting inn in the middle of the night! Ask them why.'

Gargilianus glowered at Trupo and his friends. 'Why,
soldiers?'

'We were afraid of what the witch would do,' said Trupo,
very pale but still resolute.

'So *three of you* broke into his room in the middle of the
night?' demanded the legate.

'They didn't want me to come here, sir,' Memnon said
quietly. 'They knew I have friends at court – these good
friends who've come to support me now. They were afraid that
I was going to try to get the authorities to investigate
Rogatus's death. After I got that room at the posting inn in

Luguvalium, I started worrying because I was still so close to the fort. I couldn't sleep, and in the end I just went and slept in the hayloft, thinking that nobody would expect me to be there. I thought at the time I was being stupid – but it seems not.'

'You are accusing these men of trying to kill you?' asked the legate, frowning at him.

'Sir!' Memnon protested disingenuously, 'I don't know: maybe they wouldn't have done anything except threaten me. I just know that I was *worried*, and now I can see I had good reason. There were a couple of things Trupo said and did which made me think he wanted to get rid of me. Farabert, though, had sworn that Rogatus's death was an accident, and I didn't want to inflame my comrades' feelings by making accusations – you have to realize, sir, the mood at Aballava was very tense, on both sides. I didn't want to make it worse, but I was worried about what Trupo and his friends might do if they could catch me alone outside the fort. That's why I couldn't sleep in my room.' He shrugged. 'I'd meant to get further from Aballava before I stopped, but, well, I was late leaving the fort.'

'He accuses *us*,' cried Trupo, his voice cracking with indignation and grief, 'but it's *Lord Farabert* who's dead!'

'Men die from causes other than murder,' answered Gargilianus coldly. 'Nothing you have said convinces me that your Lord Farabert was murdered, let alone that the man you accuse was responsible; indeed, he seems to have made commendable efforts to restrain his men in what was evidently a very difficult situation. You, on the other hand, have freely admitted breaking into your enemy's room at a posting inn in the middle of the night, and for that I can see no honest reason. Nothing you've said about Decurion Memnon amounts to more than hatred and superstition. I find no case to answer. The prisoner is to be released; his accusers are to be censured and . . . who is responsible for disciplining them? Oh, never mind, no flogging during the Saturnalia! They're dismissed; everyone is dismissed. Let's go home!'

The drunken usher cheered loudly, and the other court officials applauded. The soldiers of the Sixth Legion unlocked

Memnon's shackles, and Castor and Athenais hurried over to shake his hand.

'I was surprised Trupo admitted breaking into my room,' Memnon told his friends afterward, over drinks in the private room of the posting inn. 'I didn't think he'd do that. He could've been flogged for it. He would've been, if it hadn't been the Saturnalia.'

'You knew he'd done it?' asked Athenais, pouring him some more hot spiced wine. From the common room below came the sound of flutes and drums, and the occasional roar of Saturnalian laughter.

Memnon shrugged. 'I knew somebody had, and I thought it was probably Trupo.' He had a swallow of wine. 'I hope he lets it drop now. The last thing I want is some kind of blood feud with him.'

'Did you kill Farabert?' Castor asked him quietly.

'Didn't you hear?' Memnon replied easily. 'I have no case to answer.' He grinned. 'Thank you very much for pushing the legate. That lock-up was *cold*. Much better here, ah?'

Castor gazed at him ruefully. 'An evasion,' he murmured.

Memnon made a face and spread his hands in acknowledgement. 'I'm grateful to you, sir – though, come to think of it, I suppose having the hearing early means I'm going to spend next month riding about the lands of the Maeatae in the snow and the rain, under the command of that spit-and-polish Proculus. Maybe I would be better off in the prison!'

Athenais smiled. 'You have the Augusta to thank for your assignment. I told my mistress about your prefect's death and said I was afraid that the Frisian commander would victimize you. She asked her kinsman Papinian to make you prefect!'

'What!'

Athenais smiled again. 'It may seem a high rank to *you*, but, I promise you, my mistress considers it the very least that could be offered a man she's taken an interest in. Papinian, though, said it was impossible, since you aren't a citizen, and anyway, he'd already promised the position to somebody else, but once he was reminded of your existence,

he decided that it would be good if you joined this mission
to the Maeatae.'

'It's entirely appropriate that you should,' agreed Castor,
'since it's a response to, among other things, your letter. The
procurator Marcellus is supposed to make it plain to the
Maeatae that if they rebel they can expect harsh reprisals,
not concessions. Papinian thought that sending you along
would send a message to Fortrenn, at least.'

Athenais smiled again, her eyes glinting. 'That was why
the legate had to hold the hearing at once: the Praetorian
Prefect *personally* requested you for the mission – and it's
supposed to leave immediately after the Saturnalia. Oh, he
was annoyed!'

He grinned at her; she smiled back, but then her smile
faded and she asked anxiously, 'Will the people in your
fort be all right? With both the commanders dead and you
away?'

'I hope they'll be all right,' said Memnon. 'It's true things
are going to be tense – but I don't think it would help any
if I were there. Probably make things worse. Who's the new
prefect, do you know?'

'A man called Sittius Faustinus,' Athenais informed him.
'Papinian called him the nephew of an old friend. I think
he's due to arrive in Aballava some time after the Saturnalia.'

There was a burst of rhythmic clapping from downstairs,
and shrieks of laughter so loud that it was impossible to
ignore them. Memnon decided to believe that everything at
Aballava would be all right. He was out of prison with no
case to answer, a new prefect with impeccable court connections would soon be on his way – and it was the first night
of the Saturnalia! 'Sounds like they're dancing!' he told his
companions. 'Let's go down and join them!'

'And *dance*?' asked Castor incredulously.

'Why not?' Memnon grinned. 'You're not too old yet, sir,
and you've got a lovely partner!'

'I can't dance!' objected Castor.

'Listen!' Memnon told him: the clapping had been joined
by a flute and a thumping of feet. 'It's a line dance. Anyone
can do a line dance!'

Athenais giggled. 'He meant that imperial chamberlains

don't dance the line dance in the common room of a posting inn,' she explained.

'But it's the Saturnalia,' Memnon pointed out. 'During the Saturnalia, people can do anything they like.' He got to his feet. 'Come on, both of you – you'll *enjoy* it. You know you will. You're much too serious about things; you need to have some fun.'

Castor stared at him a moment – then laughed. 'I'm going to regret this,' he prophesized, and got up. He took Athenais's hand, and the three of them went downstairs and joined the line dance.

The rest of the night passed in a wild daze. They danced in the common room, arms linked with a crowd of legionaries and their girlfriends; they drank; they danced out into the street, where it was snowing. The street was white, criss-crossed with black lines of footprints, and the legionaries and their girls sang about green growing barley, until one of the girls threw a snowball and the dance broke up in shrieks and laughter and a hail of white missiles. Athenais, her cheeks flushed and her hair coming down, threw a snowball at Castor, very clumsily, then cried out in alarm when it hit him. He laughed and threw one back – but missed.

In the public square at the foot of the fortress bridge some acrobats were performing by torchlight, while a boy beat a tambourine and sang. Vendors sold chestnuts and hot wine and little honeyed pastries, and the snowflakes swirled thickly in and out of the flickering light. They applauded with the crowd, then drifted off to a quieter inn, where they sat and ate and talked.

Castor said he'd always loved the Saturnalia as a child, but that when Commodus was emperor he'd begun to hate it. 'He'd do something horrible every year. You never knew what, but it often seemed to involve someone dressed up in some stupid costume dying in agony in the arena. Immortal gods, that man was frightening! Now every time the season comes round I remember him.' He took a swallow of wine and added, smiling, 'Maybe next year I'll remember tonight, instead!'

When they were leaving the tavern to go home a group of drunken legionaries blundered into them, then noticed Memnon's colour. At once they made gestures to avert ill fortune, and one of them yelled at him to 'take his ill-omened face away'. Memnon shrugged it off, but as they were walking back toward the palace afterward, Athenais asked him if he'd minded it.

He shrugged. 'I'm used to it. It doesn't bother me much. They're just stupid.' After a moment, though, he said, very quietly, 'What bothers me is when people say I'm a demon.' That moment of oppressive memory in the courtroom seemed once again very close.

'Why?' Athenais asked quietly.

He stopped in the snowy street, his eyes searching hers. The snow was still falling, and it clung to her hair and cloak. The only light was the wash of gray off the snow, and the sounds of revelry were muffled. 'Because sometimes I'm afraid it's partly true,' he whispered. 'I'm better at killing people than seems natural or right.'

It was something she surely knew was true, but she whispered, 'Maybe you're touched by a god,' as though she'd never recoiled from him.

'Ha. It's not a god I want to worship, then.' He turned his face away and began to walk on. 'Before I crossed the desert, I was ordinary. Afterward . . . there was so much death. Sometimes I wonder if I died in the desert myself, if I only think I'm Wajjaj and really I'm something that walks around wearing his body . . . I've had too much to drink, or I wouldn't be saying this. Sorry.'

She ran after him and caught his shoulder, pulled him around to face her, and set her fingers against his lips. 'You are not a demon or a ghost,' she told him. 'You're a hero. You saved my life, and Castor's – and you didn't kill Fortrenn and his nephew, or Trupo. If you were really a monster, you would have. If a demon took hold of you in the desert, you mastered it. You crossed the desert and came out the other side still human.'

He looked at her, the intent, direct gaze meeting his, like the encounter of two naked souls. Then he took her hand and kissed it. 'Thank you,' he whispered.

Afterwards he remembered the whole night as perfect, but that moment as blessed.

Sixteen

Memnon had suspected that Proculus would be a right bastard to serve under, so when the *cornicularius* turned out to be a stickler for the rules, a fanatical devotee of armour polish, and frequently irritable with toothache, he was resigned. What he hadn't expected was that the entire embassy should prove a waste of time.

He reported to Proculus immediately after the Saturnalia, dressed in his parade tunic – worn winter-on-the-Danube style, over two thick undertunics and leather breeches. Proculus looked him over with disgust and asked what he'd done with his armour.

'Don't have any armour, sir!' Memnon told him, aghast at the expectation that he should.

'What, *none*?' asked the *cornicularius*. 'Did you pawn *all* of it?'

'African light cavalry, sir! We don't use it.'

'Oh, Hercules!' The guard commander gazed at him with deep displeasure. 'What, you're one of those bareback Numidian circus jockies who don't even use bridles?'

'Uh, we're *Moorish* circus jockies, sir!'

'Don't get smart with me, decurion! I can't possibly put you in the Horse Guard like that; you'll ruin the whole line. I'll see that you're issued some armour.'

Memnon tried to imagine riding Ghibli over the hills while encumbered with armour. The stallion would *not* like the sound or smell of it, he was certain. 'Sir!' he said desperately, 'sir, in my own unit I'm a scout. I, uh, I've never drilled as a guard, and even if you put me in armour, I'd probably still ruin your line, so . . .'

Proculus grimaced. 'It would be a solution, I suppose. If I wanted you in the Horse Guard we'd have to find you a horse, too, wouldn't we? I imagine all you've got is one of those ugly North African screws that isn't even trained to wear a saddle. Very well, we'll use you as a scout during the journey – but you were assigned as a guard for the Lord Procurator, so a guard you will be. I'll see that you're issued parade uniform and armour for the Consular Foot Guard. Borrowed, I suppose, if we can find any to fit. Let's see the state of your weapons.'

Memnon snapped to attention and pulled out his javelins. Proculus sniffed at them, but said nothing: they were obviously not weapons he thought much of, but they were undoubtedly clean and sharp. The knife, however, was another matter.

'What have you done to that?' the *cornicularius* asked in horror, when the black blade emerged for inspection.

'Grease and lamp black, sir!' Memnon informed him. 'So it won't gleam in close work at night.'

Their eyes met. 'That's what you do, is it?' Proculus asked in distaste. 'Well, you're not doing it in my guard! You'll clean that up, and while you're under my orders you'll *keep* it gleaming, you understand?'

'Yes, sir,' Memnon said unhappily.

In fact he simply bought another knife – cheap, with a weak blade that wouldn't keep an edge and which would undoubtedly snap in use, but beautifully shiny – and packed his own away in his gear. Then he went reluctantly to the fortress armoury and allowed the clerks there to try to outfit him in the uniform of the Consular Guard.

The effort was only partially successful. The Consular Guard were expected to have an impressive appearance, and were all well above average height. He was too short, below the minimum allowed. The clerks were unable to supply him with a cuirass of the usual strip-armour without making him look like a hermit crab in an outsized shell. They did give him a helmet, though – a shiny bronze one, with cheek flaps and a red crest – and they found him a large rectangular shield, red with the insignia of the procurator hastily applied in gold. A red tunic and long red cloak completed the uniform. 'Just drape the cloak like *this*,' the clerk advised helpfully, 'and hold the shield like *that*, and it won't be too noticeable that you haven't got the armour.' He grinned. 'Nothing to be done about your height, though.'

Memnon winced at the image of himself as a dwarfish dent in a rank of tall guardsmen. He was glad none of his comrades were along to witness it – only he knew they'd find it so hilarious that he supposed he'd end up telling them about it anyway.

He hoped they were all right. He'd heard no news from Aballava. Farabert's natural successor was his cousin and deputy, Trupo, but if Trupo were elevated it would prolong the feud. German chiefs were elected by their tribes from among the relatives of the previous chief; Memnon hoped fervently that the Frisians would pick someone else. He'd told Castor and Athenais that his own presence at Aballava would only make things worse, but as the days wore on he began to itch to get back there.

All of these vexations seemed unimportant, however, when the embassy finally assembled, on a cold damp morning at the end of December, and he began to suspect that it would be ineffectual.

Sextus Varius Marcellus, Procurator of Britain and the man chosen to warn the Maeatae against rebellion, was the son-in-law of General Avitus Alexianus and the husband of Julia Domna's niece Julia Soaemias. (Athenais had passed on the rumour that Marcellus had won his imperial bride through his willingness to overlook the fact that she was pregnant by her cousin Caracalla.) A Syrian nobleman from Apamea, he conversed with his staff in Greek and swore in Aramaic; he was, apparently, an able financial administrator – but he neither was nor appeared to be a soldier. He favoured silk robes and gold jewellery, and he painted his eyes with kohl and annointed himself with attar of roses; his staff included two flute-players, a kitharist and a famous singer from the mimes. It was glaringly obvious that he was not going to intimidate the northern barbarians.

His escort looked intimidating enough, though: a full cohort of men from the Alban Legion; a five-hundred-strong wing of Gaulish cavalry; a staff of eighty and a part-mounted cohort of the Consular Guard – including one Aurelian Moor.

They looked impressive when they marched out of Eboracum, their standards gleaming in the fitful winter sun.

They looked less impressive a few hours later, covered in mud and plodding along through the sleet, but they kept marching. When they finally pitched camp, Proculus had the Consular Guard up half the night cleaning off their gear.

Their first destination was the capital of the Votadini – the hill fort settlement of Fortrenn son of Talorgen. It lay about eighty miles north of the wall, on a hill overlooking the sea. They arrived there eight days after leaving Eboracum and pitched their tents facing the hill fort, as though about to lay siege to it.

Marcellus sent a slave to announce his arrival, and accepted in return an invitation to the British chieftain's hall. Proculus was displeased: he felt that the procurator should have summoned Fortrenn to meet him. Memnon was not ordinarily a supporter of the 'teach the barbarians who's master!' school of thought, but in this case he agreed with Proculus. If the Maeatae rebelled, the consequences would be bloody and bitter, for them as well as the Romans.

Marcellus agreed to call on Fortrenn the morning after the Roman force arrived. The Foot Guard was to accompany him; accordingly, when the morning dawned clear and cold, Memnon was finally obliged to pretend to be a guardsman. He'd managed to avoid putting on the helmet since it was first allotted to him; the red tunic and cloak had been harder to avoid, but he'd simply put his own hooded cape on over the top as soon as he was out of sight, keeping himself warm and drab and his fancy uniform free of mud. Now, however, he had no choice but to strap on the bronze head-piece. One of the guards handed him a spear, a legionary *pilum*: he'd been banned from carrying his own javelins because they spoiled the drape of his cloak. He took the eight-foot weapon with a sigh. It, too, was officially a javelin, but it was an infantryman's javelin, of a size and weight he had never used. He stacked it against his shield as he fastened his red cloak with Argentocoxus's brooch.

It cheered him up a bit to put Fortrenn's gold torque around his neck; he'd taken it out of the strongroom at Aballava and brought it to Eboracum in case he met the Empress again, but this seemed an even better use for it. That ought to remind Fortrenn about the dangers of angering Rome!

The Foot Guard lined up in a double file, and Proculus came and inspected them. The *cornicularius* frowned at Memnon and moved him first to one end of the line, then to the middle, then to the other end of the line – then shook his head and gave up. Memnon's neighbours gave him resentful looks. They had already made it clear that they weren't happy to have a barbarian from an obscure *numerus* of auxiliaries thrust into their illustrious company, and they were even less happy about him spoiling their parade.

Procurator Marcellus came out of his tent at last, fragrant, silken and glittering, accompanied by an interpreter and two secretaries. He mounted his beautiful white mare, the Foot Guard formed up flanking him, and the whole party moved off, down one hill, over an ice-fringed stream, and up to the gates of the hill fort.

By the time the last guards reached the gates, Marcellus was halfway to the feast hall, and the Britons on guard barely glanced at the tail of the party as it marched past. Memnon glanced up at the lintel as he marched under it and saw that there were a couple of skulls fixed there, a few locks of hair and rotting skin peeling away from the weathered bone. That was the location Fortrenn had picked for his own head. He wondered whether the dead had been Roman or more local enemies.

Fortrenn's hall was big and grand. A fire was burning in the central fire-pit, and the barn-like building felt almost warm after the cold raw wind outside. About fifty of Fortrenn's warriors were inside when the Romans arrived, lining the wall to the right of the fire-pit, but they stood quietly, saying nothing. When Memnon came in, at the end of the party, the Maeatae chieftain was just finishing his speech of welcome. The Foot Guard filed down the left of the fire-pit and stood to attention while Marcellus thanked Fortrenn for the welcome. He spoke in Greek, to the evident consternation of the British audience, and his interpreter translated his words into Latin. The procurator could usually understand what was said to him in Latin, but his command of the spoken language

was uncertain, and he evidently preferred to present the world
with dignified ignorance instead of comical competence.

'You do me honour,' replied Fortrenn. 'And you, Roman
soldiers, be welcome to my hall . . .' He started down the
line of guardsmen. 'The women will bring you mead; I hope
you will . . .' He noticed Memnon and stopped.

Memnon grinned at him. Fortrenn hurried on down the
line and stopped facing him. 'You!' he exclaimed furiously.
'You evil spirit, what are you doing here?'

'The high command thought you'd be unhappy to see me,'
Memnon informed him. He adjusted the edge of his fancy
cloak and let Fortrenn see the gold torque.

The Briton's face flushed under his tattoos. Proculus
hurried up behind him, for once looking very pleased;
Marcellus and his staff approached slowly, frowning; across
the hall, the Britons were whispering urgently to one another.

'Get out!' ordered Fortrenn vehemently. 'Get out of my
hall!'

'I don't take orders from you,' Memnon replied coolly.

'What is the problem?' asked Marcellus's interpreter.

'This dark thing did me injury!' declared Fortrenn, turning
to him. 'He will bring me misfortune: I will not have him
in my hall!'

Proculus smiled grimly. The interpreter spoke to Marcellus,
and the procurator regarded Memnon with a slight frown, as
though trying to recall who he was.

'Send him out!' Fortrenn demanded. 'You and your men
are welcome, Lord Procurator, but this evil creature is not!'

Marcellus made a slight dismissive gesture and spoke to
the interpreter.

'He says, very well,' translated the interpreter. 'The
Ethiopian is dismissed back to camp.'

Proculus stopped smiling. Memnon stood rigid a moment
– then saluted Marcellus and marched out of the hall.

He was aware as he stepped out into the chill air that a
couple of Fortrenn's warriors had slipped away from their
comrades and were following him. He began walking down
the hill quickly. The shield banged against his shin with
each step, slowing him, and the footsteps behind him were
catching up.

He dropped the shield and turned round. The two Britons stopped, facing him, their hands on their knives. Memnon longed for his own knife, stowed carefully at the bottom of his pack, and he gripped the heavy spear with both hands, hoping he could manage it. He did not have a single weapon he trusted.

'Well?' he asked the two warriors.

'Black ghost,' said one, in British, 'return our lord's . . .' Memnon didn't know the word he used, but he had no doubt the man meant the torque.

'Does Fortrenn want his prisoners back as well?' Memnon asked in Latin, 'And his nephew's foreskin?' They didn't seem to understand, so he said in British, 'I will not.'

'Give it back, or we will take it,' said the Briton.

'Fool!' Memnon told him, his voice shaking with anger and frustration. 'You take from Rome, Rome will take from you. Lands, house, wife and children, honour, life – Rome will take.'

'Your lord sent you away,' the Briton pointed out, coming a step closer. 'You do not speak for him.'

'Here!' came a shout from up the hill. Memnon, glancing up, saw Proculus descending on them, splendid in scarlet and gilding, evidently and unmistakeably high-ranking. He had rarely been so pleased to see anyone.

'Trouble, decurion?' asked Proculus, arriving behind the British warriors, who had taken their hands off their knives and now just looked sullen.

'Yes, sir,' Memnon told him, and bent to pick up his shield. 'Thank you, sir.'

Proculus grunted, eying the two Britons. They sneered back at him, then ambled off toward the feast hall, as though they'd only come out to take the air. 'I think I'd better see you out the gate.'

They started down the hill.

'Thank you, sir,' Memnon said again. 'I didn't want to fight them, and I wasn't sure I could win if I did.' His stomach was churning with rage and the aftermath of terror, and he swallowed to settle it.

Proculus raised his eyebrows. 'Even if you'd managed to keep them from killing you, soldier, you would've been in trouble. Those fellows would've said that you attacked them first, and all their friends would've said, yes, that's right, we saw it.' He walked on a few steps, and then said, in a very low voice, 'And probably the Lord Procurator would've accepted what they said, and had you flogged for quarrelling. I . . . regret what happened just now.'

It was an opening, one he'd never expected. 'Sir,' said Memnon quietly, 'there's no point in me being here. I request permission to go home.'

'You were seconded to me by order of the Praetorian Prefect,' said Proculus forbiddingly.

'To send a message to the Maeatae,' agreed Memnon. 'Sir, what sort of message does it send to them if they complain and the Lord Procurator instantly gives in? Better if I'm not here at all.'

Proculus was silent a moment, mouth twisted with disgust – at the procurator's conduct, Memnon was quite certain, and not, for once, at Memnon himself. All he said, though, was, 'I don't think the Lord Procurator remembered who you are. Soldier, you were ordered here, and it's not your job or mine to question our orders.'

Memnon stopped and turned to face him. 'Sir, I had two good friends die last summer; my unit lost a fifth of our strength. The Lord Procurator just gave the Maeatae the *wrong* message, and I'm not supposed to say anything about it? There's no point me being here, sir – worse than that! Me being here, and being sent off like that, actually hurts the mission! And you were at the hearing, you know that back at my unit they *need* me!'

'Do they indeed?' asked Proculus sourly. 'Someone else they need dead, is there?'

Memnon drew in his breath angrily.

'No case to answer, I remember,' said Proculus. 'Why do you want to go back?'

'There's a difficult situation at the fort, sir, and my unit needs all its decurions to keep order. And I'm the old prefect's heir: the men listen to me more than they do to some of the others.'

Proculus grunted and started walking on to the gate. 'I'll speak to the Lord Procurator about it,' he conceded. 'See what he says.'

* * *

He summoned Memnon the following morning. His face was sour. 'I discussed you with Lord Varius Marcellus,' he said. 'He thinks that our Praetorian Prefect made a mistake in sending you to us in the first place, that your presence is offensive to the Britons and makes his work more difficult. He is entirely agreeable to sending you back to your unit at once.'

Memnon swallowed another churning lump of bile. He understood a diplomat wanting to avoid causing unnecessary offense – but he was terribly afraid that the British wouldn't. He imagined another summer of horrible war – then found himself imagining it from the British side, picturing Sulicena and her son huddling in the bracken while legionaries searched for them; picturing the woman raped and the boy butchered.

Maybe Varius Marcellus wasn't a fool; maybe he really did know how to make his meaning clear diplomatically. Memnon feared the procurator's ignorance, cushioned behind barriers of language and custom and experience – but maybe the ignorance was his own. He had to hope so.

'I have a despatch for Eboracum,' Proculus went on. 'You're to carry it there before going on to your own unit. Since there might be trouble on the road, I'll see to it that you have an escort as far as the wall.'

To make sure that the Votadini didn't waylay him. 'Thank you, sir,' Memnon said quietly. 'I appreciate it.'

He arrived back in Eboracum in the evening, fifteen days after he left it. His escort had left him at the wall, and he entered the fortress as he had before, riding Ghibli and leading the mule with his baggage. The fortress, rather to his surprise, accepted his status as a Consular Guard despatch rider, and allotted him stabling for his beasts and a bed in the fort barracks. He handed in Proculus's despatch, then went to bed. Though tired, he lay awake for a while, staring at the ceiling and wondering what to do.

Should he do anything? It seemed presumptuous to think he understood more about the situation than Marcellus and the people who'd appointed him – except that he'd seen the machinery of government abused to support a personal grudge, seen it fail to protect its loyal servants, seen it blind to a problem growing under its nose. It was impossible to retain any faith in it.

He'd intervened in this business once already, passing on to Castor the rumours of rebellion he'd heard from Senorix. That intervention had been acted upon: Marcellus had been despatched on his unusual winter embassy. Probably Memnon's warning hadn't been solely responsible for the imperial decision that an embassy was needed, but it had probably contributed to it. Could he ask Castor to intervene again? Or should he ask Athenais? She might be the better contact in this case: Marcellus was a kinsman of her mistress.

He smiled at the thought of arranging a private meeting with the lovely Athenais. For a happy moment he dwelled on the memory of her fingers against his lips and her beautiful eyes looking urgently into his own.

Oh, gods, here it was again! It was stupid to keep wanting a woman you couldn't have, and it was dishonourable to keep wanting one who belonged to a friend.

He supposed that technically she belonged to the Empress, but it was certainly Castor she loved, and Castor was besotted with her, that was clear enough. It was a little surprising that Castor hadn't already married the girl, but perhaps he had to get permission from the Empress. Yes, of course he did: slaves couldn't marry, so the Empress would have to manumit Athenais before she was wed. At any rate, Athenais was Castor's in intent, if not in law. Castor was a friend, and friends' women were to be left scrupulously alone. If he arranged a meeting, it would have to be with *both* his friends in the Household. Maybe he should invite *them* to dinner, for a change. He was a decurion now: he could afford it.

'I wanted to give you dates,' Memnon told them regretfully, 'but the innkeeper said he didn't have any.'

'This is delicious,' Athenais assured him, taking another bite of the pastry with hazelnuts. They'd worked their way through the first two courses with small talk and reminiscences; now they were on the sweets and wine.

'Your mistress had dates,' Memnon pointed out. 'I thought maybe the innkeeper could get some, too.'

'Emperors and Empresses can get anything they want,' Castor

informed him. 'Snow in midsummer, lettuce in December –
or African dates in the far north of the world. The resources
of innkeepers are more limited. My friend, I've been pleased
to see you again so soon, but I confess I'm also a bit surprised.
Marcellus isn't expected back until the end of the month.'

'Marcellus sent me home,' said Memnon, cheerfulness
abandoning him. 'Who appointed him, anyway?'

'My patron,' replied Castor, startled. 'Though his name was
put forward by Papinian.' He wriggled his fingers. 'He seemed
suitable. He's familiar with the British situation – he's been
Procurator since we arrived. His rank is high enough to show
that we're serious, but not so high as to make it look as though
we're panicking; he's well-born, well-connected, and still
young enough that a difficult winter journey shouldn't be too
much of a burden on him. What's wrong with him?'

Memnon told them.

'He sent you away to please *Fortrenn*?' exclaimed Athenais
in outrage.

'Yes.' Memnon looked up at her with a frown. 'What
worries me is what Fortrenn made of it, what the other
Maeatae chieftains are going to make of an ambassador who's
so quick to give in to them.'

'Yes,' agreed Athenais, almost under her breath.

'I don't know what you decided about what I said in my
letter,' Memnon went on, after a moment. 'About whether
there was a connection between Caracalla asking me about
British factions, and the rumours. I thought if there was . . .
maybe somebody appointed Marcellus because they *knew*
he'd be no use.' He glanced at Castor. 'You said, though,
that you'd informed people who could deal with it.'

Castor was silent a moment, then sighed. 'I told my patron
about the rumours: he investigated and decided to send
Marcellus's embassy. On the other question . . . I took it to
the Augusta, and she said she would deal with it herself.'
He hesitated, then admitted unhappily, 'I haven't asked her
what she did. If anyone is behind those rumours – if they're
not just the idea of the Maeatae themselves – then it's more
likely to be Geta Augustus than Antoninus. Unrest among
the Maeatae means the army will have to remain in Britain
until the situation has stabilized. That's what Geta wants:

time to consolidate his position, here, where people are accustomed to see him in authority. In Rome, his brother's position is much stronger, which is why Antoninus is so eager to get back there. I *think* Antoninus was asking you questions about tribal factions because he'd seen that his brother was interested, and he wanted to know what Geta was up to – but I didn't investigate. I just . . . just can't face having *both* of them hate me. A mother can look into what her son's doing without causing mortal offence.'

'Ah,' said Memnon, in unhappy understanding.

'My mistress hasn't said anything to me, either, about what she did,' Athenais admitted. 'I'll ask her.'

Despite his anxiety about the situation in Aballava, Memnon arranged to stay in Eboracum another night, officially 'to rest my poor horse': he wanted to hear what the Empress had done. When Athenais turned up at the posting-inn that evening, he saw at once that something was wrong. She was flustered and pale, visibly shaken, and almost before they sat down she began speaking in a breathless whisper.

'I went to my mistress. I told her about Marcellus sending you off to please Fortrenn, and she was exasperated, and called him a fool. She says he doesn't understand how to deal with barbarians. She promised to send him a letter at once, telling him to be more forceful. It was everything we could've asked for. But then . . .' Athenais bit her lip. 'Then I asked her about the other matter, and she thought I was nagging her. She was annoyed with me. She said that she'd dealt with it, and that what she said to her son in private was no concern of mine. I said I didn't understand, and she said it wasn't necessary for a slave to understand, only to obey. Then she wanted to know if you two were worrying about it. I promised that I would reassure you that she had dealt with it.' She looked down and finished weakly, 'I think she was just in a bad mood. Everyone has days when every-thing seems irritating, and I *was* nagging.'

Castor was looking sick. 'Is that really what you think?'

There was a silence. Then Athenais looked up again, face very solemn. 'No. I think she asked Geta about it, and he admitted that he had leaked misleading information to the enemy

– and persuaded her to keep quiet about it. She's been afraid
Caracalla will kill him. She wanted Geta to become an Augustus
so that he could protect himself – she doesn't want him disgraced
now. He's always been her favourite son.'

Castor sat silent for a moment – then nodded. 'Yes. He
probably told her that all it was was a few words, enough
to keep the army in Britain another year but not enough to
start a war, and that it was all done with months ago. Probably
he believes that himself. Maybe he's even right.'

Memnon looked from one of them to the other in concern.
'You're saying the Empress knows her son is trying to restart
the war – and she's turning a blind eye to it?'

They both looked at him, hurt and offended. 'He's not
trying to *restart the war*,' Castor snapped. 'He's trying to
secure his position with the army. If the army stays in Britain
next summer, then there's no reason the war should start
again. And whatever Geta did, he's *done* it now.'

'But to tell the *Maeatae* . . . if they were told by somebody they *knew* had access to an *Emperor* that the Empire
won't fight if they rebel . . . how can anyone think it *won't*
start another war?'

There was an uncomfortable silence, and then Castor said,
'I'm sure that they're not getting the same reassurances now.
Marcellus was sent out to make it clear to them that the
Emperors expect them to stand by the treaty . . .'

'But he isn't doing it!'

'I think he *intends* to; I do think the confusion is only
because, as the Empress says, he's used to the sort of diplo-
macy used in the East, not the sort needed in the West. If
the Maeatae have any sense, they'll check to see what's
happening on the wall before they take up arms. They'll see
the garrisons reinforced, the troops well supplied and on high
alert, and they'll realize that rebelling would be a big mistake.'

Memnon was quiet a moment, then shook his head in
bewilderment. 'Surely the *Empress* . . .'

'She doesn't *like* to lie,' Athenais told him. After a moment,
she added, 'Probably she's already cautioned Geta not to do
anything more. The plot, if you can call it that, is already
finished, and the results have already been dealt with as much
as they can be.'

'But . . .' Memnon began, alarmed and afraid.

'My friend,' Castor said, in sudden low urgency, '*you* should forget everything you ever heard or thought about it. The Empress asked if we were worrying about it: she wanted to know if she should silence us.'

He stared in shock. 'I thought . . .'

I thought you said she was the best of the imperial house, was what he wanted to say. *I thought she, at least, deserved the devotion you and Athenais give her so faithfully!* Even as the thought formed itself, he knew that his friends had thought the same – and that the Empress had now betrayed her slave's trust, as surely as the Emperor had betrayed the trust of his freedman.

'She doesn't want to,' Athenais told him, answering his look. 'She likes you. If she decided to do anything, she'd probably just offer you a job, first off; you wouldn't have to fear for your life unless you refused to be bought. And at the moment it's all right: I convinced her that I'd reassure you and you'd accept it. But you do not, you do *not*, want to raise any question about this.' She reached across and caught his wrist. The eyes looking into his own were frightened – for him, he suddenly understood; not for herself. 'Her brother-in-law Alexianus is the general in command of your unit. Her cousin is Praetorian Prefect. If she decided to destroy you she wouldn't even need to turn to an Emperor.'

She let go. He circled the wrist she'd touched with his other hand and looked down. 'If it ends in war,' he said in a low voice, 'thousands of people will die.'

'The Emperor is aware of the rumours now,' Castor pointed out. 'He won't leave Britain until his victory is secure. There shouldn't be another war. And there's *nothing* any of us can do. Our Lord Severus has sent out an ambassador to the Maeatae; Julia Augusta will write to him to tell him to make his message clearer. We must simply trust our masters.'

'But you *don't* trust them,' Memnon pointed out – the harsh truth, which Castor always resisted.

'I trust that the divine power which raised Rome up to impose peace upon the world, will not desert her now,' said Castor, his face strained. 'No mortal can hope for more.'

Seventeen

Memnon returned to Aballava on the seventeenth of January, and found the fort quiet.

The new prefect of the Aurelian Moors, Marcus Sittius Faustinus, had arrived some time before. When Memnon went into the *praetorium* to report back, he found that all the wolfskin rugs and drinking horns had gone, and in their place were Syrian carpets and hangings of worked silk. The new prefect was in the dining room, not in the study where Rogatus had so often met Memnon. He was a plump young man, dark-haired and smooth-shaven, elegantly dressed: his tunic bore the single narrow purple stripe of equestrian rank. He had a secretary with him, a tired-looking older man.

Memnon saluted and introduced himself, and Faustinus looked him up and down with a smile. 'So,' he said, 'you are one they tell me about, yes?' Memnon had met that accent before: Syrian, like the Empress, like Marcellus. At least Faustinus was willing to make the effort to try to communicate in Latin.

'Sir?' Memnon asked respectfully.

'They say, this Memnon, he is much honours, the Empress is his patroness, you use him good, yes? I say, yes, yes, of course! You are sent with Marcellus on embassy: it goes good?'

'I don't know, sir,' Memnon replied cautiously. 'Marcellus sent me home.'

'Ah? Well, to have another decurion, that is good. The men, they are all . . .' He paused, and asked his secretary something in Greek.

'Confined to quarters when off duty,' replied the secretary.

'Confine to quartah!' agreed Faustinus, with a charming smile. 'You know the Lord Faraburr of the Frisians is dead.'

'Yes, sir.'

Faustinus leaned forward and told Memnon confidentially, 'He swore false, this I believe. The gods punish false oath. Many Frisian, they believe this, too. But there is bad feeling, there is much angah. Confine to quartah, yes. You must make thing bettah.'

'I will try, sir.'

'Good, good! The other decurion, they say, "when Memnon gets back", all the time they say it to me. You go talk to them!'

'I will, sir,' said Memnon, saluting. 'Thank you, sir.'

'Dismissed,' said the secretary wearily.

Memnon saluted him, too, before going out.

He found Donatus, Martialis and the other decurions all waiting for him outside the *praetorium*. They all retreated to the headquarters next door, where the others explained what had happened in his absence.

When Farabert's body was discovered, feelings had run high. The Frisians had at first been equally divided between the view that Farabert had been struck down by the gods for a false oath, and that he had been murdered by Memnon. Trupo, however, had been the leading proponent of the murder theory, and when he went off to Eboracum, the opposing view gained ground; when he returned with the admission that his case had been thrown out of court and that he'd narrowly escaped a flogging, his faction was routed. The Frisians held their election to determine who should be their next chief, and the choice had fallen, not on Trupo, but on a more distant cousin of Farabert's called Burcanius. This man was so quiet that Memnon could barely put a face to the name.

Both units had spent a miserable Saturnalia confined to quarters, and both were still bound to their barracks at night and for most of the day. Faustinus had arrived on the second of January and taken over the *praetorium*, though he'd graciously allowed Farabert's widow and children to keep their old rooms until they'd arranged other accommodation for themselves. The self-effacing Burcanius was still in one of the Frisian decurions' rooms, likewise waiting for Lady Ahteha to buy herself a country house and move out. It seemed that he was a poor relation of Farabert's family, and had neither the wealth nor the arrogance of the old chief. Memnon hoped that was good news.

The Aurelian decurions' opinion of Faustinus was, on the whole, positive. Until Rogatus's appointment, the Moors had usually been commanded by very similar inexperienced young equestrians. Faustinus, went the consensus, was better than most: he was willing to leave the actual management of the unit to his decurions, and merely take the credit for their successes. Bad commanders were the ones who actually wanted to run things.

'So,' said Memnon, when the others had finished their summary, 'we need to talk to the Frisian officers and try and get things back to normal. Have you had any meetings with them yet?'

The others looked at one another, then shook their heads. Memnon grimaced, wondering if they would have arranged a meeting if they hadn't been waiting for the return of Rogatus's heir.

'We should set one up for tomorrow, then,' he said. 'In the *praetorium*, if Faustinus will agree; otherwise, in the chapel of the standards.'

Faustinus had no objection to hosting the meeting, and even offered to provide wine. Memnon was relieved: the *praetorium* was heated, the chapel was bitterly cold, and he felt the meeting would work better if everyone was comfortable.

Accordingly, everyone trooped into the *praetorium* dining room next morning: ten decurions belonging to the Aurelian Moors and a dozen Frisians whose ranks and responsibilities were less defined in military terms, but who were judged by their comrades as noble and hence as deserving of a place at the conference. Burcanius was among the first to arrive: a thin, anxious looking man some years older than Memnon, white-blond with a long drooping moustache. Faustinus, who stood at the door to welcome the arrivals, shook his hand and acknowledged the salute of everyone else.

Faustinus's slaves served wine and everyone sat down, Frisians on one side of the room, Moors on the other. There was a desultory mutter of conversation. Memnon realized, with a stab of irritation, that everyone was waiting for him to open the meeting.

'Fellow soldiers!' he exclaimed – and was annoyed by the instant silence.

'All right,' he said bluntly, 'the fort's in a mess. Anybody going to dispute that?'

'Do we listen to this murderer?' asked Trupo loudly.

Memnon stared at him until the Frisian met his eyes. 'We went over that in Eboracum.'

Trupo spat. 'And you escaped justice because of your *powerful friends*!'

Memnon drew in his breath in exasperation. 'What do you want to do, call in the Commissary to investigate? See which of us can stand the rack longer? The fort's in a mess. Our comrades have been confined to quarters for a month, everyone's ready to kill, but if we start fighting, the high command will come down on us with floggings and executions all round. That what you want?'

'*I* do not want,' said Burcanius, in a deep, slow voice, looking at Memnon.

'Good,' said Memnon, nodding to him, 'because I . . . because our Lord Prefect Faustinus doesn't want it either. We need to start things working again. We need some kind of public agreement, maybe with an exchange of oaths, and then we need to make arrangements for letting the men out by turns – and *then* we need to do something to lower the tension.'

Burcanius was still looking at him. 'The big thing that make the tension,' Burcanius said in his halting Latin, 'is this that we hear, that the Aurelian Moors will keep Aballava, and we will be send away.'

Memnon drew a deep breath, then raised both hands, palms out. 'I swear by my ancestors, and by Juno Caelestis, and by the Emperors' good fortune, that I know nothing about that!' He lowered his hands. 'If you like, I'll write to my friends at court and ask them to find out,'

Burcanius nodded. 'Yes.'

'Fine. I'll do that today. What I suspect, though, is that my friends won't be able to find out, because I don't think it's been decided yet. I don't think the high command's going to make up its mind until it's ready to leave, and with the unrest among the Britons, who knows when that will be? I admit, though, that I think there's a chance they will decide to keep us here, because they found us pretty useful during the war. Now, personally I have no objection to sharing the fort. Our unit's been moved a lot, and we're used to sharing forts. I do know, though, that the high command isn't going to keep these two units in the same fort unless we give 'em some evidence that we won't kill each other – and I think they like *us* better than they like *you*. So it seems to me that if you Frisians want to stay here, you need to put some work into convincing the high command that you can get on with us.'

Burcanius's thoughtful gaze didn't alter. 'You agree to share the fort?'

'I always expected to, and I'm still willing to.'

The Frisian let out his breath slowly, frowning. 'The Lady Ahteha,' he said deliberately, 'told Lord Farabert he is no man if he lets foreigners and commoners move into his house. Now, I think that she did not understand how things are. We are not the masters here. Aballava belongs to the Romans, not the Frisians. If they send more men here, it is their right. Farabert was not wise, to see Rogatus as his enemy. There was no need to be enemies: easily he could make Rogatus his friend.'

There was a stir from among the Frisians, and Burcanius turned to glare at Trupo. 'Farabert won him easily, when he tried!' he repeated. 'We all see this, before the boar-hunt. Rogatus is all happy, trusting, glad that our Lord Farabert wants to be his friend. Why did not Farabert make him a friend when he first comes here? Then all this trouble is missed.' He turned back to Memnon. 'You agree to share the fort? You will swear this?'

Memnon spread his hands. 'Yes. Understand, I have no power over the generals. I can only swear for myself and the men who follow me. I am willing, though, to swear a peace.'

Trupo got to his feet. 'This is a dodge!' he complained angrily. 'In Eboracum he swore that he never drew his knife on Farabert – knowing perfectly well that Farabert wasn't killed with a knife!'

Memnon faced him squarely. 'I'd be willing to swear peace with *you*, Trupo, with no dodging, if you'll do the same.'

There was a silence. Trupo's face was tense and uncertain. His cloak was loose, and Memnon noticed for the first time that there was a black line on the side of his throat: lamp-black, trapped under the skin when Memnon's knife cut it.

'You wouldn't come after me?' Trupo asked at last.

Memnon realized that the man really did believe that rubbish about turning invisible and secret African arts. *I hid in a tree!* he wanted to shout. *There was nothing magical about it!* At the same time, he was tempted to play up to the stupidity, see just how much mighty-sorceror guff Trupo was willing to swallow before he gagged.

Instead he said soberly, 'I don't want a feud. Rogatus is dead, and so is Farabert: let it end there. I'll swear to leave you alone if you'll swear to leave me alone.' He glanced at the other Frisians, who were all watching him intently. 'This division in the fort is a stink, and the high command doesn't care which unit's to blame: it'll think we all smell bad. We'll *all* have the reputation of troops that can't get along with their fellow soldiers, and that won't be good for anybody. If we patch things up, though, it'll make the generals happy, and we'll all benefit.'

Burcanius nodded, then smiled, showing missing teeth. 'We hold a public ceremony, we swear oaths,' he said. 'You swear that you agree to share the fort. We agree our men are out of quarters every other day. We talk about games and marches, to make them easier.'

'Sounds good to me,' agreed Memnon, deeply relieved.

January, February: it rained, and snowed, and rained some more. Memnon wrote a letter to Castor, using the clerk Verinus as scribe, asking whether the Moors would remain in Britain or return to the Danube. Castor wrote back saying that the matter had yet to be submitted to the Emperor, and nothing was decided. A few weeks later, however, came a letter from Athenais. She said that she had made inquiries, and discovered that the legate of the Sixth Victrix was planning to ask for the Moors to be permanently assigned to

Britain, on the grounds that he needed more cavalry scouts. She'd met with the legate, she continued, and asked him about the fort of Aballava: his preference was for the Moors and the Frisians to share the fort, but he would move the Frisians elsewhere if the tension between the two units persisted.

It was a very useful letter. Memnon showed it to Burcanius, who shared the contents with the Frisian Formation: its effect on their attitude was immediate.

March, April: it rained some more. The whole winter and spring were spent in the perpetual mud, engaged upon manoeuvres intended to reconcile the Moors and the Frisians. The only good thing that could be said about it was that it seemed to be working – though sometimes Memnon thought that this was only because it united the men against a common enemy: their officers.

What the men didn't seem to realize, he thought sourly, was that those officers saw more of the mud and snow than anybody: supervising the men at all times meant you had to be out in the field with the first and return with the last. It was the prefect who got to stay in the nice warm *praetorium*, and only come out to the tribunal occasionally to award prizes. Lucky prefect.

Faustinus did not improve on closer acquaintance. He was pleasant to those he thought had power or influence that might be useful to him; everyone else he ignored. He left most of the actual work of organizing the affairs of the *numerus* to his secretary, Sabinus – who was not merely a slave, but was not even Faustinus's slave. He belonged to Faustinus's father, and had been sent to give the young man's career prospects a boost by managing the *numerus* for him. The Moors soon became resigned to following his orders, but the Frisians were disgusted.

Burcanius was more of a real commander than the Moors' prefect and his slave: the Frisian leader took his share of hardship with his men. Memnon grew to like Burcanius: a quiet, modest man, but reliable. He got on well with most of the Frisian officers, in fact – and the ones he didn't get on with, avoided him, so that was all right. Trupo and his

friends dwindled over the months from looming threat to
marginal figures griping in taverns, taken seriously by no
one. It helped when Farabert's widow, Ahteha, finally moved
out of the *praetorium* and into a country villa. Memnon
hadn't been aware of the steady stream of venom the women
had poured out, until it suddenly ended. Free of that baleful
insistence on Frisian honour and status, the Frisians relaxed
into reasonable compromises. Memnon supposed that
working together in horrible weather had some benefits after
all.

In April came a note from Castor, shockingly brief: he
had married Athenais, he said; he was sure Memnon wished
him joy.

Memnon's first reaction was to wish him in Hades. Castor
had warned him away from Athenais because she belonged to
the Empress – and had then slept with her himself. True, that
was after Athenais herself rejected Memnon – but he'd thought,
he really had, that in the last few meetings something had been
changing between them.

He'd thought, to tell the truth, that she'd begun to fall in
love with him.

Well, *that* was a dishonourable little revelation, wasn't it?
His friend's woman, and he'd been hoping that he might
succeed in stealing her away, after all! He ought to be pleased
that she and Castor had finally got to marry. She'd turned
to Castor when the young Emperor tormented her: was it
reasonable to say that Castor should have turned her down?
Memnon certainly wouldn't have! Castor loved her. He was
a respected inhabitant of the world she'd grown up in –
educated, cultured, wealthy – not a semi-illiterate barbarian.
He was a man of courage, integrity and undoubted decency.
Athenais had chosen well – and Memnon, as a friend of
both, should be ashamed of his jealous resentment.

He did feel ashamed of it. He even wrote a letter of congratulations to the happy couple, without a single snide or gloomy
word in it. But he still felt jealous and resentful. They could
at least have invited him to the wedding.

In May, Prefect Faustinus received a letter. The first part
simply confirmed what Athenais's letter had told everyone

in the fort months before: that the Moors would stay posted to Aballava. The second part, though, was news. Faustinus summoned a meeting of all the fort's officers to discuss it.

'We receive the Emperor *himself*!' Faustinus told them gleefully. His Latin had improved over the winter, but it was still erratic. 'Our Lord Severus Augustus, he wants to tour the wall before he goes home. He will stay in Uxelodunum for the night, but he will come west to Aballava next day. He will discharge the men who have served their time, give honours to the men who do bravely in the war, and then he will eat lunch *here* before he goes back to Uxelodunum!'

Memnon arranged his face in a suitably awed expression. Inwardly he was consumed with impatience. The sun was shining, hawthorn flowered in the hedgerows, and the woods were full of bluebells. First Squadron had gone to exercise their horses on the beach, and Memnon had no doubt that they'd all dismounted and were lying about in the sun gossiping – while he was stuck in the *praetorium* with Faustinus and Burcanius. Who in his right mind would want to be a decurion?

'We need to make this fort beautiful,' Faustinus went on. 'We arrange working parties, yes? To clean everything and make it beautiful. The Emperor, he is here at the third of June. That will be yes, eighteen days from now. We must work hard!'

'Yes, sir!' Memnon agreed, inwardly wincing. He'd wanted to give the men a rest after the winter's muddy exercises. He'd wanted to take a rest himself.

'Burcanius . . .' Faustinus frowned at his fellow commander. 'Maybe you buy some new clothes, yes? I can tell you a good place in Eboracum, if you want to buy something in silk.'

'I have good clothes,' the Frisian commander said in his deep voice. 'I save them for festivals.' He was, as all the fort knew, far from wealthy.

'Good, good! But . . . are they Roman?'

'*I* am not Roman,' Burcanius pointed out reasonably.

'Ah, yes, but . . . this is for a lunch with the *Emperor*! For that I think you want something in the Roman style.'

Burcanius gave him the thoughtful look, and Memnon knew that the Frisian had no intention whatsoever of spending his time and money going to Eboracum to buy silk. Too polite to say as much to Faustinus, however, he merely asked, 'What about Memnon?'

Faustinus smiled amiably at both of them. 'At the lunch will be the fort commanders, the Emperor, the staff of the Emperor. Memnon is decurion.'

Burcanius' thoughtful look darkened. 'Why should he not come to the lunch with the Emperor? He will be given honours, yes?'

'I think that he will get honours, yes, for what he does in the war,' said Faustinus testily. 'But he is decurion, and the Emperor, he has many great men on the staff. There is not space for decurions.'

Burcanius scowled. Memnon shot him a quelling look and said brightly, 'So what do you want done to the fort, sir?'

Sabinus the secretary produced a lengthy list. 'We'll arrange a welcome at the gates, of course,' he concluded. 'Fifteen of the tallest and most impressive men from each unit should form an aisle on either side of the gate, and my Lord Sittius Faustinus and Burcanius can stand before the gate to welcome the Emperor to the fort.'

'What about the officers?' asked Burcanius, frowning again.

'They will be with their squadrons,' explained Faustinus. 'On the parade ground.'

'I think it is better if the senior officers are with us,' said Burcanius.

Faustinus hesitated. 'Maybe one each. That is Donatus for me, and Rautio for you.'

'What about Memnon?' asked Burcanius, frowning again.

'He is most junior decurion,' Faustinus pointed out. 'Also, he is very ill-omened colour. I think the Emperor is offended if he is greet by black man: it is bad omen.' He gave Memnon a sunny smile. 'You do not mind?'

Their eyes met for a moment. Then Memnon ducked his head. 'No, sir,' he said mildly.

'Good,' said Faustinus, relieved. 'Well, then, that is that?'

Memnon took his leave and went off to organize cleaning rotas. Burcanius, however, followed him out of the *praetorium*.

'This is unjust,' the Frisian said seriously. 'Faustinus cheats you. He wants to steal the credit for what you do, and so he does not want you to speak to the Emperor.'

Memnon shrugged. Faustinus did try to appropriate the credit for anything and everything good in Aballava. It was often hard to persuade the Frisians to keep calm about it: they valued fame. 'Of course he takes credit for what we do,' he said casually. 'The high command *know* that. Don't worry about it.'

Burcanius gave him a doubtful look, and Memnon forced a grin. 'Don't worry!' he said again. 'I'm going to be getting a pile of medals as it is: I don't need to greet the Emperor at the gates or have lunch with him. It's going to be a pretty deadly meal anyway, from the look of things, with Faustinus trying to suck up to everyone in sight.'

'Your friend Castor the chamberlain – he will not be there?'

'He may be in the Emperor's entourage,' Memnon admitted, 'but he won't be at the lunch. The Emperor doesn't eat with his freedmen. If Castor *is* around, I'll take him off for lunch at The Bull down in the village, and, believe me, we'll enjoy ourselves much more than your lot. Don't worry!'

Afterwards, though, arranging rosters for the clean-up duties, he found his heart beating hard with anger. 'Ill-omened colour' – what a *stupid* excuse! Couldn't the aristocratic young idiot be bothered to come up with something better than that? 'I need you to supervise the rest of the men', perhaps, or, 'you'll be too busy preparing to receive your medals'? 'Ill-omened colour' – it was an idiotic idea to begin with! What did the Romans think people south of the desert did anyway? Have nothing but bad luck? Faustinus did half-believe the superstition, though: Memnon had noticed that the prefect never wanted to see him first thing in the morning. Idiot!

Memnon found that he was bending his stylus, and hastily put it down before he broke it in half. Ruefully, he admitted to himself that his anger was only partly at Faustinus: that was now an old irritation, after all. No, the real sore point was Castor. Despite his best efforts to be reasonable about it, Memnon was still hurt and angry.

Now the Emperor was coming here, and Castor hadn't warned him. There was no possible excuse for that: Castor was *a memoria*! He knew the imperial schedule before the Emperor himself did, let alone before whatever official had written to Faustinus!

Nothing to be done about it, though. He ran a finger down the roster for special cleaning duties, mentally simplifying the tasks Faustinus had requested: no need to scrub the stonework, brushing it down would do; bronze hinges could be painted instead of polished; fresh straw would be as good a mud-cover as gravel in most areas . . .

He stopped, wondering what had become of the man he'd been. Once he would've prepared for the visit of a Big General by dreaming up an elaborate joke; now he plodded along arranging *duties*. When had he become so responsible, so *joyless*?

He wished he'd gone ahead and insisted on that discharge. He hadn't wanted to abandon his friends while their situation was so delicate and dangerous – but he feared that now he'd lost his chance, that if he wrote to Castor again he'd get no reply.

Being a decurion was a bastard of a life: all the hard work of a common soldier, none of the fun, and all the misery of accounts and rosters piled on top. He'd even lost his clerk: old Verinus had handed in his resignation in April. So now Memnon was back to doing the office work himself – probably for the next thirteen or however many years. All his friends at court would disappear with the court, back to Rome, and he would remain here in Aballava, serving Faustinus and Faustinus's idiot successors – unless there was a rebellion, of course, and they all got killed. Even if he survived until his discharge, he'd probably be so old and sour by the time he made it that no pretty bright-eyed girl would want him.

He sat staring blindly at the roster, running his thumb back and forth over his lips, a hard knot of frustration and resentment in his stomach. Then he closed the tablets and pushed them aside. 'What I need is some fun,' he said out loud, and went down to the fort village to have a drink and think about things.

On the third of June he was waiting in one of the turrets of the wall, just over a mile from Aballava. He could see the fort to his right: swept and shining clean, its gate garlanded with roses. The men who inhabited it were still swarming about in such last-minute preparations as could be completed in one's best parade uniform – and no doubt asking one another if anybody had seen Memnon.

He'd slipped away without telling anyone what he intended to do. The first five or six jokes he'd thought of had required assistance, and he'd ruled them out. He couldn't ask help from his men, simply because they *were* his men now, not his tent-mates – and he had a strong suspicion that if he'd approached any of his fellow decurions, they would've told him it was a very bad idea to play jokes on an emperor. He suspected that this was indeed the case – but he was so sick of being responsible and hard-working that he didn't care. His one regret was that the only solo prank he'd managed to come up with wasn't funnier.

Memnon sat on top of his turret. It was a bright sunny morning, though banks of cloud suggested that there might be showers later. He could already make out a shadow on the road that would be the Emperor and his entourage.

As he watched, the shadow gradually resolved itself: a small party of outriders; a double file of infantry in gold and crimson, bearing the standards; another rank of gold and crimson bringing up the rear – and in the centre, a bulk of gold and purple that gradually turned into a covered litter, carried by a dozen bearers, and followed by an assortment of carriages and horsemen.

He let the outriders go by, then descended the turret, opened the door, and slid out. Nobody was watching. The watch-turrets along the wall were generally kept locked when not in use – but the decurions had access to the keys.

He was not wearing his parade uniform. He had a good tunic on, but it was black, as was the long cloak he had purchased specially. He held a wreath of dark cypress: if black was an ill-omened colour, then he was as ominous as he could make himself. He had, however, carefully left all his weapons in the fort: there was no sense in alarming the Praetorian Guard unduly.

He waited at the fort-side of the turret until the infantry had gone by, then stepped out into the middle of the road.

The litter was about fifty feet away. The curtains were tied up at the sides, and he could see the occupant: a thin old man in a purple cloak, white-haired and bearded, reclining on his side while reading a scroll. The Praetorians to either side of the litter noticed the intruder with a shout, and there was a confused flurry among them. The old man looked up and saw the obstacle. The litter bearers continued their steady pace forward, and Memnon watched in fascination as the Emperor's eyes widened and his lips contracted in something akin to terror.

Too late now to back out now. 'Severus Augustus!' he proclaimed loudly, holding up his wreath of cypress. 'Conquerer of Parthia, Conquerer of Britain! Welcome!'

Severus sat bolt upright in his litter. 'Get him *awaaay* from me!' he shrieked in horror.

The litter halted, and the Praetorian Guards surged forward. Memnon dropped his wreath and held up both hands, empty. The spears did move out of line in response, but the beefy hands that immediately laid hold of him were rough.

'Get him *away*!' cried the Emperor again, as the guards bundled Memnon off to the side.

It was, Memnon thought, entirely excessive. 'Conquerer of the whole world!' he yelled back, frightened and disgusted. 'Why don't you go conquer somewhere else?'

At that one of the guards clouted him across the mouth, so hard that he was thrown back against one of the men holding him. The man dropped him, and he fell, spitting blood, and had just time to bring up his arms to protect his head before they began to kick him.

He was appalled at their ferocity, stunned by the pain. He tried to curl up and make himself limp, to roll with the buffets, but they seemed to come from all directions at once. Someone was shouting; he hoped that they were shouting for the soldiers to stop.

Apparently they were: the kicking ended. Memnon lay curled up on the ground breathing in little whimpering gasps, wondering giddily if they'd broken his ribs. 'You!' commanded a voice. 'Get up!'

Memnon tentatively moved his arms away from his face; nobody shoved a boot into his nose, so he tried to get up.

This proved to be a mistake: a wave of dizziness swept over him and he had to drop back on to hands and knees and vomit: oh, gods, he *hurt*! Somebody grabbed him by the collar.

He groaned and sank back on his haunches. 'Maybe you could talk to me like this instead?' he asked hopefully, looking up. The man who had hold of him was a centurion of the Praetorian Guard, a tall bony man with a hatchet face under the transverse crest of his helmet.

'Who are you and what do you think you were doing just now?' demanded the centurion, not letting go of the collar.

Memnon had to turn his face aside to spit out a mouthful of blood. 'Memnon, sir!' he said, and spat again. 'Decurion, First Squadron of the Aurelian Moors, sir! I was trying to play a joke.'

'A joke?' replied the centurion indignantly. 'Our Lord Severus didn't think it was very funny!'

'No, sir,' muttered Memnon. 'I noticed that.'

A couple of the Praetorians laughed nervously. The centurion scowled. 'You say you're a decurion?'

'Yes, sir. From Aballava, the fort down the road there. We've been preparing to welcome Our Lord the Augustus, and I just thought I'd do a joke welcome first. I didn't mean to upset anybody, sir. It was only a joke.' His chin was wet; he wiped it, and his hand came away red.

The centurion snorted and let go of the collar. 'Search him!' he ordered.

The men hauled Memnon to his feet and searched him. He noticed that the last of the infantry was still marching past: the men in the ranks cast curious glances at the little group at the side. That beating must in fact have been halted very quickly. He was fervently glad of it.

'Well, decurion,' said the centurion, when the guards had ascertained that Memnon was unarmed, 'nobody liked your ugly joke. We'll take you to your fort and, if you are who you claim to be, you can spend the rest of the Emperor's visit in the lock-up. Beyond that we'll leave it to your prefect.'

'Yes, sir,' murmured Memnon: there didn't seem to be anything else he could say.

* * *

When Memnon staggered in through the gate of Aballava between two Praetorians, his appearance was greeted with consternation. The men on the gate confirmed, however, that he was indeed a decurion of the Aurelian Moors, and the Praetorian centurion had him thrown in the spare room of the southern gatehouse which served the fort as a lock-up, before going off to report the incident.

Memnon curled up on the single bench seat of the dark little room and lay quietly shaking. He was covered in bruises and he acknowledged in a quiet corner of his awareness that the men who'd kicked him would probably have killed him if the centurion hadn't stopped them. They'd taken their cue from the Emperor, but why the Emperor had been so frightened he couldn't guess. Severus was, after all, a North African: he should've been used to Ethiopians.

It was a couple of hours later and he was drowsing when there were voices outside the door, and then the unmistakeable sound of a key in the lock. He sat up and put a hand over his eyes at the sudden flood of light.

'It will be all right,' Castor told the guard, 'you can lock me in with him.'

'Yes, sir,' said the guard. He was a Moor from Donatus's squadron; his name was Koceila. 'You all right, Memnon?'

'More or less,' Memnon replied. 'Wouldn't mind a drink of water.'

'I'll fetch it.' Koceila hesitated, hand on door. 'What did you do, anyway?'

Memnon started to laugh, then stopped, because it hurt his mouth and sides. 'It was supposed to be a joke,' he explained. 'You know Faustinus said I shouldn't welcome the Emperor because I'm an ill-omened colour? I just thought I'd meet Our Lord on the road and welcome him, looking ominous. I was going to give him Faustinus's speech of welcome – well, with a few small changes – but I never got a chance.'

'Neither did Faustinus,' said Koceila, taking his hand off the door and speaking eagerly. 'The Emperor came barrelling through the gates like the Furies were after him, and went and holed up in the *praetorium*. He's still there. No presentations, no parades.'

'All that work for nothing!' sighed Memnon. He thought

about it a minute, then found himself grinning, sore lips and all. 'I wish I'd seen Faustinus's face.'

Koceila shook his head. 'It wasn't *worth* it, Memnon! Juno Caelestis, you don't play jokes on *Emperors*!' Then he shot a guilty look at Castor and went out, locking the door behind him. The room was not completely dark – a small amount of light filtered in through the wooden floorboards of the room above – but it was not enough to let him see Castor's expression.

'Why,' said Castor, in a tone of controlled fury, 'by all the gods above the earth and under it, did you pull a stupid trick like that?'

Memnon started to lean back against the wall, found that it hurt the bruises, and leaned forward instead, elbows on knees. 'It was just a joke, sir!' he protested. 'How could I know he was going to react like that? I still don't understand why he did.'

'Apparently,' said Castor tightly, 'he was approaching the furthest west he'd ever travelled, and it started him thinking about his life and his accomplishments. He'd decided to take whatever he met with next as an omen for his future.'

'Oh.' Memnon remembered the man in the litter again, the eyes widening, the terrified shriek. He thought about it a little longer, then began to laugh. He couldn't help it. 'Oh, immortal gods!' He put his hands over his mouth. 'Cypress wreath and all, o gods!'

'It was stupid!' exclaimed Castor furiously. 'Do you know how superstitious he is? Do you know how *ill* he's been? A trick like that, a *stupid, stupid* dangerous trick like that – how could you?'

'Well I didn't know it was going to be so dangerous!' Memnon pointed out reasonably. 'You think I would have done it if I had?'

'What was the *point*?' demanded Castor.

'The point was I was sick to the back teeth of being a responsible, reliable decurion, and I wanted to do something really mad and wild. Ha! I scared him, didn't I? Lucius Septimius Severus Augustus, Parthicus, Britannicus, Emperor of the Romans, Lord of the World, was scared – of me! Is there another man alive who can say that?'

Castor stood stock-still looking at him. It was still too dark to see his expression, but Memnon found that he could imagine it. 'Do you know what you've thrown away?' the chamberlain asked. 'You were going to get the citizenship, along with a whole rack of medals – and now you won't.'

Memnon drew in his breath slowly. The citizenship. The citizenship of Rome. The medals weren't important, but the citizenship . . . still, what use would it have been, without a discharge? The life he wanted, the wife and children and bit of land – they would have remained out of reach, more tantalizing for being that much closer. 'Well,' he said flatly, 'I don't suppose you'd arranged a discharge as well, without telling me?'

'We'd agreed that you'd confirm that you wanted it after the Saturnalia, and you didn't.'

'*You* never answered my last letter, sir. Or asked me to your wedding. Or slipped me a warning about *this* business. I'd about concluded that if I did write you, I wouldn't get any answer. Sir.'

That was met with silence.

'I never asked you for friendship,' Memnon said. The hurt and anger he'd been feeling for months bubbled to the surface, and he kept his voice quiet only with an effort. Only a fraction of what he felt was aimed at Castor, anyway: most was a kind of rage against the fate which had him fixed here doing work he loathed and did badly. 'I was pleased when you gave it, but I never insisted on it. You're a great man: I'm a plain one. You were generous and friendly, though, and maybe I started to presume. If I did something that offended you, though – it would have been a lot better to tell me, instead of just dropping me and leaving me guessing.'

There was another silence – and then Castor said abruptly, 'I'm sorry.' After a moment he added softly, 'It wasn't anything you did. It was just . . . Athenais likes you, and I understand why. You saved her, and I've only failed her, again and again. It made me unhappy, so whenever I had any business that concerned you, I put it off – but I didn't intend to drop you.'

'Oh, you stupid man,' said Memnon incredulously. 'You

call what I did this morning stupid, but that, that's stupid. That girl is *yours* now, your legal wife, and she's never been anything but loyal. I don't think *anybody* could steal her from you, but even if I could, I wouldn't. I don't steal from my friends.'

'Maybe I was stupid,' conceded Castor. He came over to the bench, and Memnon moved aside to give him space. The chamberlain sat down heavily. 'It's just that I still find it hard to believe my luck, and I keep worrying that one day she'll come to her senses.'

'Ha.' So, Castor was jealous! His lovely girl had taken a liking to a younger man, and he knew it, and it worried him. *That* made sense. 'She's a beautiful, clever woman, that's for sure,' Memnon said carefully. 'And she loves you, that's plain to me, however much you doubt it. Congratulations on your marriage!'

Castor nodded. 'I'm . . . sorry,' he said again. Then he went on: 'You *would've* been invited to the wedding, you know, only there wasn't one. We married very quietly, to attract as little attention as possible. My patron . . . he's been ill again, and if anything happens to me – if Antoninus . . . takes action – I don't want him to come after her as well.' He paused, then added, a little breathlessly, 'She's expecting a baby.'

Oh. That certainly explained the sudden marriage. 'Congratulations again, sir!'

'Thank you.' Castor paused again, then confessed in a rush, 'The Empress didn't want her household encumbered with a pregnant slave. She told Athenais to choose between aborting the child and leaving the imperial staff, and Athenais choose to keep the child and marry me. I . . . I was so glad!'

'Is it your first, sir?'

There was a moment's silence, and then Castor said, in a very low voice, 'My first wife had children, but they died. One lived three days; the others . . . not so long. I want this one so much – I didn't realize how much, until I knew she was expecting it. It will be freeborn, too: Our Lady Julia Augusta manumitted Athenais when she dismissed her. My child will grow up free, away from the court, away from . . . from the kind of things I've seen all my life.'

'It'll probably be clever,' Memnon offered. 'Should be, with two clever parents.'

They sat in silence for another minute, and then Castor said, 'It *was* a really stupid joke.'

'Well, yes,' admitted Memnon. 'I realize that – now.'

Eighteen

The stupidity of the joke became increasingly clear over the days that followed. Prefect Sittius Faustinus was furious that his chance to impress the Emperor had been ruined by a subordinate's notion of humour, and was – unsurprisingly – very angry with the subordinate. His first reaction, apparently, was to have Memnon demoted and flogged, but his secretary talked him out of it: Memnon's friends at court might revenge it, or it might provoke the Moors to mutiny. True, mutinies could be suppressed – but to provoke one during your first command would blight a young officer's career.

Faustinus therefore enlisted his secretary's help to make Memnon's life a misery in less dramatic ways. All the dirty jobs went to First Squadron; if none were available, an errand was found for First Squadron's decurion. Night watches were assigned for successive nights, meetings were called for early morning, or called at short notice; if Memnon turned up late, or missed one, he was reprimanded and assigned extra duties as a punishment. Worst of all, Sabinus presented him with a huge stack of indecipherable ledgers and told him to sort out the unit's books. Confronted with the malignant enigma of their pages, Memnon seriously considered setting fire to headquarters to get rid of the horrible things; the only reason he didn't was that nobody would believe it was an accident.

When the order came for the Moors to perform another reconnaissance to the north, he welcomed it as an alternative to taking his horse and deserting.

The Moors were ordered to ride up to the encampment they'd occupied the previous summer. A British legion was preparing to build a permanent fort on the site, but it would not march north until the Moors reported back. The murmurs of rebellion among the Maeatae had not died down, despite – or because of – Marcellus's embassy, and the Emperor had been obliged to postpone his departure from Britain. Other legions which had been sent north to construct garrison forts reported serious difficulties with the local tribes. Supplies of timber and iron had gone missing – and scouts had gone missing, too. Protests brought apologies, and assurances that the Maeatae had every intention of keeping the treaty; promises, too, that whoever was obstructing the building of the garrison forts would be punished – but no one ever was punished, not that the Romans heard.

It was late July when they set out, the full *numerus*, two hundred and thirty-eight men in ten under-strength squadrons. Almost as soon as they crossed the wall, they encountered signs that the Novantae were preparing for war.

As a decurion, Memnon no longer rode out ahead of his friends, but the traces were sufficiently clear that he didn't even need to wait for his scouts to report. The ripening fields were being tended by women, children and old men; the horses were missing and the cattle had been moved up towards the hill forts; there were tracks, here and there, of groups of men heading up into the hills, but none coming back.

'Sir,' Memnon told the prefect, at the end of their first day beyond the wall, 'we should go back south at once.'

Faustinus sneered. 'Scared, decurion?'

'Sir, they're *mustering*,' Donatus intervened. 'We should go back and report it at once.'

Faustinus waved it off. 'I will send report, yes. But first we complete our mission!'

'Sir . . .' began Memnon.

'This is *cowardice*!' exclaimed Faustinus with contempt. 'To run away without we even see an enemy!'

'It's not *one* enemy we're worried about, sir,' objected Donatus. 'The Novantae can put two or three thousand warriors into the field; the Selgovae even more. We're a small unit: if we actually saw them, it would be the end of us.'

'They do not dare,' replied the prefect confidently. 'Not unless they see that we are afraid: do we show fear, and make them bold? Besides, we do not know this, that they are mustering! Maybe they meet for tribal business, or for praying to their gods. No, we continue our mission!'

They rode on boldly along the road north. It made Memnon's skin crawl to take Ghibli openly along that track, and at a walk, too. His every instinct screamed that if they continued the mission, they should move fast and avoid the roads.

On the third day they arrived at the lands of the Selgovae, and found the same pattern as among the Novantae. Late in the afternoon they reached the old encampment and found that all the makeshift structures which had been put up the previous year had now been pulled down: nothing was left but the earthworks.

'*This* we can report!' Faustinus said triumphantly. 'This is against the treaty. All that before, that was just worrying.'

'Yes, sir,' said Memnon. 'Sir, we should get out of here.'

Faustinus snorted in contempt and glanced around the old encampment. Even without the shelters, it was a good camp-site, level and clear, with a stream to supply running water, and the earthworks gave it some protection. They were unlikely to find such a good site again before nightfall. 'No,' said the prefect. 'We stay here tonight, and leave in the morning.'

Memnon opened his mouth, and the prefect spat. 'They say that you were a very brave man, decurion, that you attacked a British chief with his whole warband. Is that lies, or do you lose your courage afterward?'

Memnon shut his mouth, glaring.

'Sir,' put in Donatus, 'what Memnon meant was—'

'Who commands this *numerus*?' snapped Faustinus.

There was a silence. 'You do, sir,' said Donatus.

'Yes. And I say, we camp here tonight.'

They made camp. Memnon and the other decurions quietly arranged to post double the usual number of sentries, and gave orders to have all the gear packed ready for departure, and to abandon the tents if there was an alarm. There was, however, no alarm during the night, and in the morning they struck the tents and loaded them on the baggage mules at leisure. Faustinus was smug.

Then they started back and found that there were enemy forces on the road between them and the wall.

The scouts came galloping back with the report while the enemy themselves were still miles away: between a thousand and fifteen hundred of the Selgovae, they reckoned, light cavalry armed with spears, swords and javelins, riding north toward them. Memnon and all the other decurions wanted to go westward and then dodge south through the hills: Faustinus wouldn't hear of it.

'We must first talk to them!' exclaimed the prefect. 'We must ask why they have broke the treaty, and we must ask for a guarantee of safe conduct back to the wall.'

The ten decurions all stared at him incredulously. 'Sir,' said Donatus, slowly, 'they've *declared war*! They're not going to give us safe conducts home!'

'They have not!' Faustinus replied impatiently. 'They have broke the treaty, but they have not—'

'Sir, when they tore down the old camp, that *was* a declaration of war. You don't expect them to, to send an *embassy* do you?'

'They swore a treaty! They sacrifice to the gods and make oath! We do not just ride off without even speaking to them! We go meet them, with the standards advanced and with a staff of truce, and we speak to them. Romans do not run away before they are even attacked!'

'But *sir*—'

'Order your squadrons to fall in!'

The ten men sat on their horses staring at Faustinus in horrified bewilderment.

'Sir,' said Memnon, 'what we should do is set up an ambush. Then, if you like, we can send people out to talk to them.'

'Who commands this *numerus*?' Faustinus asked, as he had the evening before.

Again there was a silence – but this time the prefect did not get the expected response. 'Memnon's right, sir,' said Donatus, and the others all nodded.

Faustinus looked at them indignantly. '*Memnon* is not prefect! I *order* you, fall in!'

There was another silence, broken only by the sound of the unit's horses shifting about or cropping the grass. Faustinus looked from one man to another, his face growing

red. 'Very well,' he said at last. 'First Squadron and Second
Squadron will come with me, to speak to the enemy under
token of truce: the rest of the *numerus* will go west into the
hills and set up an ambush. And I will not forget this.' He
turned a bitter glare on Memnon. 'As for *you* – you under-
mine my authority, you do this again and again, and now
you . . . you *mutiny*! I will see that you suffer for it!'

Not if I desert first, Memnon thought. He bowed, then
rode over to speak hastily to Donatus about where to set up
the ambush. The advantage of being in a place where they'd
spent the previous summer was that he knew the area very
well.

Second Squadron was commanded by Claudianus, an
experienced man of about Memnon's age; it contained
twenty-seven men, while First Squadron had twenty-six. The
two depleted squadrons fell into parade order, then had to
wait while the staff of truce was arranged: the Moors did
not have any such object on hand, and were obliged to
improvize one from a stick wound about with branches of
a roadside herb, with a strip of bandage tied on the end for
the white ribbon. At last they started down the road toward
the enemy, led by Sittius Faustinus and the Moors' standard-bearer, who carried the white penant under its golden
star. Faustinus himself carried the staff of truce.

They had ridden for only fifteen minutes or so when the
enemy's vanguard appeared: an unruly mob of tattooed men
riding small, shaggy horses, carrying round shields painted
white and splashed with the interlocked blue coils of the
Selgovae. Faustinus halted and raised the staff of truce,
holding it up so that the white ribbon fluttered in the summer
breeze. There was a momentary pause – and then the Selgovae
yelled and clapped their heels to their horses, lowering their
spears.

So much for talking to them! Memnon pushed Ghibli hard
with the riding rod, turning him about where he stood, then
kicked him to a hard gallop back up the road.

'What!' shrieked Faustinus. 'Come *back*!'

Memnon glanced over his shoulder, unable to believe it.
The prefect was still sitting in the middle of the road with his
staff of truce, while beyond him several hundred barbarians

charged down howling the war cry. A javelin hissed past to his right and buried itself in the muddy hillside; a scream told him that another had hit its target. '*Run*, sir!' he shouted, and leaned forward to urge his horse faster.

Other horses were galloping beside his: First Squadron, following his lead. He didn't dare look back to see what had happened to Second Squadron. There was another scream behind him.

The Selgovae paused to cut down Faustinus. It threw the front of their charge into disarray, slowing them enough that the rest of the Moors were able to draw ahead. Memnon led them back up the road, past the spot where they'd parted from the others, then turned sharply left up a drover's track. The horses scrambled up a steep hill, stones spitting from beneath their hooves, and galloped over a pasture. The animals had covered a couple of miles in minutes, and they were slowing now, their coats dark with sweat. Memnon checked Ghibli, falling back through the mass of men and horses, trying to count heads. Most of First Squadron was there, and yes, there seemed to be a lot of Second Squadron, too. They'd lost the standard; he was sorry for that – but better the standard than the men.

The pasture narrowed; the hills drew down. The southern, steeper face was forested. The Moorish horses were cantering now, and breathing hard; Ghibli, however, still had plenty of fire. Memnon galloped him back to the front and led his two diminished squadrons round the curve of the southern hill, close to the line of trees. The British followed.

Donatus and the other eight squadrons were in the wood, of course. They attacked the Britons in the skirmishers' favourite way: on the flank. There was a sudden volley of javelins striking among the pursuers; men and horses fell, and their fellows cantered over them. The Maeatae nearest the point of attack swerved away, and crashed into others; those further away turned, trying to see what was going on. Donatus and his men were already away, galloping back along the column to attack again in the rear.

The Maeatae's charge shattered into a struggling mass, some groups of men turning to face the new attack at the rear, some trying to respond to the first lash against their flank, the foremost still trying to continue the pursuit. The air filled with screams of rage and pain. Memnon checked Ghibli, turned him; all around him the two squadrons did the same. He pulled a javelin from its harness and yelled, 'First Squadron! Our turn! Hit them!' He then rode back at the enemy to the accompaniment of the shrieking war-cry of the Moors.

The few Maeatae who were still riding towards them recoiled. They turned their mounts and galloped back into the milling mob. Memnon hurled his javelin at a fleeing back – and missed; he'd never been very accurate from horseback. Some of the men, though, were better; enemies fell. The whole unwieldy mass of barbarians had turned now, though, and was galloping back the way it had come. Donatus and his men were already away from their rear, and there was nothing in their way but their own fallen: they trampled the living with the dying in their eagerness to get away.

Memnon allowed Ghibli to stop. He dismounted and stood by the stallion, patting the damp neck while the horse blew, wet nostrils swallowing the air. Donatus cantered up.

'They'll think twice about treading on our heels now!' Donatus crowed.

Memnon nodded. The Selgovae would be back, once their scouts had confirmed how few of the Romans they'd actually faced – but they'd be much more careful.

Donatus glanced about. 'Where's the prefect?'

'Dead.' Donatus gave him a shocked look, and Memnon, stung, cried, 'I *told* him to run! He just sat there, waving that damned staff of truce! It's not my fault he was stupid!'

Donatus regarded him from his horse's back, face full of misgiving. 'The high command isn't going to like it, though – specially if they hear that we mutinied first.'

'No.' Memnon sighed, then caught Ghibli's neck-rope and began walking the horse up and down, to cool him off gently. 'Let's worry about that later, though, mess-mate. Right now we've got a small army on our tail, the tribes are rising, and we're three days' north of the wall.'

Two of Donatus's men cantered up, grinning; the foremost carried the Moors' standard. The penant was covered in mud, but the gold star still glowed brightly.

'One of those bastards had it,' said the standard-bearer.
'He dropped it.'

Donatus gave a whoop of pleasure that turned every eye
toward them. He snatched up the standard and shook it, and
everyone cheered. 'Juno Caelestis!' he shouted. 'The goddess
is with us!'

'I hope so,' Memnon muttered. 'I don't know how we're
going to get home otherwise.'

The Moors' losses were light: five men from First Squadron,
seven from Second Squadron; nine from the other eight. The
losses of the pursuers had been much greater – eighty-three
men lay by the edge of the woods, most injured by their
own horses and finished off by the Moors. When the Moors
dodged away into the hills, the enemy, having lost so many
to one ambush, were wary of another, and followed much
more slowly. They fell behind – then, as far as the scouts
could tell, gave up the pursuit and turned south, perhaps
hoping to cut the Roman unit off.

It was a relief to Memnon and Donatus, who were desperately trying to work out which way to go to get back to the
wall. They had scouts out in all directions, trying to determine where the enemy had mustered and which way his
parties were riding. Apart from giving them some idea of
which routes to avoid, they hoped it would prove useful to
the high command, and perhaps atone for the loss of their
prefect.

They found the tracks of large numbers of the enemy, all
heading south. The Moors would ride along the tracks for a
few hours, to cover their own trail, then dodge away at the
first hint of more Britons gathered ahead. Their dodges took
them east, then west, but always there were enemies between
them and the wall.

On the third day, Memnon managed to work out that the
Selgovae were gathering to attack a particular target: the fort
of Castra Exploratorum. He thought of the men he'd visited
that winter and sighed: Senorix and his friends would have
to fend for themselves. Two hundred and seventeen Aurelian
Moors weren't going to be enough to rescue them.

He and Donatus led the unit west, making a wide circle

around the outpost fort, feeling their way through a hostile land. At least twice Memnon feared that they would have to fight their way through – and he knew that they couldn't, they hadn't the strength. Juno Caelestis, however, seemed to be continuing her favour: they slipped past one British force under cover of darkness, and decoyed another out of the way with a false trail. They reached Uxelodunum on the wall eight days after leaving Aballava, and five after Faustinus's death.

They were the first Romans to make it south for some days, and the prefect of Uxelodunum pounced on them: was it really the case that the Maeatae were rebelling?

Memnon and Donatus told him everything they knew about the enemy's movements. The Uxelodunum prefect, shocked and dismayed, at once began assembling a force to go to the rescue of Castra Exploratorum.

'And us, sir?' Memnon asked him respectfully. 'What do you want us to do?'

'Go home,' replied the prefect. 'You're wrung out, men and horses both. You did very well to get back here at all.'

The Moors thought so, too. They turned their exhausted mounts homewards along the Military Way.

Their arrival at Aballava caused considerable commotion: they'd been expected to spend longer at the summer encampment, checking over the supplies and inspecting the strongholds of the neighbouring clans. When they rode through the gates they were quickly surrounded by a crowd of clamorous Frisians. Burcanius came running out of the *praetorium*, anxious and alarmed.

'It's war again,' Donatus announced. 'The Maeatae have rebelled.' Everyone began shouting.

Burcanius collected the decurions and his own officers and dragged everyone into the *praetorium* to get the whole story. They were all standing about in the dining room yelling when Athenais walked in.

Her hair was wet, and dripped on to her gray silk cloak; her face was slightly flushed. The fact of her pregnancy was just starting to be evident. Memnon stared at her in amazement: her appearance at Aballava, here at the beginning of another war, was so out of place that he could scarcely take it in.

There was a pause in the shouting as everyone else in the room turned to see what he was staring at. Athenais blushed. 'My husband Castor sent me out of the city for my health,' she explained to the room at large. 'He sent you a letter to tell you, but I gather it arrived the day after you left.' She paused, then asked, 'What has happened?'

Memnon drew in a deep breath and let it out again. 'The Maeatae have rebelled.'

There was a bustle in the corridor behind Athenais, and Sabinus the secretary pushed his way into the room: too old to ride with the mission, he had remained at the fort. He looked around wildly and demanded, 'Where's my Lord Faustinus?'

There was an awkward silence. Then Memnon went over to the slave, took his arm, and led him to a couch. 'Faustinus is dead,' he said, sitting him down. 'I'm sorry.'

Sabinus gave a wail and leapt to his feet again. 'No! How can he be dead? The company's back, the decurions . . .' He glared. 'You! What have you done to him?'

Memnon winced. 'He went to negotiate with the enemy. We tried to tell him that it was too dangerous, but he wouldn't listen. I'm sorry.'

The older man glared at him in disbelief. 'Why are you back here alive, if he's dead?'

'It is a war, Sabinus,' said Burcanius quietly. 'In war, men die. Even prefects.'

Sabinus moaned. 'Oh gods, gods! What will I tell his father?' He glanced around angrily. 'His family will hear of this!' He fled the room.

Memnon sighed and rubbed the back of his neck. He glanced around the crowded room, then said wearily, 'We need to decide what to do.'

Athenais cleared her throat. 'Would you like me to take notes?' she offered. 'Or write letters?'

All the men looked at her, astonished and taken aback – and then Memnon realized that *yes*, she *could*. She had served the Empress herself: she was very much the best trained secretary in Aballava. 'Yes, please, lady!' he said eagerly.

'That –' he waved his hand at the door through which the old man had departed – 'was the prefect's secretary, and I can't ask it of him.'

Athenais sent a woman attendant to fetch writing materials and settled down in a corner of the room to take notes.

None of the Moorish or Frisian officers thought it likely that Aballava itself would come under attack, despite all those signs of Britons moving south. The British were obviously going to concentrate their attention on Roman positions north of the wall. The Frisians were, however, very concerned about friends and relatives who lived in the country surrounding the fort: it was likely that some of the British warbands would engage in raiding. They decided to send out riders at once, to warn their friends and to gather them in and bring them to safety.

The Moors' first concern was more limited: to pasture their tired horses and get a night's sleep.

Both companies, however, agreed on the need to send a letter to the high command at Eboracum at once, reporting the situation. This should have been the responsibility of Donatus, but everyone seemed to take it for granted that Memnon and Burcanius should have a part in the task as well. The other officers were assigned things to do and went off to do them; Memnon, Burcanius, and Donatus were left in the *praetorium* dining room, along with Athenais, whose note-taking had already proved useful in assigning tasks.

It was evening by now, though the long summer hours meant that it was still light. Burcanius cast an embarrassed look at Athenais. 'I am sorry we make our guest work,' he said. 'Do you want to go and rest, lady? I will give you room here; it is better if you stay inside the fort until we know how safe is the village.'

Athenais shook her head. 'I'm happy to help with your letters, Lord Burcanius.'

He looked embarrassed. 'But you have had long journey, you will have baby . . .'

'I'm quite fit enough to write a couple of letters,' Athenais said sharply. 'Lord Burcanius, this is the work I was trained for. I don't find it fatiguing.'

She seemed positively *eager* to help. Memnon grinned at

her. 'If you're willing to help us, lady, I'm happy, even if no one else is. I'm no good at reports, and these two aren't much better. Hey, Burcanius, can you tell them to bring us some food? We haven't eaten since dawn, and we must've ridden forty miles.'

Burcanius looked unhappy. 'You know that all the slaves, they belong to Faustinus,' he said. 'I will go to the kitchens myself.'

Burcanius went to the kitchens, and came back with bread, cheese, wine and a dish of stewed apricots. The four of them clustered around it and ate – the two Moors ravenously, Athenais and the Frisian more delicately – while they prepared the report to send to Eboracum.

'What do we say, though?' asked Donatus, after summarizing what had happened. 'The high command isn't going to be happy about Faustinus. His uncle's a friend of the Praetorian Prefect. And you can just bet that Sabinus will find out how we refused his order, then ran off and left him on the road.'

'You could present him as a hero,' suggested Athenais.

All three men looked at her as though she'd gone mad.

'They all do it!' she explained impatiently. 'All the generals, anyway. They all dress up their mistakes in purple to make themselves look good. Making this prefect of yours look good would be *easy*. How about something like: "On seeing the evidence that the Maeatae were preparing for war, the decurions were eager to turn back, but Sittius Faustinus resolutely determined first to accomplish the mission he had been assigned." And then: "The noble prefect was unwilling to shame the Roman name by fleeing from the treacherous barbarians without a word spoken. Accordingly, after sending the better part of his forces into the hills to set up an ambush, he took two trusted squadrons along the road to reprove the British for abandoning the treaty . . ."'

'*We* were the ones who wanted to set up an ambush!' objected Donatus. 'Faustinus would've made the whole company come with him!'

'You don't need to say that,' said Athenais. 'You need to give his family a version of what happened which *they* will like, but which also makes *you* look good.'

'How do you make it look good that he sat in the middle of the road yelling while we ran away?' asked Memnon incredulously.

'"The barbarians were overcome with elation at the sight of an enemy of rank and, flagrantly defying the sacred custom of truce, hastened to attack his party. They targeted the brave prefect, whose status they recognized from his red cloak, and cut him down, though a dozen of his loyal followers died trying to protect him . . ."'

'Ha!' exclaimed Memnon admiringly.

'You write this report, lady,' agreed Donatus eagerly. 'We'll show it to Sabinus when you've got it done, and maybe he'll decide to go along with it.'

Athenais drafted the report, including not only the account of Faustinus's death, but also, and less dramatically, the intelligence the Moors had collected on their way north and south again. When she finished and read it over, not only did Faustinus sound heroic, but the company as a whole shone as resourceful, loyal and resilient. She prepared two fair copies, one to be sent to Eboracum, the other to be kept at the fort for future reference. Donatus took that copy off to show to Sabinus.

Athenais stretched and flexed her fingers, then yawned delicately behind a hand.

'You're tired,' Memnon said apologetically. 'Umm . . . when did you get here?'

It emerged that she'd arrived at Aballava only a couple of hours before the Moors; she had a carriage with a driver parked in the fort village, and two slaves to attend her. Burcanius had treated her very courteously on her arrival, and had offered her the use of the *praetorium* baths. He had sent someone to ask about renting her a house in the village.

'You're . . . planning to stay here for a while?' Memnon asked in bewilderment. *Where was Castor?*

She gave him a bland look. 'Eboracum is very unhealthy this time of year. It's hot and overcrowded, and several people on our street have come down with an enteritic fever. As I'm sure my husband told you, we're expecting a child. Castor's very eager for it, and he thought I would be safer in the country.' She paused, then, meeting Memnon's eyes fully, she added, 'He trusts you, so he sent me here.'

Donatus returned from his call on Sabinus, looking awed. 'He burst into tears!' he told Athenais. 'He even shook my hand!'

She smiled in satisfaction. 'Good. Lord Burcanius, it's been a long day. If your man has been able to locate a house for me, I'd be pleased to move in and get some rest.'

Burcanius hesitated – then bowed. 'Lady, as I said, it is better if you stay here, until we know that the village will be safe. I will send to the village for my sister to come stay with you, it will be proper.'

She accepted the offer graciously. Memnon offered to show her to the guest room.

The room was one for which Faustinus had provided the furnishings: a couch of carved maplewood, a small table of beaten bronze, a soft rug. The bed was not made up. Athenais sat down on the plain leather and sent her woman to find a coverlet.

'Why are you really here?' Memnon asked her in a low voice.

She looked up at him, her eyes very large in a tired face. 'For my health. When Caracalla discovered that I'd married and left the Household, he made inquiries about me, with a view to resuming what his mother put a stop to. His creature Euodus turned up at my door and threatened to tell his patron everything.'

Memnon caught his breath.

'Fortunately, Euodus has concluded that he's become an embarrassment to Caracalla. He knows too much about his patron's less savoury doings – and Caracalla hasn't forgiven him for the failure of his plot to discredit Geta. Euodus agreed to keep quiet in exchange for promises from Castor and myself.'

'Promises?' whispered Memnon.

She gave him a tired smile. 'That we'd intercede for him with Julia Augusta and Geta Augustus when Our Lord the Emperor dies. He's convinced that Castor's Geta's creature – he can't conceive of any other reason for him to have foiled that plot. Anyway, we seem to be safe, for the time being, but Castor still thought it would be better if I left Eboracum, so as to stay out of Caracalla's sight.'

'I'm sorry,' Memnon told her, feeling helpless.

'No.' She shook her head, then looked away. 'No. To tell the truth . . .' She stopped, and realized that she was fighting not to cry.

'I . . .' he began.

'You don't have to be sorry!' she managed at last. 'I've been miserable since I left the Household. I love my husband, but I used to be his *partner*, his *colleague*, and now . . . now I'm just his idle, whining wife! I haven't known what to do with myself. Castor bought this house for us, and it's little, and it's cold, and none of the other women on the street will speak to me, because I'm foreign, and I've been *so* bored, so *sick,* I *wish* . . .' She stopped herself and swallowed. 'Anyway,' she resumed, in a more controlled voice, 'don't be sorry that I had to leave Eboracum. I'm happy to be away from that wretched little house, and I'll be even happier if you give me something to *do*.' She looked at him earnestly. 'I'm good, you know. I trained at Head of Africa, and I was the best among the girls. Better than nearly all the boys, too, though they never wanted to admit it.'

'What's Head of Africa?'

'Oh. It's the academy in Rome where they train people from the Household to administer the Empire. The name comes from a statue by the entrance. It's mostly for boys, but they take a few girls every year, for situations where it would be improper to employ a man. They teach shorthand, accounting, law – that sort of thing.'

Memnon remembered the stack of ledgers waiting for him in the headquarters. 'If you're really willing to help,' he said cautiously, 'we would be very, very glad of it. We're ignorant barbarians here, lady, as I've told you before. I think you may already have saved my skin with that report you drafted.'

She smiled at him, face suddenly radiant. 'Thank you. Oh – I brought you something. Not from me, from my patroness.'

'From the Empress?' he asked, puzzled and apprehensive.

She went to her satchel of supplies and took out a little lead tablet. 'Here.'

He frowned over the words carefully inscribed into the lead, and saw that they granted the citizenship of Rome to

Gaius Julius Memnon, decurion of the *numerus* of Aurelian Moors. Amazed, he looked up into Athenais's smiling face.

'I told her that it was unjust to punish you three times for the same offence, but not to reward you at all. She agreed.'

He had wanted this for so long – and now that he had it in his hand, its chief value suddenly seemed to be that *she* had won it for him, that she had brought it to give to him, and was glad that she had found something to make him happy. 'I don't . . .' he began helplessly.

'I had to point out that you'd been punished,' she explained. 'That wretched joke of yours offended her – but, from what I heard, you were given a beating on the spot, and then you were denied the honours you'd earned, and finally you were denied *this*: three punishments. My patroness agreed that it was excessive. – I hope you like your new names. "Julius" is to honour the Empress, of course, and Gaius is just because it was simplest.'

'I like it very much.' He wanted to hug her, to kiss that smile, and had to remind himself forcibly that she was another man's wife – a *friend's* wife. Castor had sent her here because he *trusted* Memnon – trusted his will and ability to protect Athenais, but trusted his honour, too. He could not betray that trust.

'Good,' she said happily. 'Good.'

Her maid returned with the coverlet for the bed, so he wished her a good night and went out, holding the leaden tablet in his hand. He made his way back to his own room at the head of the central barrack block. It was dark; he lit the lamp and propped the tablet carefully against the base of the statuette of Juno Caelestis he'd inherited from Saturninus. He read it again: Gaius Julius Memnon, citizen of Rome.

He had a flask of wine in a corner of the room. He fetched it over, and carefully poured a libation on to the floor in front of the statue. 'Juno Caelestis,' he whispered, 'Queen of Heaven, great goddess – thank you, Protectress of the Moors, thank you for getting us home! And . . . please, Mother of the Gods, protectress of marriage – keep me worthy of your protection, strengthen my heart.' He poured another libation, then prayed in the language of his childhood, 'Oh, my father and mother, and you, my little sister; Oh, my grandfathers and grandmothers, all of you, my ancestors: keep me true to the way you taught me, now that I am a Roman. Let me raise up children of our blood in honour: give me another woman to love.'

Nineteen

The rebellion had caught the Romans unprepared. Despite all the rumours, the high command had expected that if the Maeatae did rebel, they'd wait until the harvest was in. The violent rising by the supposedly conquered north saw troops frantically reinforcing the wall and scurrying to catch raiding parties which had crossed it – and while they scurried, August passed and the Maeatae brought in the harvest, ensuring that the tribes would be provisioned for another year.

The Emperor was furious. Castor wrote to Athenais that he'd quoted Homer:

> Let none of them escape from sheer destruction
> wrought by our hands; the child in the womb,
> if a boy, shall not escape from sheer destruction.

The Roman troops were commanded to go north and kill everyone they met.

By the time the order came, however, it was September. The harvest was in, and the Maeatae had retreated northward into the hills: once again, the enemy was to be found only in an ambush. The Emperor called upon the Caledones to close their borders, but the Caledones refused – and were themselves declared rebels, and sentenced to the same fate as their southern allies.

To Memnon the rest of the summer unfolded like a nightmare. He saw the woman he loved every day – and couldn't touch her. She got herself a house in the village, but came in to the *praetorium* every morning to work. She wrote reports, handled the accounts, sorted out the books, advised him on laws and policies and finance. She bought an abacus, and showed him how to use it. 'See, *this* column is tens, and this is ones, and if we multiply we move *these* beads over to here . . .' Her slim fingers flashed over the clay markers, confident and sure.

Clever girl, he thought admiringly. Brave, loyal . . . and not his, never his.

Then his thoughts would go to the other woman he'd loved in Britain, and he would wonder where she was now, and how long she would be safe. Every morning he expected to receive the order to ride north and start killing.

The summer passed, however, without that order's appearance. The death of Faustinus meant that they had no proper commander to receive the order, and the emergency meant that the high command had little time and attention to appoint one.

During the first days of the war he rode over to Uxelodunum, ostensibly to coordinate troop movements but actually to ask about his friend Senorix. The prefect of Uxelodunum had succeeded in reaching the fort of Castra Exploratorum before it was overwhelmed, and had escorted the survivors back to the wall. Memnon was anxious to know whether the British scout was safe.

Senorix, however, wasn't with the survivors. Nobody seemed to know whether he'd been killed or whether he'd deserted; Memnon queasily suspected the latter. He wished again that he'd managed to secure his own discharge before the war broke out again. He did not, not, *not* want to assist in any massacres. He dreamed of Sulicena screaming over the body of her son, and wished he'd never left Africa.

In the middle of September, though, came the real thunderbolt: he was appointed as prefect of the Aurelian Moors.

He hadn't realized he would even be considered: he'd thought his joke had killed the possibility stone dead. Apparently not: a messenger arrived with a red cloak and a letter appointing Julius Memnon to the command of the Moors. Athenais explained it to him: Eboracum had never really appreciated that the auxiliary decurion favoured by the Empress and the Ethiopian who'd presented the Emperor with that dire omen were the same man. The Empress's favour had put him in line for the prefecture; the previous prefect was dead; the high command wanted an experienced career soldier to take charge during the crisis. He now had the citizenship and a year's experience as a decurion, so he got the job. Saying, 'No thank you: I don't want anything to do with this war,' wasn't an option.

His comrades were delighted. When they heard the news they congregated outside his room, clapping their hands and shouting, and when he steeled himself to come out and accept their congratulations, they swept him up on their shoulders and carried him to the *praetorium* in triumph. They had one of their own to lead them again – Rogatus's heir, the hero who had led them to safety in war, who would protect them in peace!

The Frisians were pleased, too. Burcanius was openly delighted, and shook his hand warmly. Everyone, in fact, was so happy with his promotion that he didn't know how to admit that it terrified him, and that he would much rather go back to being a simple scout. He'd found it difficult to handle the officework that fell on a decurion: how would be possibly manage as a prefect?

Athenais, he decided afterward, was the only reason he stayed sane: when she explained the work, he actually felt he could understand it. She comforted him about the wider situation, too: 'Look, the campaign season will be over before the war can start properly. Maybe by spring Our Lord Severus will have calmed down and decided to negotiate, and there won't *be* any massacres!' He was deeply grateful to her. He found her presence a torment, but he was deeply apprehensive as to how he'd cope when she left.

Sometimes when he woke up from a nightmare, he would comfort himself by imagining that she would *not* leave: that she would stay with him. He imagined her in bed beside him, embracing him with those slim arms and wrapping those beautiful long legs around him; he imagined her sharing the *praetorium* with him, handling all the officework as he handled the men; he imagined filling the house with their children. In daylight, he was ashamed: she was Castor's wife, expecting Castor's baby, and no longer a proper subject of daydreams. Despite her confession on the evening of her arrival, the marriage seemed happy enough, too – at least, she and Castor wrote to one another all the time, long letters, which arrived or were sent off with the official despatches every few days. She never again referred to the dissatisfaction she'd described that evening. Her manner with him was friendly but distant: he noticed that she was very careful never to touch him, not even in a way as harmless as shaking hands. He suspected that she harboured some of the same feelings he did, and that she was similarly determined not to betray the man who'd sent her there.

'Don't worry!' Athenais told him, smiling, when he tentatively opened the subject of what he'd do without her. 'I'll find you a clerk before I go.'

She didn't seem to be looking for one, though. Of course, she was busy, with the officework and with her preparations for the baby.

Memnon moved into the *praetorium*. He had mixed feelings about it: he'd coveted the comfort of the big house from the first time he saw it, but he felt out of place there. He agreed with Burcanius, though, that to have the two of them amicably sharing a house sent a desirable message to the men and to the high command. Burcanius was also relieved to get the two servants Memnon had inherited from Rogatus, and to have somebody to share expenses with. Faustinus's servants had all gone back to Faustinus's father by the time Memnon arrived, and Burcanius hadn't had the money to replace them.

They had little time to rearrange the housekeeping, though: a few days after Memnon's promotion, both companies were ordered north to hunt Maeatae.

Most of the Roman army had already been doing so for a month and, to Memnon's relief, they found very few of the barbarians. The Moors scouted the hills, assisting the British legion Second Augusta in its work of looting, burning and destroying, but were not obliged to rape and murder as well. There wasn't even much to loot: farm implements in barns, occasional hides or leather goods, strayed cattle – children's toys, in one abandoned homestead they visited. They burned that, of course, and Memnon imagined the children coming home and crying over the embers – but better the toys than the children.

At the beginning of October, the weather worsened, and the troops were recalled to winter quarters. He began to hope that he'd manage to escape murdering anyone else this year – but in late November the Moors received orders to perform a reconnaissance of the territory of the Novantae and Selgovae.

It was bitter weather, cold, wet and dark – but they'd endured the same before, and were resigned to it. Memnon kept the Moors moving fast, following a zig-zag course through the hills, rotating his scouts frequently to keep them alert. For three days they saw no sign whatever of the enemy: all the deserted and ruined farmsteads remained deserted, and the hills were empty even of cattle. Memnon began to relax, confident that the Maeatae were still hiding out in the north among the Caledones.

Four days from Aballava, however, the advance scouts found the tracks of a large body of horsemen to the south west: it seemed that at least some of the enemy had moved south again. Memnon had no intention of engaging the enemy, and led the men north east, fast.

Their route brought them to a secluded hill fort. Earlier in the year it had been abandoned, but now as they approached, the dense smoke of cooking fires showed that it had been re-occupied, and by a large number of people. Memnon cursed, and ordered the *numerus* to circle to the north and ride hard: it looked like some of the Maeatae, too, had gone into winter quarters, and the Moors had just discovered where. The Britons would certainly come after them now.

The scouts soon told him that, sure enough, they were being pursued by a large force of horsemen. Memnon began the drearily familiar game of feint, dodge and retreat. He divided and reunited his company, to confuse the trail; he followed rough ground and streams to dull it. Any stray Britons who glimpsed them from a distance would never take them for Roman troops anyway: two-hundred odd muddy and weary men in shabby woollen capes, riding shaggy horses, would appear to them a British force. He had the standards packed away; his new red cloak had been stowed in a bag almost since he got it. He kept his men moving, night and day, allowing them to rest only in four-hour spells, confident that the Moors' horses would be in better condition than the British animals, which must have been enduring inadequate food and poor pasturage since the rebellion began. He circled round: east, north west, and then hard south. It worked: they ended up with the enemy to the north and the way back to the wall, so he hoped, clear and free.

He was just mounting up, on a dark morning four days after the chase began, when one of his scouts galloped up to report that the enemy had sent a party with a staff of truce out south of their main force: they wanted to talk.

He thought about it, then told Donatus to take most of the men on, while he rode back to see what the Maeatae wanted. Donatus almost refused, but eventually conceded that the British generally respected truces they'd proclaimed themselves, and that talking might provide useful information and would certainly buy some time.

Memnon took First Squadron and slunk back along a wooded valley to inspect the negotiating party. As the scouts had reported, a group of about a dozen horsemen were riding openly along the crest of the hill, led by a man in the white robe of a native priest who carried the staff. There didn't seem to be any additional forces waiting in ambush. Memnon studied them for a few more minutes from the cover of the trees, then dug his red prefect's cloak out of his saddlebag and put it on. Then he rode up out of the valley to meet them.

He saw them notice his approach. They started down the hill toward him, the priest first, holding his staff high. The man behind him had Selgovae tattoos and a gold torque: a chieftain of some sort. Then Memnon stiffened: Argentocoxus rode next after the Selgovae chieftain, and Senorix was at the back of the party. The British scout was unarmed, and he rode with another man on either side of him, but he wasn't bound. Memnon wasn't sure whether or not he was a captive.

The two parties stopped in the middle of the hillside; the Britons made their familiar gestures to avert evil. Memnon grinned at them.

'We come under token of truce!' announced the priest,

waving the staff. 'I call the gods of the earth, and of the sky, and of the land beneath the earth, to witness this truce! O, Brigida, Queen of Heaven, witness that we come to speak in peace to your favoured servant!'

Memnon inclined his head politely. 'Truce accepted. Greetings! Lord Argentocoxus, I'm sorry that we again meet as enemies. Senorix, good to see you still alive.'

Senorix inclined his head, smiling. 'Good to see you, too, Memnon. I told them it had to be you in charge when you gave us all the slip two days ago. Congratulations on the cloak.'

'I don't like it any more than I liked the sash,' Memnon told him, 'but I do like my nice warm house, and I'm eager to get back to it. What is it you want to talk to me about?'

'Tell him our conditions for peace,' the Selgovae chieftain ordered impatiently in British.

'Don't bother,' said Memnon, in British. His command of the language had improved over the year, though he still wasn't really fluent. 'The Empire will not hear them.'

'This is Ciniath, son of Ce,' said Argentocoxus quietly, nodding at the Selgovan. 'Chief of the Selgovae, my ally – and the husband of my sister Sulicena.'

'Ah. Ah.' Memnon stared at the Selgovan, who stared back in flat hostility. A tall man, he noticed, slim and not bad-looking. Memnon hoped he had a sense of humour. He thought wretchedly of the dense smoke over the hill fort: was Sulicena there?

He inclined his head to Ciniath, son of Ce. 'Congratulations, sir. Your wife is a beautiful and honourable lady. I would have proposed to her myself, but I knew she loved her people too much to accept me.'

'She loved you, Son of the Night,' said Ciniath angrily, 'and you will bring her death to her.'

'Only if you are stupid enough to leave her where she is after I get home,' Memnon replied shortly. 'If you're that stupid, you don't deserve her.'

'We have many ill,' said Ciniath, flushing angrily under his tattoos. 'Many children ill. If we go back into the hills, they will die.'

'What do you want me to do?' Memnon demanded. 'Lie

to my superiors? Even if I did, it wouldn't work: the whole
numerus saw that fort was occupied. Ask your brother-in-
law for help, not me!'

Argentocoxus was frowning at him. 'You once swore to
do no ill to me or to my clan,' he pointed out. 'Senorix has
told us that you were friendly toward our people, that you
do not want to kill our women and children.'

'This is true,' agreed Memnon. 'But of me, not the Empire.
We have orders to kill every male north of the wall.' He
grinned at the Caledonian without humour. 'Don't throw
my oath at me: you yourself were quite willing to allow
others to carry out a murder you couldn't in honour commit
yourself.'

The Caledonian ignored that. 'But where are your orders
if the Emperor is dead? I have heard you prophesized his
death – that you met him on the edge of the west, and offered
him a token of the Lady of Night.'

Memnon drew in a deep breath, suddenly cold from head
to foot: had his own stupidity fed that of the Maeatae? Or
was it even possible that the demon had been directing him
then?

'That was a joke which went wrong,' he said. 'And . . . he
received nothing from my hands. I offered him a wreath of
cypress, but he didn't take it.' In retrospect, that detail bore
a weight of significance which had been entirely absent at
the time.

The priest stirred slightly, as though it were significant to
him as well. 'Woe that he did not!' he said in British.

'It was a *joke*!' Memnon protested, suddenly very angry.
'And I'll tell you a secret: anyone who prophesizes another
man's death is going to be proved right in the end, because
all men die. If you're counting on Our Lord Septimius Severus
Augustus to save your lives, though, by dropping dead himself
before the end of next summer, then you're *fools*. A wise
man does not gamble everything on one throw of the dice,
or on one man's life. Even if you win, you are fools, and if
you lose, you are dead fools!'

'Save your breath,' Senorix put in wearily. 'I've been telling
them all year, but they won't believe anything except what
they *want* to believe. They thought that all they had to do

was show that they could still fight, and Rome would roll over and withdraw all the garrisons. Is there any way at all to get peace?'

'I don't know,' Memnon said unhappily. 'If I did, I would tell you.'

There was a silence. 'We want peace,' said Ciniath, now sounding just tired and desperate.

'So do I, man!' exclaimed Memnon impatiently. 'I can't get it for either of us. Pray to the gods that the Emperor calms down, or goes home, or dies before the spring, because otherwise all you'll get from the Empire is death.'

There was another silence.

Memnon inclined his head politely to Lord Ciniath. 'You'd better get your people away from that fort. Once I've reported, they'll send the legions. You probably have twelve days. I'll tell my superiors that you want peace, but I can tell you already that they won't grant it.' He looked at Senorix. 'You want me to tell them I saw you, and that you're being held captive?'

Senorix glanced at the men on either side of him, and Memnon understood, without a word, that the British scout had deserted voluntarily, but that he was not trusted, and was both prisoner and advisor.

'Tell them I deserted,' said Senorix flatly.

'No,' Memnon replied calmly. 'I won't mention seeing you at all.'

The Briton nodded resignedly. 'What will you do if they order you to slaughter us?' he asked.

'I'm still hoping it doesn't come to that.' He turned Ghibli and started him back down the hill. 'Sorry!' he called over his shoulder. 'I pray we all have better luck, come spring!'

Nobody followed them as they rode back. Memnon's heart ached, imagining Sulicena and her son fleeing the hill fort into the cold wet misery of the hills; imagining the Roman troops advancing on the Caledonians with the spring. Slaughtered men, women weeping, bodies hanging from the trees; more friends dying, a world of grief.

He touched Ghibli to a trot and rode on in silence, too tired and down-hearted to say anything to anyone.

*   *   *

They struggled back to the wall next day. All the horses were exhausted, and about a third of them were going lame; many of the men were ill with weariness and exposure. Memnon saw them safely back into Aballava, then staggered into the *praetorium*, took off his wet boots, and lay down on the nice warm floor of the dining room. Burcanius came in with a cup of hot wine.

'Did you find any strongholds?' the Frisian commander asked, sitting down on the floor and handing him the cup.

Memnon grimaced. 'Yes,' he admitted. He sipped the wine, lying on his stomach, feeling the warmth slide over his tongue and down his tight throat.

'Lady Athenais will not be able to write your report,' Burcanius told him.

Memnon picked up his head with a jerk, and the Frisian grinned. 'She had the baby yesterday,' he said. 'It is a boy, and healthy. The midwife says it was a good delivery, that she is well and safe.'

'Juno Caelestis!' exclaimed Memnon. He'd almost forgotten about Athenais's baby, despite the inexorable advance of the pregnancy. So she'd had it, Castor's baby! Her husband would probably want her to come home as soon as it was safe for the child to travel: whatever the chamberlain's reasons for keeping his wife away from the court, he would surely want to see his son. The dark world seemed suddenly even more bleak.

Guiltily, he shoved aside the thought that if Castor's fears were justified, and the omen he'd provided true, the chamberlain might be dead soon – that his own happiness, as well as the Britons' survival, might hinge upon the Emperor's death. Athenais, he reminded himself, was not the only pretty woman in the world. There were other girls, and other chances of happiness: he was supposed to be looking for them. Perhaps they did all look silly and plain beside Athenais – but he should look a bit harder. A man who envied his friends and wished them dead – that was not the sort of man he had ever wanted to be.

He ought to be pleased. Childbirth was dangerous: Athenais might have lost the baby; she might have died. Instead she was alive and the mother of a healthy son: he ought to be thanking the gods, not complaining to them.

'I'll have to offer something to the goddess,' he said aloud to Burcanius. 'To thank her for our safe return, and for our friend's safety in childbirth.'

He would have to get a look at the child as soon as possible, he told himself silently. A real live baby was a potent talisman: only a truly wicked man could look at it and wish its father dead.

The baby was no longer than his forearm, and weighed no more than a couple measures of flour. His eyes were the opaque blue of all newborns, and his face was wizened and red; his round skull was barely covered by its sprinkling of soft fair hair. Athenais seemed to find him utterly amazing.

'It's a marmot!' exclaimed Memnon, pretending shock.

She looked at him indignantly, and he grinned. 'Ah, no, I see now. He looks just like his father!'

'Oh, *you*!' She rocked the baby gently. 'He's *beautiful*. Aren't you beautiful, my lamb?'

'He's a fine healthy boy, anyway. Ha. Your husband will be overjoyed.'

She smiled. 'I've written to him already, to let him know he has a son. He decided what he wanted for a name ages ago, though: Ingenuus.'

Freeborn. Memnon remembered Castor speaking longingly of how his son would be freeborn, and some of his resentment dissolved. 'Septimius Ingenuus,' he said thoughtfully. 'Good name. When is he going to get to see the little marmot, then?'

Some of the animation left her face. 'I don't know.'

Castor was in no hurry. His letters continued to arrive at the fort every few days: delighted about his son, anxious about his wife – but there was no indication of when or even whether he would bring her back to the capital. It seemed that Severus was ill again, in great pain from his gouty feet and suffering from giddiness and stomach pains as well. Caracalla and Geta both were taking advantage of their father's indisposition to manoeuvre to gain control of the machinery of state, while their mother watched unhappily, powerless to influence them. The generals and their staffs continued to plan the next season's war, but their efforts were beginning to waver. The Emperor's illness, and the struggle between his two sons, seemed far more significant to the Roman state than a war against worthless barbarians.

November became December; the Saturnalia approached. Athenais wrote to her husband, trying to persuade him to visit for the festival, but he wrote back that he didn't dare leave the court. His absence might be noted, he said.

'I think Caracalla must be growing stronger,' she told Memnon, showing him the letter. 'Castor's afraid to draw any attention in this direction.'

The Moors and the Frisians celebrated the festival together, with bonfires and feasting and music. There were hunting parties, too – but Memnon did not participate.

January came, with deep snow. Memnon feared that the Moors would be sent out on another reconnaissance, but no orders came: the court was paralysed by the Emperor's illness.

He was in the heated dining room of the *praetorium*, arguing with Donatus over whether it would be possible to train British horses Moorish-fashion, when one of the old servants knocked on the door, then opened it to admit Castor.

Memnon stared in astonishment. The chamberlain wore a thick travelling cloak which was heavy with melting snow; his nose was red, his lips were blue, and he was shivering.

'Gods and goddesses!' Memnon exclaimed.

'I had . . . a few days,' Castor said, in a hoarse voice. 'I wanted to see Athenais, and my son. Are they . . . ?'

'They're in the village,' Memnon informed him. 'In her house. You want to go there straightaway, or stop here and warm up a bit first?'

Castor wanted to go straight there. Memnon went with him to point out the house. He declined to go inside though. 'You enjoy your reunion with your wife,' he said. 'Get to know your son. I'd like it if you came to dinner in the *praetorium* tomorrow, though, you and her both. We can talk then.'

When Castor had gone in, however, he stood outside in the snow for several minutes, imagining the embraces, the kisses. Then, ashamed of himself and angry at his weakness, he turned aside and went back to the fort.

At dinner the following day, Castor made it clear that he

had no intention of taking his wife and son home. The Emperor was very ill, he told them, in a frightened whisper: he had no engagements for twelve days, by order of his doctors. 'Everything's overturned, nothing's in its accustomed place – so I thought I could disappear for a few days without anyone wondering where I've gone. I had to come; I had to see my son, at least once.'

'He's a very fine boy,' Memnon told him, and Castor smiled and thanked him.

He left the following day, on a mule which he'd hired from a livery stable in Eboracum. Memnon offered to ride with him on the first stage of his journey.

That mule carried a whole burden of significance along with its rider. Memnon had never before seen Castor ride astride; the freedman had always used a carriage. Hiring a carriage, however, meant hiring a driver, who would know where his passenger had gone.

Of course, Athenais had been making no secret of who she was. The Commissary could easily find out *where* she was if it wanted to, hired driver or not. The Commissary, however, presumably still served Severus, rather than his sons. Castor was trying to avoid unofficial, rather than official, attention.

'Will you keep her safe?' Castor asked, after a long silence. Memnon had offered to escort him from Aballava precisely so as to give him just such a guarantee. 'I will,' he said solemnly. 'I swear it by my ancestors.' They rode on a little way, and then he asked, very softly, 'You think your patron will die?'

Castor closed his eyes in pain. 'He may recover. He always has been a strong man; he may recover.' He looked soberly at Memnon. 'It's just better to be prepared for the worst.'

Memnon nodded, though he couldn't bring himself to say anything. He couldn't say anything, between pity and indignation for his friend's plight, and the fierce, if disreputable, hope that the Emperor's death would end the British war. He did his best not to think of the further possibility that Severus's death would free Caracalla to make Athenais a widow. Whatever his guilty imaginings in the middle of the night, Memnon did not long for Castor's death. 'I will die myself before allowing anyone to harm your wife or your son,' he promised instead.

Castor drew in a long breath. 'Thank you.'

They rode on for a few minutes in silence. The sun had come out, and shone off the snow, dazzlingly bright. On their left, the bulwark of the wall rose golden, edged with black shadows. Memnon wondered whether the Selgovae he'd met were camping out in the snow, or whether they'd gone back to their stronghold. He imagined mothers of young infants shivering in the cold, and wished them safe and warm.

It was wicked, as well as sacrilegious, to hope that the Emperor died.

'If I die,' Castor said abruptly, 'you can marry her with my blessing, so long as you protect the child.'

Memnon had prepared his answer to this suggestion. He could not eliminate the shameful part of himself that hoped Castor died – but he could, and would, disown it completely. 'Ha!' he exclaimed, and checked Ghibli. The stallion snorted, laying his ears back and rolling his eyes at Castor's mule, which bared its teeth. Memnon slid off his back.

'If it comes to the point, sir,' he said, catching the mule's bridle, 'yes, I like your wife, a lot.' He met the other man's eyes honestly. 'I liked her when we first met, and I like her even more now I know her better. But that's nothing to do with whether I protect her and that baby. I'm going to do that because you're my friend, and because she's my friend, and because it's what I've sworn to do. You trusted me to look after her and keep her safe, and I have, haven't I? You don't have to bribe me with marriage to make me keep on doing that, and neither does she, all right?' He made himself grin. 'There are plenty of pretty girls who'd be happy to marry a prefect. I am not a man who can't get a woman except by stealing one.'

Castor was very surprised and taken aback. 'I . . . never thought you were!' he protested. 'I only thought . . . she would be safe with you.'

'She will be as safe as I can make her,' said Memnon fiercely. 'She and your son Ingenuus. As for marriage, though – I won't press her in any way.' He raised both hands, palm up. 'I swear that I will never even *ask* her! If I fail my oath,

may my ancestors disown me and the gods destroy me!' He
lowered his hands, grimly satisfied. He wanted Athenais, but
he wanted her honestly and honourably, not coerced by need.
He did not want any shame or guilt attaching to either of
them from Castor's death. He would deal honourably with
his friends, and pray that Castor lived. There were, as he'd
just said, other girls, and if he didn't want them now, he had
no doubt that a spirited young woman might change his
mind.

'I thank the fate that linked us,' Castor said fervently, and
held out his hand.

Memnon took it and pressed it in both his own. 'I pray
the gods grant that we see you again, sir, in good health.'
He grinned. 'Cheer up, sir! Maybe your patron will just
retire to sit in the sun, and you can retire too, to raise your
children.'

Castor smiled again, more widely. 'I'll hope for it! May
the gods keep you in health!'

They received a letter from him on the twenty-fifth, reporting
that he'd arrived home safely and that his patron the Emperor
was still ill. It was followed by an official despatch, which
for the first time admitted publicly that the Emperor was ill
and asked all the people of the Empire to pray to the gods
for his recovery.

The Empire prayed. In Aballava, the Frisians and the Moors
offered three white heifers for the recovery of the Emperor
Lucius Septimius Severus. Afterwards it was remarked that
people all over Britain ate beef dinners for the Emperor –
but in vain.

> Septimius Castor, freedman of Augustus, sends greet-
> ings to his beloved wife Athenais.
> My dearest joy, it is with deep regret that I must tell
> you that my patron, Our Lord Septimius Severus
> Augustus, has passed from this sad world and taken his
> place among the gods. He remained alert in mind even
> to the end; his last words were, 'If we have anything
> to do, come, give it here!'
> Before he died, he spoke to his sons, and urged them

to agree with one another. Beyond that, he advised them to 'enrich the soldiers, and despise everyone else,' advice I fear they will honour as much as they disregard his injunction to unity.

His funeral is being prepared even as I speak. His sons are both expected to take a prominent role in the ceremonies. Although Geta still has much support among the legions, it is clear that the position of Antoninus is paramount and unassailable, and I very much fear that he will be able to accomplish whatever he desires, short of the immediate death of his brother, who is now surrounded by troops wherever he goes. If Antoninus remembers me, I fear that I am lost.

My dear love, you have been a treasure to me, the more joyful for being so much beyond my expectations. If the worst comes to pass, my boast is that I loved you, and that I have served the Empire all my life in integrity and truth. I can rejoice that I leave behind me a son to carry my name and my blood into the ages to come: that is the great gift you have given me. If I am fortunate and my enemy overlooks me, I will send for you as soon as it is safe.

May the gods keep you and our son in health and safety until then! Farewell.

It was the last letter Athenais received from her husband. She brought it up to the *praetorium* to show to Memnon, and spoke agitatedly of what Castor might do, and how the Empress might help, and where she and her husband and infant son might go. Then she began to cry. Memnon gave her wine and agreed with all her more hopeful utterances, feeling helpless.

The official news arrived three days later: Septimius Severus was dead, and his sons, Aurelius Antoninus and Septimius Geta, had succeeded him. There was a large donative to all the troops in honour of the new emperors' accession. The messenger who brought the news also carried a letter for Athenais. It was from the Empress.

Julia Augusta greets her freedwoman Athenais.

It is with deep sorrow that I must inform you of the

death of your husband, Septimius Castor. The order for
his execution was given last night by my son Antoninus
Augustus. I tried to intercede, but by the time I became
aware of what was happening, it was already too late.

Those who witnessed it said that your husband died
well and bravely. He was arrested during the night and
led out to execution at dawn, together with several
others, including my sons' tutor Euodus, for whom
Castor had also sought my protection. The soldiers who
escorted them say that Euodus wept and pleaded for
his life, but that Castor only smiled. When the execu-
tioner asked him why he was smiling, he said, 'Because
I shall never see Caracalla's reign.'

The prisoners were beheaded with a sword; believe
at least that your husband's death was swift. I have had
his body collected and given the sacred rites of burial,
though I thought it wiser not to order a memorial, for
fear that it might be desecrated.

Believe that I grieve deeply for this crime, which I
pray will not be an omen for the years to come.

Your husband's fortune has been confiscated to the
state, but before his sad end he had deposited certain
goods with me, beseeching me to forward them to you
if any harm should befall him. This I will do, adding
to them as much again, to honour that good man and
provide for his family. Expect the gold as soon as it
can be arranged discreetly.

Dear child, I granted you your freedom, and I am
glad of it. Do not come back to court; stay far away
from Eboracum until we have gone back to Rome. Pray
that the divine power softens my sons' hearts, and that
they return to the ways of justice and virtue. Farewell.

There was no offering Athenais wine for this. She locked
herself in her room and wept bitterly.

Memnon was guiltily aware that he'd advised the Selgovae
to pray for the Emperor's death – and certainly it provided
the peace he had hoped for. Caracalla had no interest in his
father's war. He sent envoys into the territory of the Maeatae

immediately, offering to abandon all claim on the lands north of the wall in exchange for an agreement that the tribal leaders would punish any man who raided south of it. The Maeatae accepted the offer with alacrity. They sent embassies to Antoninus to swear their agreement to the new treaty, and Antoninus gave orders to his staff to start for Rome as soon as the weather permitted the voyage.

The Aurelian Moors, however, were given official notice that they were to remain in Britain, sharing the fort of Aballava with the Formation of Frisians.

The formal notice of his appointment to remain in Aballava came at the end of March. Memnon took the letter down to the fort village as soon as he got it, and hesitantly knocked on Athenais's door. The slave Carpus answered it, and admitted him at once.

Athenais was in the small dining room, copying a scroll, with Ingenuus on a blanket on the floor beside her. The baby was four months old now, and had learned to roll over. Ingenuus beamed toothlessly at Memnon and gurgled: this was a visitor he was well accustomed to. Memnon stooped down and swept him up. He set the letter down on the table beside Athenais and lifted the baby high in the air.

'What's that?' asked Athenais, setting down her pen. Her hair was coming down, and her face was shadowed by sleeplessness and grief. Memnon found her impossibly beautiful.

'Official letter,' he explained. 'I thought you should see it.'

He played with the baby while she read the letter. 'Oh!' she exclaimed, when she'd finished it. 'Well – that's good news, isn't it? At least, it is for the Frisians; I don't know if you . . .'

'It's good news,' said Memnon firmly. He sat down on the couch beside Athenais and balanced the baby on his knee. 'I couldn't have looked Burcanius in the face if the high command decided to throw him out, after all he's done to get his men to like us.' He made a face at the baby, who laughed.

'You did a lot, too,' she said, giving him a warm look.

'I'd much rather make friends with people than fight them,' he agreed.

She laughed, and he gave her a questioning look.

'None of the Frisians would dare say that,' she explained. 'You can get away with it. They always have to prove their courage, but nobody ever doubts yours.'

He shrugged. Ingenuus caught hold of his index finger and dragged it into his toothless mouth, and he play-wrestled with the child, pulling the finger out and letting the baby pull it back again. 'I'm afraid of lots of things.'

'Such as?'

'Lions,' he said promptly. 'Battles. Big barbarians with ten-foot spears. And, oh Juno Caelestis, yes! *Accounts*, may all the gods defend me!'

She laughed.

'Easy for you to laugh! You just look at the things and they all lie down fawning and whining, "oh, please, put me in order, mistress!" Me, they jump up and bite!'

She laughed again. 'No, no! You're well on your way to taming them!'

I'm afraid of you, too, he thought to himself. When she had looked at him with horror, it had struck him to the soul; when she had met his eyes and called him a hero, he was blessed. How he could he not be afraid of a woman who had so much power over him? He didn't dare speak his mind to her – and it was as much from fear of her as from fidelity to his oath to Castor.

'Did you want to stay in Britain?' she asked, after a silence.

He nodded. 'I think the troops here in Britain are the lucky ones. We'll be left where we are to guard the wall and keep the new peace. The troops on the Danube – they're the ones who'll get called on if there's a civil war, them and the Albans and the Praetorians. I'm glad to be out of it.' He frowned at her. 'What about you? You have family in Rome, don't you? Your father?'

'I'm going to stay away from Rome,' she said, and shivered.

'Britain's not so bad – except for the climate.'

'I like it here,' she admitted. She looked down at her hands in her lap, then looked up again. 'I suppose I really mean that I like it *here,* in Aballava.'

'Ah, well. You *like* accounts. I don't understand how!'

She smiled. 'I like the work, yes. I've never been *in charge

in an office before; I've always been somebody's underling.
I was miserable in Eboracum.'

He was silent a moment. 'You said you were lonely. In
that house.'

'I was miserable before then, too. When I was first chosen
to work for Julia Augusta I was so proud and happy – and
then I . . . well, it was all intrigues, and manoeuvring for
position among the staff: you've no idea. And then there was
Caracalla. That was horrible.

'Castor was different. He never played their games. He
was so good, so kind, so *brave*.' She wiped her face. 'But I
never really wanted to *marry* him. Wives are, are *dull*. I
wanted things to stay as they were, with the two of us working
together. Only I got pregnant.' She looked over at the baby
perched on Memnon's knee and gently stroked the child's
head. 'I'm not sorry I chose Castor and the baby instead of
the Empress and the Household. I'm glad I gave Castor a
son: he wanted one so much. But . . .' She stopped.

He sat very still, not daring to breathe: he felt that he was
stalking some fabulous beast, some creature never seen in
all the world before. If he managed not to alarm it, it would
come to him.

There was a long silence. He felt her eyes on him, and
concentrated judiciously on the baby. 'It was the Caledonian
woman who really made me see it,' she resumed softly. 'I
wasn't jealous, don't think that. But she spoke of you as a
great warrior, a hero, and my first thought was, "Oh, she's
wrong; he's just a common auxiliary!" Then I saw that no,
I was wrong, that she'd seen something I'd been blind to.
Castor had seen it: he knew very well that what you'd done
wasn't common by any standard. My mistress knew it, too:
she thought it was a matter of course that you should become
a prefect. Me, though – I'd thought that all honour and
value comes from the imperial court. And it doesn't: I saw
that then, and I've been seeing it more and more ever since.
The court doesn't produce loyalty and honour and devotion: it *eats* them. Then I thought that you'd been in love
with me, and I'd never really taken you seriously – and I
was ashamed.'

He looked away from the baby, silently meeting her eyes.

She looked back, unflinchingly. 'I loved Castor. He was a very good man, and he loved me, and I was carrying his child. I had to marry him, and I would have been faithful.'

'I wasn't blaming you.'

'It was you I wanted, though,' she whispered. 'I realized that, after that Saturnalia in Eboracum. But by the time I realized, it was too late.'

He had not asked her: he had kept his oath. By some miracle of Juno Caelestis, or the cajoling of his ancestors, he didn't have to ask her: *she* was asking *him*.

'It isn't too late now,' he told her, very softly.

She looked away. 'Castor told me that if I wanted to marry you, after he died, I would have his blessing. He was thinking of that, in the last months – thinking of my happiness, and my safety. He was like that.'

'*Do* you want to?' he whispered back.

She was silent for a long moment, looking at him again: the same raw meeting of soul to soul. Then she drew in a deep breath and whispered, 'Yes.'

The Usual Historical Epilogue

The spark that set this book off is historical. In chapter 22 of the life of Severus in the *Historia Augusta*, there is an account of an Ethiopian who presented Severus with an omen of death during the emperor's visit to the western end of Hadrian's Wall. Now, the *Historia Augusta* isn't exactly the most reliable of historical sources – it's a collection of sensationalist imperial biographies, some of which are frankly fictional – but in this case, its record has received some support from inscriptions found at the fort of Aballava, now Burgh-by-Sands, which show that during the third century a '*Numerus* of Aurelian Moors' was posted there. There could well have been black soldiers among its ranks. I was intrigued: as far as I know this unnamed auxiliary is the first black person attested to in Britain. I thought that merited a story.

What I've come up with as a result is, of course, fiction, not history. Real history – especially ancient history – is complicated, so full of gaps, questionable evidence, and contradictory interpretations that it is sometimes completely incoherent. To use it as background to a story you have to simplify it: otherwise it simply won't fit. On the other hand, I do research my books very carefully. It annoys me when reviewers accuse me of anachronism: while I accept that my interpretation of the evidence could be wrong, I am at least familiar with that evidence, and I find it galling to be corrected by people who show no signs of ever having heard of it. Can I therefore ask anyone who wants to accuse me of anachronism to cite their own evidence that I've got it wrong?

My account of Severus's Scottish campaign is based on the three principal primary sources: the history of Dio Cassius, the history of Herodian, and that same unreliable *Historia Augusta*. I also consulted a great many secondary sources in trying to

make sense of the period and the events in it. I don't have
space to mention them all, but I owe a particular debt to Anthony
Birley's biography, *Septimius Severus: the African Emperor*. I
also would like to pay tribute to Anne Hyland's book, *Equus:
the Horse in the Roman World*, which was extremely useful
for its hands-on account of Roman cavalry, to P.R.C. Weaver's
Familia Caesaris; and Lloyd A. Thompson's, *Romans and
Blacks*. The website, www.roman-britain.org, is a wonderful
resource – details on every Roman site in Britain at the stroke
of a key! Finally, may I express my gratitude to the Ermine
Street Guard, particularly Derek Forrest, who ran down the
answers to several questions about the circumstances and the
legal rights of auxiliary soldiers which had me completely
stumped. (The Ermine Street Guard are real enthusiasts; they
love that sort of stuff. They make me feel normal.)

The Roman world may well have feared a fratricidal civil
war on Severus's death, but it didn't happen. Dio Cassius,
the chief historian of the period and a contemporary of the
events he recounts, tells the story in Book LXXVIII of his
Roman History:
    'After this Antoninus assumed supreme power, for though
in word he reigned jointly with his brother, in fact he reigned
alone from the start . . . When he got back to Rome, he did
away with (Geta). Since many soldiers and athletes guarded
Geta, day and night . . . Antoninus induced his mother to
summon them both, unattended, to her room, for a recon-
ciliation . . . but when they were inside, some centurions
picked by Antoninus rushed upon Geta and struck him down,
though he had run to his mother . . . crying, 'Mother, Mother
who bore me, help, I'm being murdered!' And she, thus
deceived, saw her son perish in this unholy way in her very
arms . . . for she was drenched in his blood, to say nothing
of a wound she received on her hand. Nor was she permitted
to mourn . . .
    'Antoninus . . . took possession of the legions . . . on
entering the camp he said, "Rejoice, O fellow soldiers, for
now I can do favours for you . . ." Of the imperial freedmen
and soldiers who had been with Geta he put to death some
twenty thousand, men and women both, wherever in the

palace they happened to be; he also killed eminent men, Papinian, among others.'

Once he'd actually obtained unrivalled power, however, Antoninus had very little interest in government. He left most of the work to his mother, who had to struggle to fund the extravagant pay rises with which he'd bribed the army. His most famous edict – that granting Roman citizenship to all who were citizens of the Empire – was probably promulgated to enlarge his tax base: he was otherwise a bloody and brutal dictator. He was murdered after six years by his praetorian prefect, Macrinus, and his mother, in a Stoic repudiation of the world, starved herself to death.